Mistresses

AFTER HOURS
WITH THE BOSS

MAISEY   MELANIE   SCARLET
YATES   **MILBURNE**   **WILSON**

Mistresses Collection

November 2016

December 2016

January 2017

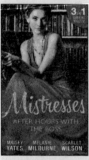

February 2017

March 2017

April 2017

Mistresses

AFTER HOURS
WITH THE BOSS

MAISEY   MELANIE   SCARLET
YATES   **MILBURNE**   **WILSON**

MILLS
BOON
&

Published in Great Britain 2017
By Mills & Boon, an imprint of HarperCollins*Publishers*
1 London Bridge Street, London, SE1 9GF

MISTRESSES: AFTER HOURS WITH THE BOSS © 2017
Harlequin Books S.A.

Her Little White Lie © 2013 Maisey Yates
Their Most Forbidden Fling © 2013 Melanie Milburne
An Inescapable Temptation © 2013 Scarlet Wilson

ISBN: 978-0-263-92759-7

24-0217

HER LITTLE
WHITE LIE

MAISEY YATES

For my grandma, who passed on her love of
books and romance to me.

USA Today bestselling author **Maisey Yates**
lives in rural Oregon with her three children and
her husband, whose chiselled jaw and arresting
features continue to make her swoon. She feels
the epic trek she takes several times a day from
her office to her coffee maker is a true example of
her pioneer spirit. Visit her online at her website
www.maiseyyates.com.

CHAPTER ONE

"EXPLAIN this, or pack up your things and get out."

Paige Harper looked up from her seated position and into her boss's dark, angry eyes. Having him here, in her office, was enough to leave her speechless. Breathless. He was handsome from far away and, up close, even enraged, he was arresting. It was hard to look away from him, but she managed. Then she looked down at the newspaper he'd thrown onto the surface of her desk and her heart sank into her stomach.

"Oh…" She picked up the paper. "Oh…"

"Speechless?"

"Oh…"

"I said explain, Ms. Harper. 'Oh' is not an explanation in any language that I am aware of." He crossed his arms over his broad chest and Paige suddenly felt two inches tall.

"I…" She looked back down at the paper, open to the lifestyle section, the main headline reading Dante Romani to Tie the Knot with Employee. Underneath the headline were two pictures. One of Dante, looking forbidding and perfectly pressed in a custom-made suit. And one of her, on a ladder, in a window at Colson's, hanging strips of tinsel from the ceiling in preparation for the holiday season.

"I…" She tried again as she scanned the article.

Dante Romani, notorious bad boy of the Colson Department Store empire, who just last week made

> headlines for the callous axing of a top exec, and for
> replacing the family man in favor of a younger, less-
> attached man, is now engaged to one of his employees.
> We can't help but wonder if playing games with his
> staff is a favored pastime of the much-maligned
> businessman. Either firing them or marrying them at
> will.

Her stomach tightened with horror. She couldn't fathom
how this had ended up in the paper. She'd done a fair amount
of panicking over how she was going to fix the lie she'd
told the social worker, but she'd thought she would have
some time. She hadn't expected this, not even in her wildest dreams.

But there it was, the lie of the century, shouting at her in
black and white.

"That's hardly more eloquent, or more informative."

"I told a lie," she said.

He looked around her office, and her eyes followed his,
over the stacks of fabric samples, boxes with beads hanging
out of them, aerosol cans of flocking and paint sitting in the
corner and Christmas knickknacks spread over every surface.

He looked back at her, his lip curled upward. "On second
thought, why don't you skip packing and just walk out. I can
have your things express delivered to you."

"Wait…no…" Losing her job was unthinkable, as was
getting caught in her lie. She needed her job. And she really didn't need child services to find out she'd lied during
her adoption interview. Well, what she really needed was a
time machine so that she could go back and opt not to lie to
Rebecca Addler, but that was probably a bit too complicated
as solutions went.

She looked back down at the article.

> It's hard to imagine that a man who so recently fired
> someone for being, reportedly more devoted to his

family than to the almighty dollar, could settle down and become a family man himself. The question is: Can this thoroughly average woman reform the soulless CEO? Or will she become another in the long line of professional and personal casualties Dante Romani leaves in his wake?

Average woman. Yeah, that sounded like her life. Even in her lie, where she was engaged to the hottest billionaire in town, she came out of it as the average woman.

She swallowed and looked back up at her boss's blazing expression. "This is horrible journalism. Sensationalist nonsense, really. All but an opinion piece, one might say. Fluff, even."

Dante cut her off, his black eyes hard, flat. "What did you hope to accomplish with this? Was it fun gossip you didn't think would spread around to this degree? Or was it something you wanted?"

She stood, her knees shaking. "No, I just…"

"You might not be newsworthy, Ms. Harper, but I am."

"Hey!" The assessment burned, especially on the heels of the descriptor of her as "average." Of course, she had to admit, looking at their pictures side by side, that *average* was a pretty kind descriptor.

"Did I offend you?"

"A little."

"I guarantee it is not half so offensive as coming into work to discover you're engaged to someone you have barely had four conversations with."

"Actually, I'm sort of in the same boat you are. I didn't expect for this to be in the paper. I didn't…I didn't expect for anyone to ever find out."

"Be that as it may, they have. And now I have. It would be best if you were to see yourself out. I do not wish to call security." He turned and started to walk out of the room and she felt her heart slide the rest of the way down.

"Mr. Romani," she said, "please, hear me out." She was nearly pleading. No, who was she kidding? She *was* pleading. And she wasn't ashamed. She would get down on her knees and beg if she had to, but she wasn't going to let him ruin this.

"I tried. You had nothing of interest to say."

"Because I don't know where to start."

"The beginning works for me."

She took a deep breath. "Rebecca Addler frowns on single mothers. Not every social worker does, but this one…this one doesn't like them. I mean, not that she doesn't like them personally, but in general. And she asked me why Ana would be better off with me as opposed to a real, traditional family with a mother and a father and I just sort of told her that there would be a father because I was getting married and then your name slipped out because…well, because I work for you, so I see it a lot and it was the first name I thought of."

He blinked twice, then shifted, his head tilted to the side. "That was not the beginning."

Paige took another deep breath, trying to slow down her brain and find a better starting point. "I'm trying to adopt."

He frowned. "I didn't know."

"Well, I have my daughter in the day care here."

"I don't go to the day care," he said, his tone flat.

"Ana's just a baby. She's been with me almost from the moment she was born. I…" Thinking of Shyla still made her throat tighten, made her ache everywhere. Her beautiful, vivacious best friend. The only person who'd really enjoyed her eccentricity rather than simply bearing it. "Her mother is gone. And I'm taking care of her. Nothing was made official before Shyla…anyway she's a ward now."

"Meaning?"

"Meaning the state has the final say over her placement. It's been fine for me to foster her, I'm approved for that. But… but not necessarily for adopting. I've been trying and I had a meeting with the worker handling the case two days ago. It was looking like they weren't going to approve the adoption.

And yes, I lied. About us. And about…the engagement, but please believe it had nothing to do with you."

A slight lie. It had a lot to do with the fact that he was much better looking than any man had a right to be. And she had to go in to work in the same building as he did, and chance walking by him in the halls. Being exposed to all that male beauty was a hazard.

So, yes, there were times she thought of him away from work. In fairness, he was the best-looking man she'd ever encountered in her entire life, and she was in a dating dry spell of epic proportions, which meant, pleasant time with images of Dante was about all she had going on in her love life.

And she saw the man all the time, and that made things worse.

As a result of the exposure, when pressed for the name of her fiancé by Rebecca Addler, the only man she'd been able to picture had been Dante. And so his name had sort of spilled out.

Another gaffe in a long line of them for her. When it came to "oops," she was well above average.

So there, newspaper reporter.

One of his dark eyebrows shot upward. "I'm flattered."

She put her hand on her forehead. "There is no way for me to win trying to explain this," she said. "It's just awkward. But…but…I don't really know what to do now. It wasn't supposed to be in the paper, and now it is, and if it turns out we aren't engaged they'll know that I lied and then…"

"And then you'll be a single mother who is also a liar. Two strikes, I would think." His tone was so disengaged, so unfeeling.

She swallowed. "Well, exactly."

He was right. Two strikes. If not a plain old strikeout. It wasn't an acceptable risk. Not where Ana was concerned. Ana, the brightest spot in her life. Her helpless little girl, the baby she loved more than her own life. There was nothing and no one else she would even consider stooping to this level of subterfuge for, nothing else that could possibly compel her to do what she was starting to think she had to do: propose to her boss.

The man who practically stole the air from her lungs when he walked into a room. The man who was so far out of her league, even thinking of a dinner date with him was laughable.

But this was bigger than that. Bigger than a little crush or her insecurity. Her fear of outright rejection.

"I…I think I need your help."

There was no change in his expression. Dante Romani was impossible to read, but then, that wasn't really new. He was the dark prince of the Colson empire, the adopted son of Don and Mary Colson. The media speculated that they'd adopted him because he'd shown profound brilliance at an early age. No one imagined it had been his personality that had won over the older couple.

She'd always thought those stories were sad and unfair. Now she wondered. Wondered if he was as heartless as he was portrayed to be. She really hoped he wasn't, because she was going to need him to care at least a little bit in order to pull this off.

"I'm not in the position to give this kind of help," he said, his tone dry.

"Why?" she asked, pushing herself into a standing position. "Why not? I…I don't need you forever, I just need…"

"You need me to marry you. I think that's a step too far into crazy town, don't you?"

"For my daughter," she said, the words raw, loud and echoing in the room. And now that she'd said them, out loud, she didn't regret them. She would do anything for Ana. Even this. Even if it meant getting thrown out of the office building.

Because for the first time in her memory, something mattered. It mattered more than self-protection or fending off disappointment. It was worth the possibility of adding to her list of failures.

"She's not your daughter," he said.

She gritted her teeth, trying to keep a handle on the adrenaline that was pounding through her, making her shake. "Blood isn't everything. I would think you would understand that." Probably not the best idea to be taking shots at him, but it was true. He should understand.

He regarded her for a moment, a muscle ticking in his jaw. "I will not fire you. For now. But I will require further explanation. An explanation that makes sense. What do you have on your agenda for the day?"

"I'm working on Christmas," she said, indicating the array of decorations spread out in the room. "For Colson's and for Trinka." She was working on a series of elegant displays for the parent store, and for their offshoot, teen clothing store, something mod and edgy.

"You'll be in the office?"

She nodded. "Just fiddling today."

"Good. Don't leave until we've spoken again." He turned and walked out of her office and she sank to her knees, her hands shaking, her entire body wound so tight she wanted to curl in on herself.

She was so stupid. Nothing new. She'd spoken without thinking. As per usual. Only this time it had landed her in serious trouble, with the man who signed her checks.

Everything was in his hands now. Her future. Her family. Her money.

"Time to learn to think before you talk," she said into the empty office. Unfortunately, it was too late for that. Way, way too late.

Dante finished with the last item of work on his agenda and turned to his file cabinet, placing the last document on his desk into its appropriate spot. Then he put his elbows on the desk and leaned forward, staring at the newspaper on the shining surface.

He'd studied the news story again when he'd come back

into his office. A scathing piece on how the impostor of the
Colson family moved people around like pawns on a chess-
board. It was stacked with details about the man, Carl Johnson, he'd fired last week for skipping out on an important
meeting to go to a child's sporting event.

The press had covered it a week ago, too, since Carl had
gone screaming to the papers over discrimination of some
kind. In Dante's mind, it wasn't discrimination to expect an
employee to attend mandatory meetings, no matter whether
it was the last game of a five-year-old's T-ball season or not.

Still, it had been another of those juicy bits the media had
latched on to to further stack the case against him and his possession of human decency. It generally didn't matter to him.

But one thing in that article stood out to him: Can she
reform him?

Could Paige Harper reform him? The idea amused him.
He had the bare minimum of contact with her. She did her
job, and she did it well, so he never had a reason to involve
himself. But he had noticed her. Impossible not to. She was a
blur of shimmer when she moved around the office. Bound-
less energy and a sense of the accidental radiated from her.

He would be lying if he said he wasn't intrigued by her.
She was a window into so many things he would never seek
out: chaos, color, motion. So many things he would never be.
Combined with the fact that she had a figure most men would
be hard-pressed to ignore, and yes, he was intrigued by her.

But no matter how intrigued, she simply wasn't the sort
of woman he would normally approach. Until this.

"Can this thoroughly average woman reform the soulless CEO?"

He had no desire to take part in a reformation, but the idea
of an image overhaul in the media? That had possibilities.

He could have demanded a retraction the moment he'd
walked in that morning. Or he could let it run. Let them build
off the image they'd created for him when he'd been thrust
into the spotlight. A fourteen-year-old boy, adopted, finally,

and suspected of being capable of all manner of violence and sociopathic behaviors.

His story had been written in the public eye before he'd had a chance to live it. And so he had never challenged it. Had never cared.

But suddenly he had been handed a tool that might help change things.

He turned around and faced the windows, looked out at the harbor. He could still see the look on her face. Not just the expression, but the depth of fear and desperation in her eyes. The press had a few things right about him, and one of them was that feelings, emotions, mattered little to him. And still…still he couldn't forget. And he thought of the baby, too.

He had no use for children. No desire for them. But he could remember being one all too well. Could remember being passed around the foster care system for eight years of his life. Could remember what it was like to be at the mercy of either the State, or, before that, adults who brought harm, not love.

Could he consign Ana to that same fate? Or to a family who might not feel that same desperate longing that Paige seemed to feel for her?

And why should he care at all? That was the million-dollar question. Caring wasn't counted among his usual afflictions.

The door to his office opened and Paige breezed in. Maybe breezed was the wrong term. A breeze denoted something gentle, soothing even. Paige was more a gale-force wind.

She had a big, gold bag hanging off her shoulder, one that matched her glittering, golden pumps that likely added four inches to her height. She also had a bolt of fabric held tightly beneath the other arm, and a large sketchbook beneath that. She looked like she might drop all of it at any moment.

She plunked her things down in the chair in front of his desk, bending at the waist, her skirt tightening over the curve of her butt, and pushed her hand back through her dark brown hair, revealing a streak of bright pink nearly hidden beneath the top layers.

She was a very bright woman in general, one of the things that made her impossible to ignore. Bright makeup, lime-green on her lids, magenta on her lips, and matching finger-nails. She made for an enticing picture, one he found himself struggling to look away from.

"You said to come in and see you before I left?"

"Yes," he said, breaking his focus from her for the first time since she'd come in, looking at the items she'd chucked haphazardly into the chair. He had a very strong urge to straighten them. Hang them on a hook. Anything but sim-ply let them lie there.

"Are you going to fire me?"

"I don't think so," he said, tightening his jaw. "Tell me more about your situation."

A little wrinkle appeared between her brows, her full lips turning down. "In a nutshell, Shyla was my best friend. We moved here together. She got a boyfriend, got pregnant. He left. And everything was fine for a while, because we were working it out together. But she got really sick after giving birth to Ana. She lost a lot of blood during delivery and she had a hard time recovering. She ended up…there was a clot and it traveled to her lungs." She paused and took a breath, her petite shoulders rising and falling with the motion. "She died and that left…Ana and I."

He pushed aside the strange surge of emotion that hit him in the chest. The thought of a motherless child. A mother the child had lost to death. He tightened his jaw. "Your friend's parents?"

"Shyla's mother has never been around. Her father is still alive as far as I know, but he wouldn't be able to care for a child. He wouldn't want to, either."

"And you can't adopt unless you're married."

She let out a long breath and started pacing. "It's not that simple. I mean, she didn't say that absolutely. There's no…

law, or anything. I mean, obviously. But from the moment Rebecca Addler, the caseworker, came to my apartment it was clear that she wasn't thrilled with it."

"What's wrong with your apartment?"

"It's small. I mean, it's nice—it's in a good area, but it's small."

"Housing is expensive in San Diego."

"Yes. Exactly. Expensive. So I have a small apartment, and right now Ana shares a room with me. And I admit that a fifth-floor apartment isn't ideal for raising a child, but plenty of people do it."

"Then why can't you do it?" he asked, frustration starting to grow in his chest, making it feel tight. Making him feel short-tempered.

"I don't know why. But it was really obvious by the way she said…by how she was saying that Ana would be better off with a mother and a father, and didn't I want her to have that? Well, that made it pretty obvious that she really doesn't want me to get custody. And…I panicked."

"And somehow my name came into this? And into the paper?"

Her cheeks turned a deep shade of pink. "I don't know how that happened. The paper. I can't imagine Rebecca… If you could have met her, you would know she didn't do it. Maybe whoever handled the paperwork because I know she made a note."

"A note?"

Paige winced. "Yeah. A note."

"Saying?"

"Your name. That we'd just gotten engaged. She said it was possible it would make a difference."

"You don't think it has more to do with the fact that I'm a billionaire than it has to do with the fact that you're getting married."

He was under no illusion about his charm, or lack of it. And neither was the world in general. The thing that attracted women to him was money. The thing that made him acceptable in the eyes of the social worker would be the same thing. Monetarily, he would be able to provide for a child. Several children, and that *did* matter. A sorry way to decide parentage in his opinion.

But that was the way the world worked. Coming from having none, to having more than he could ever spend, had taught him that in a very effective way.

"Possibly," she said, sucking her bright pink bottom lip into her mouth and worrying it with her teeth.

His phone rang and he punched the speaker button. "Dante Romani."

His assistant's nervous voice filled the room. "Mr. Romani," he said, "the press have been calling all afternoon looking for a statement…about your engagement."

Dante shot Paige his deadliest glare. She didn't shrink. She hardly seemed to notice. She was looking past him, out the window, at the harbor, twirling a lock of hair around her finger, her knees shaking back and forth. She was the most… haphazard creature he'd ever seen.

"What about it?" Dante asked, still unsure how he was going to play it.

As far as the press was concerned, he was marrying Paige and he was adopting a child with her. To go back on that a day later would kill the last vestiges of speculation that he might possess honor or human decency. That wasn't exactly a goal of his. Yes, by the standards of some, he lacked charm. Really, he just wasn't inclined to kiss ass, and he never had been. But it didn't mean he was angling for a complete character assassination by the media, either.

If things got too bad, and they were headed that way, it might affect business. And that was completely unacceptable to him. Don and Mary Colson had adopted an heir to their fortune, to their department store empire, for a reason. It was not so he could let it fail.

And then there was Ana. Dante didn't like children. Didn't

want them. But the memories from his own childhood, memories of foster care, of going from home to home, sometimes good, sometimes not, were strong.

Perhaps Ana would be adopted right away. But would they care for her? Would they love her? Paige did; that much even he could recognize.

This concern, for another human being, was unusual for him. It was foreign. But he couldn't deny that it was there. Very real, very strong. The need to spare an innocent child from some of the potential horrors of life. Horrors he knew far too well.

"They want details," Trevor said.

Dante's eyes locked with Paige's. "Of course they do." *So do I.* "But they'll have to wait. I have no statement at this time." He punched the off button on the phone's intercom. "But I will need one," he said to Paige. A plan was forming in his mind, a way to take this potential PR disaster and turn it into something that would benefit him. But first, he wanted to hear an explanation. "What do you propose we do?"

Paige stopped jiggling her leg. "Get married?" Her expression was so hopeless, so utterly lost looking. "Or…at least let the engagement go on for a while?" The desperation, coming from her in waves, was palpable.

No one had ever cared for him with so much passion, not in the years since he'd lost his birth mother. He didn't regret it. It was far too late in life for that.

But it isn't too late for Ana.

He looked back down at the newspaper. It wouldn't only be for Ana anyway. It was a strange thought…the idea of being able to manipulate the image he'd always had in the press.

He'd grown from sullen teenage boy to feared man all in the eye of the public. For years he'd been painted as an unloving, ungrateful adopted child who had no place in the Colson family. As he'd grown up, his image had changed to that of a hard boss, a heartless lover who drew women in with sexual promises, sensual corruption and money before discarding them. It colored the way people saw him. The way they talked to him. The way they did business with him.

What would it be like to have it change? It wouldn't last, of course. He wouldn't stay with her. Wouldn't pursue anything remotely resembling a real marriage. An engagement though, at least for a while, had interesting possibilities.

But to be seen as the angel rather than the devil…it was an interesting thought. It might make certain transactions easier. Smoother.

Dante was past the point where negative character assessments bothered him. Unless they affected a business. And in the past, he knew people had shied away from dealings with him thanks to his reputation.

A womanizer. Heartless. Cutthroat. Dangerous. It had all been said and then some, most of it spun from speculation and created stories. Would it change things if he were considered settled? A family man? Even if it wasn't permanent, it could quite possibly shift how people saw him.

An interesting thought indeed.

Can she reform him? The real question was, could he use her to reform his image?

For a moment, a brief moment, he allowed himself to think of the many ways he could use her. Fantasies that had been on the edge of his consciousness every time she breezed through the office. Fantasies he had not allowed.

He gave them a moment's time, and then shut the door on them. It was not her body he needed.

"All right, Ms. Harper, for the purposes of keeping the facade, I accept your proposal."

Her blue eyes widened. "You…what?"

"I have decided that I will marry you."

CHAPTER TWO

PAIGE was pretty sure the floor shook underneath her feet. But Dante didn't look at all perturbed, and everything appeared to be stable, so maybe the shaking was all internal.

"You…what?"

"I accept. At least on a surface level. At least until the furor in the media dies down."

"I… Okay," she said, watching her boss as he stood from his position behind his desk. His movements were methodical, planned and purposeful.

He was always like that. Smooth and unruffled. She had wondered, more than once, what it took to get him to loosen up. What it took to shake that perfect, well-ordered control.

She'd wondered, only a couple of times, if a lover ever managed to do it for him. Loosen his tie, run her fingers through his hair.

Now she knew she had the power to do it. Not in the way a lover would, but by inadvertently leaking a fake engagement to the press.

"Excellent," he said, his tone clipped. Decisive. "I see no reason why this can't work."

"I… Why?"

"Is this not what you want? What you need?"

Her head was spinning. This morning everything in her world had been on the verge of collapse, and now—now it seemed like she might actually be able to keep it all standing.

"Well…yes. But let's be honest. You aren't exactly known for your accommodating and helpful nature, sorry, so it seems… out of character."

He bent and picked up the paper from his desk, his dark eyes skimming it. "Can you imagine what the media would say if I backed out? They're already salivating for the chance to rip me to pieces if I would just give it to them. This article is practically a setup for the following piece where they will gleefully report that I have dropped my subordinate fiancée, who I was likely playing power games with, for my own debauched satisfaction, and ruined her chances of adopting her much-loved child. It would have an even darker angle to it, considering I myself am adopted. I can see that headline now."

"Well, yes, I can see how that would be…not good. But I'm surprised they just…believed that we were engaged anyway." *Average woman.* That was what they'd called her in the paper. And Dante Romani would never be linked with a woman who was average.

In so many ways it was like a bad joke. A cruel high school flashback.

"Been reading stories about me?" he asked, his lips curving into a half smile.

"Well, I mean, I see them," she said, stuttering. He didn't need to know that sometimes she looked at pictures of him for a little longer than necessary. It wasn't like anyone could blame her. She was a woman; he was a stunningly attractive man. But she knew she had no shot with him, ever. And no desire to take one. "But also, we haven't really been seen together in public, so it seems odd that they would just assume, based on a random tip, that we're engaged."

He shrugged. "It sounds like something I would do. Keep a real relationship under wraps. In theory. I haven't had one, so I wouldn't know."

"Right. Yes. I know that."

"You do read the stories, then."

Her cheeks heated and she cleared her throat. "That and I have keen powers of observation and… Oh, no!"

"What?"

Paige looked at the clock on Dante's wall, positioned just above his head. "I have to go pick Ana up. Everyone is probably waiting on me."

"I'll come with you," he said.

"What?" She needed to get away from him for a minute. Or have flustered-angry Dante back. Now that he had a plan he had taken firm control over everything and it was making her feel dazed.

"Well, I am your fiancé now, am I not?"

Paige's head was swimming, her fingers feeling slightly numb. "I don't know…are you?"

He nodded once. "Yes. For all intents and purposes."

"Oookay then."

"You seem uncertain, Paige," he said, taking his coat off the peg that was mounted to the wall and opening the door.

Paige scrambled to collect her things from the chair. "I…I'm not, not really. I just don't know how you went from spitting nails in my office to…agreeing."

"I'm a man of action. I don't have time to be indecisive."

She walked past him and out into the lobby area of his floor. His assistant, Trevor, was positioned behind his desk, his eyes locked on to the both of them.

"Have a nice evening, Mr. Romani," he said.

"You too, Trevor. You should go home," Dante said.

"In a bit. So…"

"Oh, yeah," Paige said. "We're engaged."

"You are?" he asked, his expression skeptical.

Paige nodded and looked at Dante who looked…uncharacteristically amused. "Yes," she said.

He nodded. "Yes."

"I…didn't know," Trevor said.

"I'm a private man," Dante said. "When it suits me."

"Apparently," Trevor said, looking back at his computer screen.

"See you tomorrow," Dante said. Trevor made a vague nod in acknowledgment.

Paige followed Dante to the elevator and stepped inside when the doors opened. "So…Trevor doesn't seem thrilled," she said. Really, she was surprised at the dynamic between Dante and his assistant. Dante was something of a fearsome figure in her mind, and the fact that Trevor hadn't been fired on the spot for his obvious annoyance with the situation wasn't exactly what she'd expected.

"Trevor is mad because he didn't know," Dante said. "Because he likes to know everything, and make sure it's jotted down in my schedule at least six months in advance."

"And you don't mind that he was…upset?"

Dante frowned. "Why? Did you expect me to throw him from the thirtieth-floor window?"

"It was a possibility I hadn't ruled out."

"I'm not a tyrant."

"No?" He gave her a hard stare. "Well, you fired Carl Johnson. For the baseball game," she said.

"And it makes me a tyrant because I expect my employees to show up during work hours and earn the generous salaries I pay them?" he asked.

"Well…it was for his child's T-ball game…"

"That meant nothing to anyone else in the meeting. It might have personally meant something to Carl, but not to anyone else. And if everyone was allowed to miss work anytime something seemed like it might take precedence for them personally, we would not be able to get anything done."

"Well, what about when you have something in your personal life that requires attention."

"I have neatly handled what might have been a dilemma by having no personal life," he said, his tone hard.

"Oh. Well…"

"You expect me to be unreasonable because of what is

written about me," he said, "in spite of what you see in the office on a daily basis. Which only serves to prove the power of the media. And the fact that it's time I manipulated it to my advantage."

Her face burned. "I...suppose." It was true. Dante was a hard man but, other than this morning, she'd never heard him raise his voice. As bosses went, he'd never been a bad one. But she'd always gotten an illicit thrill when he was around. A sense of something dark. And it was very likely the media was to blame.

"And you *do* read the stories they write about me," he said, as if he was able to read her mind.

She pursed her lips. "Fine. I've read some of what's been written about you."

"Being a tyrant implies a lack of control, in my opinion, Paige. And it shows an attempt to claim it in a very base way. I have control over this company, of my business, in all situations, and I don't have to raise my voice to get it."

She cleared her throat and stared straight ahead at the closed elevator door. At their warped reflections in the gleaming metal. She came just past his shoulder, and that was in her killer heels. She looked...tiny. A bit awkward. And he looked...well, like Dante always looked. Dark and delicious, supremely masculine, completely not awkward and just a little frightening.

"You raised your voice when you were in my office," she said, still looking at reflection Dante, and not actual Dante. Actual Dante was almost too handsome to look at directly, especially when standing so close to him.

He laughed, a short, one-note sound. "It was deserved in the situation, don't you think?"

"Was it?"

"How would you have felt if the situations were reversed?"

"I don't know. Look, are you serious about this?" she asked, turning to face him just as the doors to their floor slid open.

"I don't joke very often, if at all," he said.

"Well, that's true. But in my experience when men say they want to date me, it can turn out to have been a cruel joke, so I'm thinking my boss agreeing to get engaged to me could be something along those same lines."

"What is this?"

She shook her head. "Nothing, just…high school. You are planning on following through with this, right? Dante, if I get caught—committing fraud, basically—it might not just be Ana that I lose."

"As previously stated, Paige, I do not joke. I am not joking now."

"I just don't understand why you're helping me."

"Because it helps me."

He said it with such certainty, and no shame.

Paige sputtered. "In what regard?"

"People see me…well, as a tyrant. If not that, a corruptor of innocents, and perhaps, the personification of Charon, ready to lead people down the river Styx and into Hades."

He said it lightly, with some amusement, though his expression stayed smooth. Paige laughed. "Uh, yes, well, I suppose that's true."

"Already there is speculation that you might manage to reform me. The idea of giving that impression…I find it intriguing. An interesting social experiment if nothing else, and one with the potential to improve business for me."

"Of course you would also actually be helping me and Ana," she pointed out.

He nodded once. "I don't find that objectionable."

She could have laughed. He said it so seriously, as if she might really think he would find helping others something vile. And he said it like that perception didn't bother him.

"Okay. Good." She continued on down the hall with him, on the way to the day care center that she'd come to be so grateful for.

She opened the door and sighed heavily when she saw

Genevieve, the main caregiver, holding Ana. They were the last two there. "I'm so sorry," she said, dumping her things on the counter and reaching for Ana.

Genevieve smiled. "No worries. She's almost asleep again. She did scream a little bit when five rolled around and you weren't here."

Paige frowned, a sharp pain hitting her in the chest. Ana was only four months old, but she already knew Paige as her mother. There had been such few moments in Paige's life when she'd been certain of something, where she hadn't felt restless and on the verge of failure.

One of those moments was when she'd been hired to design the window displays for Colson's. The other was when Shyla had placed Ana in Paige's arms.

Can you take care of her?

She'd only meant for a moment. While she rested and tried to shake some of the chronic fatigue that came with having a newborn. But Shyla had lain down on their sofa for a nap that day and never woken up. And Paige was still taking care of Ana. Because she had to. Because she wanted to. Because she loved Ana more than her own life.

Genevieve transferred Ana and her blanket into Paige's arms, and Paige pulled her daughter in close, her heart melting, her eyes stinging. She looked back at Dante, and she knew that she'd done the right thing.

Because she would be damned if anyone was taking Ana from her, and she would do whatever she had to do to insure that no one did. Ana was hers forever. And even if marriage to Dante wasn't strictly necessary, she would take it as insurance every time.

Genevieve bent to retrieve Ana's diaper bag, then popped back up, her eyes widening when she registered the presence of their boss. "Mr. Romani, what brings you down here?"

Paige thought the girl had a slightly hopeful edge to her voice. As if she was hoping Dante had come to ravish her against the wall. Something Paige could kind of relate to, since Dante had that effect. Even Paige, who knew better than to fantasize about men who were so far out of her league, struggled with the odd Dante-themed fantasy. It was involuntary, really.

"I'm here to collect Ana," he said.

Genevieve looked confused. "Oh…I…" He reached over the counter and took the diaper bag from the surprised-looking Genevieve.

"With Paige," he finished. "It was announced in the news today, but in case you haven't heard, Paige and I are to be married."

Genevieve's mouth dropped open. "Oh, I…"

"Let's go, *cara mia*," he said, sweeping Paige's things from the counter and gathering them into his arms. Her big, broad-chested Italian boss, clutching her sequined purse to his chest, was enough to make her dissolve into hysteric fits of laughter, but there was something else, another feeling, one that made her stomach tight and her chest warm, stopping the giggles.

She wiggled her fingers in Genevieve's direction and walked through the door, which Dante was currently holding open for her with his shoulder.

Paige continued down the hall, heading toward the parking garage. Dante was behind her, still holding all of her things. She stopped. "Sorry, I can take that."

"I've got it," he said.

"But you don't have to…I mean…you don't have to walk me out to my car."

"I think I do," he said.

"No. You really don't. There's no reason."

"We have just announced our engagement. Do you think I would let my fiancée walk out to her car by herself, with a baby, a diaper bag, a purse and…whatever else I'm currently holding?"

"Maybe not," she said. "But then, you don't really have a reputation for being chivalrous."

"Perhaps not," he said, "but I'm changing it, remember?"

"Why exactly?"

"Walk while you talk," he said.

Not for the first time, Paige noticed that he didn't look at Ana. She seemed no more interesting to him than the inanimate objects in his arms. Most people softened when they saw her, reached out and touched her cheek or hair. Not Dante.

"Okay," she said, turning away from him and continuing on. "So…how are we going to do this?" she asked.

She paused at the door, a strange, new habit she seemed to have developed just since coming down from the top floor with Dante. And he didn't let her down. He reached past her and opened the door, holding it for her as she walked into the parking garage.

"Where are you parked?" he asked.

"There," she said, flicking her head to the right. "I get to park close now because of Ana."

"Nice policy," he said. "I don't believe I was responsible for it."

"I think your father was."

A strange expression passed over his face. "Interesting. But very like Don. He's always been very practical. One reason he put in the day care facility early on. Because he knew that employees with children needed to feel like their family concerns were a priority. And better for the company because it ensures that there will be minimal issues with employees missing work because of child care concerns. Of course, missing baseball games cannot be helped sometimes, and I am not putting a field in the parking garage," he finished dryly.

"I imagine not." She shifted, not quite sure what to do next. "Well, I've never met your father, but judging by some of the policies here, he's a very good man."

Dante nodded. "He is."

Paige turned and headed toward her car. "Oh…purse," she said, stopping her progress and turning to look at Dante. He started trying to extricate the glittery bag from the pile in his arms. Then she checked the door. "Never mind, I forgot to lock it."

"You forgot to lock it?"

"It's secure down here," she said, pulling the back door open and depositing the sleeping Ana in her seat.

"Locking it would make it doubly secure," he said, his tone stiff.

She straightened. "How long have you lived in this country?"

He frowned. "Since I was six. Why?"

"You just…you speak very formal English."

"It's my second language. And anyway, Don and Mary speak very formal English. They are quite upper-crust, you know."

"And you call them by their first names?"

"I was fourteen when they adopted me, which I'm sure you know given your proclivity for tabloids."

"Wow. Exaggerate much? Proclivity…"

"And," he continued as if she hadn't spoken, "it would have seemed strange to call them anything other than their first names. I was adopted to be the heir to the Colson empire, more than I was adopted to be a son."

"Is that what they told you?"

His expression didn't alter. "It's the only reason I can think of."

"Then why aren't you a Colson?" She'd often wondered that, but she'd never asked, of course. Partly because until today she'd never had more than a moment to speak to him.

"Something Don and I agreed on from the start. I wished to keep my mother's name."

"Not your father's?"

His face hardened, his dark eyes black, blank. "No."

Paige blinked. "Oh." She looked back down at Ana, who was sleeping soundly and was buckled tightly into her seat. She closed the door and leaned against the side of the car. "So…I guess I'll see you tomorrow then."

"You'll see me tonight," he said, turning away from her.

"What?"

"We're not going into this without a plan. And if I'm going to help you, you will help me. It's in both of our best interests that it look real, once we take one step into confirming this, there is no going back. You understand?"

She nodded slowly.

"And you need to remember this. It's essential for you, much more than it is for me. If this blows up it would simply be another bruise on my reputation, and frankly, what's one more beating in that area? You on the other hand…"

"I could lose everything," she said, a sharp pang of regret hitting her in the stomach.

"So we'll make sure we don't misstep," he said. "I'll follow you to your apartment."

The thought of him, so big and masculine and…orderly, in her tiny, cluttered space, made her feel edgy. Of having a man, any man really, but a man like him specifically, in her space, was so foreign. But really, there was no other option. And she couldn't act like he made her nervous. He was supposed to be her fiancé.

And people were somehow supposed to believe that he had chosen her.

"I feel dizzy," she said.

He frowned. "Should I drive?"

She shook her head. "I'll be fine," she said, opening the driver's side door. "I'll be fine," she repeated again, for her own benefit more than his.

And she really hoped it was true.

CHAPTER THREE

PAIGE'S house was very like her. Bright, disordered and a bit manic. The living area was packed with things. Canvases, mannequins, bolts of fabric. There was a large bookshelf at the back wall filled with bins. Bins of beads, sequins and other things that sparkled. Her office had simply been the tip of the iceberg.

This was the glittery underbelly.

"Sorry about the mess," she said. "You can just dump my stuff on the couch." She set the baby's car seat gently on the coffee table and bent, unbuckling the little girl from her seat, drawing her to her chest.

He looked away from the scene. Watching her with the baby reminded him of things. He wasn't even sure what things exactly, because every time a piece of memory tried to push into his mind, he pushed it out.

He focused instead on trying to find a hook of some kind, something to hang her bag on at least.

"Just dump it," she said, shifting Ana in her arms.

"I don't…dump things," he said tightly.

She rolled her eyes. "Then hold Ana while I do it."

He drew back, discomfort tightening his throat. "I don't hold babies."

She rolled her eyes. "Pick one," she said.

He set her purse on her kitchen counter and then went farther into the living room, depositing her fabric on another pile of fabric, and placing her sketchbook next to a bin that had paints and pencils in it.

That had some reason to it, at least.

She laughed. "You couldn't do it. You couldn't just dump it."

"There's nothing wrong with caring for what you have."

"I do care for it."

"How do you find everything in here?"

She cocked her head to the side and he caught sight of the flash of pink buried in her hair again. "Easily." She put her hand on Ana's back and patted her absently, pacing across the living room.

There was no denying that she looked at ease in her surroundings, even if he couldn't fathom it. He needed order. A space for everything. A clear and obvious space for himself. He prized it, above almost everything else.

He cleared his throat. "What size ring do you wear?"

"Six," she said, frowning. "Why?"

"You need one."

"Well, I have rings. I can just wear one of those," she said, waving her hand in dismissal.

"You do not have the sort of ring I would buy the woman I intended to marry."

She paused her pacing. "Well, maybe you wouldn't buy the sort of ring I would want."

"We'll come to a compromise, but your engagement ring must be up to my standards."

She groaned and sank onto the couch, baby Ana still resting against her chest. "This is bizarre."

"You're the one who said we were engaged."

"Yes. I know. And I knew the minute I said it I was in over my head but it just…popped out."

For some reason, he didn't doubt her. Probably because he was the least logical option to choose. If she'd been thinking, she would have chosen a different man. One who liked children and puppies and had some semblance of compassion.

He was not that man, and he knew it as well as everyone around him.

"I can't lose her," she said, her focus on the baby in her arms. "I can't let one stupid mistake ruin her life. And mine."

He looked at Paige, at the baby nestled against her, ignoring the piece of his brain that demanded he look away from the scene of maternal love. Ana took a deep breath, almost a sigh, that lifted her tiny shoulders and shook her whole little frame. She was content, at rest, against the woman she knew as her mother.

Unexpectedly, genuine concern wrenched his gut. It was foreign. Emotion, in general, was foreign to him. But this kind even more so.

"I understand," he said. And he found that he did. "But that means this can't just look real, it has to be real."

It occurred to him, just as he spoke the words. The engagement wouldn't be enough. It would have to be more. It would have to be marriage.

"You want to keep Ana."

"More than anything," she said.

"Then we have to be sure that the adoption is final before we go our separate ways. We need to get married, not just get engaged."

She blinked twice. "Like…really get married?"

"I think a government office would be especially concerned with the legality of our union so we can't very well jump over a broom on the beach."

"But…but a real marriage?"

"Of course."

Her blue eyes widened. "What do you mean by that?"

He almost laughed at the abject horror evident in her expression. Most women didn't look horrified if it was implied they might sleep together; on the contrary, he was used to women being eager to accept the invitation or eager to seek him out.

Though he turned his share down. Far too many were out

to reform the bad boy. To make the man with the heart of stone care, to reach him, save him, perhaps. Something that simply wasn't possible.

He wasn't a sadist and he had no interest in hurting people. He could easily take advantage of wide-eyed innocents with a desire to reform him. But he didn't. He wouldn't.

Still, he found Paige's clear aversion to it interesting.

"I don't mean in that way," he said.

Her blue eyes widened further. "What way?" As if she had to prove her thoughts hadn't even gotten near the bedroom door. She was a very cute, unconvincing liar.

"I don't intend to sleep with you." Even as he said it, he wondered if the underwear she had on beneath her clothes was a bright as the rest of her. Bright pink, showing hints of pale skin beneath delicate lace? He could imagine laying her down on white sheets, the filmy garments electric against the pristine backdrop.

Color flooded her cheeks and she looked down at the top of Ana's head. "I…of course not. I mean…I never thought you did."

He shouldn't. He shouldn't be toying with fantasies of it, either. He had to stay focused. He tightened down on the vein that seemed to bleed a never-ending flow of erotic, Paige-themed imagery through his brain.

"The look on your face said otherwise."

"It was just an honest question. And anyway, you're taking this a step deeper, and I'm entitled to ask some questions, and I just need to know what 'real' would mean to you. Other than the license, I guess."

"What I mean by it being real, has to do with our activities outside the bedroom. You will need to accompany me to any events I might need to attend. We will have to get married, and you will have to move into my home. It has to look real."

Dante didn't like the idea of it. Not in the least. Of bringing this little rainbow whirlwind into his personal space. And not just Paige, but the baby, as well.

He gritted his teeth. His house was big. It would be fine. And it would be temporary. He didn't question the decisions he made. He simply made them.

She nodded slowly. "I know. But I mean…it seems crazy and extreme."

"It's hardly extreme. Understand this, Paige, you've gotten us both into a bit of a dangerous game. There could be very real consequences if we're caught in the lie. Very real for you, especially."

She looked away, pulling her lush bottom lip between her teeth. "You're right."

He pulled his focus away from her mouth. "Of course I am. Do you have anything to drink?"

"Uh…there's a box of wine in the fridge."

Dante didn't bother to keep the disapproval from showing on his face. "A box?"

"Yeah," she said. "Sorry if that doesn't meet with your standards. Maybe you can choose me some wine and a ring?"

"I'm not opposed to it. However, when you move into my home, there will be a wine selection waiting for you. And none of it will be boxed."

"Well, la-dee-da," she said, standing. "I'm going to put Ana in her crib. Do you think you can stand here for a minute and keep the internal judgment to a minimum?"

"I'll do my best," he said drily.

He watched her walk out of the room, his eyes drawn to the sway of her hips and the rounded curve of her butt. He was only human, and she was beautiful. Not his type in the least, and yet, it wasn't the first time he'd noticed her.

He liked women who were cool. Contained. In both looks and manner. And Paige was none of those things, which made her both a fascination and impossible to ignore.

Paige returned a moment later, hands free, a wet spot on her shirt near her shoulder. "You have something on your shirt," he said.

She looked down. "Oh. Yeah. She's really drooly right now. No teeth to hold it back."

He let out a long breath and sat down on the couch. "I think I will take some wine."

The idea of having this woman and her explosion of belongings and a baby who was, by Paige's description, drooly, in his home was enough to send a kick of anxiety through him.

Paige shrugged and headed to the kitchen, reaching up into a high cabinet and taking down two mismatched pieces of stemware. A green champagne flute and a clear wine goblet. Then she opened up the fridge and bent down, dispensing wine from the plastic tap that was jammed into the cardboard box, into the cups.

She kicked her shoes off and pushed them to the side as she walked to the couch, wineglasses in her hands. "I haven't had anyone over in a long time. You know, other than the social worker." She handed him the clear glass and moved to a chair that was positioned next to the couch. She sat down on her knees, her feet tucked up under her.

"In how long?"

Paige looked down into her wine. "Since Shyla died."

"That must have been difficult." It was hard for him to find the words you were supposed to say when people were grieving. Hard to know what they wanted to hear. He had experience dealing with death, and yet, he couldn't remember what people had said to him. If they had said anything.

Paige took a sip of her wine and nodded. "Yes. She was my best friend. She and I moved to San Diego from Oregon together shortly after we graduated."

"Why here?"

She shrugged. "It's sunny? I don't know. A chance to start over, I guess. Be new people. She met her boyfriend really soon after we got here, and she ended up moving in with him. Then she got pregnant and he freaked out. And I had her move in with me. It was crowded but great. And then…

and then Ana was born and it was so fun to have her here. So amazing." Paige looked down into her glass, tears sparkling on her lashes like shattered crystal. "We were making it work. The three of us."

"How old are you, Paige?" he asked. She looked young. Beneath all the makeup, he was sure she looked like a girl who could still be in school. Her skin was smooth and pale, her blue eyes round, fringed with long, dark lashes. Her lips were full and pink, turned down at the corners, giving the illusion of a slight pout.

"Twenty-two."

"You're only twenty-two?" Ten years younger than he was. And yet she was willing to take on raising a child by herself. "Then why do you want to raise a child right now? You have so many years ahead of you. And don't you want to get married?"

She shrugged. "Not really. And anyway, I guess…no this isn't the ideal time for me to have a baby. And if you had asked me a few months ago if I was ready to have a baby, I would have told you no. But that would be a hypothetical baby. And Ana isn't hypothetical. She's here. And she doesn't have anyone. Her birth mother is dead, my friend, my best friend is dead. The line on the birth certificate that should have a father's name on it is blank. She needs me."

"She needs anyone who will care for her. It doesn't have to be you." She flinched when he said the words.

"It does," she said, her voice thin.

"Why?"

"I don't know for sure if anyone else will love her like I do. And I…I knew Shyla. I knew her better than anyone, and she knew me. I'll be able to tell her about her mother." Paige's throat convulsed. "And Shyla asked me to. She asked me to take care of her."

That answer hit him hard in the chest and the memories he'd been pushing away from the moment they'd picked Ana up at the nursery crowded in, too fast and forceful for him to hold back anymore. He'd been much older than Ana when he'd lost his mother, so he remembered a lot on his own. Memories that he often wished he didn't have. Of soft lullabies, gentle hands…and blood. In the end…so much blood.

He blinked and shook off the memory, reclaiming control, lifting the glass of wine to his lips and grimacing when the chilled, acrid liquid hit his tongue. There was no buzz on earth worth that. He set it back down on the table.

"I understand that."

"It's not just for her. It's for me, too. I love her. Like… like she really is my baby. I saw her come into the world. I cared for her from the start, did the midnight feedings and visits to the doctor. I can't…I can't just let her go. Let her go to someone else. Someone who might not love her like I do. How could anyone love her like I do? I love her so much that sometimes it overwhelms me."

Paige spoke with conviction, so much it vibrated from her petite frame. Dante couldn't imagine emotion like that. It was so far beyond where he was now.

In truth, he couldn't imagine a good emotion that strong. Fear, grief, the type that had the power to reduce a man to a quivering, raw mass of anguish…that he knew. But nothing like it since. Nothing that even came close. He was numb to feeling.

But he could sense hers, could feel them radiating off her. She didn't hide them, didn't sublimate them to try to deal with them. He doubted she could. She was too honest.

Well, except for that one little lie. The one he was currently enmeshed in.

"You cannot keep the pink in your hair," he said. He needed to tone her down, to make her less distracting.

"What?" she sifted her fingers through her dark hair, the movement unconsciously sexy.

"I would hardly become engaged to a woman with pink hair."

"Um…but you did. You totally just did."

"I didn't know about the pink stripe until recently. When I found out I nearly broke it off with you, so you promised to go to the hairdresser."

"You can't even see it if I have my hair down."

"I saw it when we were in bed." Again, the images of her skin against his sheets hit him hard.

Her cheeks colored a deep rose. He couldn't remember the last time he'd made a woman blush, discounting Paige, and he certainly couldn't remember ever finding it so fascinating.

"Uh…and that was your predominant thought? My pink hair? We did something wrong, in that case." She looked away from him and took another long drink of her vile wine.

"Just color over it," he said.

"I have an appointment in a few weeks. It'll keep."

"You seem to forget that I'm doing you a favor."

"I didn't think that was your predominant motivation. And anyway, I'm doing you a favor, too."

He shrugged. "Maybe. Maybe not. I don't know what the reaction will be. I'm curious to find out."

"So, this is just a social experiment to you?"

"It's interesting, yes. Ultimately though, it's with a mind to improving business."

"And deceiving people doesn't bother you?"

"Does it bother you?"

She frowned. "Usually. But not now. Not for…not for Ana. I would do anything for her."

"So I gathered."

"I'm far more bothered by the fact that we're actually… that we'll be getting married." She looked down, giving him a view of long, dark lashes spread over pale skin, and lids that were lined in emerald green, a sprinkling of golden glitter adding sparkle.

"If you can think of another way…"

She raised her focus, her expression open, honest. "I can't. Nothing this certain."

"Then don't trouble yourself over it."

She frowned. "I won't. So, now what do we do?"

"I'll text your ring size to Trevor and send him to procure something suitable. You will have it on your desk by lunch. Then…then we have a charity event to go to."

"I don't have anyone to watch Ana."

"I'll pay Genevieve to do it. She's good with Ana, isn't she?"

"Well, yes, but…I'll have been away from her all day."

"Leave early," he said. "I'll come here and pick you up before the event."

"Why do you keep having answers to all of my problems?" she asked, her tone petulant.

"I would think that would be a good thing, especially since you have so many problems at the moment."

She let out an exasperated sigh. "Granted."

He stood, taking his glass of nearly untouched wine off the coffee table. "Good night, then. I'll be by to pick you and Ana up at seven-thirty tomorrow morning."

"Wait…pick me up?"

"You're my woman now, Paige, and that comes with a certain set of expectations."

She blinked. "I didn't…I didn't agree to this."

"You brought me into this. That means you aren't making all the rules anymore." He turned and walked into the kitchen, pausing at the sink and dumping the contents of his glass down the drain. "That wine is unforgivable. I will teach you to like good wine."

"And you'll teach me to like good jewelry, and the sort of hair you deem 'good.' Tell me, Dante, what else will you teach me to like?" She crossed her arms beneath her breasts—rather generous breasts—and a rush of heat assailed him. Intense. Impossible to ignore.

The desire to lean in and trace her lips with his fingertip, with his tongue, was nearly too strong for him to overcome. But he would. He would keep control, as he always did.

He took one last, lingering look, at her pink lips. "That's a very dangerous question, Paige," he said. "Very dangerous."

CHAPTER FOUR

THAT'S a very dangerous question.

Yes, it had been a dangerous question. Only Paige hadn't realized just how dangerous until it had come out of her mouth. And she was certain that Dante didn't realize how much truth was behind it. How much teaching she would need.

Oh, dear.

Just thinking about it again made her feel hot, all over. And that was exactly why she wasn't going to think about her futile, one-sided attraction anymore

She looked at the clock and shifted in her chair. Genevieve was already here, and Ana had been happily passed off to her. It hadn't taken the little girl more than a moment to recognize her daily caregiver and the two were happily playing on the rug in the living room.

Paige sighed and realized that she was jiggling her leg. She stopped herself. Her little nervous habit wasn't a good look with the long, silky gown she was wearing.

Yes, she was wearing a dress, to go on a date. Which was something she hadn't done in…almost ever. She wasn't the girl that men went after. She was the screwup, the funny one. The one with a pink stripe in her hair, although Dante was putting the kibosh on that.

She didn't get dressed up in slinky gowns to go to fancy charity dinners with billionaires. She also didn't get engaged to billionaires. Oh, yeah, she didn't really marry them, either, though that was now in her future. All because her stupid, impulsive brain had spit out the most ridiculous lie at the worst time.

Desperation wasn't her best state. She more or less had a handle on the blurting these days. When she'd been a kid, all the way up into high school, it had been really bad. She was always saying stupid things and embarrassing herself, which was one reason she'd opted for class clown rather than trying to be sexy or cool or anything like that. Letting it go, instead of wishing she could be something she wasn't, had been much easier.

Or rather, as the case had been, she'd had one incredibly defining, humiliating moment that never let her forget that there were certain guys, who liked certain kinds of girls. And she was not one of them.

There was a heavy knock at her door and she scrambled up out of the chair, grabbing her handbag and wrap. She scurried into the living room and bent down, dropping a kiss onto Ana's soft, fuzzy head.

"I won't be too late," she said to Genevieve.

"I wouldn't blame you if you were," Genevieve said.

Paige's cheeks got hot and she was sure they were a lovely shade of red. "I...we won't be late." She had to get a handle on the blushing, too. There was no reason to blush. Dante Romani was hardly going to ravish her in the back of his car.

She straightened and draped her bright purple wrap over her bare shoulders, giving herself a little look in the small mirror that hung in her living room on her way to the door of her apartment.

The door opened just as she reached it.

"Were you going to leave me freezing on the front step?"

"It's San Diego. It's not freezing. And you're in the temperature-controlled hallway."

"It's the principle," he said.

"I had to say goodbye to Ana. Do you want to see her?"

A strange look crossed his face. Confusion, fear, then boredom. "No."

"Oh, sorry. Most people like babies, you know," she said, stepping out into the hall, closing the door behind her.

"I have no interest in having any of my own. I'm not certain why it would be important for me to like babies."

"They're cute."

"Yes, so are puppies but I don't want one."

"A baby isn't a puppy," she said.

He shrugged. "It doesn't matter to me for the reason previously stated."

She rolled her eyes and pushed the button on the elevator. "Right. Well. I hope Ana and I don't disturb you too much when we live in your home, as you don't want a wife or a child."

"It's a large house," he said, his words carrying a stiff undertone, as if he didn't believe it would be large enough.

The doors to the elevator slid open and they both stepped inside. She'd never noticed how small elevators really were before she'd taken to riding in them with Dante Romani. He made everything feel smaller. Tighter. Because he filled the space he was in so absolutely.

It wasn't just because he was well over six feet tall and broad, either. It was his charisma, the dark energy that radiated from him. He was so unobtainable, so uninterested in what was happening around him. It made you want to go and grab his attention. Made you want to be in his sphere. To make him seem interested. To make him smile.

To make him laugh.

At least she did, but she was good at that. Making people laugh and smile. Defusing tension with antics and jokes. And she had, apparently, not learned her lesson about unobtainable men.

She nearly opened her mouth to make one when her eyes locked with his and the breath leached from her body.

His dark eyes roamed over her curves, taking in every

inch of her. And she was reminded again of their exchange last night.

What else will you teach me to like?

Oh, no, no, no. She wasn't going there. She never had before, no reason to start now.

Besides, Dante could have any woman he wanted, on the terms he chose. He had no reason to start lusting after her pink-striped self.

She'd grown up in a small town, and every guy she knew had known her from the time they were in kindergarten together. They knew that she talked too much, and that she very often laughed too loud. That she had trouble paying attention in class. That she'd cut a boy's tongue with her braces during her first kiss. They knew that she'd been the focus of what had essentially been the senior prank. They knew that she'd barely passed high school, that her parents hadn't seen the point of paying for her to go to college when she just wouldn't apply herself. They'd watched her get a job at a coffee shop instead of going away to school like everyone else.

They had all watched her grow from an awkward kid, to an awkward teen, to an awkward adult. It was like living in a fishbowl. And being the slow fish with the crippled fin. Nothing like her straight-A achieving sister and her football-star brother.

She was just…Paige. And it had always seemed like a pitifully small accomplishment, just being her. For most of her life, she'd accepted it. She'd just put on the image they'd applied to her and owned it. So much easier than trying to be anything else.

But there was a point, as she was pouring a cup of coffee for her fiftieth customer of the day, who asked her about her brother or sister, and not about her, that she couldn't do it anymore.

A week later she'd moved. Just so she could be new to a place. So she had a hope of finding who she was apart from the painful averageness that marked her life.

It hadn't been an instant transformation, no sudden rise to the top of the social heap. But she'd made a small group of friends. She'd found her job at Colson's. That provided her with the first real sense of pride she'd ever had in a job.

They'd seen her raw talent and they'd hired her based on that, not based on classroom performance. Colson's, and by extension, Dante, was her first experience with being believed in.

Strange.

She cast him a sideways glance. He was tall and…rigid in his tux. Each line of his suit jacket conforming to his physique with precision. Dante was never ruffled. She envied that a little bit. Or a lot of a bit, truth be told. She was captivated by it, really, his control. His perfection. His beauty. It was a dark, masculine beauty, nothing soft or traditionally pretty about him. It made her want to look at him, and keep looking.

The elevator doors slid open and they walked out of her apartment building and to the street. There was a black car parked against the curb, waiting for them, she assumed.

Dante opened the back door for her and she slid inside. She'd never ridden in a car with a driver before. Not even a taxi. She always drove her own seen-better-days car.

"It will be nice not being the one fighting traffic for a change," she said when Dante got in on the other side and settled into the seat beside her.

"Mmm," he said, taking his phone out of his pocket and devoting his attention to checking his email.

And just like that, the hot guy wasn't looking at her anymore. Typical.

She let her gaze wander to her left hand, to her still-bare ring finger. "Oh…didn't you…you were going to give me a ring before tonight, weren't you?"

He set his phone down. "Yes," he said. "I don't know why you're intent on spoiling the surprise."

"Uh…because it's not a surprise."

"Perhaps I had something planned."

She didn't think he was serious. But with Dante it was hard to tell. Still, she couldn't help but wonder what it would be like, to have a man like him do the get-down-on-one-knee thing and ask her to be his wife. To look at her with intensity in those dark eyes and...

"So, ring?" She held out her hand and tried to shut out the little fantasy that was playing in the back of her mind.

Forget a dream proposal. She should aim for a kiss that wasn't a disaster first.

Her reached into the inner pocket of his suit jacket and produced a velvet box. "Be my wife, et cetera," he said, opening the box, revealing a pear-shaped emerald surrounded by diamonds.

"It's...wow." Hard not to be completely floored when a gorgeous man was giving you a beautiful ring. "How did you know I liked green?"

"Your eye shadow," he said.

She looked up, as if she could see it. "Oh."

"And I thought the color and style would suit you. Sedate doesn't seem to be your thing."

"Uh...no. Not so much."

"Put it on," he said.

"What? Oh, yeah." She looked down at the ring and a clawing sense of dread made her chest tighten. Was she really going to do this? To put on his ring and go all the way with this?

Yes. Yes, she was. She'd never believed in anything more in her whole life. She'd never been the goal-oriented one in her family. She'd never been the top achiever. She'd never wanted anything so much it made her ache.

That wasn't the case now. Now there was Ana. And she made Paige want to be the best mother. Made her want to do everything she could to give her baby the best life possible. To encourage her, to love her as she was.

She took a deep breath and lifted the ring from its silken

nest, sliding it onto her finger. "There. We're engaged now," she said.

He nodded slowly and leaned back in the seat. She couldn't tell what he was thinking. If he was thinking.

"What?" she asked.

"What do you mean by that?"

"I was just wondering what you were thinking. I mean… this is weird." She wondered if he was thinking of a beautiful blonde, or stunning, dark-haired beauty he would rather have given a ring to. The thought made her chest feel odd. Tight. "We don't really know each other and…were you planning on getting married ever?"

"No," he said, definitively. Decisively.

"Oh. Not even if you meet the right person?"

"There is no right person for me. Or at least not one who's right for more than a couple of days. And nights."

Dante watched Paige's face, the confusion, the little bit of judgment. What he'd just said wasn't true in the strictest sense. The part about marriage was true, but the way he'd spoken of his relationships made it sound like he and the women he slept with met and spent a few days locked in a passionate embrace.

Nothing could be further from the truth.

He'd had arrangements with a few different women over the course of his adult life. Women who were just as busy and driven as he was. Women who were just as averse to relationships.

The women he usually took to the charity events, the models, the actresses…he didn't sleep with them. They were the bit of flash, the ones who looked good in pictures and who wanted to be in them.

But they were too young, many of then. Too starry-eyed and not nearly cynical enough. The women he took to bed, all they wanted was a couple of hours and a couple of orgasms. They wanted what he wanted. They didn't want forever and fireworks; they wanted a basic need to be met. And that's what happened. Basic, simple pursuit of release.

Still, there was no way to explain that without making it sound even worse.

And when had he ever cared what anyone thought? Never. He'd come into the public eye amid speculation and criticism. The Italian orphan that had somehow weaseled his way into the Colson family. That had been named as the heir of a billion-dollar fortune. There had been endless speculation about him, about how it had happened. As if he, even at fourteen, had known some sort of dark secret about the older couple who had taken him into their home. Something that would have enticed them to take on such a sullen, angry child.

He had never once tried to correct the rumors.

But something about the look in Paige's eyes made him want to clarify, to change her assumptions. Or at least make an excuse.

"What about you," he asked, happy to redirect the focus of the conversation to her. "Do you want to get married? Beyond this, I mean."

"Well, I wasn't really at the point where I was thinking about it."

"All women think about it."

"That's a gross generalization and there's no way you can know that. Or rather, you *can* know that you're wrong because I wasn't. Not in a serious way."

"Why not?"

"I've been too busy discovering who I am. Apart from the small town I grew up in, I mean. I've been down here for about three years and I've been kind of…finding myself. Which sounds maybe a little bit geeky but it's true. Back at home there were all these preconceived ideas about me. Who I was, what I was capable of. And when the town is as small as mine, those ideas don't just come from your parents, they come from…everyone. I moved here and decided to really figure out who I would be if there was no one around expecting anything different."

"A noble quest," he said. And interesting, considering that he was doing the same thing, in a way. On a surface level, at least. He had no interest in finding himself, whatever that meant. But the idea of changing perceptions, that one grabbed him.

"Not really," she said. "Just a desire to be seen as something other than a terminal dork."

"I can't imagine you being thought of as a…as that."

"Well, I was. Scrub off the makeup, add a ponytail…I revert right back. Actually, I don't think I'm evolved all that far beyond dork status—it's just that I have a better handle on confusing people by presenting a more polished appearance."

"Polished but flashy."

"Distract them with something shiny, right?"

In some ways he understood that philosophy, too. Bring a beautiful, bubbly date and people might not notice how much he hated being at public events. Might not notice how little he smiled.

"Right," he said, his eyes on her ring. He took her hand in his, ran his thumb over her smooth skin, to the gem that glittered on her finger. "This should do it," he said, looking up, meeting her gaze.

Her eyes were round, her lips parted slightly and he knew that he could lean in and kiss her and she would kiss him back. The desire to do it, the need, tightened his gut. They would have to do it in public eventually. It would be perfectly reasonable to give it a try now. To press his lips to that soft, pink mouth. To dip his tongue inside and find out if she tasted as explosive as she looked.

He turned away from her sharply, putting his focus back on his phone. He wouldn't kiss her. Not now. Not because he wanted to. Not because the desire, pumping hot and hard through his veins told him to. No, when there was a need for it, he would do it. Not before then.

He was in absolute control of his body, and his desires. Always. It would be no different with Paige. They were playing a game that bordered on dangerous, and that meant he had to be sure that he kept things tightly in line.

Paige cleared her throat. "Right. It certainly is...distracting."

"Yes," he said, clenching his teeth tight, "it is."

You can't have more champagne. You'll make a total ass of yourself.

She'd already rolled her ankle twice while walking around the lavishly decorated ballroom and had stumbled obviously, teetering sharply to the right thanks to her three-inch heels.

She wasn't exactly making the best appearance as Dante's brand-new fiancée.

But this had all happened so fast she hadn't had time to adjust. And that was one of the many reasons that alcohol felt slightly necessary.

The other was that moment in the car, just before they'd arrived, when Dante's dark eyes had been focused on her mouth. When heat and desire had spread through her, flushing her skin, making her heart race. When she'd looked like a total fool, drooling over a man who didn't have the slightest interest in her.

Yeah, there was that.

"Enjoying yourself, *cara mia*?" Dante appeared, holding two glasses of champagne. He offered her one, and she took it, in spite of herself.

"I'm not really sure," she said.

"You aren't sure?"

"No. I mean, I don't know anyone here but you so I'm basically just standing next to you smiling and no one is really talking to me and...my cheeks hurt."

"Your cheeks?"

"From the smiling."

"Ah." He frowned. "I must confess most of my dates aren't

here for conversation so I imagine the assumption has now been made about you."

"What are they here for?" she asked. The obvious, she imagined. The pleasure of having Dante later.

"For the publicity," he said, uprooting her previous assumption. "There will be several pictures of you, standing next to me and smiling, published in various places online and in print by tomorrow morning."

"So, women date you to get their picture in the paper?"

"I'm not really vain, but I don't think that's the only reason."

Paige's heart slammed hard against her breastbone as she thought of all the other reasons women might date Dante. Oh, yeah, she could see that for sure. "Well, I mean...I'm sure your sparkling wit and effusive personality also net you a few dinner engagements."

He laughed, a more genuine, rich laugh than she'd heard from him before. "I doubt it, somehow, but thank you for the confidence in me."

"Or course," she said. "It's the least I can do considering what you're doing for me."

"I'm getting something in return."

"You say that like you have to convince yourself you aren't being altruistic," she said, regretting the two glasses of champagne she'd already had, and the candor that came with them, the moment she said it.

"Because I never am."

"So can never be?"

"Mr. Romani, and your lovely fiancée!" They were interrupted by an older woman with a broad smile.

Dante inclined his head. "Nice to see you again, Catherine, and please, call me Dante."

"Dante, of course." Catherine began regaling Dante with stories of her country club, gossip, both personal and business related. She noticed that Dante managed to appear vaguely interested, his expression politely pleasant.

And yet she could see something behind his eyes. Calculation. She could almost see him filtering out the unimportant, retaining bits about failing businesses and mistresses who might cause trouble in someone's professional life.

Then he smiled, a smile that some might call warm, and bid the older woman goodbye.

"Who was that?" she asked.

"A friend of my…parents," he said, the word coming out in a few, halting syllables.

"Oh."

"I'll confess, I don't like these things, either," he said. "But, you do hear interesting information. It's worth it. So that about sums up my altruism, really. It's for charity, which is nice. But I get something out of it, too. Nothing is purely altruistic."

She thought of Ana, of how much joy Ana brought to her life. How much love and purpose. "I suppose not."

"Does the purity of motivation really matter anyway? As long as no one is hurt. As long as people are cared for?"

"I always imagined it did."

"Nobody gets points for good intentions."

"I suppose not." The champagne spoke for her again. "Does anyone hold bad intentions against you if you don't act on them?"

"Speaking of yourself, or of me?"

She shrugged. "Just curious if it works both ways."

"In my experience, intentions, and sometimes actions, don't really matter at all. What matters is what people think."

"Now that is true," she said, sighing heavily, thinking back to how people had perceived her in her home town. Of how the social worker perceived her and her situation.

He lifted his glass. "To reinvention," he said.

She lifted her glass in response but opted out of taking a sip. She needed to get her feet back on solid ground, needed to get her words back under control. And she really needed to get her thoughts in regards to Dante back under control.

"Perhaps when we're through with this you and I will both be totally different people," she said. "Or at least, in your case, people will think so."

A smile curved his lips. Not a friendly smile. One that was dangerous. And, though it really shouldn't have been, sexy. "Perhaps."

CHAPTER FIVE

PAIGE took her latte off the counter and waved to her favorite barista as she walked out the door of the coffee shop.

She paused and put her sunglasses on, taking a sip of her drink while admiring the afternoon light filtering through the palm trees. It was a perfect day. The light glinted on her new engagement ring and it put a slight dent in her moment of zen.

There was a flash to her left and she turned to look. It was not a little flare of afternoon light. There was a photographer, standing there, holding his camera up, not even trying to be subtle.

"Uh...could you not do that?" she asked.

"Ms. Harper?"

"What?"

"When are you and Dante Romani getting married?"

She clutched her sequined purse to her side and strode down the sidewalk, away from the man with the camera, her heart pounding. She turned back to look and saw that he was still there, snapping off shots casually. Like she was a monkey in a zoo.

Her purse vibrated and she reached inside, casting another glance behind her as she retrieved her phone and answered the call. "Hello?"

"Ms. Harper, this is Rebecca Addler with child services. I wanted to speak to you about your case."

She quickened her pace, heading back to the office building. Back to Ana. Back to Dante even. She could hide behind his broad chest. And she wasn't even ashamed for wanting to hide behind him right now.

"Right. Great to hear from you. What about the case?" she asked, scurrying through the revolving door to the Colson's corporate building and walking quickly to the elevators.

"We're going to have to interview your fiancé. He's going to be involved in the process, of course."

"Well, of course."

"And he'll be adopting Ana, as well."

Damn.

"So there will be paperwork for that," she finished.

Paige had overlooked that bit. She'd overlooked it completely. "Of course," she said, her throat dry. She took another sip of latte and scalded her mouth. She punched the up button on the wall and waited for an elevator.

She dashed inside as soon as the door opened.

"And we'll want to do a parent interview with him."

"Naturally. Dante will be delighted—" like Dante was ever delighted about anything "—to participate."

"We'll do a little meet-up this Friday if that works for you."

"Of course it does!" she said, far too brightly.

The elevator reached her floor, and she stood inside, waffling. Then she hit the button that would take her to Dante's floor and the door slid closed again.

She tapped her foot while she finalized the details of the appointment with Rebecca. She ended the phone call as quickly as possible and tapped her fingers on the wall, waiting for the elevator to stop. When it did, and the doors opened, she nearly ran out, past Trevor, and to Dante's office.

She didn't bother to knock.

"I just got my picture taken. Like…a hundred times by some photographer. And then Rebecca Addler called and said we need to start doing interviews as a couple. Oh, I just realized there will be a home study, and we'll have to start over and do it at your house because as far as everyone is concerned that is where we'll be living. And you're going to adopt Ana legally. Which is sort of…obvious but I didn't think of it until now and…and I'm officially panicking a little bit."

"Don't," he said, standing from his position behind the desk, his large, masculine hands planted palms down on the pristine surface. He didn't even have the decency to look surprised that she'd burst into his office. He just looked… smooth and calm and unaffected as ever.

It was just unfair, because her cage was well and truly rattled.

"Don't panic?"

"No. There's no need. When we divorce I'll sign custody of Ana over to you. You have my word on that."

"Oh." She let out a breath she didn't know she'd been holding in a rush. "That does make me feel better."

"I thought it might."

"Then there's the home study."

"You and Ana should move in with me. Soon." That he said with a kind of grim determination that let her know exactly what he thought of it.

"I can see you're completely thrilled at the idea."

"I value my own space," he said.

"Well, as you mentioned, it's a big house. I'm sure we won't be on top of each other."

He lifted one dark brow, and horror crept over her as she realized the double meaning of her words. As she pictured just what it might be like to be on top of him.

Or to have him on top of her.

Her entire face heated, prickling awareness spreading over her skin. Her heart was racing and she was…turned on. And it was obvious. She was certain it was.

She was such a dork. A side effect of spending her school years as the funny one. She didn't know how to be smooth; she knew how to go for a joke. Another side effect of that was that guys didn't flirt with her.

Well, that might have also been because of the time Michael Weston had tried to make out with her at a party and had ended up cutting his tongue on her braces. No one had wanted to kiss her after that. Kissing her became a running joke, and very firmly kept her in her place as school screwup.

Well, after that someone had made her *think* he wanted to kiss her, and more than that. It had all been a gag, of course. Thinking about that reduced the horror of the situation a little bit, because nothing, nothing in the history of the world, was quite as bad as meeting a guy under the bleachers after prom to…to…and having the popular kids standing by, waiting for just the right moment, waiting for the top of her prom dress to come down, for her "date" to pull her out from beneath the bleachers onto the field so they could throw eggs at her. And laugh. And take pictures of her humiliation for posterity.

Yes, that put a woman off dating for a while.

As a result, she wasn't great at handling men. Unless they were more like buddies. And Dante didn't feel like a buddy. Not even a little.

"You know what I mean," she said. "Don't look at me like that."

"Like what?"

"You know," she said, narrowing her eyes.

"As for the parent interview…" He neatly sidestepped the moment.

"What about it?"

"I don't see how it will be a problem."

"You may have to grow a personality between now and then."

"And you may want to tone yours down."

"Why because a fun-loving, smiley person might not make a good parent? Do I need to be a bit more dour?"

"Are you calling me…dour?" he asked.

"If the scowl fits."

"You're going to have to keep yourself from taking shots at me in the presence of the social worker. Actually, you should probably keep yourself from taking shots at me because I'm your boss."

She bit her lower lip. "Yeah. Okay, that could be…"

"And don't bite your lip like that." He leaned forward and extended his hand, putting his thumb on her chin, just beneath her mouth.

She slowly released her hold on her lip, her heart pounding heavily, butterflies taking flight in her stomach and crashing around, making her insides feel jittery.

She could only stare at him, at his incredibly handsome face, his dark, compelling eyes.

"I'll try not to," she said, not sure why she agreed with him. She should be annoyed that he was being so dictatorial, and yet she found she wasn't. But that could be because he was touching her, and men didn't make a habit of touching her.

It didn't mean she didn't want them to. It just hadn't really happened for her for many and varied reasons. A huge reason being she was too afraid to let a moment like that happen. Because she was afraid to acknowledge she wanted it, for fear of it all being a joke again.

"Good. You're also going to have to work on not blushing like a schoolgirl every time I get near you."

"I don't blush." She could feel the heat creeping into her face, calling her bluff.

"You blush more than any woman I've ever seen."

"I'm very pale. It's hard to hide when you have no pigment to disguise it."

"I imagine," he said. "Even so, if we were truly engaged we would be well past the point where I could make you blush with just the casual brush of my hands. Unless…" he said, rounding the desk, coming to stand near her. "Unless you were thinking of all the things my hands have done for you."

His voice changed, became rougher, more ragged. Something in his expression changed, too. Hardened. Never, ever, ever had a man looked at her like that before. Not even close.

She wanted to say something to defuse the tension. Something funny, or random, something to break the spell. But she couldn't. A part of her didn't want to. She wanted to stand there, and have Dante Romani look at her like she was the most fascinating thing he'd ever seen. She wanted to get closer to him, see if he was as hot as he looked. To see if the fire smoldering in his eyes would burn her.

"I…suppose that could be a possibility." She looked down, trying to catch her breath. But her eyes connected with his hands, and that did not help her regulate her breathing. "Subtext, right? Like when you're acting? You make sure that even your thoughts match those of your character. And…stuff."

"Something like that," he said.

Of course to really have good subtext she would have to know exactly what he could do with his hands, and frankly, some of that information was a little hazy for her. And she was in no position to change it. Not now, not with him. And, given that she was going to be single mother of a small child for quite a few years, maybe not anytime soon.

That had never really been her plan. But she'd been too afraid to put herself out there after the way she'd been treated. Too afraid of rejection.

Dante picked up his phone and dialed a number. "Trevor, I need you to hire some movers. Send them to Paige's apartment. The address is on file. Personal items only, no furniture, all of the baby supplies. It needs to be done by the end of the day." He hit the end button on the phone and put it back in the holder on his desk.

"Did you just…evict me?"

"You'll keep the apartment, for later. I assume that's the place you'll go back to."

"Yeah, I think I'll need my home. But what's going to happen with it in the meantime?"

"There's no reason to do anything with the apartment. I can handle the rent for you for the duration of your stay at my home."

"I pay the rent. I'm not having trouble with the rent—there's no reason for you to pay it for me!"

He shrugged. "But I can, so I don't see why it's an issue."

"Because *I* can," she said.

"Don't be stubborn."

"Me? You're telling me not to be stubborn? That is funny, Dante, real funny."

"This ruse really ought to be easy. In fact, they may assume we've been married for twenty years given the way you argue with me."

"I argue with you? Hmph."

"Yes, you do. Just like that."

"Well, I'm annoyed with you."

"Then you had better get un-annoyed, *cara*. Remember, this whole thing is of your making. I never would have sought you out." His words made her flinch internally. "I will take advantage of the situation, yes, but I would not have sought you out. You're completely unsuitable, obviously, and if I had felt the need for a wife pressing I would have one already."

Stupidly, a little pang of hurt hit her square in the chest, knocking the wind out of her, making her eyes sting. "I'm... unsuitable? Wh–why?"

She shouldn't have asked why. Not when she really didn't want to hear it all.

"Am I suitable to you?" he asked, his tone incredulous.

"No," she said. "No, you're rude. And obnoxious. And you don't know how to laugh."

He took a step toward her, his dark eyes intent on hers. "And you are disorganized and scattered."

"I must not be too bad since you keep me on here. Clearly I know how to do my job."

"As do hundreds of my employees, but that does not mean they would make a good spouse for me."

She took a step toward him, tossing her hair back over her shoulders. "I'm sure they feel the same way about you."

He reached out his hand and took a lock of her hair, her

pink hair, between his thumb and forefinger. "I would clearly never become involved with a woman who has pink hair."

She leaned in, up on her tiptoes, trying to make herself eye level with him. "And I would never become involved with a man who's more starched than his shirt collar."

He reached out and wrapped his arm around her waist, drawing her up against his hard body. She squeaked as her breasts came up against the muscular wall of his chest. "You think I'm too serious, is that it?" She nodded mutely, no words coming to her. "That I don't know how to have fun." His fingers flexed against her back, sending little pops of sensation from the point of contact all throughout her body.

"Yes," she managed, heat flooding her.

He dipped his head so that his lips were nearly touching her cheek, his breath hot on her skin. "I think I might surprise you."

She was trembling, actually trembling, and in danger of having a knee-buckling experience. No man had ever held her like this before. With such purpose, with such strength. No man had ever made her feel so wanted. No man had ever made her want to arch against him, press her breasts harder into his body.

And most especially, no man had made her want to kiss him while she was angry at him.

But here she was, quivering with the need to touch Dante, even while thinking murderous thoughts about him and his autocratic behavior.

Dante released her suddenly and she stumbled back, trying hard to catch her breath. She looked at him, searched his face for some sign of what he was thinking. To try to figure out if he was as affected, as shaken, as she was.

But he wasn't. He was just standing there, his hair smooth, his suit crisp, as though he had never taken her into his arms. As though he hadn't just held her so close she could feel his heart beating, hard and heavy against her chest.

"You had better figure out a way to forgive me," he said.

And that was when she realized that he was affected. Because he might look as smooth as ever, but his voice was rough, his shredded control evident in each word he spoke. "Because at the end of the day, you're coming home with me."

CHAPTER SIX

DANTE'S home was his most prized possession. The lawn was immaculate, cut perfectly and kept in top condition by his team of groundskeepers.

The house itself was a triumph of architecture. Clean lines, an open design, windows that made the most of the ocean view. The interior was white, the carpets, the walls, the furniture. Evidence of how orderly it was.

Evidence of the control he now held over his life.

And as Paige, with her glittery high heels, walked over the threshold, carrying a bright-eyed baby girl with drool running down her chin, he felt a pang of absolute dread hit him in the gut.

There was nothing orderly about either of them, and he could feel the hard-won control of his surroundings slipping away from him.

"This is…" Paige looked around, her mouth open, her blue eyes round. "This is incredible. Gorgeous. I don't… I've never seen anything like it."

"I had it built five years ago, shortly after the control of Colson's passed to me."

"I'm thinking the social worker will like this place better than she liked mine."

"Probably," he said, thinking of her cluttered little apartment. "I apologize for my lack of boxed wine. I suppose something from the cellar with have to do."

"Now, now, nobody likes a show-off."

"That depends on what they're being shown."

"Heh. No, it depends on how much money and power the show-off possesses, and then the person will pretend to be suitably impressed based on how much they figure ingratiating themselves will help them out."

"So you think my admirers are merely out to use me for my wealth and fame?"

She shrugged. "Not so far-fetched, is it?"

"You're not very good for my ego, Paige, as you seem to think no one would suffer my company without heavy compensation."

"That's not what I meant. Oh…pfft. I like your house—that's the important thing right now."

"I assume the location of your bedrooms are important, as well?"

"Bedrooms?"

"Ana will have a nursery. I called my housekeeper earlier and ensured that all of her things have been put in there."

"A nursery?"

He let out an exasperated sigh. "Did you think I would cram you both in the basement to keep you out of the way?"

"Well, I didn't know. I didn't… We really need to discuss this more."

"I agree, which is why we're having dinner together later."

"Oh."

"Here, so you don't need to worry about a babysitter. Now come with me." He started up the stairs and down the hall. He could hear Paige's footsteps behind him, slow and methodical. He turned and saw that she was practically getting whiplash. "What is it?"

"Your art!" she said.

"What about it?"

"It's so beautiful. And it really stands out in the white space. You have fabulous taste."

"Fabulous? Rarely am I accused of being fabulous."

"Well, in this instance, you are. I'm going to have to take the time to study it all later."

"So, you like art?"

She smiled and her entire face brightened, her blue eyes glittering. "Love it. I'm not just into dressing windows. I paint, too. Well, I started with painting. And some sculpture. It was about the only thing that held my attention in school. Unfortunately, one cannot graduate with art credits alone."

"I would guess not." The enthusiasm she felt for the subject, for the paintings—paintings he hardly looked at anymore—was fascinating. She was so different than most of the people he knew. She was open. She wore her passion all over her, for anyone to read. Not just her passion, her anger, her happiness. Everything was just laid bare with her.

And she evoked something in him. Emotions, things he hadn't felt in longer than he could remember. As a result, he'd made a mistake in his office earlier, and he didn't make mistakes.

But she'd been standing there, all challenge and fire, angry as hell. And she'd made him angry. More than that, she'd tempted him. He hadn't been able to stop himself from walking forward, from wrapping his arm around her and drawing her body against his.

She challenged him. No one challenged him. But she did. And she picked at his control, pushing and pushing until he'd been unable to do anything but push back.

He didn't like it. Emotion was destructive. Painful. But he wouldn't give in to it. What he hadn't lost the day his mother died had been drained from him over the course of eight years in foster care.

Now, he doubted there was even enough in him to cause problems, even if he wanted it to. No, what had come over him in his office was lust. Pure and simple. Normally, that wasn't a problem for him, but he was only a man, so it wasn't too surprising.

Paige had the added benefit of being forbidden fruit, another thing that had never appealed to him before, but he could certainly understand why it might.

"Ana's room is here," he said, redirecting his thoughts, indicating a door on the left. As he pushed it open, a strange flash of anxiety ran through him. It was unfamiliar. Completely different than it had been that morning when he'd left for work. It gave him a strange sense of being back in his childhood. Opening the door to a new bedroom for the first time, seeing what was there.

Whether it would be spare, or crowded. Clean or dirty. Nothing that belonged to him.

The space that had been organized for Ana was immaculate.

Plain white walls and a double bed had been replaced with an ornate, dark wood crib with pink bedding and a mobile hanging over it. There was a rocking chair, a matching dresser and a closet filled with pink clothes.

"Oh." Behind him Paige made a little noise. Then she brushed past him and into the room. "Ana, look. It's your very own room."

His chest seized up tight, his breath locking in his lungs. The light in Paige's eyes as she presented Ana with a space that belonged to her was…he had never seen anything like it. All of Paige's unruly enthusiasm was, in this moment, focused on her daughter.

How anyone could doubt that she would be a good mother was beyond him. It was hard for him to remember his birth mother, hard because thinking about her always dredged up other memories that he wanted to keep firmly locked behind a closed door in his mind.

Mary Colson, his adoptive mother, had been a firm and constant presence. Both she and Don had invested in him, into his education, into guiding him, putting him on a path that would lead to success. He was grateful to them, and their distant, tough sort of parenting had been ideal for him.

But for a moment, he wondered if anyone had ever looked at him the way Paige was looking at Ana.

It didn't matter. He closed the door on the yawning, empty well inside of him. He wasn't a child. He didn't need obvious displays of emotion. Far from it, he avoided them if at all possible. And being around Paige didn't seem to allow for that. She was constant bubbling energy, and emotion. And glitter.

"Thank you," she said, her blue eyes bright.

"Don't thank me," he said, trying to find some way to loosen the knot in his chest. "You're here under false pretenses, due to a situation of your own making. And it's hardly permanent, so don't get too attached."

She blinked, a flash of genuine pain visible on her face. So open. So real. Did the woman have no sense? Had she no defenses at all? "Okay, I…I mean I know that, but this is beautiful and I just got really excited and I didn't mean anything by it." All of her words ran together, coming faster as she rambled, the tension she was feeling palpable. She projected her feelings. So strongly he felt like he was being hit with a wall.

"Relax, Paige," he said. "Take a breath."

She snapped her mouth closed, her eyes still pooling with confused emotion.

"I'm sorry," he said, the word foreign on his tongue.

Almost instantly, the tension left her, her face brightening. "It's awkward. For everyone. I know. I'm not picking out china patterns or anything, I'm just…making the best of things. Making the best of living in a mansion by the sea, which, I admit, is not so hard."

"You may not be so optimistic when you hear what I have to say next," he said.

"You're putting me on a hide-a-bed. No, my window has an ocean view, but the beach is a nude beach. Or maybe…"

"You're going to have to at least appear to be sharing a room with me."

"Say what?"

"Come now, Paige, are you so naive? If we've moved in together, we'll obviously be sharing a room. A bed."

Paige bit her bottom lip. "I don't know about that. What about good, traditional values?"

"Does anyone have them these days?"

"My social worker, it seems. Since she was so concerned about Ana having a mom and dad."

"Which means she needs to be confident that that is indeed what Ana is getting. And my staff needs to believe it, as well. The last thing I need is for someone to slip up and make a comment that winds up in the paper. I'm not being dragged into a public farce. A private farce, it seems, is unavoidable, but I will not be humiliated in a public forum."

"That's not my intent," she said. "But hey, as long as I don't actually have to sleep with you, I'm okay with having to dig through your closet to find my clothes."

He wasn't. He'd never lived with a woman before, had never had feminine things mingling in with his suits. His space was highly prized and this element of their arrangement didn't sit well with him.

But while she was comfortable with her things being put anywhere, there was clearly one area that made her uncomfortable. And he had the uncontrollable urge to push at her, just a little.

"You're the first woman I've ever encountered who was so opposed to sleeping with me she had to remark on it every couple of days."

He was rewarded by the flood of color that bled into her cheeks. "That's not… I'm just clarifying…"

"One might think," he said, taking a step closer to her, "that you protest too much."

She pulled Ana in tighter to her chest, a tiny, living shield. "Hey now, that is not true. I protest just enough for a woman who isn't interested in having a…a fling with a playboy."

"Playboy," he said. "Such a strange label, and not one I've ever felt applied to me."

"You change lovers often enough."

"The dates I go to events with are not my lovers. I am very discreet with my lovers. And selective."

She cleared her throat. "Well, then, I doubt I have anything to worry about. If you're as selective as you say, I mean."

Paige felt like melting beneath Dante's intense, dark gaze. She didn't know what had possessed her to bait him like that. To tempt him to say something derogatory about her appeal. She was aware of how far short she fell when it came to sexual allure.

The problem was, it wasn't looks, not specifically. It wasn't the way she dressed. She'd actually managed to score dates since moving to San Diego; it was just that…when they got that serious look, like they might miss her, she sort of freaked out. The idea of failing again, with someone new, was too painful. The thought of wanting someone who wouldn't really end up wanting her…she hadn't been willing to take the risk.

Which was why she really hadn't bothered with dates for a long time. Getting herself sorted out was her top priority after all. Finding her way. And anyway, she didn't need a hundred guys. She only needed the one right guy. And she was certain that one right guy would look nothing like Dante Romani.

Which was fine. Looks weren't everything after all. The guy didn't have to have a square jaw, and golden skin. Or a broad chest with incredible muscles that could not be hidden by the dress shirts he wore. He didn't have to look like the essence of temptation wrapped in a custom suit. No. There were much more important things than that.

Like…way more.

She was sure of it.

"Is that what you think?" he asked.

Something in his eyes changed, the look becoming hungry, wild almost, as far from cool, calm, stuffed shirt Dante Romani as she could possibly imagine.

"I…obviously," she said, her throat suddenly dry.

"What is obvious about it?" he asked.

"I'm…I'm…"

"Attractive," he said.

She blinked. "Even with the pink stripe?"

"It's growing on me."

"Maybe I *will* get it colored over next time. In that case."

"You just like to be difficult."

She shrugged. "I'm a contrary beast, on occasion, I admit it." She was doing it again, deflecting with humor, so he couldn't see how much it had meant for him to call her attractive.

"I like a challenge."

"I'm not a challenge," she said, nerves skittering through her, making her feel shaky and off-kilter.

"You aren't?"

"No. That makes it sound like I'm some sort of a…a game and I don't like that. I don't play games. What you see is what you get."

"I've noticed. But I didn't mean that I intended to play a game with you."

"You didn't?"

He shook his head, his dark eyes intent on hers. "I don't play."

She tried to swallow again. Her throat felt like it was coated in sand. "Right. Neither do I."

He chuckled, dark and rich like chocolate. "I got the impression that you did very little besides playing."

She looked down at the top of Ana's fuzzy head. "And where did you get that idea? Between working for Colson's and taking care of Ana, I don't have a lot of playtime."

He frowned. "I suppose that's true. But it's more the way you are. The things you say. You're…happy."

She laughed, the sound bursting from her with no decorum or volume control, as always. "I guess so. I mean, there's plenty of crap I'm unhappy about. Like losing my best friend and having to contend with the adoption stuff. But I suppose…I mean in general I suppose that's true." She studied Dante's face for a moment, the lines that feathered out from the corners of his eyes, the brackets by his mouth. "Are you happy?"

He shrugged. "I'm not really sure what that means. I'm content."

"Content," she repeated. She smoothed her hands over Ana's back and a rush of love, or pure joy and pain filled her. "How can that be enough?" It wasn't for her. Not now. It never would be again.

"Because emotion, strong emotion, is dangerous," he said. "You don't seem to realize that yet, Paige. But that's the truth of it." His voice was rough. Savage, almost. And coming from Dante, who was always smooth, and never ruffled, it meant something. It reached down deep inside of her and twisted her stomach.

"Was it the truth for you?"

"It's just true," he said. "If emotions control you, you have no control over yourself. In my mind, that's unacceptable. Now come, and I'll show you to your room."

CHAPTER SEVEN

AFTER you put Ana to bed, come down to the dining room for dinner.

Paige touched the note Dante had left her earlier. A note. Who wrote a note? She'd have to introduce the man to the mighty power of the text message. Or, better still, making human contact when you lived in the same house as someone.

She touched one of the letters on the paper. He'd pressed too hard on his pen, made dents, each letter precise and perfect, gone over two or three times she guessed. Dante didn't do spontaneous very well, that was for sure.

Well, she supposed their arrangement fell under spontaneous, but then, even when he'd had that headline sprung on him he hadn't acted with any sense of wild abandon. It had been with frightening calm, and complete confidence in the fact that he'd made the right decision.

Whereas, she, after blurting out the idiot untruth to Rebecca, had eaten a pint of ice cream and spent the night beating her head against the arm of her couch.

Decisive wasn't really her thing. She needed to start getting there, though. She had a baby. A baby that would grow, and who would need a mother who could stand strong in decisions and discipline and…stuff.

The idea of it made her a little anxious. But for now, it was all about loving her. And that she had down just fine.

At least her room was nice. And yeah, all her clothes and

her toiletries were in Dante's room, but she'd managed to get her dress for dinner and her makeup essentials over to her room without running into him. Which suited her fine. She'd been feeling a little rumpled and frumpy after what had been a very long day.

But a shower and a sparkly minidress had done a lot to fix the way she felt. Her newfound sense of flashy style was something she'd acquired on arrival in San Diego, and it had done wonders for the way she felt about herself. About the outside of herself, anyway.

She leaned into the mirror and swiped her lipstick over her bottom lip, painting it with a streak of fuchsia, then spreading it evenly. She smiled. She felt better when she was bright. Like showing the world her mood, so that she had to bring herself up to match it.

She let out a long breath and opened her bedroom door, padding quietly down the hall to Ana's room first, to make sure she was sleeping soundly, then continued to the stairs. She took the stairs two at a time, anxious now to hear what Dante would say.

To see if he would tease her again. Flirt with her? No, he wouldn't flirt with her. There was no reason for that.

She tripped on the last step, her focus splintered over her thoughts.

"Careful."

She looked up and her heart slammed hard against her breast. Dante was standing in the doorway of the dining room, his eyes on her. On her nearly falling on her face. He, on the other hand, looked immaculate as always. Perfectly pressed in a crisp white shirt that was open at the collar, showing a faint shadow of chest hair that she couldn't help but notice, and black slacks that showed off his trim waist and powerful thighs.

Since when had she ever noticed a man's thighs? What was he doing to her?

"I like to make an entrance," she said, doing a very lopsided curtsy in an attempt to defuse the tension. All she really succeeded in doing was making herself look like a bit of an ass. That seemed to be her specialty. But it didn't matter really. She just kept smiling. If she didn't care, no one else seemed to. No one else seemed to notice how hard things were, how awkward she felt, if she didn't.

She straightened and smiled, hoping she didn't blush.

"You certainly do that." He walked toward her, the easy grace in his movements filling her with one part envy and nine parts desire. He really was gorgeous.

"Ha. Yeah. My blessing and my curse."

He put his hand on her lower back and heat fired through her from that point to the rest of her body. He propelled her forward into the dining room and she was afraid she might wobble again. Not because she was that big of a klutz, not usually, but because his touch was making her limbs feel rubbery.

She sucked in a breath when she saw the table. It was laid out special—gorgeous platters with appetizers and there were candles. It was very real, suddenly. Like an actual date, which she knew it wasn't.

And she shouldn't let it make her feel any kind of pressure. He wasn't interested in her that way, and that was fine with her. She didn't have the time or inclination for it.

"This looks great," she said, too brightly.

He pulled her chair out for her and looked at her, waiting for her. She just stared.

"Would you like to sit down?" he asked.

"Oh, uh...yes. I'm not used to men pulling my chair out for me."

"Then you need to associate with better men."

"Or maybe find men to associate with in general."

"I imagine your dating life is somewhat hobbled by recent developments."

"Yeah, recent developments. That's what's hobbled my dating life." She sat down and he abandoned his post at her chair and went to sit across from her. She took a salmon roll off the platter and put it onto her plate, her stomach growling, reminding her it was late for dinner. "So," she said, "you want to talk?"

"We need to talk. I'm not sure I particularly want to talk. But we need a plan. If we're going to be a couple, to both child services and the media we need to know about each other."

"And how do you propose we get to know each other?" she asked, taking a bite of the sushi.

"I'm not proposing we get to know each other. I'm proposing we learn things about each other. The two are different."

"Less involved, I suppose," she said.

"Much." He took a roll off the platter with a pair of chopsticks. Effortless for him, as ever. "Where are you from?"

"Silver Creek. Oregon. Small, bit of a nothing town. Everyone knows your business. Everyone knows you. The entire population is kind of like your extended family."

"Which is why you moved."

"Yes. To somewhere that didn't have people with…expectations." Expectations of her failure. Of her continuing to drift through life without a goal, without any success. "And you, where are you from?"

"Rome originally. Then moved to Los Angeles. And then…when my mother died," he said, his voice too smooth, too controlled, as if he was saying words he'd rehearsed to perfection, "I went into foster care. I spent a few years with different families before the Colsons adopted me at fourteen."

"I could have found all that out by reading a bio online somewhere."

"But had you read one?"

"No."

"So, I still had to tell you."

"Fine, you did. What else do I need to know?" she asked.

He slid two covered plates over from the edge of the table and placed one in front of her, and one in front of himself. She uncovered it and took a moment to appreciate the tantalizing look and smell of the fish dish before directing her focus back to Dante.

"My sign?" he asked, his tone dry.

She laughed. "I don't even know my own sign. I don't pay attention to that stuff."

"That surprises me—you seem like you would."

"Why?"

"Because you're very…free-spirited. And you're an artist."

"I see. Well, sorry to disappoint you. What's your favorite color?"

"I don't have one."

"That's stupid. Everyone has a favorite color."

He arched one dark eyebrow. "Did you just call me stupid?"

"No. Your lack of favorite color is stupid."

"Fine, what's yours?"

"Well, I'm an artist, so I have a close relationship with color. I like cool colors—they're very calming. And of course warm colors are quite passionate. So I have to say my favorite color is…glitter."

He laughed and she felt a small tug of gratification that she's managed to pull an expression of humor out of him. "That isn't a color."

"Sure it is. I'm an expert. I don't question you about merchandising and advertising and everything else you have a hand in. Siblings?" she asked.

"No," he said. "You?"

"Two. My sister is a pediatrician and my brother is a second-string quarterback for the Seahawks. Impressive, I know."

"Very. So how did you get into art?"

She fought off the sting of embarrassment that always came when she had to talk about Jack and Emma. It wasn't fair, really. They deserved their success. They earned it. They had talent, and they worked hard.

They didn't deserve for her to make it about her. Still, it

was never fun to talk about. But talking about it was better than living in a town where everyone knew that you were, without question, the big letdown of your family.

"I've always been interested in it. Started drawing and painting really young."

"Did you go to school for it?"

"No." She shook her head, kept her tone light. No big deal. It was no big deal. "I never really liked school. Just wasn't my thing."

"And what did your parents think of that?"

"Would you like me to lie down on the couch before you continue?"

"Just a question."

"Well, uh…they've never been that impressed with my interests. My grades in school were bad, and they were spending a lot of money sending Jack and Emma to school already, even with the help of scholarships and…and they didn't want to pay to send me too when they knew I wouldn't apply myself. So the not going to school was a mutual decision."

She could feel Dante's dark gaze boring into her. "A mutual decision?"

She shrugged. "I mean, I might have gone if they…"

"But they wouldn't."

"No."

"Should we tell your parents about the wedding?"

The subject change threw her for a moment. "Oh, it's… No, probably not. It's not like it will be huge news outside of our circle here. Your circle here, I should say and anyway… they won't really approve of the whole thing with Ana." An understatement. She could just hear her mother's skepticism.

Do you think you can handle it, Paige? Filled with concern, and a bit of condescension.

But she could handle it. She was sure she could. She was almost completely sure. Again, the bigness of it all threatened to swamp her completely. She couldn't remember the last time she'd really wanted something. The last time succeeding had been so important, if it ever had been.

It was so much easier to just not care. But with Ana, she couldn't.

"They don't approve of you adopting?" he asked.

She shrugged and put her focus back on her food. "I haven't talked to them about it, but I figure if I save it until everything is final I can spare everyone a lot of angst. It still might not work out." Her throat tightened, terror wrapping icy fingers around her neck.

"It will," he said, total confidence in his tone. "We have the media involved which, now that I think of it, is very likely going to work in your favor. I doubt social services want reports out about how they denied an adoption to a child's lifelong, primary caregiver."

"You may have a point. I have to ask, though, what's really in it for you? Because I don't have any guarantee that you won't back out. I know you talked about easing business deals but clearly you make deals just fine without me, so I can't fathom why it would suddenly be important."

He shrugged one shoulder. "I have opportunistic tendencies. This opportunity presented itself and I decided to follow it to its conclusion. There were two options in this situation—do what was expected of me, accept the negative press. Or, try to change things."

"And that's all? Because truly, with that as your only motivation, I'm not really filled with comfort and warm fuzzies."

His gaze sharpened, his dark eyes intense. "It's important for you to know something. When I say I will do something, I do. There is no going back."

He said it with such purpose, such unequivocal certainly that she couldn't help but believe him.

"You didn't have to do this," she said. It was the truth. She was the one in the stranglehold. She was the one who was in a situation that was too big for her, nothing unusual there. She was the one who needed help.

But instead of giving up, like she usually did, she'd done whatever she'd had to in order to secure her success. Unfortunately, that had meant lying. It had meant dragging Dante into the situation, and she really did sort of feel bad about that.

"I am doing it. I made the decision. I won't change my mind."

"But is the media thing…that's all you want?" she asked. Seriously, it was a stupid question because she didn't exactly have anything to give him if changing his image in the press wasn't enough.

He put his fork down, and took in a deep breath, his expression one of barely contained annoyance. "I have been the target of malicious rumor and speculation by the media since I was fourteen years old. I came onto the stage a villain. I thought it might be interesting to see if I could end up a hero."

There was no real venom in his words, none of the emotion that was so easy for her to think should be there. That the media had been attacking him since he was a young teenager seemed unforgivable. But he just said it like it was an interesting fact. And he talked about changing public perception as if it were no more than a fascinating experiment.

"What did they…say about you?"

"That I had somehow tricked the Colsons into adopting me. That I was holding something over their heads, that I was a plant for the Mafia—racially motivated attacks are always nice. That I might murder the poor, trusting older couple in their beds."

He spoke so casually, without inflection. Cold horror settled in her stomach, making her shiver. He continued. "Some thought Don Colson had 'imported' me because I was some sort of financial genius and he lacked an heir."

"But you knew the truth," she said, her heart tightening, aching for him. Things with her family were hard, and sometimes she felt like she didn't belong, but she didn't have the media weighing in on it.

He paused for a moment. "That's the thing. Paige, I don't

know the truth. Why they would take me in is somewhat beyond me. A fourteen-year-old boy with no people skills and no inclination to find any. But I was smart," he said, as if trying to reason it out. "I did well in school."

Oh, good, he was a genius, too.

"I'm sure it was more than that," she said. Because she really needed to believe that getting good grades in school wasn't the deciding factor on a person's value. Otherwise she was sunk.

"Perhaps. I'll have to ask them sometimes."

"You never have?"

"It doesn't matter."

"But it does."

"No," he said, his voice hard, "it doesn't. They gave me a future, the best education possible, the best job opportunity possible. They gave me the means to support myself." He chuckled. "That might be an understatement. They gave me the means to thrive. They owe me nothing. No explanation. No frilly words. I don't need them. I have everything I need. And I think you and I have everything we need, too."

He stood from the table, his food less than half-finished. "I'll see you in the morning. We'll all drive to work together. It would look wrong to go separately."

She nodded and watched him walk out of the room. She picked up her fork and started eating again. She wasn't going to go to bed starving just because he'd decided to get upset about something and leave.

And he was upset. For all that he'd stayed calm, she could tell that the conversation had disturbed him.

There was so much more to her poker-faced boss. Finding out just what lay beneath the surface should be the furthest thing from her mind. It didn't matter. Nothing mattered but Ana.

But it was Dante dominating her thoughts tonight. She sighed and tried to focus on her dinner, and not think so much about the deep, overwhelming darkness that she'd glimpsed in his normally expressionless eyes.

Dante unbuttoned his shirt and took a hanger out of his closet. He put it on the hanger and buttoned the top few buttons, then put it in its place in the closet

He moved his hand to his belt buckle, then paused for a moment. He walked into his en suite bathroom and braced his hands on the vanity countertop, looking at his reflection in the mirror.

He didn't look at himself often. He didn't see much point in it. But he did now. And he wondered what other people saw.

He chuckled, the sound bitter, hollow in the empty room, and turned the sink on, running cold water onto his hand, splashing it onto his face. He knew what people thought about him. They wrote it in on society blogs and people, people from all over, were able to leave comments with their explicit opinions.

Sexy, but dead behind the eyes.

Amoral.

Italian bastard.

Impostor.

Yes, he knew what people thought of him. How they saw him. And he knew that it didn't matter. Not because he was so at peace with who he was, but because he genuinely didn't care.

A man makes his own destiny. If he is in control of himself, he can control everything around him.

Words from Don Colson when he'd first come to live with them. From the man he thought of as his father. The man he'd never felt worthy of calling father. It was what made him strive to be worthy. The Colsons were the only people who'd inspired that feeling in him.

Control was the key. It was what put him on Don Colson's side. And not on the side of his real father. The man who'd spilled his mother's blood. The man whose blood ran through his veins.

He shut off the water and turned, walking back into his room. His bedroom door opened and Paige stopped short, one foot in the room, a sharp squeak escaping her lips.

"I thought you were…that is…you didn't say anything when I knocked, and my pj's are in here. I'll…come back."

It took him a moment to realize that her wide eyes were glued to his bare chest. It gave him a strange sense of satisfaction to know that, in spite of her constant reminders that she didn't want to sleep with him, she wasn't immune to him.

Something that shouldn't matter.

"No need. Find your pajamas," he said. "Don't mind me."

"Right," she said, sliding into the room and moving quickly to the closet. She opened it and walked in. He watched her rummaging in the corner that had been designated for her clothing. He would have to ask his housekeeper to lay things out more nicely for her. His closet was huge, and his clothes always well spaced out so he could see what he had. There was no harm in crowding things in a little bit for Paige's sake.

Although, just when the idea of giving her some substantial room in his home had stopped bothering him, he wasn't sure. Maybe, *stopped bothering him* wasn't the right way to put it. More that it didn't make his eye twitch.

"Got them." She emerged a moment later, clutching a pair of flannel pants and a white T-shirt to her chest. "So I'll go."

He found that he was reluctant to let her leave. If she left, he would be alone with his thoughts, and tonight, his thoughts were on a dangerous path.

"Those don't look like I imagined they might," he said, extending his hand, taking the flannel between his thumb and forefinger.

"No?" she asked. He noticed that her chest pitched sharply, in time with a sudden breath. That his drawing nearer to her was making her nervous. That he was right in his earlier assessment of her. She wasn't immune to him.

"No," he said. "Something diaphanous and flowing, I thought. Something with glitter."

"And slippers with heels and feathers?" she asked, her voice thin and shaky.

"Also a tiara." He took a step closer to her, heat firing in his blood. He was thinking too much tonight and being near her made him feel less like thinking, and more like acting.

He lifted his hands and brushed his finger along her cheekbone. Her mouth dropped open, her lush lips forming an O. Oh, yes, this was simpler.

He slid his hand around, cupping her head, his thumb stroking her face still. "Even so, this has a certain appeal to it. As does the dress you have on now."

"D-Dante…"

"If we are going to be a couple, do couple interviews and things like that, you will have to look comfortable with me touching you."

"I'm comfortable," she said, the high pitch of her voice proving her a liar.

He wasn't comfortable, either. He was shaking, he was hard as hell and he couldn't fight the need that was coursing through him, not anymore. He had seen her, he had wanted her. Wondered what it would be like to taste all that color and light. To absorb it into himself.

But he had denied himself. No more.

Without thought for consequence, without even trying to gentle his movements or ask her if she was all right, he leaned in and pressed his lips to hers. She was so warm. So alive. Her breath filled him, the soft sound of shock she made when he slid his tongue over the seam of her mouth, made his stomach twist.

Keeping one hand on the back of her head, he curved his other arm around her waist and pulled her to him. Her arms were pinned between them, still clutching her pajamas, keeping him from feeling her body against his.

He reached between them and tugged the clothes from her

hands, scattering them over the bedroom floor. She pressed her hands flat against his bare chest, her palms warm, her touch sending a shock of heat and fire through him.

He traced her bottom lip with his tongue and she opened to him, offering him entry into her mouth. He felt like drowning in her. Like losing himself completely.

He didn't realize he'd starting moving until Paige's back came up against his bedroom wall. She was pinned between the hard surface and him, her breasts pressing into his chest. So he deepened the kiss. Took more. Demanded more.

Her hands were still pressed tight against his chest and for a moment, he thought she might be pushing him away.

No. No, he needed more. He continued to kiss her, devouring her, until she relaxed against him, until her hands crept upward, fingers curling around his neck, clinging to him.

Yes.

His heart was pounding, sweat beading over his skin. She dug her fingernails into his neck, holding on to him tightly, pressing in closer so that his heavy length was resting against her stomach.

There was no room for rational thought. There was no thought at all. Not beyond the next hot, wet slide of her tongue on his. Not beyond the next gasp of pleasure that came from her lips. There was nothing but bright lights bursting behind his closed eyes, and a pounding need to take her, join himself to her. Go deep inside. So deep he would lose himself completely.

It would be the easiest thing to push her dress up, tug her panties down, free his aching erection and push inside her tight, wet body. Find solace in her release, and in his. To let go.

He jerked back, his heart thundering, his body protesting. This was not how he operated. Not why he had sex. Not how he allowed himself to live. He couldn't allow it. Not ever.

He would never give in to that creeping darkness inside

of himself. To the monster that lived in him. The thing that he hated most.

"I'm sorry," he said, his words clipped.

She blinked. "Why?"

"It shouldn't have happened," he bit out. It was inexcusable. The loss of control. The desperation he'd felt. To use her as a salve for his wounds. To let go of everything completely.

"I see," she said. She bent down and started collecting her clothes, her movements jerky, awkward. She seemed angry, upset.

"You think it was a good idea?" he asked, frustration pounding his temples, arousal pounding in his groin.

"What? Oh…it's just…" She stood up. "Whatever." She waved her hand in dismissal. "It was a kiss. It's not like it was anything serious. No big deal. Lips. Tongue. Not a big…I'm gonna go now." She sidestepped out of the room and closed the door behind her.

Dante wrenched his belt off and threw it on the ground, stalking into his bathroom and turning the shower on cold. He dropped his pants and underwear and stepped beneath the spray. He let the icy water roll over him, making him shiver, his body shaking from the inside out. It wasn't about cooling the heat in his body. He was paying penance for losing his control.

It would not happen again.

Paige leaned against her bedroom door, her heart sill pounding heavily, her lips still burning. Just a kiss? No big deal? She was getting good at lying.

She'd never been kissed like that, by a man like him, in her life.

And of course, the first words out of his mouth had been that it was a mistake. Of course it had been. How could it be anything else? A man like him would not want to kiss a woman like her. Not really.

Sometimes she felt like she was changing. Finding out who

she was apart from the labels she'd been given at home, back in high school. Tonight, she felt like she'd reverted. Back to the painfully awkward girl she'd been.

The one she still was beneath the makeup and sequins.

She changed into her pajamas as quickly as possible and tried to ignore just how conscious she was of the fabric sliding against her skin. Of how sensitive she felt. He'd lit her skin on fire, made her feel like she was burning from the inside out.

The memory of the kiss, of how it had made her feel, took the edge off her humiliation. He'd made her want to do something stupid, like run her fingers over that finely muscled chest. To feel him, firm flesh, heat and a hint of chest hair, beneath her palms.

He'd made her want more than that. Her entire body heated at the thought of exactly what he'd made her want.

And he thought it was a mistake. Had he even wanted her? Even a little? Or had he just been horny and wanting sex? And she was in his house instead of one of the women he'd *selected*.

He wouldn't have stopped with one of them. Wouldn't have called it a mistake.

She opened her door and padded down the hall, cracking open the door to Ana's room. She pushed Dante, and the arousal, the need, the hurt he'd inflicted on her, out of her body. A sense of calm washed over her as soon as she entered her daughter's room. She didn't need blood relation, or a government document to feel like Ana was hers. She was, in every sense of the word, no question.

She walked over to the crib and leaned up against the rail, not minding that the wood was digging into her ribs. She bent down and ran her hand over Ana's fuzzy head, down her stomach. Ana sighed and wiggled beneath Paige's hand, making a little smacking sound with her mouth.

So much perfection. So much love. So much responsibility. Paige had never succeeded at anything in her life. And she had to succeed at this.

No matter how hot the kisses, Dante Romani was just a means to an end. She couldn't let him distract her.

And that meant no more kissing. Unless they had to. For the press or for social services.

Suddenly she felt very tired. Like a weight had come to rest on her shoulders. It was harder than she'd imagined it would be. And she couldn't pretend that she didn't care. Couldn't pretend that there wasn't pressure pushing in from all sides. Couldn't pretend that losing would mean nothing.

Not when it would mean everything.

"I'll do my very best, sweetie," she whispered, an ache in her throat, a tear rolling down her face. She just hoped that for once, her best would be good enough.

CHAPTER EIGHT

PAIGE managed to avoid Dante for the next few days. As best as she could avoid someone when she lived with him and drove to work in the same car with him every morning.

She was definitely much more careful when trying to sneak into his room for clothes. Not because she was afraid of him, but because she was afraid of herself.

She'd liked the kiss too much and she was in serious danger of longing after the man. She didn't do the longing thing. It ended in disappointment. And sometimes humiliation. Whether it was test scores or boys, that had been her experience. Longing just made the impossible hurt more.

There was no time for longing. She had to focus on Ana, not her suddenly perky hormones.

She growled into her empty office and bent down, rummaging through the box of glass, glitter-covered ornaments and gathered a few of them in her arms, taking them over to the work space she had cleared for herself in the back of the room.

The sunlight streamed in, bright and perfect for Paige to get an idea of just how everything would glitter in the windows of Colson's department stores at Christmastime. The Christmas designs took up so much of her year, because every year there was the pressure to do bigger, better, more intricate. She loved it.

They moved her wooden frame, the same size and shape

of a standard Colson's window, so that it was right in the path of the sun and she started hanging the ornaments from the top with fishing line.

They caught the light, and they glinted. But it wasn't enough. She needed flash. She needed something no one would walk by and ignore.

She dug through her big box of sparkle, as she'd dubbed it, and produced a canister of silver glitter, one of gold and some deep purple gems. She set to it.

The finished product was much better. They caught fire when the sun hit, and beneath the display lights they would be fantastic.

She brushed her hands on her black skinny jeans and grimaced when she noticed the trail of glitter she'd put down her thighs.

"You've been working hard."

She turned at the sound of Dante's voice and ignored the fact that her heart had slammed into her chest and then started pounding hard and fast.

"Eh, you know the old joke. Hardly working and all that," she said. She wasn't sure why she was so quick to dismiss her work, and yet, she always did. Making light of it seemed to be her default setting. She was only just noticing it, and she didn't like it.

"Doesn't look that way to me," he said, crossing the threshold and moving to her work area. "I like it."

"There will be more. The mannequins, of course. Plus, about fifty more of these hanging at different heights. Snow. A Christmas tree. This is just for one of the side-street windows. But the main window display is going to be pretty amazing. I'm excited."

"I can tell."

"I put a lot of work into it," she said, for herself more than for him. "And I work really hard."

"Of course you do, Paige, or you would hardly still be on my payroll. This will be our third Christmas with you at the helm, and everyone has said how much higher the quality has been on the displays since then."

"Well...thank you."

"Tell me about the main window."

"It's going to be called Visions of Sugarplums. It will be a bunch of Christmas fantasies. And I think I want to have them like they're sort of springing from a dream. So some mist and icicles and lights. Very whimsical and beautiful."

"And all the same at each location?"

"I think each one should be slightly different," she said. "At least the big destination stores in Paris, New York, Berlin, et cetera. So that each one is an attraction."

"Do you have the budget for it?"

"Um, now that you mention it, I do need a slight budget increase."

"I thought you might."

"But you said my displays are high quality."

"I did. How much more do you need?"

She named a sum in the several thousands and Dante didn't bat an eye. "All right, if that's what you need, I will make sure you have it."

"Thank you," she said.

She stopped and really looked at him for the first time since he'd walked in. She'd glanced at him, but she'd avoided careful study. She knew why now. Looking at him full-on was a bit like staring into the sun. He was so beautiful it made her ache. She could no more reach out and touch him, have him for her own, than she could claim a star.

It made her feel so achingly sad. Just for a moment. She didn't have time to worry about Dante or the fact that she had the hots for him. Or the fact that, in all honesty, it felt like more than just having the hots for him.

"Ready for the couples interview?" she asked him.

"Of course," he said, his tone sounding thoroughly unconvincing. Which was funny, because if Dante was one thing, it was certain.

"What are you worried about?"

He looked at her and arched one dark brow. "I don't worry, *cara mia*."

"About anything ever?"

"No."

"What are you doing in business? You should be teaching self-help classes."

He chuckled, a dark sound. "I don't think I'm in much of a position to be telling people how to help themselves. I'm just very good at ignoring things I don't want to deal with."

It was shockingly honest, and it was also something she recognized.

"Yeah, me, too."

"Something we have in common," he said.

"Who would have thought?"

"Not me. Do you think it's enough to play the part of convincing couple?" He took a step closer to her and her stomach quivered. She could taste him on her tongue, the memory of his kiss so strong it was enough to make her knees shake.

Enough to make her take a step toward him. Stupid, really, because she shouldn't kiss him again. He didn't even want to kiss her, she was sure. Because that first time had been a mistake. He'd said so.

He tilted his head to the side, his expression intense, as though he was studying her.

"We certainly have chemistry," he said, his tone rough.

She laughed, shaky, nervous. "You think so?"

He nodded and took another step toward her. "Yes, and it's a good thing, too. Many things can be faked, Paige, and some of them even quite convincingly. But the heat between us? That's real. And no one will question it."

"I don't really know if one kiss constitutes as heat," she said. "One kiss that you said was a mistake."

His lips curved upward. "Are you challenging me?"

"No. I'm not that stupid."

"No, you are certainly not stupid." Strange, but that made

her chest feel warm, made her heart lift. "But you might be trying to bait me into kissing you again."

"Why would I do that?" she asked.

"For the same reason I'm hoping you are baiting me. I'd like to kiss you again."

"You…want to kiss me?"

He nodded.

"B-but last time you said…"

"I said it shouldn't have happened, because we both have goals to focus on. And I think we might both find it hard to focus while we're tangled together in bed. And that, Paige, is where a kiss like the one we shared in my bedroom leads."

"Oh."

"I'm going to kiss you again."

"I don't think that's a great idea."

"Perhaps not, but in just an hour we will be interviewed as a couple, and it's imperative we have no awkwardness between us." He took another step toward her and she could feel his heat, smell the scent of him. Clean skin, soap. Man.

She took a step toward him. His gaze dropped to her mouth and she pulled her lower lip between her teeth.

He reached out and put his thumb on her lip. She raised her focus, her eyes clashing with his. "I find I envy your lip," he said.

He couldn't possibly mean… She touched her tongue to the tip of his thumb, tasting salt, tasting Dante. Then she took a breath and a chance, and bit him gently. He closed his eyes, a rumble of satisfaction vibrating through his chest.

Emboldened, she repeated the action, biting harder this time.

He moved quickly, wrapping both arms around her and pulling her up against his hard body. She pushed up onto her toes and kissed him. It felt so familiar and so foreign at the same time. So wickedly exciting.

He thrust his tongue between her lips and she recipro-cated, the slide and friction sending a shot of heat through her veins. Making her breasts ache to be touched, making her feel hollow.

He put both hands on her hips and gripped her tightly, pulling her against him, letting her feel the hard jut of his arousal against her stomach.

He backed her against the desk and she adjusted so that the edge was just under her butt, supporting her weight. He moved in closer to her, parting her thighs slightly, settling between them.

He pressed his lips to her jaw, her neck, her collarbone.

She never wanted it to stop. She wanted more. And she didn't want to have to look him in the face when it was over and see the same regret she'd seen last night.

The kissing was safe. The kissing was good. She wanted more of that.

But it ended, and when he pulled away, it wasn't horror or regret she saw on his face. It was worse. It was nothing. Nothing but a smooth, beautiful, unreadable mask. Like he hadn't just pushed her to a point she'd never reached before. Like he hadn't introduced her to a whole new side of attraction.

Like the world hadn't just tilted on its axis. Her world certainly had.

"That, I think, proves my point," he said.

She wanted to hit him. Kick him in the shins. Sing a show tune. Something that would get him to react. Because his coolness, his totally unruffled state, was killing her.

"That we have chemistry? Yeah, thanks. I'm really glad I got to be a part of the experiment." She touched her lips. They were hot. And swollen. Overly sensitive just like the rest of her body.

Dante moved slightly and she caught a glimpse of gold shimmer on his suit jacket with the movement.

She frowned. "Could you move to the light here?" She indicated the shaft of sun coming through the window.

He complied, and the order did earn her a strange look,

which, all things considered, she would take and feel somewhat satisfied with.

The light hit his front and a giggle climbed her throat, bursting from her lips. "Oh, my gosh. I'm so sorry!"

"What?"

"Your suit."

He looked down at the spray of golden glitter that was pressed against the entire front of his suit in a little Paige-shaped pattern.

He uttered a curse and brushed his hand over his jacket. Paige tried to hold in her laughter, and succeeded in snorting.

He gave her a dirty look.

"I'm sorry! Oh, brushing it like that isn't going to help. Glitter is the cold sore of the craft world. It spreads easily and it's hard to get rid of."

"Yes," he bit out, "thank you. I actually figured out the reference without it being explained."

"You were the one who pulled me all up against you. I was working, as we established, and that involves…"

"It's fine, Paige," he said, his annoyance, probably with the whole situation, coming through now.

"I am sorry. Because that suit must have cost…"

"A lot," he ground out, "but I have a lot so it's not a big deal."

Except that he was meticulous with his things to a degree she couldn't wrap her mind around, so she knew on some level it was a big deal.

"Well, then…"

"I have some things to finish up and then I'll meet you at the day care to pick Ana up."

Dante had been forced to walk through the office advertising intimate contact with his own personal glitter fairy. Which, he imagined, he should be somewhat grateful for or at the very least, okay with.

She was, after all, supposed to be his fiancée, and that

meant they were expected to touch. To kiss. To have interludes in her office during the workday.

He should be fine with it, but he wasn't, and it had nothing to do with the possible ruination of his suit and everything to do with the flashing sign on his chest that was advertising his loss of control.

There were only a few minutes left until their interview. He stepped out of a cold shower and into his bedroom. He dressed quickly, ignoring the ache in his body that reminded him that no amount of icy-cold shower could steal the desire he had for her.

He gritted his teeth and turned sharply, hitting the solid wood bedpost with his open palm. The pain, he hoped, would remind him to keep himself under control. A reminder that passion had its price. That any loss of control had a cost.

Nothing was free. Nothing was without consequence.

The sting in his palm reminded him, for a moment, of her teeth grazing over his thumb. Of the reaction that faint pain had had on his body.

He closed his eyes and hit the bedpost again, the hard wood pushing past flesh and making contact with the bone in his wrist. He lowered his hand and shook it.

There was a timid knock on his door. "Come in."

"Oh, hi. I was wondering if you were ready?" Paige opened the door wide to reveal her and Ana. They were both dressed in pink. Paige in a bright, silk dress and Ana in pale pink one, her chubby legs swinging back and forth.

"I am now," he said, running his stinging hand over his hair.

"Good, she's almost here." Paige turned and flitted out of the room and he followed her. Paige had adjusted Ana so that she was up against her chest, Ana's bright eyes peeking over Paige's shoulder. Looking right at him.

He had no experience with babies, and no particular desire to become experienced with them. And this one, this tiny, perfectly formed human, seemed to look straight into him. As if she could see everything. And yet, her expression remained clear and bright. As if she saw it all, and it made no difference.

He realized then that there was one thing that had been neglected. He and Paige were meant to present themselves as a couple, but he'd forgotten that Ana would be with them. That he would have to find some ease with her, as well.

Suddenly, Ana's little face crumpled and she let out a high-pitched whine. Paige stopped completely, adjusting the baby's position, stroking her little cheek. It was amazing to see the effect Ana had on Paige. The little whirlwind of a woman was serene with her daughter in her arms. Her focus entirely on her.

Ana squeaked again and Paige started to sing. A soft, sweet sound. A lullaby. Terror curled around his heart, terror he hadn't anticipated, and couldn't shake off.

Paige bent forward, her necklace falling toward Ana as she continued to sing.

Cold sweat broke out over his skin, a sick, heavy weight hitting him in the gut and just lying there in him.

He knew one lullaby. And it was in Italian. If he closed his eyes, he could see his mother, leaning over his bed, her necklace hanging down, just as Paige's was doing now. Singing softly, her hand comforting on his forehead.

Stella, stellina,
la notte si avvicina
Star, little star, the night is approaching…

He shook off the memory, but it tried to hold him, tried to make him see it all. His mother, first alive and so beautiful, and then…

He swallowed hard and took in a breath. "Let's go," he said, his voice too rough, too harsh.

Paige's head snapped up and she looked at him with startled eyes. It made his heart twist. "Sorry," she said.

He shook his head. "No, I'm sorry. I am not myself today."

He wished that were true. Sadly, he feared he was more himself today than he ever usually allowed himself to be.

"Well, get it together. If you blow this…if we blow this… I can't lose her."

He looked at the little, fussing baby, and back at the woman who was, in every way that mattered, her mother.

"I know," he said, teeth gritted, heart pounding.

They couldn't blow it. Paige couldn't lose Ana, he knew that. But more importantly, Ana couldn't lose her. Because he knew, better than most, just how much of a loss it would be.

"Did it go well? I think it went well." Paige knew she was chattering, but she couldn't help herself.

The interview was over and they were out on the terrace on the second floor of the house. Dante's housekeeper had barbecued for them, and they were sitting now, their plates empty, looking out at the ocean. Ana was lying happily on her stomach on a large cushion that had been placed out for her, rocking back and forth and flailing her hands and feet.

"I think it went fine," Dante said.

There was no sign of the dark, angry man who had been in the hall earlier. There hadn't been any sign of him from the moment Rebecca Addler had walked through the door.

He'd charmed her, utterly. Clearly, the media's stories about him hadn't bothered her in the least or, if they had, Dante in the flesh had erased them in a moment.

He had that effect, that ability to make everything seem fine and easy. He exuded total and complete confidence, no matter the situation. He certainly interviewed better than she did, which was galling, because it showed her just how faulty something like this could be. She was the one who loved Ana, with all of her heart, and yet, he was the one who had charmed the social worker.

Thank God he was on her team.

"Well, I'm glad you're feeling confident."

"Why worry, Paige, the outcome will be the same either way."

"Easy for you to say. She's…everything to me."

"I know," he said, his tone serious. "And, I swear I will not let you lose her. Whatever it takes."

"Really? Why? Why would you…why would you do that?"

"Because I know what it is to lose a mother," he said, his tone cold. "I know what it is to drift from home to home, no one wanting you. That she is being spared the brunt of it, because of you… I will always have her be spared from it, and if I can help in any way then I will."

She looked over at Ana, and for the first time, she let the fear that was always ready to pounce on her, overtake her fully. "Can I do this? Am I really the best person?" She looked at Dante. "Tell me. Because I'm scared I'm going to mess it up."

He looked stunned for a moment. "I…I confess, I'm not the best person to judge how healthy a family is. But you love her. I remember love. I remember when I could feel it. I remember my mother. And the way you hold her, the way she feels when you're near, that's what it is."

A lump in her throat tried to block her words. "But I mess everything up," she said. "Ask anyone. My family, my teachers, my friends. I always got such bad grades in school. In math and science and history. I liked to read. I did well in English and art. But the other stuff…I could hardly pass a class. I did so poorly that my parents wouldn't help me get to college. And of course I couldn't get a scholarship. And no one was surprised. Because they just…expect it from me." She blinked back tears. "I have messed up about every major life moment a person has. First kisses, prom, getting into college. What if I screw this up, too?"

"You haven't messed everything in your life up," he said, taking on that confident tone that was so familiar to her now. "You do well at your job. Exceedingly well. You lost your best friend and you carried on, both with work and with raising her child. Do you know how many people would have been content to simply let the State take over? So many, Paige. And you didn't do that. You come through when it matters."

"But I'm scared to want it," she said. "I'm scared of how much I care for her."

He frowned and looked out at the sea, the lines by his eyes deepening. "Emotion is the single most dangerous thing I can think of. The kind that controls you. Makes you do things you never thought you were capable of. But…I can see the way it pushes you with her. You told the social worker you were engaged to your boss. You were willing to do anything, take any risk, for her. There is power in that. And your love seems to have power for good. Trust that."

His words were encouraging in a way, but so laced with a bitter sadness that they settled in her like lead.

"And what about your emotions?" she asked. "What power do you see in them?"

He looked at her, his dark eyes glittering. "I looked in myself, and saw the potential for terrible things. And since that day I haven't felt anything. I find my power from somewhere else, a place I can control."

She felt like someone had reached into her chest, grabbed her heart and squeezed it tight. "Dante…you're helping me. I look in you and I see so much good."

"Then you are blind." He stood up and walked off the terrace into the house, and all she could do was stare at his back retreating into the shadows.

She'd seen that emptiness again. That same look he'd gotten in the hall just before he'd snapped at her. That same look he'd had in her office when they'd kissed. She'd taken it for emotionlessness but it wasn't that.

It was something else. Something worse. Something she was afraid she couldn't help him with.

CHAPTER NINE

He heard crying. He moved to a sitting position in bed and swung his legs over the side, his feet planted on the carpet.

Ana was crying.

He stood and walked out of his room, striding down the hall. He opened the door to the nursery, casting a sliver of light into the room. He saw Paige, sitting in the rocking chair, holding Ana, rocking her, patting her back. Ana was crying still. And so was Paige. Glittery tracks down her cheeks.

His first instinct was to turn away. To walk away from the scene as quickly as possible, go back to bed. Shut down the strange emotions that were rising up, pressing on his throat.

"Is everything okay?"

"No," Paige said thickly. "She's been crying for an hour and she won't stop. I've tried everything. I fed her, I changed her. I'm holding her. I turned the light on, I turned it off. I don't know what else to do."

"I'm sure it's nothing you're doing wrong."

"What if it is?" she whispered, despair lacing her voice.

He took a step into the room, ignoring the tightness in his chest. "Babies cry, for no reason sometimes."

He'd heard that said, though he wasn't sure where.

"But Ana doesn't, usually."

"Does she have a fever?" That seemed a logical question.

Paige put her cheek down on Ana's head. "I don't think

so." She smoothed her hands over the baby's brow. "She doesn't feel warm to me. Does she feel warm to you?"

He couldn't bring himself to touch her. She was a tiny creature, fragile. Small-boned. Delicate. He didn't want to put his hands on her.

"I don't think she's warm," he said.

Paige put her hand on the baby's forehead. "No, you're right. I don't think she is. Could you sing to her?"

"Sing?" he asked.

"A lullaby."

His breath stalled in his throat, got trapped there. "I don't know any lullabies," he lied.

"Oh...that's okay." She patted Ana on the back. "I tried to sing and she just cried harder so I thought maybe you could..."

"Sorry," he said, curling his fingers into fists, fighting the urge to run from the room.

For that reason alone he had to stay. Dante Romani did not run. He would not.

Ana hiccuped, her tiny shoulders jerking with the motion. Her cries slowed, quieted, until they became muffled, sporadic whimpers.

He watched her for a few moments, silence settling between them as Paige continued to rock Ana until the whimpering ceased altogether.

"See, she was just crying," he said, trying to sound certain. Trying to feel some control over the situation when the simple fact was, he had none. There was a nursery in his home. There was a baby here. A woman. She had her things in his closet.

No, nothing was in his control anymore.

"I guess she was," Paige whispered.

She got up from the chair and walked over to the crib, placing Ana gingerly onto the mattress, then straightening, freezing for a second while she waited to see if the baby would wake up.

The room stayed silent.

"She seems like she's asleep now," Paige whispered.

"You should sleep, too," he said. She looked tired. Sad.

She wrapped her robe around herself, a little tremor shaking her body. "No. I don't...I don't think I could sleep right now."

The desolation in her tone did something to him. Made his stomach feel tight.

"Hungry?" he asked.

She shook her head. "Not really. But do you have chocolate?"

He let out a long, slow breath. Paige was upset, obviously, and while he would usually walk away and get back in bed without a twinge of guilt, he couldn't do that now. He wasn't going to take the time to analyze why. "We'll have to go raid the cupboards and find out. I'm not certain."

"How can you not be sure if you have chocolate?" They walked out of the nursery and left the door open so they could hear Ana if she woke.

"I'm not accustomed to raiding my kitchen at odd hours."

"I guess that's why you have washboard abs and I don't." Her eyes were trained meaningfully on his bare torso. Her complete lack of guile amused him, and aroused him. She didn't try to hide her open appraisal of him. And yet, it was different than the sort of open gazes he was used to seeing. There was no extra motive with Paige, only admiration.

He looked back at her, treating her to the same, intense study she'd treated him to. Her T-shirt molded to her breasts, her pajama pants sitting low on her hips. Too baggy for his taste. He wanted to see the curves beneath. "I have no complaints about your figure."

She stopped and turned sharply. "Oh, really?"

He shouldn't have said that. There was no point in fostering the attraction between Paige and himself. It wasn't good for either of them. She did something to him. Tested him in ways he'd never been tested before.

Detachment was normally simple for him. This time, not

so much. But he couldn't pull the compliment back now. He wasn't the sort of man to lie to a woman, or charm her to get her into bed, but he still knew enough to know that this was a subject to tread carefully with. Could sense that the wrong words could break her, or lead her to believe he could give things he simply could not.

"Every inch of you is beautiful," he said. It was the truth, not flattery. Though why he was compelled to speak it in that way, he wasn't certain.

She flushed scarlet. "You haven't seen every inch of me."

"Yet," he said, the word escaping without his permission and hanging between them, heavy and, he realized in that moment, stating the inevitable.

"No," she said, turning away from him and continuing down the stairs and into the kitchen.

"No?"

"You and I both know it would be a very bad idea."

"Why is that, Paige?" he asked. "What harm could come from a bit of fun?" There was so much wrong with that sentence. He knew exactly what harm resulted from sex and passion. Which was precisely why his sexual encounters were void of passion. Passion wasn't required for release. It was perfunctory. The right contact in the right place and his partners found their pleasure, then he was free to take his. Find a moment of blinding oblivion. But it had very little to do with the woman he was with, and even less to do with feeling.

And *fun* was a word he wasn't sure he put any stock in. He wasn't sure if he ever had any.

"Quite a few bits of harm, I think," she said, crossing to the stainless-steel refrigerator and opening the freezer, rummaging through the contents. "What ho! Chocolate ice cream!"

She pulled the carton out and held it high like a frozen trophy before setting in on the granite countertop. "Get spoons," she said. "And bowls."

"And the previous discussion is closed?"

"Yep."

He complied with her order and produced bowls and spoons. He set them out and scooped them both some ice cream. He pulled up on the edge of the counter and sat, and Paige did the same on the counter across from him.

"Maybe I won't be such a terrible mother," she said, eating a spoonful of ice cream.

"You won't be. But what has led you to the conclusion?"

"I used my stern voice and got you to change the subject and dish my ice cream," she said, her grin impish. But the impishness didn't reach her eyes. She still looked sad. Scared.

"I want to tell you something," he said. He lied. He didn't want to tell her what he was about to say, but it seemed important. It was all he had to offer.

She nodded and took another bite of ice cream, her eyes trained on his.

"Do you know what I remember about my mother?" he asked.

She blinked hard, her eyes glistening. She set her bowl and spoon down on the counter beside her. "No."

"I was six when she died. But I do remember her. How good it felt when she put her hand on my forehead before I fell asleep. The way her voice sounded, soothing, kind. The way she sang to me." He cleared his throat. "It's not about getting everything right. It's about those things, those small things. That's all that matters. You do that for Ana. You may make mistakes, but you'll be the constant, comforting presence in her life. That's what matters," he repeated.

He remembered more about his mother. Her fear. When his father would come home from work in a dark mood. Her tucking him in, locking his door with a key. So he couldn't get out and see. So his father couldn't get in and cause him any harm.

And he remembered her lying on the floor, too still. Too pale. The sparkle gone from her eyes forever.

He remembered lying with her on the floor and singing her

a lullaby until the police came. His hand on her head, stroking her hair, like she had always done for him.

Stella, Stellina. Star, little star.

He left that part out. If only he could leave it out of his mind. If only he could scrub the memory away. Hold on to the good, leave out the bad. But it wasn't possible.

The good always came with bad. Always.

A tear slipped down Paige's cheek. "She must have been wonderful."

"She was," he said.

"I have failed at so many things," she said. "And I don't know why. I don't know why things are harder for me. I tried to do well in school...I just couldn't. And my parents...I think they tried to be supportive of me, but I don't think they really believed that I was trying. My brother and sister, they were extraordinary, and they worked for it. But I had to work for ordinary. I had to bust my butt just to be average. And that meant no college for me. In their minds...I suppose I was a failure. I mean, I had my art but art doesn't translate to much, not to them."

"And that's why you moved."

She nodded. "To find out what it would be like if I wasn't surrounded by people who expected nothing from me. People who had given up on me. Shyla always believed in me. She said I was smart. No one ever said that. No one else. She encouraged me to go out for the position at Colson's and I thought...I thought there was no way. I had no degree, no experience. But your hiring manager...she saw something in me, too. In my work. She took a chance on me, and the only reason I was brave enough to take a chance on myself was because of my friend. I can't let her down," she said, her voice shaky. "There is so much at stake here and I can't fail. But failure is something I'm so good at, I'm afraid history will just repeat itself."

"Tell me, are your bother and sister artists?"

She shook her head. "No."

"Your parents, are they artists?"

"No."

"Could any of them imagine the window settings that you do? Not only that, could they find the materials, imagine the lighting, the colors, everything that you do, to make them a reality?"

"Probably not."

"Then maybe you haven't failed. You've simply succeeded in different areas. Areas that those other people couldn't, and so don't understand."

"I…" She blinked rapidly. "You're the first person who's ever…said it like that."

"It's true, though. We can't all be great at everything. I couldn't design the windows for the store, so I hired you to do it."

"Your hiring manager did."

"Fine, but you get the idea. I don't do everything. I don't have the ability to do everything. Why should you?"

"It's just that what I do has never been important to my family."

"That's their problem. You're good at what counts. You stand firm when you're needed. You're coming through for Ana. Your instinct, when you were being interviewed by the social worker, was to protect her, to keep her with you no matter what. If that doesn't prove that you're strong enough to do this, nothing will."

She slid down from the counter, her hands balled into fists at her sides. She took a sharp breath and crossed to him, standing in front of him, eye level to his chest. She reached up and put her hands on his cheeks, then tugged his face down as she drew up onto her tiptoes, pressing her lips against his.

He held on to the edge of the counter, letting her lead the kiss, letting her part his lips with her tongue. Letting her set the pace, the intensity.

He could taste the salt from her tears on her mouth, could feel the barely contained sadness in each shaking breath.

He ached to take control. To tug her up against him and to kiss her with every bit of pent-up passion, sorrow and pain that was buried inside of him. That was threatening to claw its way out through his chest if he didn't find a way to release it.

But he couldn't allow it.

This was for her, to have what she would. He would give it to her, and feel no sense of sacrifice. Whatever she wanted, she could have. As long as the true control belonged to him.

Paige pulled back from Dante, her heart thundering, her hands shaking. She didn't know what she was thinking, if she was thinking. All she knew was that she wanted to feel something big. Something real and affirming. She wanted Dante's actions to confirm his words.

She wanted to prove that she could want someone, and have them want her. That she wasn't broken. That she wasn't a joke. She wanted the unobtainable, beautiful man all for herself.

She didn't want happily ever after from him. She didn't want love. And she didn't want to thank him. It was something else, a need so deep and raw that she could hardly understand it.

All she knew was that his touch would make things better. His kiss would heal so many wounds, be the confirmation for what he'd spoken.

To prove that she wasn't a failure with men. That she wasn't undesirable. That someone could want her.

She smoothed her hands over his chest, his muscles hot and hard beneath her palms, his chest hair crisp. So sexy and masculine. So different from her own body.

"I want you," she said, her lips still pressed against his.

The silence that followed seemed to last forever. He might reject her. He probably would. But this was the first time she'd ever been willing to take the chance. It felt like a chain had been loosened on her, like she could move more freely.

He slid down from the counter, locking his arm around

her waist and drawing her hard up against his body. "You want to kiss me? Or you want more?"

"M-more."

"I have to hear you say it," he said, his tone stretched, tortured.

"I want to…to sleep with you tonight." A sudden, horrifying thought occurred to her, and her stomach sank to her toes. "Unless you don't want to." Why would he? He'd pulled away from every kiss they'd shared. He was a bronzed god of a man with a physique that looked too good to be real. A man with tons of sexual experience. A man who could have, and had had, any woman he wished. For a crazy moment she'd been convinced she could have this, could have him. But maybe she'd been fooling herself. Again.

He chuckled, rough and humorless. "How can you think I don't want you?"

"I'm average, remember?"

He moved his hand up to her hair and pushed his fingers through it, tugging on a pink strand, rubbing it between his thumb and forefinger. "I have never seen anyone quite like you. Which means the description cannot be accurate."

"You hate my hair."

He shook his head. "It's growing on me."

He pressed his other hand against her lower back and brought her into closer contact with his body. With the evidence of his desire for her.

Her eyes widened. "You do want me."

"I'm sorry it's so hard for you to believe. But by the end of tonight, it won't be."

She wished she had a witty reply, something to defuse the tension. Something to loosen the knot in her stomach and lessen the ache between her thighs. To lessen the importance of the moment. But there was nothing. Her brain was too busy spinning around all the ways he could show her.

Never before had discovering what she'd been missing with sex been so important. Been so essential. But it was now.

He kissed her again, intensifying it. He moved his hand down to the waistband of her pajama pants and let his fingertips drift beneath the flannel fabric, and down low so that he was palming her butt, his touch hot and rough and perfect. He squeezed her and a shot of liquid, sexual heat poured through her, zipping straight to her core.

She arched into him, rubbing her breasts against his chest, looking for a way to dull the ache there, squirming as the one between her thighs intensified, the hand on her bottom so close to where she needed him, the nearness making it all the more frustrating.

"We have to find a bed," she said, pulling away from him, her breath coming in out-of-control gasps.

"We don't need a bed," he growled, leaning in, kissing her neck.

"Oh. *Oh…*" Her mind went blank for a moment as his tongue swirled over the hollow in her throat. "Yes. We do. I don't feel like…I don't have the experience to…" She was not going to say virgin. She was going to avoid that word at all costs. "I'm remedial. At this. I need something standard. And soft. In case I fall or something."

He stopped for a moment, his dark eyes searching hers. "I won't let you fall."

You might not be able to stop me. The words hovered on the edge of her lips, but she didn't speak them. She didn't dare. She wasn't even sure what they meant. Only that they terrified her down to her bones.

"I know but…please?"

He nodded and swung her up into his arms. She squeaked and clung to his neck as he walked out of the kitchen and to the stairs, taking them two at a time. He didn't put her down until they were in his room, at the foot of his bed.

"Will this bed do?"

She nodded, her throat dry. "Yes. Now come here and kiss me. I promise not to get glitter on you."

He moved to her, cupping her cheek and brushing his thumb across her skin. "Your wish is my command."

He kissed her, deeply, sensually, his hands roaming over her curves. He cupped her breast, teasing her nipple with light contact, making her ache for more. For his flesh on hers. His mouth on her body.

He tugged her shirt up over her head. The cold air hit her breasts, and she didn't have any time to feel self-conscious about what he was seeing. He tugged her against him and she gasped as her breasts brushed against his chest, the heat of his skin warming her through her whole body, his chest hair abrading her sensitized nipples.

She moved her hands over his back, his muscles shifting and bunching beneath her fingertips.

He pushed her flannel pajamas and underwear down her hips, letting them pool at her feet. She was thankful he hadn't paused to look at her panties. A sexual interlude had been the last thing on her mind when she'd selected the purple cotton garment after her shower that evening.

She wanted to take his clothes off him, but her hands felt heavy suddenly, clumsy. She wasn't sure if it was her move or not. Or if he liked it when a woman undressed him. Or… anything.

He was so perfect, so beautiful, just like the moment. She didn't want to do anything to mess it up.

Thankfully, he was more than ready and willing to discard his own clothes, and after he disappeared into the bathroom briefly, he returned, fully erect, more gorgeous than any man had a right to be, and carrying a box of condoms.

She couldn't stop staring at him. At the thick erection that stood out from his body. She'd never seen a naked man in person before, and pictures of classical statues really didn't do them justice. Or at least, they didn't represent Dante.

"I want to touch you," she said, shocked at her boldness. But for some reason, the moment he'd come back into the bedroom, all of her nerves had evaporated. She was standing there, naked, and he was there, naked. And they were about to share the most intimate connection two people could possibly share.

There was no room for fear. Or shame, or awkwardness. She was sure. It was such an unusual feeling for her. And yet, with him, in the moment, everything felt right.

"Feel free," he said, his voice rough.

She moved to him, ran her fingers from his chest down to his abs, to the dark line of hair that led from there and to his hard, thick shaft. She wrapped her fingers around him, testing his weight.

"What do you like?" she asked, her heart thundering hard, her stomach quivering.

"This," he said, his breath hissing through his teeth.

"Just me touching you?"

"Yes," he said. His breathing increased, his chest rising and falling quickly.

"And this?" She squeezed him gently and was rewarded with a groan that bordered on tortured.

"Yes," he bit out.

"Harder?"

He put his hand over hers and stilled her movements. "Only if you want me to come right now."

She pulled her hand back. "No. Not yet. You aren't allowed yet."

"I thought not." He captured her lips in a fierce kiss, bringing her down onto the bed with him.

She looped her thigh over his hip, opening herself to him. She moved against him, each brush of his arousal against the bundle of nerves at the apex of her thighs sending a streak of white heat through her.

He lowered his head and sucked her nipple deep into his mouth. A raw moan escaped her lips and she gripped his shoulders hard, her nails digging into his skin. He lifted his head, letting it fall back. She gripped him harder and he winced, his hold tightening on her back.

"Don't stop," she said.

And he obeyed, lowering his head to her breasts again, licking her, sucking her, bringing her to the edge and back with the sensual assault from his mouth. He moved his hand from her back, down to her waist, to her hips, holding her hard, kissing a path down her body until he came to the place that was wet and aching for him.

His tongue moved over her clitoris and she lifted her hips off the bed, sensation so deep, so intense hitting her that she couldn't hold still. He held her, continuing as though she wasn't whimpering beneath him, as though her body wasn't trembling, her world crumbling inward, reducing to pleasure, to Dante.

She laced her fingers into his hair, holding him to her, so close now, so close to the peak that she had no desire to fight it. No desire to fight him.

He released his hold on her and his hand joined his mouth, one finger sliding deep inside of her as he flicked his tongue over her clitoris again. The world exploded behind her eyelids. Stars raining down on her, leaving her blanketed in heat and light.

She shook, her body trembling as each wave of release passed through her.

Dante lifted his head and kissed her hip, the space just beneath her belly button. Her stomach. Between her breasts. Then he settled between her thighs, his hardness probing the soft, wet entrance to her body.

He cursed and paused, reaching beside them and picking up the condom box. He fished inside of it for a moment, producing a small packet that he tore open quickly. He rolled the condom onto his length with deft efficiency, and she was grateful he hadn't asked her to do it.

Then he was back over her, pressing into her. She felt a brief, searing pain as he pushed inside of her, her body stretching to accommodate him.

He paused for a moment, his dark eyes blazing, his expression pained.

She shook her head. And he didn't speak. Instead, he thrust into her to the hilt, his body coming up hard against hers, making contact right where she needed it, pleasure erasing the pain, slowly, but oh so perfectly.

He retreated, thrusting home again, establishing a steady rhythm that built up tension inside of her again. It was deeper this time, reaching farther inside of her, calling up the need from somewhere new. It was shared desperation, shared need.

She met each thrust, working with him, moving with him, toward completion. Everything blurred, blending together, the room beyond Dante turning fuzzy, insubstantial.

His movements became erratic, evidence of his fraying control, and hers began to shred, too. Her grip on the world loosening. When they fell, they fell together, raw sounds of completion filling the room as they reached the peak.

She held on to him tightly, trying to keep from getting lost in it all. Anchoring him to her.

When his muscles stopped trembling, he let out a long, slow breath and pressed his forehead against her chest. She wrapped her arms around him and held him there. Held his body against hers, skin to skin, every inch of him against every inch of her.

She didn't want to speak. She didn't want to move. She didn't want to face reality.

But she knew that they would have to.

But not yet.

CHAPTER TEN

Dante cursed himself. To hell. To any level of hell. He'd heard every reference about his name in connection with the place of suffering and damnation that the media could possibly create, and this time, he found it appropriate.

He belonged there for this.

He had let her lead, but what he hadn't realized was that she hadn't known the dance.

A virgin. A damn virgin.

He should have known. He should have seen it in every wide-eyed glance, in every sweet, perfect blush. In the way she didn't seem to know the sort of power her body could wield.

But he hadn't, or worse, he'd ignored it. That black part of his soul rising up to choke out the control, choke out the small seed of human decency that had still rested inside of him.

He avoided women who didn't know the game. Who didn't understand that with him sex was only about one thing: release. Even if the woman had had a hundred partners, he had to be sure she understood that.

But a woman who had no experience with sex? She was not the kind of player he picked for the game. Ever.

The voice in his head whispering that Paige was different was silenced completely.

"Dammit, Paige," he said, his voice rough.

"Oh, no. Don't do that please."

She scooted away from him and burrowed under his covers. In his bed. Like she was planning on staying the night, which he was sure she was. Women didn't stay the night with him. They never had. Not once.

They met in hotels. They got the itch scratched. They left. A long encounter lasted a couple of hours. Never more.

"Don't get upset about you not telling me you were a virgin?" he growled.

"Yes!" She threw her arms up and brought her hands back down on the covers. "It's stupid. You're not a mustache-twirling villain who just ripped away my maidenhead. I knew what I was doing."

He moved into a sitting position on the edge of the bed and forked his fingers through his hair, his heart pounding heavily. Too quickly. He hadn't gotten his control back yet. "I cannot even wrap my head around that sentence."

"I *wanted* it. I told you I wanted it. You asked me to say it, and I did. I wanted to sleep with you. I wanted you to be my first. No, you know, that's not even it. It wasn't about first. It was about wanting you. End of story."

"Paige, I don't... I can't offer you anything."

"Oh, you mean you can't offer me anything other than a temporary marriage to help me keep custody of my daughter? You can't offer me anything more than that and multiple orgasms? Is that what you mean?"

"Paige," he growled.

"Get into bed, Dante."

"I don't..." He was about to tell her. To tell her that his lovers did not share his bed. His lovers didn't usually enter his home.

But the words stuck in his throat. He should tell her, tell her that if she wanted sex, she could have it, but if she wanted to make love she would have to look somewhere else. But for the first time in his memory, the blunt words, the true words, stuck in his throat.

He stood. "I need to go and take care of things."

She nodded, her hands clutching the covers like talons, as if proving to him that she was well and truly rooted to the spot.

He walked into the bathroom and disposed of the condom, then for the second time in only a few days, he gripped the edge of the sink and regarded the man in the mirror.

He released his hold and straightened, turning away from his reflection. And he weighed which sin would be greater. To give her what she asked for, with no intention, no ability, to offer emotion. Or to show her now, that with him, there would be no softness.

He walked back into the bedroom, his chest tightening when he saw Paige, deep in the blankets, rolled onto her side, her eyes open.

"You did come back," she said.

"I did," he said.

His stomach tightened, painfully, a raw, intense tremor of terror working its way beneath his skin and straight into his heart. The closer he got to the bed, the sharper the feeling became.

He stopped, trying to catch his breath. She looked...angelic. Her lips swollen and flushed pink, her skin still flushed, too. Her blue eyes filled with an innocent expectancy, a need that he knew he could never meet.

And still, the desire to slide beneath the sheets and tug her bare body against his was strong. The need to feast on her beauty, to sate himself on that need, so great, so powerful, it threatened to take over.

He took a step backward. "You are welcome to stay in here for the night, Paige," he said, his words stilted. "But I have work to do."

He bent and retrieved his pants from the floor, tugged them on, then did the same with his shirt. And without looking back, he walked out of the room and closed the door firmly behind him.

* * *

Paige opened her eyes slowly, squinting against the light coming through the curtains. Her first thought was that it was strange that Ana hadn't woken up.

Her next thought was about how strange it was that she was naked. She never slept naked. She wore her pajamas. But she hadn't last night.

Oh, yes, and now she remembered, very, very clearly why she hadn't worn pajamas.

Dante. His hands. His mouth. His body. He was…everything a man should be. No wonder she'd been so fascinated with him for so long. Somehow, some part of her, must have known, instinctively, that that man was capable of giving pleasure that went well beyond anything she'd previously imagined.

A smile curved her lips. Okay, so she hadn't waited for marriage, or even true love, which she was sure her perfect sister had done. But it had been worth it. So, so worth it.

She pushed away the dreaded suspicion that she might feel differently about it later, and instead, focused on the warm satisfaction that was still resting in her body. She shifted and winced. Oh, yeah, there was also a little bit of *ow* resting in her body, but that seemed worth it, too.

Her muscles hurt. And so did…things that had never hurt before.

She rolled over and realized that the sheets were cold where Dante should have been. And then she remembered him walking out, his expression shuttered, blank, and she wondered if he had ever come back to bed.

The door to the bedroom swung open and Dante entered, wearing the clothes from the night before.

"Good morning," she said, feeling slightly less blissful than she had a second earlier.

He frowned. "It is morning." He tugged his shirt up over his head and her brain stalled at watching the play of perfect, golden skin over shifting muscles.

A little thrill assaulted her. He was hot, so supposedly

out of her league, and yet, last night, he'd been hers. He had wanted her. Her.

She'd gotten the hot guy, and for a moment, she just wanted to celebrate that. Before reality hit.

"Yes, it is morning," she said, sounding far chirpier than she imagined he might like.

"Are you okay?"

She sat up, holding the covers to her chest, and poked herself in the arm. "I…feel okay."

"Very funny, Paige. You know what I'm asking." He dropped his pants and her stomach followed the trajectory, sinking around her toes.

"If I'm angry that you made love with me and left me for the rest of the night?" she asked, keeping her eyes trained on his tight butt as he looked through his closet, shoving her clothing aside with rough, frustrated movements. "I'm a little angry about that, yeah."

"That isn't what I was asking."

She really hoped that he wasn't actually asking what she thought he might be asking, because that was just too stupid. "You want to know if I regret the sex."

"Yes."

She let out an exasperated breath. "I don't regret the sex, Dante. But I am a little put out by the way you acted after. And actually, the way you're acting now."

"It sounds to me like you regret anything happened at all."

"I told you I wanted it," she said, exasperation lacing her tone.

He draped a pair of black slacks and a white shirt over his arm, still completely naked. "I know, but that was before you knew…"

"Just because I was a virgin doesn't mean I didn't know anything about sex. You can know about things without actually doing them."

"But you don't know how they'll make you feel."

"I feel—felt, because now I'm a little annoyed—satisfied. And warm. And…happy until you ditched me to work or whatever it was you did."

"So, you have it all figured out then, do you?"

"Yes. If you stop treating me like a child, or a stranger who invaded your bedroom, I think we can work something out."

His expression turned dark, fierce. He stalked over to the bed and leaned in, planting his hands on the foot of it. "So you think we can just go on and have an affair while you're living here? Just sex. You, me, this bed, no clothes, no emotions—is that what you think?"

He was challenging her, trying to make her back off, trying to make her say no. And she knew it wasn't for her benefit, not really. She didn't know how she knew, but she did.

"Yeah," she said, shrugging one bare shoulder, "I think we could do that."

He raised both eyebrows. "You do?"

"Yeah. Last night was…really fun."

"Fun?" he asked, his tone deadly.

"I can't believe I waited so long. Well, I can, because you know…this is really embarrassing, but when I was in high school, I made out with this guy, but I had braces, and he cut his tongue."

Dante blinked. "He…cut his tongue?"

"Yeah, on the braces. Only because he kissed like an over-zealous puppy. You're much better, by the way."

"Thank you," he said, drily.

"You're welcome. Anyway, that's hard to live down." She drew her knees up beneath the covers and studied the stitching on the comforter. "And so, already I was sort of a running joke at the school. And then…senior prom, this guy who was…waaaay out of my league, asked if I would be his date. And I said yes. And then after the dance part, he told me he had a blanket and some drinks waiting for us under the bleachers which means…well, you know what that means. Well, no guy had paid attention to me in a couple of years thanks to the braces incident and so I…I was going to do it."

"But clearly you didn't," he said, straightening.

"Clearly," she said. "Because that wasn't really what I was there for."

"What happened?" he asked.

She bit her lip. "I don't know why it's so hard to talk about. It's been what…four years? Stupid." She shook her head, trying to stop the burning sting of tears in her eyes, the echoing burn of shame in her chest. "We went out to the football field, under the, um…bleachers. It was prom, you know, so…you know."

"Yes," he said, his tone hard. "I know."

"Anyway things were going well. We were kissing, I hadn't injured him. He started to take my dress off…." She blinked hard, trying to keep her tears from falling. She'd cried enough about it. "Then he grabbed my arm and pulled me out onto the football field, and the big lights came on, and a huge group of my *friends* in the senior class threw eggs at me. Laughed at me. They took pictures of me, half-naked like that and trying to cover myself up. They made fliers later to pass out in school."

She bit her lip hard. "You know, I would have gotten in serious trouble, for being out there unauthorized, but I think the principal thought I'd suffered enough. My parents thought so, too. Because everyone saw it. Everyone knew. I don't know why…I don't know why I walked into that. As one of the girls put it, did you really think he came out here to be with *you*?" A tear slid down her cheek and she brushed it away. "I had. I had really believed it. But not after that. And they never let it go. They brought it up all the time, even after graduation, and they would just…laugh like it had been the funniest, cleverest prank of all time. And I learned to laugh, too. Because my only other option was showing how much it hurt and I wouldn't…I didn't want to do that."

"But then you moved here. Away from those people surely…"

"And take a chance at being rejected again? Obviously not

on a scale that grand, but still. My entire senior class made a joke out of my half-naked body."

Dante swore harshly. "There's nothing wrong with your body."

"Maybe not. No...I mean I know there isn't but...they said there was. And in high school that's all that matters."

"Paige, why did you sleep with me?" he asked.

She looked up at him. "You wanted me."

She could see the horror that passed through his eyes clearly. "Is that all? Because you thought I was the only man who would want you? Those people you went to school with were stupid. As limited as your family when it comes to see-ing beauty and value," he bit out. "I cannot imagine any man not wanting you. So I sincerely hope that this wasn't some desperate act of someone who believed they could never have anyone else."

She shook her head. "No. No, that wasn't it. It was... you wanted me, yes, and I could see it. But also...I wanted you. Enough to risk the rejection. I've never wanted anyone enough to put myself out there again. But I wanted you that much. And that seems like a good enough reason to have sex to me."

"And now...now that you've seen that I'm not a support-ive, caring lover. Do you regret it?"

Yes, his abandonment of her had stung, and yet, she knew it had to do with him, not with her. She wasn't sure why she was so certain of that, but she was. "I can't regret it. It was a lot more about me than it was you, by the way, so maybe take some comfort in that."

A shadow passed through his eyes, intense, dark. But be-fore she could analyze it, it was gone.

A high-pitched wail shattered the moment. "Ah," Paige said. "There she is. It's a little past time for that."

She looked at him, and his total, casual nudity, and down at her blanket-covered breasts. "This is a little different now," she mused.

"What is?"

"Uh, the idea of being naked in front of you. When I was turned on things were a bit more hazy. Also, the room was darker. And I wasn't irritated with you."

"You're irritated with me now?"

She nodded. "Yes. I'll get over it, but for now, yes."

He nodded. "I'm going to shower now, so, you're safe." He turned and strode into the bathroom and she watched his butt the whole way, until he closed the door behind him.

Oh, he was so hot. And yes, that was maybe shallow. And yes, she was angry at him, which was just an even-greater testament to that hotness. But he was like four-alarm-fire hot, and she'd had sex with him. It was hard not to feel a little bit of smug triumph over that.

Sure, he hadn't gathered her into his embrace and held her all night long, but Dante had never promised romance. And she wasn't going to forget that.

She slipped out of bed over to the closet, grabbing a pair of sweats and a T-shirt, dressing as quickly as possible, doing a victory hop-step down the hall to Ana's room.

A little ray of joy broke through everything else when she saw Ana in her bed, kicking her feet, her eyes bright, her expression indignant. The memories, the confusion over Dante, for a moment, it all lessened.

"Morning, baby!" She leaned over and plucked her from her crib, kissing her soft head. "Let's go get breakfast."

She carried Ana downstairs and set her in her bouncy chair, letting her watch as Paige got her bottle ready. Then Paige picked her up and sat in one of the kitchen chairs to feed Ana. She smiled at the contented look on her face. Her fists were balled up by her face, her eyes round.

"Okay, take a break." Paige pried the bottle from Ana's lips, which earned her an indignant squeal. Then she propped her up over her shoulder and patted her back until she burped.

"Now you can have the rest." She returned her to her feeding position.

"My housekeeper isn't in on the weekend," Dante said when he entered the room.

"That's fine. I can pour a bowl of cereal. What do you usually do?"

"I can pour a bowl of cereal," he said.

"But you didn't even know if you had chocolate, so I assume you don't."

"I go out," he said.

"Ah."

"I take it you don't want to?"

"You can," she said. "I want to stay home with Ana. Spend more time on the terrace. She really liked it out there and it looks like it's going to be a beautiful day."

"I can pour a bowl of cereal," he said. "I can pour two. We can eat together."

He made it sound like he was submitting to mild torture. "You don't have to."

"It's the right thing," he said.

"Why? You think it's what you have to do because I was a virgin?"

"Yes. Don't protest. I've never slept with a virgin before. Allow me to salve my conscience."

"Bleah," she said. "Don't let your conscience be wounded on account of my hymen."

"*Dio*, Paige," he said, pulling a bowl out of the cupboard and slamming it onto the counter. "Must you say things like that?"

"I'm a blurter. I blurt. That's how we got into this situation in the first place."

"I remember."

"I thought you might. It's one of those defining moments in one's life. When someone lies about being engaged to you and you read about it in the news."

"That does stay with you."

She looked down at Ana. "You think I'm capable of taking care of Ana, right? Or being a mother, and seeing that she grows into a functional, happy human being?"

"I've said as much."

"Great. So why would you think I can't handle this?"

"I…"

"Exactly. You have no grounds. Either I'm tough enough to raise a child and fight to keep her, or I'm too wimpy to know my own mind and can't be trusted to make decisions about who I sleep with. But I can't be both."

"You could never be accused of being a wimp."

"Didn't think so. It would be like accusing you of being too effervescent."

He took a box of cereal out of the pantry. "You don't think I am?"

"No offense, but no."

"What am I then?" he asked.

Yet again, she could sense a strange, underlying seriousness to the question. And she had to wonder if sleeping with him had formed some sort of deeper connection, or if sex just made him philosophical.

"I'm not sure," she said. "Whatever you are, you're good underneath all that hardness on the outside."

"You think so?" he asked, a humorless smile curving his lips.

"I know so."

"How?"

"Here I sit in your kitchen, with Ana. And you're helping us. No matter how many layers of self-serving motivation you wrap it in, that's still the heart of it."

"I was paid back in full last night, don't you think?" His tone hardened, his eyes turning to cool chips of coal.

"Okay, now you've gone from misguided gentleman to a-hole. Not sure what happened there."

He crossed to the table and set her cereal in front of her.

She looked up at him. "I want coffee." Caffeine just might make this morning, and him, bearable.

"I don't make coffee."

"Oh, for the love of…" She stood up. "Hold her, please."

He looked stricken, his face frozen. "Hold her?"

"So I can make coffee, so we don't have to figure out a way to mainline the grounds directly into my bloodstream."

He took a step back, his expression closing off slowly, his black eyes going flat. "Let's go out."

"What?"

"All of us. It will make a nice photo-op for the press, don't you think?"

"I…suppose so."

"Why don't you go and get ready," he said.

"Okay." She stood from her chair and held Ana close as she made her way out of the kitchen and up to her room.

And that was when she realized that it had been her request for Dante to hold Ana that had triggered his idea of going out. And that in all the time since they'd come to live at his house, Dante had never once touched Ana.

After breakfast, Dante had spent the day in his office, working, avoiding Ana and Paige to the best of his ability. But it was impossible when they seemed to be everywhere. On his deck, in the living room. Paige's clothes were in his closet.

He stood from his desk and stalked out of the office, walking down the hall. He would go out and get some air. It was late and the lights were off in the house. Everything was quiet, blessedly so.

He walked down the stairs and to the living room, headed out toward the deck. And stopped cold. Paige was there, cradling Ana, who was wrapped in a blanket, in her arms.

He could hear her, singing softly, even through the closed doors.

It all came into focus slowly, and for a moment, he couldn't move, couldn't breathe. Paige smoothed Ana's hair with her hand, her expression so loving, so serene.

It choked him. Pain rose up in him, tightening its hold on him. Memories of another lullaby. Of his mother.

He loosened his tie, trying to get breath, clawing at the button on his shirt collar. He felt surrounded, crowded. Like nothing was his own anymore. Like his control was being pried from his hands.

He walked away from the scene, taking the stairs two at a time. He threw his bedroom door open, feeling his hold on his emotions, on his control, slipping from his grasp.

He turned and hit the wall with his open fist. It wasn't enough. It didn't take away from the explosion of feeling in his chest. He drew his arm back and punched the wall, pain biting into his skin, a dent in the plaster, a smear of blood on the paint that had been perfect and white a moment ago. He looked at his hand and dropped it back to his side, his eyes on the damage he had done.

Damage that he couldn't simply wash away. He could have someone come and fix it, of course, but that wasn't the point.

He stood there for a long time and simply looked. At what he had done. At the evidence of what happened when he lost his control.

Then he went into the bathroom and ran cold water over his stinging knuckles, focusing on the pain, on this consequence. Letting it overtake the suffocating emotion that had risen up inside of him. Letting it bring back his clarity of mind.

He needed space. He would spend the night in his office in the city. Anything to get away from this scene of domestic bliss. The vision of the kind of love that had been torn from him so many years ago.

Just a little space. That was all he needed. And he would be back in control.

CHAPTER ELEVEN

ANA was finally asleep, at eleven-thirty, and Paige was avoiding Dante. Which seemed pointless in some ways, as he'd been avoiding her since breakfast yesterday.

After they'd eaten, he'd disappeared into his home office. And then last night he'd disappeared completely, leaving a quick note saying he'd had a work emergency he'd had to go in for. At ten-thirty on a Saturday night. And today, she'd hardly seen him at all.

She'd spent time on the deck with Ana and a canvas, painting bold, brash colors that had nothing to do with the scene in front of her.

The ocean was too serene and beautiful. And nothing inside of her felt serene.

And now, Dante was in his home office, and she wasn't sure if, when she saw him again, he would be rude, or if he would get all "I have deflowered you and must make amends" again. If he would want her. Or if he would leave the house rather than face sleeping with her again.

She rolled her eyes and tiptoed down the stairs, headed for the kitchen and the rest of the chocolate ice cream.

She opened the freezer and let the cool air wash over her face. She felt confused. And lonely. She didn't know why the loneliness was hitting so hard now. When Shyla had died, it had been hard. So very hard. But Ana needed her. Ana had needed her from that moment and every moment since then and there had been no time to dissolve.

There was still no time to dissolve. And in the absence of total dissolution, perhaps there could be an ice-cream binge and a few tears.

"I was looking for you."

She turned and closed the freezer, forgetting the ice cream. Dante was there, looking end-of-the-day rumpled. Which for Dante meant he'd discarded his jacket and had obviously run his hands through his hair a few too many times. Otherwise, he remained well pressed, his black tie in place, his white shirt tucked into white slacks. She had the overwhelming urge to ruffle him.

To really find the man beneath the layer of rock and stone he kept around himself. To find out who he really was.

She'd seen glimpses of it. When he spoke of his mother. When he'd expressed genuine concern for her well-being after they'd slept together. And in each of those moments, there had been so much. Tenderness, love even, when his mother had been mentioned. But also a haunting sadness and fear that tore at her insides.

The fear she saw when he looked at her and Ana. Dark, endless. She wished she could watch it for a moment, to try to understand it. But he always covered it too quickly, taking control again as soon as he could.

She felt compelled to seek it out. Compelled to unbury it all. The good, the ugly. She had a feeling she could never reach the good if she didn't uncover the bad, too. Expose it to the sunlight.

A few days ago, she would have rejected the idea. Because Ana was her world. And Ana was still her world. But Dante was starting to be a huge part of it, too. Not a separate part, or a bigger part, or even a smaller part. He was folded in. Impossible to extricate.

And that was just damned terrifying.

"I figured you had lots more work to do. Since it's Saturday and you put on a tie."

"I work, Paige. It's what I do."

"And what do you do for fun?"

He took a step closer to her. "I can think of one thing."

Her heart slammed into her chest. "Oh, well, yeah. Eating chocolate ice cream is what you mean, right?" She turned back to the freezer trying to defuse some of the tension between them. Because, given her recent realization, she was more than happy to defer any intensity between them.

"Not quite."

Dante watched Paige's valiant effort to ignore him by digging through the freezer for much longer than necessary. She was probably making the smart choice, denying the fire that ignited between them.

He'd tried to do it all day. Work punctuated by push-ups, bicep curls until he was sure his arms were going to drop out of their sockets. Anything to build enough pain to block out the intense need that had been rioting through him from the moment he'd gotten out of bed the other night and left her there alone, when he'd wanted nothing more than to take her again. And again. And again.

He wanted even more to try to eradicate the pain in his chest that seemed to hit him, so hard and strong whenever he looked at Paige holding Ana. A mother and her child. The love that passed between them. The truest love he'd known. The love he had lost.

He wanted to crush those feelings. Bury them beneath something stronger. Lust. Sex. Desire.

Yes, Paige was being the wise one.

And for once, he wasn't. Couldn't be.

He moved behind her and put his hand on the freezer door. She froze in front of him, her petite frame stiff.

"Don't ignore me, Paige," he said. He swept her hair to the side and bent, pressing a kiss to the side of her neck. "Ever."

She shivered beneath his touch. "I wasn't."

"You were trying to ignore this—" he traced the line of her neck with the tip of his tongue "—and you know we can't."

"I don't know. Maybe I don't know, because I'm just so gosh darn innocent."

He put his hands on her waist, drawing her backside up against his growing erection. "Don't make a joke of this. Don't put distance between us."

"I… Okay."

"I've had the day to think about it and the conclusion I've come to is that yes, you were a virgin. But you were right— you knew what you were doing. And you certainly seem to know what you want. So, let me ask you now, what do you want?"

"Ice cream," she said.

"Too sticky." He reached past her and took an ice cube out of the bin that sat in the back of the freezer, the chill burning his fingertips before it started to melt. "This, on the other hand, has some possibilities."

He held the ice cube above her shoulder, a drop of water hitting the curve of her neck and rolling down her pale skin. He leaned in and followed the trail of the drop with the tip of his tongue, warming the cold places.

She put her hands on the fridge, as if bracing herself.

"Good?" he asked.

"I would never have thought of that," she whispered. "So maybe I'm more innocent than I thought."

He pressed the corner of the ice cube to her neck, then removed it, following up with a hot kiss. "Do you want me to stop?"

He felt like he was poised on a razor's edge, waiting for her answer, watching the rise and fall of her petite shoulders with each intake of breath. He would stop if she asked. He would.

"No," she whispered. "Don't stop."

Relief flooded him, the sweeping intensity of it pulling on something inside of him. Pulling something loose. The chains to his tightly bound control fell and he felt, for the first time, a kind of deep and growing intensity that he was certain could consume them both.

And he wanted it. Welcomed it. He wanted to drown in it. Lose himself completely.

Never in his life had desire felt like this. Lust was a focused thing for him. Find release, and satisfy it. But this wasn't about release. This was about the softness of Paige's body. About the cold, salt and heat in her skin.

This was about the way it would feel to slide inside her again. So tight and perfect.

This was about the journey. About making it take as long to get to the destination as possible.

"I was hoping you would say that." He gripped the hem of her shirt and she helped him tug it up over her head. Then he turned her, shutting the freezer behind her.

Her round blue eyes were focused on him as she unhooked her bra, revealing those small, perfect breasts to him. Her nipples were puckered, from arousal, from the cold.

He placed the ice cube on her collarbone, water spilling down as he let it drift over her flesh, the droplets curving over the shape of her breasts, tightening her nipples even further, changing them to a deeper shade of blush.

He leaned down and ran his tongue over her breast, then sucked the tightened bud between this lips, the taste of her sending a jolt of painful need through him, making his shaft pulse, the ache in his stomach intensify.

She arched into him, her back against the door of the refrigerator. He continued to suck her breast, one hand anchored on her hip, the other directing the ice, leaving drops on her stomach that rolled downward. She squirmed, a sharp moan of pleasure on her lips.

"Good," he said, his lips still at her breast.

"Yes," she whispered.

He straightened and touched the ice to her lips, then kissed her there, deeply. Her lips were cold, the inside of her mouth, her tongue, hot.

He'd never imagined a sexual game could be exciting. He'd never played a sexual game, because sex had never been about the journey.

Until now.

He pulled his mouth from hers and she looked at him, her lips parted. He slipped the remaining bit of ice cube into her mouth, letting it melt on her tongue.

She leaned in and pressed her cold lips to his throat, the tip of her icy tongue tracing a line on his skin. Cold had long been a method he'd used to regain a handle on his emotions. Of stopping himself from getting out of hand. Of forcing his mind blank, effecting a reboot.

But this wasn't cooling him. It was heating him, burning him from the inside out, the chill on his skin evaporated by the heat running through his veins.

Paige turned and opened the freezer again, producing her own ice cube, a wicked grin on her face. She separated the top four buttons on his shirt and pressed the ice to his chest. Burning cold assaulted him, but it did nothing to cool the fire that was streaking through his body.

He was shaking, his entire body in pain with the need to free himself and sink into her. To be joined to her. Lost in her. To find the ultimate heat and burn alive in it.

He pushed her back against the fridge, every last ounce of his control gone. He pressed her hand against his chest, letting the ice burn, then numb, melting against his skin as he kissed her lips, as he devoured her.

She freed her hands and reached around behind him, tugging his shirt up out of his pants and unbuttoning it quickly, shrugging it off his shoulders and leaving it on the ground. And he didn't care.

He pushed her pajama pants down, along with her panties—the panties that proved just how little she'd expected to be having another sexual encounter with all their sensible cottonness—and kicked them to the side. He reached around, cupped her butt and lifted her so that her legs were wrapped around his waist, her arms around his neck.

He moved, turning them both, and pinning her against the wall. He used one hand to open his belt, undo his slacks and jerk his pants partway down, releasing his erection and sliding it through her moist folds.

She tightened her hold on him, her fingernails biting his skin, sharp pain piercing his flesh, ramping up his need.

"*Dio*, yes." He slid inside of her, her body hot around him, perfect. So wet and sweet. He thrust up hard and she gasped, blue eyes opening wide. "Okay?"

She bit her lip, nodding. She was so perfect. So very Paige. There was no woman like her anywhere, no woman who had ever made him feel this way.

And then there was no thought. There was only feeling. Burning in his chest and lungs, tightness in his gut, the pressure of impending release, building, building until he was certain he would burst with it. He gritted his teeth, tightening his hold on her hips as he thrust hard into her.

She let her head fall back against the wall, a strangled cry on her lips, her internal muscles pulsing around him, heightening his own need.

Finally, he gave in, pushing into her one last time, orgasm exploding through him, pleasure that was almost pain curling itself around every muscle, every vein, overtaking his entire body as he spilled himself inside of her.

His thighs shook, trembled. He set her down, making sure her feet were planted firmly on the floor before letting himself sink to his knees in front of her, his hands braced on the wall.

He put his head down, trying to catch his breath, trying to clear his mind. He felt full, and completely drained at the same time. Weak, depleted. In need. But there was no room for anything else in him, nothing but the intensity of the desire that was still ignited in his chest, in his bones.

He pushed away from the wall, away from her, and stood.

"I'm going to shower," he said. He had to escape. Had to put distance between them. As much as he'd needed it after the first time, he needed it more now.

He turned and walked away from her, leaving her there, naked against the kitchen wall, regret clinging to him like a film on his skin.

When he got to his bathroom, he turned the water on cold and put himself directly under the spray, trying to ease the feeling. To numb himself inside and out. He put his hand on the tiled wall and leaned forward, struggling to catch his breath beneath the icy assault.

Cold that would normally have wiped his mind clean, now made him think of the ice cube on his chest, followed by the warmth of her hands, her lips, her...

He had been out of his mind. Absolutely and completely. She had done it to him, had pushed him past the point of return. And he knew better. He *knew.*

For every loss of control there was a cost. He had lost his control. He had taken her without a condom. Without any consideration for how innocent she really was. For how sweet she was. For the fact that she wasn't the kind of woman you pinned to the wall and screwed.

He hit the tile with his fist, the stone hard beneath his hand, the grout biting into his flesh. He did it again. And again. Again until the pain shot up his arm, burned in his shoulder, left the skin on his fist raw, bleeding.

Nothing blacked out the pleasure that was still moving through him. Stronger than the regret. Stronger than the punishment.

So he lowered his head, and let the water wash over him. And waited. Waited for it to wash his feelings away.

Paige managed to collect her clothes and eat a bowl of ice cream. She was a little too stunned to face Dante. He had done...he had done things to her that she'd never imagined in her wildest fantasies. And she'd done things to him she'd never…

Oh, boy.

And then he'd left. And she didn't know why. Reasons, reasons she made up, were buzzing around in her head, but they probably weren't true, or they were at least only true in part. Dante wasn't an easy man to figure out and she knew she wasn't going to do it in five minutes over a bowl of Rocky Road.

She stood up and put the bowl in the sink, then made her way up the stairs. Ana was still sound asleep, completely unaware of the disaster that the two adults in the house were making of everything. And Paige had a choice to make: her room, or Dante's room?

Yes, they had said they would do this while she lived here. But if his behavior after their first time was an indicator, he didn't really want to share her bed.

Well, he was going to have to meet her in the middle. She wasn't having sex with him and then creeping back to her own room like they were sneaking around. She just wasn't. Yes, she did want to keep her heart uninvolved, and yes, she did fear that in some ways it was too late. But still. She wanted what she wanted, and he would have to deal with it.

Granted, she wasn't an expert but she felt like falling asleep next to each other was an essential piece of the sex equation. She also felt a new surge of confidence, one she'd never felt before. He wanted her. He desired her. That meant she had some negotiating power here.

She walked into Dante's room without knocking, and saw that he wasn't in it. She could hear the water running in the bathroom, but there was no cloud of steam. No extra warmth from what, by her quick calculations, had to have been a thirty-minute shower.

She walked into the bathroom, her hands shaking a little bit.

"Dante?"

He didn't answer. There was nothing, only the sound of the water.

"Dante," she said, this time more forceful.

She pulled open the shower door and her heart stopped. Dante was standing, his hands braced on the wall, his head down, as water, cold water, rained down on his back. His muscles were shaking, his skin bright red.

"What are you doing?" she asked, certain she didn't want to know. But equally certain that she had to know.

He lifted his head, his expression blank, his lips gray, his eyes black, bottomless pools. A shiver racked his frame.

Paige jolted into motion, grabbing a towel off the rack and holding it out to him. "Get out of there."

"It didn't work," he said, his tone dark, a tremor running through his words.

"What didn't work? You didn't freeze your balls off yet?" she snapped. "Come here."

"You have to pay for it somewhere, Paige," he said, his tone rough, unsteady. "Every ounce of pleasure has a price."

Her heart curled in on itself. He didn't make any sense to her, but the undertone to his words was so raw, so very serious. She might not understand his words, but he did. And they carried a weight that she feared could crush them both.

She put her hand on his back, on his ice-cold skin. "A little bit of cold is sexy, but this isn't." She draped the towel across her arm and planted her hands on his shoulders, tugging on him. It wasn't her strength that got him out of the shower, it was the fact that he complied.

He didn't feel like himself. He was usually solid, hot beneath her fingertips. The muscle beneath his ice-cold skin trembled now, his stance weak. And his eyes…they weren't blank now. The anguish was evident, there for her to see, to examine like she'd wanted. And now, she wanted to look away, because the rawness of it was simply too much. The pain too great.

But she didn't. She met his gaze as she brushed the towel

over his skin, drying him, her hands trembling, her stomach sick. "Come on. Let's go to bed."

He complied again, following her into the bedroom and sliding between the covers.

Paige stripped her clothes off and got in beside him, pushing her breasts against his freezing-cold back, wrapping her arms around him as he shivered against her.

A tear rolled down her cheek and she pressed her face to his shoulder blade. "You're so cold," she said.

"That's the idea," he said, his voice stronger now.

"Why?"

"A habit, I suppose."

"You take cold showers after sex?"

"No. Not so simple. I pay penance."

"For what?" she asked, trying to keep the horror from her tone. "For sins?"

"For feeling. For losing control. I've used it to train myself." His tone was flat, lifeless.

"Why?" she asked, her voice barely a whisper.

"Because, *cara mia*, nothing in life is free. Everything has a cost. Especially deep emotion. Most especially passion. Life is made of light and dark, good and bad. The other side of love is hate, and the line between the two is thin."

"I've never thought so," she said. "I don't think love and hate are anywhere near each other."

"And that's where you're wrong." He shivered again. "Because you haven't seen it turn. But I have. I told you about my mother. That she died. That I remembered her soft touch, and her singing. But I also remember how she died. How she was killed. My father killed her. While I watched from behind the couch, helpless to do anything but cover my ears to block out the sound. I will never forget what it's like to watch someone die. My mother. My own mother. I won't forget holding her in my arms as she faded. That's what happens when you have no control. When you are ruled by passion. That's what it can become. And that's why I remind myself that when you lose control, someone pays."

She tightened her hold on him, more tears sliding down her cheeks. "Why do you have to pay, Dante?" They were the only words she could voice. There were so many words she wanted to say. So many. And they weren't enough. They never would be.

"So no one else will."

She just held him then, her eyes stinging, her entire body, down to her soul exhausted. But she couldn't sleep. So she held him, warming him, until the darkness faded and light started to invade the room.

If only she could find a way to do the same for him. To shine a light on his soul and banish the darkness.

CHAPTER TWELVE

"WE'RE moving the wedding up to a week from yesterday."

Dante strode into her office midway through the day on Tuesday, a strange sight considering he had ignored her all day Monday and then had gone out to the office after hours on Monday night and not come home.

She'd driven Ana and herself to Colson's that morning, and she was still more than slightly peeved at him over the disappearing act.

She knew why he'd done it. The phrase running scared seemed a nice way to describe it. Still, she'd been imagining him dead on the side of the road. She'd called, but he hadn't answered, and pride prevented her from doing it more than five times. So she'd paced the hall instead. And she'd gone to sleep in his bed, inhaling the scent of him on his pillow, because it turned out that sex made her feel somewhat mushy about a guy.

"You can't reschedule what was never scheduled," she said, dryly, her heart hammering. "And that's way too soon."

"No, it's not. It's time we got everything going. I'm not running a bed-and-breakfast."

His words were like a slap to the face. "Right. Oh, my mistake. That's what I thought I was doing at your house. In my defense you shouldn't have put a little check-in desk with a bell right by the front door."

"Paige…"

"Dante," she said, her tone mocking.

"You know what I meant."

"You're being an insulting bastard. Is that what you meant? Because if that was the aim, great job. You did it."

"I meant this isn't permanent."

"Yeah, I do know that. You keep reminding me of it, actually."

"Do you want to get the adoption finalized as soon as possible or would you like to continue with your wounded maiden routine?" he asked.

"The adoption."

"I thought so."

"So we're getting married on Monday and…and what's with the adoption?"

"I have made a very generous donation to the local child services department. They like me a lot. I'm imagining that the rest of the process should go off without a hitch."

"You…bought the adoption?"

"More or less. But I imagine if they found something terrible about us they wouldn't allow it."

"That's…oh, that just makes me so mad!" She stood up and kicked a box of decorations aside. "I had to work so hard to prove I was fit, all because I was single and lived in a small apartment or whatever, and you waltz in with your—sorry, but it's true—bad reputation, but oh, you have money, so no problem let's get this adoption show on the road."

"I'm sorry you're frustrated but I imagine the relief of knowing it will be finalized soon will take the sting out of it."

She covered her mouth and sat on the edge of her desk. "Oh, you're right. Oh…she's really going to be mine." She popped up and took two leaping steps toward him and threw her arms around him. "Thank you so much."

He just stood, stiff, unmoving.

She stood up on her tiptoes and brushed a kiss to his cheek. "No glitter today," she whispered.

He pulled away from her. "That's good."

"Will your parents be at the wedding?" she asked.

He paused, his jaw hardening. "They'll have to be invited. I don't…I would rather not lie to them."

"I don't want anyone to know," she said. "And I know maybe it's selfish, but if anything were to jeopardize my getting Ana…"

"I understand," he said, his voice firm.

"And I understand why you don't want to lie to them. They're your parents and…"

"Yes. They are."

"They were good to you, weren't they?" He always spoke of them so formally, no warmth in his tone.

"Yes," he said. "Very. They gave me firm guidance, which I needed desperately. Gave me everything I needed. My own space, which I never had before. My own things."

She'd noticed how meticulously he cared for everything, and suddenly, she realized why. He had been in foster care for around eight years and that had likely meant a lot of moving, and owning very little.

"Love?"

He shrugged. "I don't need that."

The statement shocked her, even though, after the other night, it probably shouldn't. "But…don't they?"

His expression froze. "I…it's not that I don't…"

But he couldn't say it, or think about it really, she could see that. "I know. And I'm sure they know."

"They'll probably enjoy a wedding far too much. Though I'm not sure what they'll think about one on notice this short."

"I'm sure they'll be fine with it."

"I'm sure Mary will pitch a fit about finding a mother of the groom dress on such short notice." The ghost of a smile touched his lips.

"Well, yeah, but most women would."

"There's something else I need to say."

An apology maybe? That would be nice. She would happily take an apology.

"What?"

"I didn't use a condom the other night."

Her stomach sank a little. Not an apology. "Oh."

"I need to know if you're pregnant. I'll need you to tell me."

She nodded. "I would. I will."

For a moment, she was afraid her knees might give out. What would she do if there was a baby? What would it mean for Ana? For the adoption? Would she be a single mother of two children? She wasn't entirely certain she could handle one. The idea of juggling both…it terrified her.

"Good."

"I'm not, though," she said, because she had to believe it. The alternative was too frightening. Another example of her taking something that was working and making an impossible jumble out of it.

"You don't know that."

"Dammit, Dante, I have to believe I'm not."

He laughed, a humorless sound. "I don't blame you for not wanting my baby. You've heard about everything lurking in my gene pool. Hell, I've treated you to a front row seat."

"That's not it," she said, ice trickling through her veins. "But be honest with me. If I were, would you even stay? Or would I be on my own with two children?"

"You would be better off without me."

"I suppose that answers my question."

"Sadly, it doesn't. I would stay. But it's better you don't need that. Better I don't have to."

"I don't want to be someone you're forced to be with."

"If you're having my baby, then you will be. I will take care of my responsibilities, make no mistake."

Her stomach tightened. He looked…resigned. She didn't want that. Not for the rest of her life. "You would…you would love our child wouldn't you?"

"I don't think I could."

"You don't mean that. You just…you need to put the past behind you and…and…"

He exploded then, a dark flame in his eyes burning bright, stealing the light from the room. "Look around you, Paige. I own all of this. Things have already happened for me. What do you think, that I need to talk about my feelings? That I need a psych? To what? To listen to me? Because that will fix it? That will bring my mother back? It will make it so I don't share half my blood with a violent killer? Is that it? It will fix me. Make me happy and able to love?" He shook his head. "You live in fairyland. But the real world has less glitter. You can't fix everything."

"Dante that's not… I'm not trying to trivialize…"

"You did. I have a business trip that I need to go on this week. I'll be back in time for the wedding. Everything is being planned. All we have to do is show up."

"You're leaving?"

"I have business," he bit out.

"Fine." She went back to her desk and sat behind it, her heart in her throat. She had no idea where they stood. Except that they were both angry at each other. And that he was leaving while still angry at her. But she couldn't figure out how to fix it, even though she hated it.

He walked to her desk quickly and braced his hands on the surface, leaning in and taking her mouth in a hard, intense kiss. She was lost in it, in him, the moment his lips touched hers. She pushed her fingers through his hair, slid her tongue against his.

He pulled away, straightening. Dark and dangerous. "When I get back, we'll have the wedding. Then we'll have the wedding night."

The media had often accused Dante of atrocious behavior, and very often it had been a part of the myth they'd spun around him for their own enjoyment.

This time, with no witnesses other than Paige, he would have deserved it.

But his world was ordered, well controlled, just as he needed it and she seemed bound and determined to come in and challenge him at every turn.

He didn't know why he'd told her so much about his mother. About why he took cold showers, and hit things. It sounded crazy when voiced, and maybe in some ways it was. But it had been necessary. The way he'd controlled his emotions as a young boy moving around in the foster system. Anger had to have a release, but if he gave the consequence to himself, no one got hurt. It had flooded over into every emotion until it had been easy to simply not have them.

He hadn't needed the intense, physical reminder for years. Not until Paige came into his life.

Even with those precautions, everything had crashed down around him. He might have gotten her pregnant. A child. His child. He wasn't the man for that. He couldn't even look at Paige and Ana without being taken over by memories of his mother. Couldn't bear to touch the child because she reminded him too much of what it was to be so helpless.

And he couldn't, wouldn't allow himself, to imagine what it would be like to have a child of his own. To share his poisoned blood. The blood he shared with his father. The blood he worked so hard to keep under control.

He was failing. He had failed, in every way that mattered.

And Paige might be the one to pay for it. Someone always paid. Paige. Ana. The child, if there was one. All tied to him because of an act of carelessness.

The truth was, this business trip could be deferred. But he had to get his control back. He had to get distance.

And as long as Paige was around, as long as he had to see her, with her petite curves and tendency to dress in sequins, to listen to the sound of her voice, that voice that he'd heard moaning with pleasure, as long as he had to smell that sweet

floral scent combined with the fresh smell of her clean skin...
he wouldn't be able to master his emotions.

And he had to. There was no other option.

Even if it might already be too late.

Midnight, the day of the wedding, Dante arrived back at his
San Diego home. It had been a long trip. And his bed had
seemed cold, empty.

He had made promises, threats, really, about a wedding
night, but he had no doubt Paige wouldn't be too thrilled if
he tried to make that happen. And he wouldn't blame her.
He'd acted like an ass to her.

About everything. About the potential baby.

But he had everything contained now. One thing the time
away had been good for was to start feeling like himself
again. To start feeling like he had some semblance of control
over his mind and body.

Whatever was ahead for them, they would handle. So long
as he maintained his distance, in an emotional sense, everything would be fine.

He walked into the house, expecting silence, and heard
Ana's indignant wailing instead. He walked up the stairs,
toward her room, expecting Paige to be there as she'd been
their first night together.

But she wasn't there.

He could hear the water running in the next room. Paige
was in the shower, and since it was the time when Ana was
normally asleep, she was probably stealing what had been
her first chance of the day.

But now the baby was crying. Deep sobs. A sound so sad,
so pitiful. And so full of helplessness that it called to him,
resonated in him.

He walked into the nursery, an image in his mind of a
small boy on the floor, crying endless tears, with no one there
to comfort him. Crying for a mother who would never return.
He approached Ana's crib, his heart pounding in his head.

He swallowed and looked down at her. "Why are you crying, *principesa*?"

She looked at him, her owlish eyes wide and furious, and continued bawling.

He reached out to her slowly, placing his hand flat on her round tummy. She quieted and wiggled beneath his palm, her expression morphing to one of curiosity. When he didn't satisfy it immediately, she started to cry again.

He could go and pull Paige out of the shower, which she had done to him. Of course, his had been a shower with a self-destructive bent, rather than one intended for cleanliness. Or he could handle this himself.

He couldn't remember if he'd ever held a baby before. He doubted if he had. But he had seen the way Paige held her, with infinite care and sweetness. Close to her body to keep her safe. And if…if his carelessness had resulted in a pregnancy, he would have to learn.

He bent forward and scooped her into his arms, pulling her up against his chest. The discomfort that bordered on fear whenever he saw Ana started to fade, replaced with that tenderness he always saw on Paige's face when she held her daughter. He didn't want to acknowledge it, that softening in his chest. But surely it was right to feel tender toward a baby? A sign that perhaps not everything in him was frozen.

Ana stopped crying, her heart beating fast like a little bird's as she nestled into his chest. "Is that all you wanted?" he asked, his voice breathless. "To be held?"

She melted into him, her little body supported by his hands. The trust she had in him humbled him, broke something deep inside of him.

She shifted, a sharp cry of discontentment on her lips.

He sat down in the rocking chair, hoping the back-and-forth movement would calm her.

Sing to her.

He remembered Paige asking him to do that the first night.

I don't know any lullabies.

A lie.

Ana wiggled against him, her crying becoming more insistent.

He took a deep breath, moving his hand over her back. For a moment he could not force the words out. They stuck in his throat, stuck, along with the image in his mind of the little boy curled up on the floor. That was the last time he had sung the song. The last time he had let the words out.

He moved his hand over Ana's back, felt her warmth. Her breath. Her life. She was not cold. She was not gone.

She would hear the song. She would take comfort in it.

He took a breath. *"Stella stellina, la notte se avvicina."* She quieted at the sound of his voice, her wide eyes trained on his face. His chest felt tight, his throat threatening to close, but he kept on. Up until the end. *"Nel cuorre della mamma."*

And all are sleeping in the mother's heart.

Ana rested her head on his chest, relaxed her body against him. And he put his cheek on top of her feather-soft head.

"Papa's heart, too," he said, without thinking.

His own words jolted him back to reality. Ana didn't have a father. He certainly couldn't fill that place in her life. He couldn't fill the place at Paige's side, either. A husband. A father. He wasn't meant to be either of those things.

He had nothing in him to give. A few moments in a rocking chair, a song, didn't change that. He was bound up too tight, everything in him ordered, set, unable to be moved. If he opened up at all, if he changed one thing, he was afraid it would all collapse. Afraid that his control would slip. That the pain, the ugliness, that lived in him would be unleashed on the innocent people around him.

That couldn't happen. Not ever.

Still, he stayed, in this moment outside of reality. A quiet moment, the kind a man like him had never been given before. To hold someone so helpless, so precious, who trusted him so completely for no other reason than that life had always handed her people who cared for her. Because she had never been touched by someone who intended evil.

He wasn't the kind of man who prayed, but in that moment, he prayed that she never was.

CHAPTER THIRTEEN

It was her wedding day. Strange because she'd never given a lot of thought to her wedding day. Although, when her mind had wandered to the event she'd imagined—the very few times she'd imagined anything—a lot of color.

Glitter, naturally. Having some friends and family present, no matter how fraught the relationship, would have been nice, too.

But she'd opted out of it because she simply hadn't told her parents, or siblings, that she was engaged, so that made it easy.

And now, in her gorgeous but sedate satin gown, with her hair pinned up, so that her pink stripe was covered, as commanded by the hairdresser, she felt a little sad about her lack of support. About the fact that she hadn't put more of her own personal stamp on things.

Which was stupid, because this was a very temporary marriage to a man who meant nothing to her. A man who was just her boss. And who was just the most fascinating, interesting, sexy man she'd ever met. And who was, oh, yeah, also her lover.

So there was that, too, but it was still no big deal and not worth getting worked up over.

Too bad she was worked up.

She blamed some of the worked up on getting out of the

shower last night and finding Dante sitting in the rocking chair, holding Ana against his chest. Singing.

That had made something crack apart in her chest. Had left her feeling vulnerable, tender. Different.

She took a deep breath and bunched up handfuls of her slippery skirt. She didn't have time to get all moony. Ana was already in the church, with Genevieve who was acting as an attendant and babysitter. They'd opted to include Ana in the ceremony because, honestly, the party was for her. The whole thing was for her.

Paige hoped, sincerely, that Ana never doubted how loved she was. Because this was nothing, only a small piece of what she was willing to go through in order to secure her daughter's safety and happiness. In order to keep her in her life.

She would walk through fire. All today required was a corset and mascara. And some vows. In a church.

So maybe she *would* walk through fire for all this eventually.

At least now she felt equipped to do it. Felt like she had the strength. She didn't know what had happened to her over the past few weeks, but something in her had changed. She wasn't afraid that everything she touched would turn to sand and blow away in the wind. Wasn't afraid that she was destined to fail. She felt…powerful. Like she had the power to do what had to be done.

"Ms. Harper?" The wedding planner, the one who had thrown everything together at the last minute without batting an eye, poked her head into the waiting area Paige was standing in.

"Yes?"

"It's time to queue up."

Paige nodded and walked out of the quiet little entryway into the foyer of the church. Two wooden double doors loomed in front of her. She could hear people talking quietly, and she could hear music.

"Dante, Genevieve and Ana are already in place. You just wait until I signal you."

Paige nodded, unable to come up with any words.

Then, way too quickly, the wedding planner gave her the signal and the doors swung open. Paige took a deep breath and started to walk slowly down the aisle, her heart pounding in her head.

She didn't really like having everyone's eyes on her, because there was a very high likelihood of her tripping or otherwise making a fool out of herself, and she really didn't relish a thousand people bearing witness to her clumsiness.

One foot in front of the other.

She concentrated on that. On making it down smoothly. And she didn't once look up at Dante. She found Ana first, clinging to Genevieve, her frilly white dress bunching out around her, a headband with an oversize flower decorating her short hair.

Only at the end, when she had nowhere else to look, when it was time for her to take Dante's hand, did she look at him.

And it was like the whole sanctuary, the whole city, the whole world, cracked apart around her and fell away. He was beautiful, but he was always beautiful. The tuxedo highlighted the hard lines of his trim physique, the candlelight casting shadows in the hollows of his face, making his cheekbones sharper, his jaw more square.

But that wasn't it.

He took both of her hands and the pastor began the ceremony. She managed to say the vows, managed to repeat them when it was her turn, to keep from stumbling over her words.

But when the command was given to kiss the bride and Dante's lips touched hers, she realized what it was. And it filled her with a sense of bone-deep terror, and a kind of pure, intense elation that she'd never experienced before in her life.

Dante wasn't just her boss. He wasn't just a man who was helping her. He wasn't just her temporary husband. He wasn't even just her lover.

Dante was the man she loved. The only man she'd ever loved. The man who was worth the risk. The man who had made her fear of being unwanted seem like nothing. Because she was willing to fight for him. Willing to risk herself, her heart, for him.

Because she loved him.

And she knew that the admission would send him running back up the aisle alone.

So, she said nothing, and she kept on kissing him.

"And now I pronounce them, not only husband and wife, but a family," the pastor said.

Genevieve handed Ana to Paige and Paige took her, held her daughter close against her chest, her heart thundering, as Dante took her free hand.

"I am proud to present the Romani family."

Dante was grinning, the kind of grin designed to make the headlines. The kind of grin designed to impress child services. The kind that Paige knew was a fake. Because she could see the emptiness in his eyes.

She was finding it a little hard to fake it, considering the revelation that had just slapped her in the face.

She wasn't sure when it had happened, the love thing. When a crush had changed into something real, something deeper. Sometime in between when he'd stood in front of her desk like an avenging angel demanding an explanation, and when he'd cradled Ana against his chest and sang to her with the most profound tenderness she'd ever seen from him.

They walked down the aisle, to thundering applause, and she wondered, for the first time, who the people in attendance were. Friends of Dante's family. And friends of their friends, she imagined.

Paige forced a smile, and tried to keep a hold of Dante's hand. He leaned in, the motion likely seeming like an affection nuzzle to their audience. "Smile," he said.

"I am," she whispered back.

The double doors opened for them and they entered the empty foyer.

"You aren't," he said, once the doors closed behind them.

"Well, I'm not as good of an actor as you," she said.

He looked stricken by that statement and she couldn't understand why. It's what he was doing, she could tell.

"Well, you had best become better at it. We are headed to the reception now, and you are going to meet my parents."

Dante watched as Paige, pale and drawn, attempted to converse with guest after guest in the massive ballroom. He could tell she was fading. Ana had faded long ago, and was asleep in his arms, her face pressed hard against his shoulder.

Strange, how easy it was to get used to carrying the little girl, when he had avoided it for so long. It seemed natural now. Right.

Don and Mary, his mother and father by every right, caught his eye and made their way across the ballroom, their hands unlinked, but touching lightly with each step. They weren't overly affectionate and never had been. But they presented a strong front of solidarity. One that went well beyond a front, he was certain.

"Dante." Mary leaned in and pressed a kiss to his cheek, resting her hand on Ana's back. "We're so very happy for you."

He nodded, discomfort assaulting him. He hadn't wanted to lie to them. Not for anything.

Don smiled. "We were certain you'd never settle down, and then this. Out of the blue. Instant family. A granddaughter for us, too."

Guilt stabbed him. "A surprise for me, as well." That was the strict truth.

Paige looked over at him, and in moments she was flitting across the room. She came to his side, her hand on his arm.

"You must be Dante's parents," she said.

"And you're the world's most unexpected woman," Mary said. "We never thought Dante would choose family life."

"Ah, well," Paige said. "I sort of roped him into it. He didn't have a choice really."

Don and Mary laughed, because it sounded too ridiculous to be true. Even if it was. Though, that he'd had no choice was where Paige was wrong. He had a choice. He could walk away at any moment, but something was keeping him from doing it.

If only he knew what it was. Ana shifted against him, and a strange tightness invaded his chest.

"We do have a bit of a surprise for you," Don said. "Dante told us you weren't planning a honeymoon because of the baby. So Mary and I thought we would offer to take Ana for the night, and that we would send you to a hotel downtown."

Heat flooded through Dante's veins at the thought of a night alone with Paige. Not the best moment to be flooded with heat, all things considered. "One of your hotels?"

Don laughed. "Naturally."

"Oh," Paige said. "I don't know. I…"

Mary put her hand on Paige's. "I know you don't know us, but Dante does. And we're Ana's grandparents now. We want to be involved."

The statement made Paige look even more sallow than she had all day. "Right. Of course."

Dante handed Ana over to Mary, and Ana stirred, pinning her sleep-clouded eyes on the older woman. But she didn't shriek or make a fuss. That was one thing he found fascinating about Ana. She seemed to make instant assessments about people and then decide how to react according to that assessment.

In so many ways, she could have been his daughter. She was decisive. Focused.

The thought doused the fire that had been raging through him, killed it off with a streak of ice. She wasn't his daughter. She never would be.

Just like Paige wasn't really his wife. And they shouldn't

be. For their own sakes, it was a blessing they were not. And he could only hope that there would be no other child. That Paige wasn't pregnant.

He ignored the faint, treacherous feeling of hope that burned in him. The hope that she was. That he could keep her with him.

No. He would go on their mini honeymoon and enjoy their wedding night. But the fact that they'd signed a document didn't change anything. It didn't make any of it real. It didn't make any of it possible.

Forgetting that wasn't an option.

The suite was stunning. And Paige was shaking.

She'd hardly said two words to Dante for a week, and now they were going to get naked again, and have amazing sex, which was great. Except that sex with him had such a high cost to her emotions and while she was willing to pay it, she did have to gear up for it.

"That was very nice of your mom and dad," she said.

A muscle twitched in Dante's cheek. "It was."

"So this is your dad's hotel?" She knew he called his parents by their first names, but she felt awkward about it.

She walked across the sleek, modern room, to the window that provided a view of the lights in the Gaslamp Quarter. The city was glowing, still alive in spite of the late hour. And yet up in the top of the hotel, everything seemed so distant. Unreal.

It felt like an alternate reality up there. Both safer for its separation from the world and more dangerous for it.

She turned around to face Dante and her heart crumpled. He looked so perfect in his tux, his tie open, the top buttons on his shirt undone. He looked less than perfectly pressed for once. As if the day might have actually pierced that armor he valued so highly.

And she knew why now. She saw it clearly. What the press took as aloofness, a kind of unfeeling detachment, she knew had been a survival technique. To protect the little boy who had felt too much.

The boy whose world had broken before his eyes one horrible day, at the hands of the man who should have loved him. Should have loved his mother.

She also saw, clearly, that Dante's parents loved him. That Don and Mary had deep, real affection for the boy they'd brought into their home as a teenager. And she saw that Dante didn't realize it. That he kept himself from returning it, or at least showing that he did.

Still protecting himself. Still guarding himself against pain.

She recognized it clearly. It was a grand scale version of what she'd done for most of her life. Don't care, don't hurt. Don't try, don't fail.

"Champagne?" she asked, walking over to the full kitchen area in the suite, touching the top of the bottle that was sitting on ice, two crystal flutes set out for the newlyweds.

"Why not?" he asked. "It seems a traditional thing to do on one's wedding night."

"Yes," she said. "And fitting, since you promised me the rest of the night would be traditional, too."

He looked down, a lock of dark hair falling forward. "I did. And I must apologize for that. For the way I treated you before I left."

"I'm over it, Dante."

"Don't be," he said. "I behaved like an ass and I deserve for you to be annoyed with me."

"I'm not, though. Since that first night with you I didn't have any intention of going to bed alone on our wedding night, so your demand was well in line with my plans."

He glowered at her, so serious and irritated she nearly laughed at him. "You're impossible, Paige."

"Yeah, I've been told that." She took the champagne out of the bucket and worked the cork, wincing when it popped out. She poured two glasses and held one out to him. "I've been told I'm quite impossible, in fact, but I never seem to change. And there was once a man who told me that maybe the problem isn't with me, but with other people."

He took the glass from her hand and held it up in salute, and she did the same.

"To your impossibleness," he said.

"I'll drink to that." She took a sip of the dry, bubbly liquid, her eyes never leaving his. "You know what's funny?"

"What?" he asked, leaning against the counter.

"The other times I've been called impossible...it wasn't because I was stubborn. Actually, I've spent my whole life being very, very not stubborn. I was impossible because I wouldn't apply myself. Because I never listened when my mother told me I should try harder. Or, rather because I stopped listening at a certain point."

"Explain."

"You know I'm going to. At length."

"Yes, I do know that about you."

"Anyway, the thing is, it became clear very early on that school was hard for me. My brother and sister, they were brilliant. My sister in academics, my brother in academics and in sports. They were stars. From day one they were like hometown heroes. My sister would go to national spelling bees and science fairs. My brother brought the high school football team to the state championships and scored the winning touchdown. My sister was the valedictorian of her graduating class."

She took another sip of her champagne and tried to stop the tears that were forming. It shouldn't hurt. Not after all this time.

"So then there was me. And I struggled to pay attention in class. To pull average grades. And it wasn't good enough. I was accused of not trying when I was. And I did try. I tried to do well. I tried to make friends and...and fit in. But it didn't work. And so I just...stopped. Because if I didn't care, then it didn't hurt so much. You remember I told you about the braces incident? That was another one of those moments. If I laughed with everyone else and made it a big joke, it was funny that I cut the hell out of a guy's tongue during my first kiss. If I could just laugh, when I got a flier handed to me in the halls that had a picture of me, covering my chest, with eggs on my face, well, then maybe I could be part of the joke instead of just being the butt of it. But I shut down inside. And I stopped trying."

Dante frowned, his dark eyebrows drawing together. "I have never looked at you and seen a woman who wasn't trying, Paige. Never."

"Not now," she agreed. "I've been changing, slowly over the past three years, since I moved. Since I got the job at Colson's and I saw that I could be really good at something other than just splashing paint on a canvas."

"People make a lot of money splashing paint on a canvas," he said drily.

"Yes, but I wasn't. And no one thought it had any kind of value, not in my family. Not in my community."

"Blind and stupid," he said, his tone harsh. "You have a gift for color and design. I still don't understand how they couldn't see it."

His anger on her behalf warmed her. Caused a little trickle of satisfaction to filter through her veins. But that wasn't why she was telling him about herself, about what she'd been through.

"And then there was Ana," she said. "Suddenly another person was depending on me caring. On me making a success. Throwing myself into it and not giving a thought to failure. Because I couldn't afford to think of failing. For Ana, it's been a pursuit of success at all costs and suddenly I realize that I can achieve things. With your help, I grant you. But…"

"But it was your bullheaded stubbornness that got me to help," he said.

"And that was something I didn't know I had." She looked into her drink, watched the bubbles rise to the surface as she picked her next words carefully. "But I had to be willing to stop trying to protect myself. I had to be willing to be hurt in order to grab anything worthwhile."

His expression flattened, light leaching from his dark eyes. "I'm happy you were able to do that."

So, he wasn't going to understand what she was saying. Or he was going to pretend that he didn't.

But she'd changed. And just because it wasn't easy, didn't mean she wasn't going to try. Because whether or not Dante ever loved her, Dante deserved to feel loved. He deserved to be healed. And he was worth any level of pain or disappointment she might face.

Because he was worth something. Everything.

Of all the realizations she'd had about Dante, the most terrifying, heart-wrenching one, was that her enigmatic, alpha boss, didn't see himself as valuable. He saw himself as a liability. As a roadblock to the happiness of others. As a danger, in many ways.

She would change that. No matter what happened between them in the end, she was determined to change that. She wasn't going to be the happy-go-lucky Paige Harper of three years ago. She wasn't even going to be the Paige she'd been a few weeks ago.

She was stronger now. She knew she had power. She knew she could succeed.

She set her glass on the counter, walked back over to the window, sensing Dante's gaze following her movements.

With the curtains open, the lights from the city casting a pale glow on the living area, Paige reached behind her back and gripped the tab on her zipper, sliding it down slowly, the fabric parting, exposing her back to the cool air.

The straps on the gown loosened, and she pushed them off her shoulders, the gown slipping down her body and pooling in a silken mass at her feet. She stepped away from it, keeping her back to him.

The strapless, lace undergarment she was wearing pushed

her breasts up high, contoured her waist, ending at her hips, just above the white, lace thong that barely covered anything. She left her stilettos on, bright pink and shocking, with glitter dusting the heels.

Confidence—unfamiliar, empowering—burned inside of her, along with a steady pulse of desire that beat a rhythm through her entire body, centered at the apex of her thighs.

"I can tell you something else I want," she said. "Something I'm determined to have."

"What's that?" he asked, his voice a low growl.

"You. Tonight, I'm going to have you."

"Do you think so?" His voice was closer now, feral. Arousing.

"I know it." She turned to face him, and the lean, hungry look on his face gave total evidence of her victory.

"My little innocent has become a seductress?"

"I always have been," she said. "I just needed to find her. She was always there. But you helped bring her out. Because you…knowing you, has changed me."

She could see it, clear and quick, a flash of fear in his eyes. "Have I?" he asked, his voice rough.

"Yes. You've helped me find my power. My peace with myself."

"How did I do that?" he asked.

"By being you."

She took a step toward him, her heart thundering, the need burning in her like fire overtaking any insecurity that might threaten to ruin the moment. Her moment. His moment.

She reached behind her back and started to undo the hooks and eyes on the corset bra, letting it fall to the floor, her breasts bare for his inspection.

He was watching her, motionless as stone, his body tense, his expression blank. But there was a wealth of information in that blank slate. She knew him well enough to know that now. That the less she saw, the more there was. The more desperately he was trying to hide. To keep control.

She wouldn't let him have it. Not tonight. She wanted more. More than their first night, more, even, than the night in the kitchen. She wanted it all. All of him.

She hooked her fingers in the sides of her panties and tugged them down her legs, kicking them to the side. Then she closed the distance between them, pressing her body against his, still fully clothed in his tux. She wrapped her arms around his neck and pressed a kiss to his lips.

"Handy thing about the high heels," she said. "I don't have to get up on my tiptoes. But I do think they leave me a little overdressed." She toed them off and shoved them out of the way. "And you are way overdressed."

Paige put her hands on his shirt and concentrated on undoing every last button, shoving it, along with his suit jacket, onto the floor.

"Relax, Dante," she whispered. "Don't you ever relax?"

"Show me a man who can relax while you're doing this to him. He does not exist." His voice was strangled, affected.

She planted her hand on his chest, feeling the heat of flesh and muscle beneath her palm. "I don't know very many women who could relax with you looking like this. I know I'm not exactly relaxed. Just incredibly turned on."

A groan escaped his lips and she captured it with hers, sliding her tongue over his, pressing her breasts to his bare skin. She pulled away from him, kissing his neck, tasting the salt of his skin, before traveling lower to his chest.

She traveled lower, lavishing attention on each ridge of muscle, his stomach contracting beneath her lips, his fingers tangling in her hair, working at the pins that held it in place.

She stopped at the waistband of his pants, tracing the line where flesh met fabric with the tip of her tongue. Then she started loosening his belt, pulling it slowly through the loops, watching the effect each movement had on her captive.

The muscles in his stomach jumped as her hand brushed the hardness of his cloth-covered erection, his eyes like black fire, burning into her, his attention rapt on her. There was no disinterest now. No flatness. Nothing veiled, nothing hidden.

She pushed his pants down his lean hips, leaving him gorgeous, naked and aroused for her exploration. She circled his length with her hand, testing the weight of him, the hardness. She squeezed him gently and earned a rough growl of pleasure. So uncivilized. So uncontrolled. So everything she wanted from him.

"I've been wanting to do this for a while," she said, on her knees in front of him, a subservient position. Ironic, because in that moment she knew, for a fact, that she was the one with all the power.

"What is that?" he asked. She could hear the strain in his voice, could hear the edge, how close he was to losing his control completely.

And she pushed. She leaned in, flicking her tongue over the head of his erection. Tasting him, testing him. So good. So perfect.

She dipped her head, taking him inside of her mouth, her lips sliding over his length. He pushed his fingers deeper into her hair, her curls falling out of the pins and cascading over her shoulders.

"*Dio*, Paige."

Her name on his lips was fuel for the fire. She continued to explore him with her mouth, her tongue, pushing him higher, harder. Pushing herself right along with him. She could feel him shaking, the muscles in his thighs, his hands in her hair unsteady.

"Enough," he said, his tone pleading. "I can't hold back."

And part of her didn't want him to. But another part, the selfish part that won, wanted to stop so that she could join him in release.

She pulled away from him, moving into a standing position, her eyes never leaving his. In the dim light, she could see the dull flush of arousal staining his high cheekbones, could see his chest rising and falling sharply with each labored breath.

Could see that she was close to uncovering the man beneath the armor.

"Come to bed with me," she said.

And he complied.

There were condoms in the bedside table, and Dante quickly rolled one on, joining her on the bed, stroking the silken seam between her thighs with his fingers, sliding a finger deep inside of her, testing her readiness.

"Oh yes," she breathed, the white-hot friction created by his touch sending a streak of pleasure through her each time he brushed his fingers over her clitoris.

"Ready for me?"

She bracketed his face with her hands, her eyes locking with his as she pressed a kiss to his lips. "Always," she said.

He slid inside of her, his eyes never leaving hers as he filled her, joined himself to her, in the most primal, basic, profound way possible.

This was why they called it becoming one. Because she couldn't tell anymore where he began and she ended. Couldn't tell whose pleasure she was feeling, whose desperation.

The need for release pounded through both of them, and each thrust of Dante's body within hers, each press of hers against his, brought them closer. She moved her hands over his back, felt the tension in his muscles, tension that echoed through her, tightened more and more, unbearably so.

He thrust hard into her one last time and pushed them both over the edge, a rough growl on Dante's lips.

She lay there, holding him against her body—her world, her defenses, at his feet. Somehow, it wasn't just about him anymore. It was about her. Not about breaking him down, but being broken in front of him. Of offering him everything, regardless of the consequences.

She ran her fingers through his hair, pressed a kiss to his shoulder. "I love you."

* * *

I love you.

It shouldn't matter how she felt. Ultimately, it changed nothing. It didn't alter the plans he'd been making, slowly, since the wedding. Since the moment she'd appeared at the church. Since he'd seen his parents with Ana.

What she felt changed nothing. On one thing, he was sure Paige was absolutely right: her love had no darkness to it. There was nothing in Paige but pure, beautiful light. And there was nothing more than that in her feelings.

She was all strength, determination and generosity.

He was the one who had to be kept on a leash. Of that he was certain. He had the blood of a monster in his veins. He had seen what love had done to that man. How he had let it get twisted inside of him. Love becoming about hurting someone else, controlling her, never controlling himself.

He would never do that. Would never allow it.

He had lost something of his control back in that bed with Paige, but he would not allow it to happen again. The feeling, though, with her, was proving addictive. The temptation to drown in passion, in her arms, was strong.

He gripped the rail of the balcony and looked out at the city below. The air was warm, but he was cold to his bones. There was no need for him to exact punishment on himself tonight, no need to remind himself of the destruction he was capable of.

I love you.

Paige loving him, what it might do to her, that was the cruelty. That was the punishment.

Maybe it's a good thing. Maybe it will keep her with you.

Not a kindness on his part, perhaps, but he had been considering it, strongly. To keep Paige and Ana in his life. In his house. Something to thank his parents for all they had done, a source of stability and warmth for his home. A place for them to be protected and to live in luxury.

Feelings he hadn't counted on, hadn't wanted from her. But

it wasn't the end of everything. He could keep her. He could make her happy. And he could do it without endangering her.

Without exposing himself.

It was wrong to want this. But he did.

He turned and walked back into the bedroom, looked at Paige curled up in bed. He slipped beneath the covers with her and gathered her close, pressing a kiss to her hair.

This could work. He would make it work. Tomorrow, when they were back home, he would tell her he wanted her to stay with him. And she would.

She had to.

CHAPTER FOURTEEN

PAIGE was overjoyed to be reunited with Ana, who had grown spoiled overnight in the company of the people who now considered themselves her grandparents. Her heart ached at the thought of what their deception was doing. Over the people it could hurt.

She hadn't counted on this. On how far it would spread. No, she hadn't thought at all. And now it had all become one big emotional tangle. Don and Mary Colson loved Ana, and she loved them. Ana loved Dante. Paige loved Dante and she had been foolish enough to tell him so.

And he hadn't said a thing back. Hadn't said a thing about it since, not even in denial of it, or rejection of it.

With his parents around, she hadn't really thought he would. But once they were gone and a very cranky Ana who was coming off being treated like her Royal Highness the Grand Duchess had been put down for her nap, she'd expected something.

Instead, Dante had retreated to the office. Really, it was Tuesday and they both could have gone in, but she'd felt sulky over his behavior, and reluctant to leave Ana, and he hadn't pressed.

Paige put the finishing touches on her sketch and looked out at the ocean. She had another window designed for Christmas, and with only one more main display to concern herself with, she was running well ahead of deadline.

Dante's seaside house was certainly good for inspiration.

Even if the man himself was turning her into a quivering ball of nerves.

She set her sketchbook down on the table and stood, stretching her arms up over her head, then shaking her hands out, trying to get rid of some of the adrenaline that was running through her.

Thinking about Dante had that effect on her. Remembering being in bed with him did that to her. Most especially, remembering that she'd told him she loved him had that effect on her.

She took a deep breath of the ocean air and put her hand on her stomach. Dante's parents, their feelings, were just a part of the unintended side effects of this whole thing. It was still possible that she was pregnant.

The idea had panicked her at first. The thought of caring for two babies. Of what it might do to the adoption. Now... now she felt like she could do it. Like no matter what happened, it was within her power to handle it.

Because she wasn't the same person she had been. Or rather, she didn't see herself the way her family, or the people back in her hometown had anymore. She wasn't deficient. She had everything in her that she needed to succeed. Most importantly, she knew just how much power love had. How it had changed her. With Ana, and now with Dante.

Another baby would mean more love. And no matter how difficult it might be to manage everything, she couldn't regret that.

She turned and walked back into the house, and nearly ran into Dante, who was walking through the living room with long, purposeful strides.

"You're back."

"Yes," he said. "I am."

"It's before five, so it surprised me."

"There was pressing business for me to take care of here."

"What...what's that?" she asked, sure she didn't want to know. Because she was sure she already knew. It had something to do with the I Love You incident and while she had wanted to talk to him about it, she found that, as she was faced with it, she was changing her mind.

"I've been thinking. The coverage of the wedding in the media has been very positive."

She grimaced. "Yeah, I hadn't really looked at it." Frankly, she hadn't wanted to see pictures of the moment she'd realized she was in love with the world's most impossible man.

"I had Trevor send me the highlights. But, as I thought, the wedding, the relationship in general, has had a very positive effect on my image."

"Well, that's nice." This was about as far from feelings as it got, and she found she was more annoyed than relieved.

"There is the possibility you're pregnant."

"I'll know soon-ish," she said.

"Also," he said, pressing on as if she hadn't spoken, "it didn't escape my notice how quickly Don and Mary took to Ana. And how quickly she took to them."

Her stomach fell. "Oh. Yeah, I feel bad about that."

"Why? There's no reason to. If anything, it confirms what I already suspected we should do."

"And what's that?" she asked, not sure she was going to like the answer. Afraid she might love it.

"I think this should be a permanent arrangement."

She did love it. A rush of joy, of complete and utter joy, filled her. "Really?"

"It seems the best thing to do, all things considered."

"Yes," she said, walking to him and throwing her arms around his neck. "Yes." Her mind went blank of everything, everything but the moment. Everything but him.

He pulled her in tightly, kissing her lips, his hands roaming over her curves. They kissed as they went up the stairs before Dante swung her up into his arms, holding her to his chest, his mouth devouring hers as he set her on the bed, stripping his clothes and hers as quickly as possible.

* * *

In the aftermath, she lay there replete, the room spinning, her heart pounding. She rolled over, ready to pull Dante into her arms, but he was already up and getting dressed, his expression tight, shuttered.

"I think we've proven that there are even more reasons for us to stay together," he said, as he tugged his pants on, his tone conversational. "The chemistry between us is incredible."

"The chemistry?" she said, feeling thick and fuzzy from her release still. Chemistry didn't sound right, though. It sounded like nothing more than a base, chemical reaction and yet she felt like there was so much more between them. There was for her, at least.

"It's the best sex I've ever had."

She felt struck by that comment. So bald and so basic. At any other time, she might have found it sexy to hear him say that, felt complimented. But when she'd offered love twelve hours before, and this was her gift in return, no, it didn't feel so good.

"And is that…all?" she asked.

"There's nothing more, Paige. Nothing else that matters."

"Dante…"

"Now that we've settled things, I do have more work to do." He tugged his shirt on and buttoned it with deft, steady fingers. He slicked his hair back with his hand and it was like nothing had just happened between them. As if a storm hadn't just blown through the room, blown through them.

He turned and walked out of the room, closing the door firmly behind him. Paige pulled her knees up to her chest and sat there, stunned. She felt…sad. Drained. Used.

She let the feeling wash over her, wash through her. But only for a moment.

Then she remembered the look in his eyes. That awful blank look that she knew so well. Dante was running scared. Trying to have the basest arrangement with her without giving anything of himself. Only his money, his body.

But she wouldn't accept that. The old Paige would have. She wouldn't have tried for more.

But this Paige, this woman who was, in part of Dante's making, was going to try for everything. All she needed was a plan.

Dante couldn't concentrate on his work. He could concentrate on nothing. He had left work at three in the afternoon, come home and had passionate, intense… It was sex and yet at the same time, something more, with a woman who seemed determined to break him open with a battering ram.

And she was close. Too close.

Three hours on and his body still burned. His chest aching like there was a hole in it.

"Dante."

He turned and his heart nearly stopped. Paige was standing there, a chiffon gown that had no substance at all wound around her curves, the light behind her showing the silhouette of her body beneath the gown.

"What are you doing?" he asked, his throat tightening, threatening to choke him.

"I'm here to talk."

"You don't look like you're here to talk," he said.

"But I am. I'm here to lay it out for you, as clear and honest as I can."

"Lay what out?"

"Everything. What I feel. What I feel for you. I'm not going to do it while I'm half-asleep, while you can pretend you didn't hear. I'm going to tell you now, to your face."

She crossed the threshold of his office and came to stand in front of his chair, her blue eyes bright, determined. She cupped his face, her eyes never leaving his as she leaned in and pressed a kiss to his forehead.

"I love you," she whispered. She kissed his cheek. "I love you." Then his lips, the touch feather-soft and perfect. "I love you."

He gritted his teeth, trying to fight against the pain, the need, that was building in his chest, threatening to overwhelm him, to consume him completely. "I'm glad, Paige. If that makes you happy, then I'm glad."

"Is that all?" she asked, searching his face, demanding honesty.

He gritted his teeth and looked away. "It's all I have to give."

"You're a liar, Dante."

Anger flooded through him, unreasonable and hot. "I'm a what?"

"A liar. And not just about this. Your entire life is a lie. Your whole existence."

He pushed up from his chair and she leaped backward, her eyes wide with shock. "Of course," he snarled, battling against the pain in his chest. "How could I forget? I'm the Italian bastard, adopted by a respectable family. The one who doesn't belong. Of course my existence is a lie. I have spent years pretending to be civilized, pretending to be a man of honor, when we both know I am not. I don't share their blood," he said, speaking of his parents. "I have the blood of a killer in me. The blood of a low-class, violent coward who abused women. Killed them. That's who I am…of course this is a lie," he said, sweeping his hand around the well-ordered, perfect room. The lie he had built for himself.

He stared her down, stared into her wide eyes, waiting for the fear to win. Waiting for her to realize that what he said was true. That he wasn't the man she thought he was. That he wasn't the man he pretended to be. That beneath his armor, was a darkness that no one would ever want to touch.

"No," she said, shaking her head. "You idiot. You think I don't know that's what you think of yourself? You think I buy what the press writes? What you show everyone? Don't forget I'm the one who dragged you out of that cold shower. I'm the one who warmed you with her own body, so don't try to scare me now with the same lie you tell yourself every day.

Because this is the lie, Dante Romani. That you're broken. That you can't love or be loved. Look around you...people love you. Because you're worthy of it. Don and Mary love you. Ana loves you. I love you. And you won't let us. Because you're too damn afraid."

"Hell, yes, I'm afraid," he growled, feeling the walls he'd erected around his heart crumbling. "I am half of that man, Paige. Do you know what that means? Passion is poison for me. It could be."

"It's not true."

"You think it's not true. Why? Because you love me? *She* loved him, Paige." He shouted the words, desperate to make her understand, to make her believe him. "That's why she didn't leave. She loved him...she thought he could be different. That he could change. Don't you understand? Love doesn't fix anything. It hides flaws. Makes people blind to them. But love is not all brightness and sunshine. It can't heal a damned thing." His voice broke, the memories of his mother flooding his mind. "It has a dark side. Everything does."

She shook her head. "Only if you choose to dwell in the dark. He made a choice, Dante. You can't blame love for that. That wasn't love."

"Passion then. Emotion. A lack of control. I won't let myself do that. Do you see this?" he asked, sweeping his arm across his office. "Order. Control. That's who I am. It's what I've made myself. What I've trained myself to be. So that I will never hurt someone like that. So that I will never become that man."

"So that you'll never be hurt," she said, her voice soft.

"That, too," he said, everything in him feeling exposed now. Raw.

"This isn't real," she said, looking around the room. "It's just stuff. It's just the outside. It doesn't fix who you are."

He laughed, the sound divorced from humor. "Nothing can, I'm afraid. All I can do is keep hiding who I am. Keep it locked up."

She bit her lip and shook her head. "You're a good man, Dante. I don't know why you don't know it. Why you don't believe it. Look what you've done for me. For Ana. You keep almost every bit of yourself locked up tight and you make me work to reach it, but when I do, that's when I know."

"When you know what?" he asked, his lungs frozen, incapable of drawing breath.

"When I know that I love you. And not just that, but why. Because you are so strong. And so broken. And yet, in spite of everything you've been through, you've grown up to be a good man. A man who puts the needs of others before himself. A man who is capable of great love, if only he would let himself feel it."

He shook his head. "That's not me, Paige. I'm sorry you're confused about that."

"You love me," she said.

Something inside of him broke completely, opening up a flood of emotion, of need so strong he wasn't sure he could withstand the onslaught. But he stood still, composing his face into a mask, doing what he had to do.

"No."

She shook her head. "I don't believe that."

"Then you have fooled yourself."

A tear spilled down her cheek, then another, each track of moisture a stab in his chest, a drop of his own blood shed inside, bleeding him dry. She shook her head. "No, Dante. Stop now. How long will you punish yourself for sins your father committed?"

"Love only means one thing to me, Paige. It is rage, and loss and grief so deep it consumes everything in its path. It puts you on your knees, steals your breath with the pain that it causes."

"That isn't love, Dante. That's evil. It was evil that tore love from you, that made your father do what he did. There was no love in it."

"Then it's the potential for evil I see in myself. Thank you for making it clear."

"You say you're half of your father like that makes everything certain. Like you aren't half of your mother. Don't forget that. Don't forget she gave you life, and that she would want you to live it fully. And don't forget what Don and Mary gave you, not through genetics, but what they taught you. You're bigger than one man, bigger than one event."

"And you speak like you have anything more than frivolous thoughts in your head," he growled, hating the insult, hating the words even as they left his lips. He was a coward. And in that moment, he knew it. Knew he was using anger to make her leave so he wouldn't have to listen to her anymore.

Because she was too close to tearing the veil away. To exposing him, not just to her, but to himself, for the first time.

"Out," he said. "Get out."

She stood for a moment, her blue eyes fixed on his, windows into her soul. Her pain, her sadness, worst of all, her love. For him. Love he didn't deserve. Couldn't accept.

"Get out, Paige. I don't want you here. I don't want you." The last words were torn from him, taking a piece of his soul with them. A lie he had to tell. A lie he hated.

She bit her bottom lip and nodded, then turned and walked out of the room, closing the door behind her. He didn't want to follow her. He didn't want to watch her walk out of the house, drive away. Out of his life. He would deserve it. He should want it.

But he didn't. He so desperately didn't. He wanted to cling to her words. To tell her that she was right. To will himself to believe it no matter what. So he could have her. So he could have Ana.

He looked around his desk, it was well-ordered. So perfect. And for the first time, he realized that everything around him was a lie. He was broken. Disheveled. Destroyed. And no amount of cleaning his surroundings would fix it.

He put his hand on his desk, on top of a mug that was

placed at a right angle, in the exact spot it needed to be for him to reach it with ease when he was seated. He picked it up by the handle and looked at it, felt the weight of it in his hand.

And he looked back down at the surface of his desk. A place for everything, everything in its place. And he hated it.

He growled and hurled the mug at the wall, splintering it into a hundred pieces. He braced himself on the desk, then he pushed everything to the floor.

His pencil holder. Stapler. The lamp. The damn zen garden that was supposed to make him feel calm. A stack of papers. Until his office was littered with the kind of destruction that mirrored the man he was within.

Piece by piece, he exposed himself. Tore away the walls. Tore away the facade until he had to look at it. Until he had to look at himself.

Pain tore at his chest. For once, he didn't have to strike out to cause physical agony as punishment. It was all in him, burning him alive from the inside out. He dropped to his knees, leaned forward, his forehead and forearms touching the floor.

She was right. He was a liar. He was scared, of himself. But not only of that, of caring and losing again. So much so, he had spent his life training himself never to care, on the excuse that he was protecting everyone from himself.

When he was really protecting himself from everyone else. Still a scared child, hiding behind a sofa, waiting, waiting for the monster to find him. A monster from outside, or a monster inside of himself.

He had believed, wholly, that he had banished his every emotion. But it was a lie, too. He hadn't. He had simply embraced fear and allowed it to dictate everything he did. Who he was.

For a brief moment in time, he'd had love in this house. A woman who loved him. A child who trusted him completely.

And he had thrown it away. The final punishment for his sins. The ultimate penance. He had fallen in love. The thing he had sworn he must never do. And he had done it. So he had pushed her away, pushed them away.

And now he was reduced to nothing. Raw and bleeding, all of his protection gone. All of his defenses, his ways of dealing, exposed for the flimsy nothings they were. He could do nothing. Nothing but lie there and embrace the pain, the love, the misery, the loss. Not just for Paige, not just for Ana, but for every moment in his life.

The walls he'd built to protect himself burned to nothing, reduced to ash before his eyes. He was not the man he pretended to be. He was not the man the media thought he was. And he let himself hope, for a moment, that he was the man that Paige saw. A man worthy of her love, worthy of Ana's admiration. Worthy of the Colsons' adoption.

For a long time he lay there, stripped of his protection. Of everything. Anguish washing over him, beating against him.

Finally, he stood, his hands shaking, and dialed his mother and father's phone number.

"Dante?" His mother answered on the second ring.

"Why did you adopt me?" he asked. He had never asked. He had always feared the answer. Had always feared that the media was right. And over the years, he had simply started to assume they were.

More than that, he was afraid of loving again. Of caring and losing. But that fear had carried him nowhere. That fear had nothing for him. Had given him nothing.

"Because," she said, her tone simple, matter-of-fact, "we fell in love with you the moment we saw you. An angry teenage boy with so much potential, in so much need. We knew you were our son. The one we'd been waiting for."

"I wasn't ready to hear that," he said, swallowing hard, holding the phone tight to his ear. "Until now."

"I know," she whispered.

He closed his eyes and released his hold on fear. "I love you," he said.

CHAPTER FIFTEEN

PAIGE felt like she was dying. Ana hadn't slept the whole night. She couldn't really blame her. She was in her little bassinet, rather than her crib, and crammed back into Paige's old room, in her old apartment. As a result, Paige hadn't slept, either.

She'd thought coming back to her little apartment would give her some clarity. Make her feel more…more like Dante and everything else had never happened. But it hadn't helped. She was too different. Too changed from her time with him. There was no way to even pretend it hadn't happened.

Now she was sitting at her desk, after having weathered a sea of congratulations from the other employees on her way into the office, feeling like death and having just spent the night away from her new husband, who was probably never going to speak to her again.

She would have to go back to Dante's house, she knew that. But one night couldn't have hurt. No one would find out. It would hardly compromise the adoption. And she needed space. Needed to not be sharing the same air as Dante.

She knew that he'd lashed out because she'd challenged him. Because he was frightened. She knew it down in her soul. But just because she was right, didn't mean he would change his mind. Didn't mean he would decide to change a lifetime of thinking and feeling a certain way. Didn't mean he even wanted to.

Maybe she was wrong about him loving her—that could be true. He loved Ana, though. She could see that. And she knew, given the chance, that he would be an amazing father. The kind of man who offered support and love to his children.

She'd known it the moment she'd seen him there, singing Ana his lullaby. She knew that had cost him, and that Ana's needs had transcended his grief. She'd known in that moment that he was a man capable of great love. And that he'd let fear cripple him.

Stupid man. Stupid, fantastic, lovely man.

"Mrs. Romani?"

It took Paige a moment to realize she was being addressed, even though she was in her office. She looked up and saw a young man standing at the door, a newspaper in his hand.

"Yes?"

"I'm supposed to deliver this to you." He came in and set the paper on her desk.

"Oh…" She looked down at her desk, frowning. "Oh…I… thank you…" She looked up and the man was gone.

She picked up the paper and started to turn each page, looking for…she didn't know what. Had someone wanted her to see pictures of the wedding? She flipped to the style section, and the headline stopped her cold.

She put her hand over her mouth, a sob climbing her throat. She picked up the paper, gathered it close to her chest, stood and ran out of her office.

"Explain this," Paige said, throwing the newspaper onto Dante's desk, a tear rolling down her cheek. She was shaking. Everywhere.

Dante looked up at her, his eyes haunted, the veil well and truly dropped. There was no armor covering up his emotions, nothing protecting him. He was as bare and vulnerable as she was.

"I told the truth," he said, his voice rough. "For the first time in so long, I told the truth."

She read the headline out loud. "Recently Wed Dante Romani Proclaims: I Love My Wife."

"It's true," he said.

Another tear slid down her cheek and she looked down at the paper, reading out loud.

"It was speculated only a few weeks ago, about whether or not Ms. Harper could reform ice-cold Dante Romani, and today he has confirmed that, indeed she has. 'I love my wife,' Romani says, 'and love changes you.'"

She looked back up at him. "This is a fluff piece," she said, sniffling. "No hard-hitting journalism, just a page of you talking about h-how much you love me, and your parents. And Ana."

"I admit that maybe doing it in a public forum wasn't the best thing but...all things considered..."

"Turnabout's fair play."

"Yes," he said. "Yes, it is. But this doesn't replace what I need to say to you now. I love you."

Paige's heart expanded in her chest, more tears falling. "Dante, you're ruining my makeup."

"And you completely destroyed the way I saw myself, and life, so I'd say it's a fair trade." He stood and walked around his desk, his eyes intent on hers. "You were right, Paige. I lied to myself. Because I was afraid. Of everything. Part of me was locked up tight, and I never intended on letting it out. Not ever. But you've shown me, consistently, that the reward for bravery is worth the risk. You've been so brave, so much braver than I. You took a risk to protect Ana... You took a risk in confessing your love to me. You put yourself out there time and again and opened yourself up to rejection when you didn't have to do that. And I was too cowardly to do the same."

Paige tried to swallow past the lump in her throat. "We've

had different life experiences, Dante. I can't even imagine what you went through. What that does to someone."

"It changes you," he said, his eyes filled with pain. "There's no way around that. But what you said…it's very true. And I can't let my fear of a man so far in my past be more important than the woman here in my present, and my future. You were right. People do love me, and I have been afraid to accept it. To look for it. To see it. Because I didn't want pain or grief to touch me ever again. And because of that, I've been living a cold life. I thought that by keeping everything well-ordered around me, that by accumulating more things, more success, I would somehow change from who I was into who I needed to be. But none of it mattered. None of it was real. None of it changed me. It just let me hide. From myself. From everyone. Everyone except you. You dragged me into the light. And I've learned something, Paige."

"What's that?" she asked.

"Light is stronger. I used to think that the two of them were different sides of the same coin. That with one, always came the other. That way of thinking…it helped me reason out what had happened when I was kid. It helped me find a way to believe that by behaving a certain way, I could control things. And now I've realized two things, the first being that I can't control everything. And the second is that light casts out darkness. When you shine it bright, it fills every corner, and it eradicates anything dark. There is nowhere for it to hide. That's what you've done for me. You shone a light on my soul, and now I'm filled with it. With your love."

She threw her arms around his neck and kissed him hard on the mouth. "I love you so much."

"I love you, too, Paige. I am so thankful for everything you are, because it's everything I needed. You are perfect in every way."

"Even when I get glitter on you?"

"Even then. Maybe especially then. Because I love that you come with color, and paint, and glitter."

"And a baby?"

"Most especially a baby. I want to be your husband," he said, "forever. And I also want to be Ana's father. Her real father. I never let myself realize just how much this is true, but I have a wonderful example of what a father should be in Don Colson. And I want to be that for Ana. I want to guide her, support her and love her. I'm afraid I'll mess it up, but I want to try."

"And if she wants to be an artist slash window dresser like her mother?"

"She's welcome to it. I'll build her an art studio."

"What about if she wants to be a CEO like her father?"

"She could do that, too. She can do anything."

"I think she can, too," Paige said, happiness filling her, suffusing her.

"And one of the most important things I hope to teach her, is through example," he said, his voice getting rough. "I hope to show her what love looks like, every day. By loving her as a father should love a daughter. And I hope to show her the kind of love that should exist between a husband and wife, by loving her mother, every day, as long as we both shall live."

EPILOGUE

ANA started crawling the day the adoption was finalized.

"She's really moving now," Paige said.

Dante watched Ana rock back and forth on her hands and knees before moving forward again, heading straight for the coffee table. He scooped her up into his arms, keeping her from certain disaster. "You have to watch your head, *stellina*," he said.

Ana had most definitely become his little star, not just because she was one of the two people at the center of his universe, but because she had healed so much pain in him.

He had vowed to teach Ana what love was, and yet, he found she was the one who taught him. Every day.

"Before you know it, she'll be dating," Paige said, giving him a mischievous smile.

He frowned. "No. I'm not thinking that far ahead."

"Why? Are you afraid some handsome Italian is going to come and sweep her off her feet?"

"Yes," he said.

Paige laughed. "You do have to watch those Italians. I should know. I'm a terminal case for the one I married."

She looped her arms around both him and Ana and kissed him on the cheek.

"So you don't regret it?" he asked, knowing she didn't, but liking to hear it anyway.

"Nope. Not one bit. There is one thing that will be hard to explain to Ana, though."

"What's that? Why you and I disappear behind closed bedroom doors for hours on end?"

She laughed. "Uh, I don't plan on explaining that. But that isn't what I meant."

"What then?"

"It'll be hard to explain to her why telling a lie led to the best thing that ever could have happened to me."

* * * * *

THEIR MOST FORBIDDEN FLING

MELANIE MILBURNE

Melanie Milburne read her first Mills & Boon novel at age seventeen in between studying for her final exams. After completing a Masters Degree in Education, she decided to write a novel in between settling down to do a PhD. She became so hooked on writing romance the PhD was shelved and her career as a romance writer was born. Melanie is an ambassador for the Australian Childhood Foundation and is a keen dog lover and trainer and enjoys long walks in the Tasmanian bush.

CHAPTER ONE

MOLLY SAW HIM first. He was coming out of a convenience store half a block from her newly rented bedsit. He had his head down against the sleeting rain, his forehead knotted in a frown of concentration. Her heart gave a dislocated stumble as he strode towards her. The memories came rushing back, tumbling over themselves like clothes spinning in a dryer. She didn't even realise she had spoken his name out loud until she heard the thready sound of her voice. 'Lucas?'

He stopped like a puppet suddenly pulled back on its strings. The jolt of recognition on his face was painful to watch. She saw the way his hazel eyes flinched; saw too the way his jaw worked in that immeasurable pause before he spoke her name. 'Molly...'

It had been ten years since she had heard his voice. A decade of living in London had softened his Australian outback drawl to a mellifluous baritone that for some reason sent an involuntary shiver over her skin. She looked at his face, drinking in his features one by one as if ticking off a checklist inside her head to make sure it really was him.

The landscape of his face—the brooding brow, the determined jaw and the aquiline nose—was achingly familiar and yet different. He was older around the eyes and mouth, and his dark brown hair, though thick and glossy, had a few streaks of silver in it around his temples. His skin wasn't quite as weathered and tanned as his father's or brothers' back on the farm at home, but it still had a deep olive tone.

He was still imposingly tall and whipcord lean and fit, as if strenuous exercise was far more important to him than rest and relaxation. She looked at his hazel eyes. The same shadows were there—long, dark shadows that anchored him to the past.

'I was wondering when I'd run into you,' Molly said to fill the bruised silence. 'I suppose Neil or Ian told you I was coming over to work at St Patrick's for three months?'

His expression became inscrutable and closed. 'They mentioned something about you following a boyfriend across,' he said.

Molly felt a blush steal over her cheeks. She still wasn't quite sure how to describe her relationship with Simon Westbury. For years they had been just friends, but ever since Simon had broken up with his long-term girlfriend Serena, they had drifted into an informal arrangement that was convenient but perhaps not as emotionally satisfying as Molly would have wished. 'Simon and I have been out a couple of times but nothing serious,' she said. 'He's doing a plastics registrar year over here. I thought it'd be good to have someone to travel with since it's my first time overseas.'

'Where are you staying?' Lucas asked.

'In that house over there,' Molly said, pointing to a seen-better-days Victorian mansion that was divided into small flats and bedsits. 'I wanted somewhere within walking distance of the hospital. Apparently lots of staff from abroad set up camp there.'

He acknowledged that with a slight nod.

Another silence chugged past.

Molly shifted her weight from foot to foot, the fingers of her right hand fiddling with the strap of her handbag where it was slung over her shoulder. 'Um… Mum said to say hello…'

His brows gave a micro-lift above his green and brown-flecked eyes but whether it was because of cynicism, doubt or wariness, she couldn't quite tell. 'Did she?' he asked.

Molly looked away for a moment, her gaze taking in the gloomy clouds that were suspended above the rooftops of the row of grey stone buildings. It was so different from the expansive skies and blindingly bright sunshine of the outback back home. 'I guess you heard my father's remarried…' She brought her gaze back up when he didn't respond. 'His new wife Crystal is pregnant. The baby's due in a couple of months.'

His eyes studied her for a beat or two. 'How do you feel about having a half-sibling?'

Molly pasted on a bright smile. 'I'm thrilled for them… It will be good to have someone to spoil. I love babies. I'll probably babysit now and then for them when I get back…'

He continued to look at her in that measured way of his. Could he see how deeply hurt she was that her father was trying to replace Matt? Could he see how guilty she felt about *feeling* hurt? Matt had been the golden child, the firstborn and heir. Molly had lived in his shadow for as long as she could remember—never feeling good enough, bright enough.

Loved enough.

With a new child to replace the one he had lost, her father would have no need of her now.

'You're a long way from home,' Lucas said.

Did he think she wasn't up to the task? Did he still see her as that gangly, freckle-faced kid who had followed him about like a devoted puppy? 'I'm sure I'll cope with it,' she said with the tiniest elevation of her chin. 'I'm not a little kid any longer. I'm all grown up now in case you hadn't noticed.'

His gaze moved over her in a thoroughly male appraisal that made Molly's spine suddenly feel hot and tingly. As his eyes re-engaged with hers the air tightened, as if a light but unmistakable current of electricity was pulsing through it. 'Indeed you are,' he said.

Molly glanced at his mouth. He had a beautiful mouth, one that implied sensuality in its every line and contour. The shadow of dark stubble surrounding it gave him an intensely male look that she found captivating. She wondered when that mouth had last smiled. She wondered when it had last kissed someone.

She wondered what it would feel like to be kissed by him.

Molly forced her gaze to reconnect with his. She needed to get her professional cap on and keep it on. They would be working together in the same unit. No one over here needed to know about the tragic tie that bound them so closely. 'Well, then,' she said, shuffling her feet again. 'I guess I'll see you at the hospital.'

'Yes.'

She gave him another tight, formal smile and made to move past but she had only gone a couple of paces when he said her name again. 'Molly?'

Molly slowly turned and looked at him. The lines about his mouth seemed to have deepened in the short time she had been talking to him. 'Yes?' she said.

'You might not have been informed as yet, but as of yesterday I'm the new head of ICU,' he said. 'Brian Yates had to suddenly resign due to ill health.'

She gripped the edges of her coat closer across her chest. *Lucas Banning was her boss?* It put an entirely new spin on things. This first foray of hers into working abroad could be seriously compromised if he decided he didn't want her working with him. And why would he want her here?

She was a living, breathing reminder of the worst mistake he had ever made.

'No,' Molly said. 'I hadn't been informed.'

'Is it going to be a problem?' he asked with a direct look she found a little intimidating.

'Why would it be a problem?' she asked.

'It's a busy and stretched-to-the-limit department,' he said. 'I don't want any personal issues between staff members to compromise patient outcomes.'

Molly felt affronted that he thought her so unprofessional as to bring their past into the workplace. She rarely spoke of Matt these days. Even though she had lived with her grief longer than she had lived without it, speaking of him brought it all back as if it had happened yesterday—the gut-wrenching pain, the aching sense of loss. *The guilt.* Most of her friends from medical school didn't even know she had once had an older brother. 'I do *not* bring personal issues to work,' she said.

His hazel eyes held hers for a beat or two of silence. 'Fine,' he said. 'I'll see you in the morning. Don't be late.'

Molly pursed her lips as he strode off down the street. She would make sure she was there before he was.

Lucas glanced pointedly at the clock on the wall as Molly Drummond rushed into the glassed-in office of ICU. 'Your shift started an hour ago,' he said as he slapped a patient's file on the desk.

'I'm so sorry,' she said breathlessly. 'I tried to call but I didn't have the correct code in my phone. I'm still with my Australian network so I couldn't call direct.'

'So what's your excuse?' he asked, taking in her pink face and the disarray of her light brown hair. 'Boyfriend keep you up late last night, or did he make you late by serving you breakfast in bed?'

Her face went bright red and her grey-blue eyes flashed with annoyance. 'Neither,' she said. 'I was on my way to work when I came across a cat that had been hit by a car. I couldn't just leave it there. It had a broken leg and was in pain. I had to take it to the nearest vet clinic. It took me ages to find one, and then I had to wait until the vet got there.'

Lucas knew he should apologise for jumping to conclusions but he wanted to keep a professional distance. Out of all the hospitals in London, or the whole of England for that matter, why did she have to come to his? He had put as much distance as he could between his past and the present. For the last ten years he had tried to put it behind him, not to forget—he could never, would *never* do that—but to move on with his life as best he could, making a difference where he could.

Saving lives, not destroying them.

Molly Drummond turning up in his world was not what he needed right now. He had only recently found out she was coming to work here, but he had assured himself that he wouldn't have to have too much to do with her directly. He had planned to become director at the end of next year when Brian Yates formally retired. But Brian being diagnosed with a terminal illness had meant he'd had to take over the reins a little ahead of schedule. Now he would have to interact with Molly on a daily basis, which would have been fine if she was just like any other young doctor who came and went in the department.

But Molly was not just any other doctor.

She wasn't that cute little freckle-faced kid any more either. She had grown into a beautiful young woman with the sort of understated looks that took you by surprise in unguarded moments. Like yesterday, when he'd run into her on the street.

Looking up and seeing her there had made his breath catch in his throat. He had been taken aback by the way her grey-blue eyes darkened or softened with her mood. How her creamy skin took on a rosy tinge when she felt cornered or embarrassed. How her high cheekbones gave her a haughty regal air, and yet her perfect nose with its tiny dusting of freckles had an innocent girl-next-door appeal that was totally beguiling. How her figure still had a coltish look about it with those long legs and slim arms.

He had not been able to stop himself imagining how it would feel to have those slim arms wrap around his body and to feel that soft, full mouth press against his. He had his share of sexual encounters, probably not as many as some of his peers, but he wasn't all that comfortable with letting people get too close.

And getting too close to Molly Drummond was something he wanted to avoid at all costs.

'I haven't got time to give you a grand tour,' Lucas said, forcing his wayward thoughts back where they belonged. 'But you'll find your way around soon enough. We have twenty beds, all of them full at the present time. Jacqui Hunter is the ward clerk. She'll fill you in on where the staff facilities are. Su Ling and Aleem Pashar are the registrars. They'll run through the patients with you.' He gave her a brisk nod before he left the office. 'Enjoy your stay.'

'Dr Drummond?'

Molly turned to see a middle-aged woman coming towards her. 'I'm sorry I wasn't here to greet you,' the woman said with a friendly smile. 'Things have been a bit topsy-turvy, I'm afraid.' She offered her hand. 'I'm Jacqui Hunter.'

'Pleased to meet you,' Molly said.

'This has been such a crazy couple of days,' Jacqui said. 'Did Dr Banning tell you about Brian Yates?' She didn't wait for Molly to respond. 'Such a terrible shame. He was planning to retire next year. Now he's been sent home to get his affairs in order.'

'I'm very sorry,' Molly said.

'He and Olivia just had their first grandchild too,' Jacqui said shaking her head. 'Life's not fair, is it?'

'No, it's not.'

Jacqui popped the patient's file, which Lucas had left on the desk, in the appropriate drawer. 'Now, then,' she said, turning to face Molly again. 'Let's get you familiarised with the place. You're from Australia, aren't you? Sydney, right?'

'Yes,' Molly said. 'But I grew up in the bush.'

'Like our Lucas, huh?'

'Yes, we actually grew up in the same country town in New South Wales.'

Jacqui's eyebrows shot up underneath her blunt fringe. 'Really? What a coincidence. So you know each other?'

Molly wondered if she should have mentioned anything about her connection with Lucas. 'Not really. It's been years since I've seen him,' she said. 'He moved to London when I was seventeen. It's not like we've stayed in touch or anything.'

'He's a bit of a dark horse is our Lucas,' Jacqui said, giving Molly a conspiratorial look. 'Keeps himself to himself, if you know what I mean.'

Molly wasn't sure if the ward clerk was expecting a response from her or not. 'Um...yes...'

'No one knows a whisper about his private life,' Jacqui said. 'He keeps work and play very separate.'

'Probably a good idea,' Molly said.

Jacqui grunted as she led the way to the staff change room. 'There's plenty of women around here who would give their eye teeth for a night out with him,' she said.

'It should be a crime to be so good looking, don't you think?'

'Um…'

'He's got kind, intelligent eyes,' Jacqui said. 'The patients love him—and so do the relatives. He takes his time with them. He treats them like he would his own family. That's rare these days, let me tell you. Everyone is so busy climbing up the career ladder. Lucas Banning was born to be a doctor. You can just tell.'

'Actually, I think he always planned on being a wheat and sheep farmer, like his father and grandfather before him,' Molly said.

Jacqui looked at her quizzically. 'Are we talking about the same person?' she asked.

'As I said, I don't know him all that well,' Molly quickly backtracked.

Jacqui indicated the female change room door on her right. 'Bathroom is through there and lockers here,' she said. 'The staff tea room is further down on the left.' She led the way back to the office. 'You're staying three months with us, aren't you?'

'Yes,' Molly said. 'I haven't been overseas before. The job came up and I took it before I could talk myself out of it.'

'Well, you're certainly at the right time of life to do it, aren't you?' Jacqui said. 'Get the travel bug out of the way before you settle down. God knows, you'll never be able to afford it once the kids come along. Take it from me. They bleed you dry.'

'How many children do you have?'

'Four boys,' Jacqui said, and with a little roll of her eyes added, 'Five if you count my husband.' She led the way back to the sterilising bay outside ICU. 'One of the registrars will go through the patients with you. I'd better get back to the desk.'

'Thanks for showing me around.'

Molly spent an hour with the registrars, going through each patient's history. Lucas joined them as they came to the last patient. Claire Mitchell was a young woman of twenty-two with a spinal-cord injury as well as a serious head injury after falling off a horse at an equestrian competition. She had been in an induced coma for the past month. Each time they tried to wean her off the sedatives her brain pressure skyrocketed. The scans showed a resolving intracerebral haematoma and persistent cerebral oedema.

Molly watched as Lucas went through the latest scans with the parents. He explained the images and answered their questions in a calm reassuring manner.

'I keep thinking she's going to die,' the mother said in a choked voice.

'She's come this far,' Lucas said. 'These new scans show positive signs of improvement. It's a bit of a waiting game, I'm afraid. Just keep talking to her.'

'We don't know how to thank you,' the father said. 'When I think of how bad she was just a week ago...'

'She's definitely turned a corner in the last few days,' Lucas said. 'Just try and stay positive. We'll call you as soon as there's any change.'

Molly met his gaze once the parents had returned to their daughter's bedside. 'Can I have a quick word, Dr Banning?' she asked. 'In private?'

His brows came together as if he found the notion

of meeting with her in private an interruption he could well do without. 'My office is last on the left down the corridor. I'll meet you there in ten minutes. I just have to write up some meds for David Hyland in bed four.'

Molly stood outside the office marked with Lucas's name. The door was ajar and she peered around it to see if he was there, but the office was empty so she gently pushed the door open and went inside.

It was furnished like any other underfunded hospital office: a tired-looking desk dominated the small space with a battered chair that had an L-shaped rip in the vinyl on the back. A dented and scratched metal filing cabinet was tucked between the window and a waist-high bookcase that was jammed with publications and textbooks. A humming computer was in the middle of the desk and papers and medical journals were strewn either side. Organised chaos was the term that came to Molly's mind. There was a digital photo frame on the filing cabinet near the tiny window that overlooked the bleak grey world outside. She pressed the button that set the images rolling. The splashes of the vivid outback colour of Bannington homestead took her breath away. The tall, scraggy gum trees, the cerulean blue skies, the endless paddocks, the prolific wildflowers after last season's rain, the colourful bird life on the dams and the waters of Carboola Creek, which ran through the property, took her home in a heartbeat. She could almost hear the *arck arck* sound of the crows and the warbling of the magpies.

Her parents had run the neighbouring property Drummond Downs up until their bitter divorce seven years ago. It had been in her family for six generations, gearing up for a seventh, but Matthew's death had changed everything.

Her father had not handled his grief at losing his only son. Her mother had not handled her husband's anger and emotional distancing. The homestead had gradually run into the red and then, after a couple of bad seasons, more and more parcels of land had had to be sold off to keep the bank happy. With less land to recycle and regenerate crops and stock, the property had been pushed to the limit. Crippling debts had brought her parents to the point of bankruptcy.

Offers of help from neighbours, including Lucas's parents, Bill and Jane Banning, had been rejected. Molly's father had been too proud to accept help, especially from the parents of the boy who had been responsible for the death of their only son. Drummond Downs had been sold to a foreign investor, and her parents had divorced within a year of leaving the homestead.

Molly sighed as she pressed the stop button, her hand falling back to her side. The sound of a footfall behind her made her turn around, and her heart gave a jerky little movement behind her ribcage as she met Lucas's hazel gaze. 'I was just…' she lifted a hand and then dropped it '…looking at your photos…'

He closed the door with a soft click but he didn't move towards the desk. It was hard to read his expression, but it seemed to Molly as if he was controlling every nuance of his features behind that blank, impersonal mask. 'Neil emails me photos from time to time,' he said.

'They're very good,' Molly said. 'Very professional.'

Something moved like a fleeting shadow through his eyes. 'He toyed with the idea of being a professional photographer,' he said. 'But as you know...things didn't work out.'

Molly chewed at the inside of her mouth as she thought about Neil working back at Bannington Homestead when he might have travelled the world, doing what he loved best. So many people had been damaged by the death of her brother. The stone of grief thrown into the pond of life had cast wide circles in the community of Carboola Creek. When Lucas had left Bannington to study medicine, his younger brother Neil had taken over his role on the property alongside their father. Any hopes or aspirations of a different life Neil might have envisaged for himself had had to be put aside. The oldest son and heir had not stepped up to the plate as expected. Various factions of the smallminded community had made it impossible for Lucas to stay and work the land as his father and grandfather had done before him.

'It wasn't your fault,' Molly said, not even realising how firmly she believed it until she had spoken it out loud. She had never blamed him but she had grown up surrounded by people who did. But her training as a doctor had made her realise that sometimes accidents just happened. No one was to blame. If Matt had been driving, as he had only minutes before they'd hit that kangaroo that had jumped out in front of them on the road, it would have been him that had been exiled.

Lucas hooked a brow upwards as he pushed away from the door. 'Wasn't it?'

Molly turned as he strode past her to go behind his

desk. She caught a faint whiff of his aftershave, an intricately layered mix of citrus and spice and something else she couldn't name—perhaps his own male scent. His broad shoulders were so tense she could see the bunching of his muscles beneath his shirt. 'It was an accident, Lucas,' she said. 'You know it was. That's what the coroner's verdict was. Anyway, Matt could easily have been driving instead of you. Would you have wanted him to be blamed for the rest of his life?'

His eyes met hers, his formal back-to-business look locking her out of the world of his pain. 'What did you want to speak to me about?' he asked.

Molly's shoulders went down on an exhaled breath. 'I sort of let slip to Jacqui Hunter that we knew each other from…back home…'

A muscle in his cheek moved in and out. 'I see.'

'I didn't say anything about the accident,' she said. 'I just said we grew up in the same country town.'

His expression was hard as stone, his eyes even harder. 'Why did you come here?' he asked. 'Why this hospital?'

Molly wasn't sure she could really answer that, even to herself. Why had she felt drawn to where he had worked for all these years? Why had she ignored the other longer-term job offers to come to St Patrick's and work alongside him for just three months? It had just seemed the right thing to do. Even her mother had agreed when Molly had told her. Her mother had said it was time they all moved on and put the past—and Matthew—finally to rest. 'I wanted to work overseas but most of the other posts were for a year or longer,' she said. 'I wasn't sure if I wanted to stay away from home quite that long. St Patrick's seemed like a good place to start. It's got a great reputation.'

He barricaded himself behind his desk, his hands on his lean hips in a keep-back-from-me posture. 'I've spent the last decade trying to put what happened behind me,' he said. 'This is my life now. I don't want to destroy what little peace I've been able to scratch together.'

'I'm not here to ruin your peace or your life or career or whatever,' Molly said. 'I just wanted some space from my family. Things have been difficult between my parents, especially since Crystal got pregnant. I'm tired of being the meat in the sandwich. I wanted some time out.'

'So you came right to the lion's den,' he said with an embittered look. 'Aren't your parents worried I might destroy your life too?'

Molly pressed her lips together for a moment. Her father had said those very words in each and every one of their heated exchanges when she'd broached the subject of coming to London. 'Do you want me to resign?' she asked.

His forehead wrinkled in a heavy frown and one of his hands reached up and scored a rough pathway through his hair before dropping back down by his side. 'No,' he said, sighing heavily. 'We're already short-staffed. It might take weeks to find a replacement.'

'I can work different shifts from you if—'

He gave her a dark look. 'That won't be necessary,' he said. 'People will start to ask questions if we make an issue out of it.'

'I'm not here to make trouble for you, Lucas.'

He held her gaze for an infinitesimal moment, but the screen had come back up on his face. 'I'll see you on the ward,' he said, and pulled out his chair and sat down. 'I have to call a patient's family.'

Molly walked to the door, but as she pulled it closed on her exit she saw that he was frowning heavily as he reached for the phone...

CHAPTER TWO

LUCAS WAS GOING through some blood results with Kate Harrison, one of the nurses, when Molly came into the ICU office the following day. Her perfume drifted towards him, wrapping around his senses, reminding him of summer, sweet peas and innocence. How she managed to look so gorgeous this early in the morning in ballet flats and plain black leggings and a long grey cardigan over a white top amazed him. She wasn't wearing any make-up to speak of and her shoulder-length hair was pulled back in a ponytail, giving her a fresh-faced, youthful look that was totally captivating.

'Good morning,' she said, her tentative smile encompassing Kate as well as him.

'Morning,' he said, turning back to the blood results. 'Kate, I want you to keep an eye on Mr Taylor's white-cell count and CRP. Let me know if there's any change.'

'I'll ring you with the results when they come in,' Kate said. She turned to Molly. 'Hi, I'm Kate Harrison. I heard on the grapevine you're from Dr Banning's neck of the woods.'

Molly's gaze flicked uncertainly to Lucas's. 'Um... yes...'

'I looked it up on an internet map,' Kate said. 'It's

a pretty small country town. Were you neighbours or something?'

'Sort of,' Molly said. 'Lucas's family ran the property next door but it was ten kilometres away.'

'I wish my neighbours were ten kilometres away,' Kate said with a grin, 'especially when they play their loud music and party all night. Nice to have you with us, Dr Drummond.'

'Please call me Molly.'

'We have a social club you might be interested in joining,' Kate said. 'A group of us hang out after hours. It's a good way to meet people from other departments. Nobody admits it out loud but it's sort of turned into a hospital dating service. We've had two marriages, one engagement and one and a half babies so far.'

'Dr Drummond already has a boyfriend,' Lucas said as he opened the file drawer.

'Actually, I would be interested,' Molly said, sending him a hard little look. 'Apart from Simon, I don't have any friends over here.'

'Great,' Kate said. 'I'll send you an invite by email. We're meeting for a movie next week.'

Lucas waited until Kate had left before he spoke. 'I'd be careful hanging out with Kate's social group. Not all the men who go have the right motives.'

She gave him a haughty look. 'I can take care of myself.'

'From what I've heard so far about your plastics guy, he doesn't seem your type.'

Her brows came up. 'And you're some sort of authority on who my type is, are you?'

He gave a loose shrug of his shoulders. 'Just an observation.'

'Then I suggest you keep your observations to yourself,' she said, her eyes flashing like sheet lightning. 'I'm perfectly capable of managing my own private life. At least I have one.'

'Just because I keep my private life out of the hospital corridors doesn't mean I don't have one,' Lucas clipped back.

Jacqui came into the office behind them. 'Whoa, is this pistols at three paces or what?' she said. 'What's going on?'

'Nothing,' they said in unison.

Jacqui's brows lifted speculatively. 'I thought you guys were old friends from back home?'

'Excuse me,' Molly said, and brushed past to leave.

'What's going on between you two?' Jacqui asked Lucas.

'Nothing,' he said with a glower.

'Could've fooled me,' Jacqui said. 'I saw the way she was glaring at you. It's not like you to be the big bad boss. What did you say to upset her?'

'Nothing.'

Jacqui folded her arms and gave him a look. 'That's two nothings from you, which in my book means there's something. I might be speaking out of turn, but you don't seem too happy to have her here.'

The last thing Lucas wanted was anyone digging into his past connection with Molly. It was a part of his life he wanted to keep separate. The turmoil of emotions he felt over Matt's death was something he dealt with in the privacy of his home. He didn't want it at work, where he needed a clear head. He didn't like his ghosts or his guilt hanging around.

'Dr Drummond is well qualified and will no doubt be a valuable asset to the team at St Patrick's,' he said. 'All new staff members take time to settle in. It's a big change moving from one hospital to another, let alone across the globe.'

'She's very beautiful in a girl-next-door sort of way, isn't she?'

He gave a noncommittal shrug as he leafed through a patient's notes. 'She's OK, I guess.'

Jacqui's mouth tilted in a knowing smile. 'She's the sort of girl most mothers wish their sons would bring home, don't you think?'

Lucas put the file back in the drawer and then pushed it shut. 'Not my mother,' he said, and walked out.

Lucas was walking home from the hospital a couple of days later when he saw Molly coming up the street, carrying a cardboard box with holes punched in it. He had managed to avoid her over the last day or two, other than during ward rounds where he had kept things tightly professional. But as she came closer he could see she looked flustered and upset.

'What's wrong?' he asked as she stopped right in front of him.

Her grey-blue eyes were shiny and moist with tears. 'I don't know what to do,' she said. 'My landlord has flatly refused to allow me to have Mittens in my flat. He's threatening to have me evicted if I don't get rid of him immediately.'

'Mittens?'

She indicated the box she was carrying. 'Mittens the cat,' she said, 'the one that got hit by a car on my first day? I had to take him otherwise the vet would've sent him to the cat shelter and he might've been put down if no one wanted him.'

'Didn't the owner come and claim him?' Lucas asked.

'It turns out he doesn't have an owner, or none we can track down,' she said. 'He hasn't got a collar or a microchip. He's only about seven months old.'

He angled his head, his gaze narrowing slightly. 'What were you planning to do with him?'

Her expression became beseeching. 'One of the nurses mentioned you lived in a big house all by yourself. She said you had a garden that would be perfect for a cat. She said you'd—'

Lucas held up his hands like stop signs. 'Oh, no,' he said. 'No way. I'm not having some flea-bitten cat sharpening its claws on my rugs or furniture.'

'It's only for a few days,' she said, appealing to him with those big wide eyes of hers. 'I'll find another flat, one that will allow me to have a cat. *Please?*'

Lucas could feel his resolve slipping. How was he supposed to resist her when she was so darned cute standing there like a little lost waif? 'I hate cats,' he said. 'They make me sneeze.'

'But this one is a non-allergenic cat,' she said. 'He was probably hideously expensive and now we have him for free. Well…not free exactly…' She momentarily tugged at her lower lip with her teeth. 'The vet's bill was astronomical.'

'I do *not* want a cat,' he said through tight lips.

'You're not getting a cat,' she said. 'You're *babysitting* one.'

Lucas rolled his eyes and took the box from her. His fingers brushed against hers and a lightning strike of electricity shot through his body. Her eyes flared as if she had felt it too, and two little spots of colour pooled high in her cheeks. She stood back from him and tucked a strand of hair back behind her ear, her gaze slipping from his. 'I don't know how to thank you,' she said.

'My place is just along here,' he said gruffly, and led the way.

Molly stepped into the huge foyer of the four-storey mansion Lucas owned. The house was tastefully decorated with an eclectic mix of modern, art deco and antique pieces. Room after room led off the foyer and a grand staircase to the floors above. There was even a ballroom, which overlooked the garden, and a conservatory. It was such a big house for one person. It would have housed three generations of a family with room to spare. 'You don't find it a little cramped?' she asked dryly as she turned and faced him.

The corner of his mouth twitched, which was about the closest he ever got to a smile. 'I like my space,' he said as he shrugged off his coat and hung it on the brass coat rack. 'I guess it comes from growing up in the outback.'

'Tell me about it,' Molly said with feeling. 'I'm starting to feel quite claustrophobic at that bedsit and I've barely been there a week. I don't know why Simon suggested it.'

'Does he live there with you?' he asked.

'No, he's renting a place in Bloomsbury,' she said. 'He offered me a room but I wanted to keep my independence.'

'Are you sleeping with him?'

Molly frowned to cover her embarrassment. She had only slept with Simon once and she had instantly regretted it. She couldn't help feeling he had only slept with her as a sort of payback to his ex Serena because he'd been so hurt by her leaving him. Molly had mistaken his friendliness as attraction, but now she wasn't sure how to get out of the relationship without causing him further hurt. 'I can't see how that is any of your business,' she said.

His eyes remained steady on hers, quietly assessing. 'You don't seem the casual sleep around type.'

She felt her cheeks heat up a little more. 'I'm not a virgin, if that's what you're suggesting. And there's nothing wrong with casual sex as long as it's safe.'

His gaze slowly tracked down to her mouth.

Something shifted in the air—an invisible current that connected her to him in a way Molly had never felt quite before. She felt her lips start to tingle as if he had bent his head and pressed his mouth to hers. She could almost feel the warm, firm dryness of his lips against her own. Her mind ran wild with the thought of his tongue slipping through the shield of her lips to find hers and call it into erotic play. Her insides flickered with hot little tongues of lust, sending arrows of awareness to the very heart of her. She ran the tip of her tongue out over the surface of her lips and watched as his hooded gaze followed its journey.

The mewling cry of Mittens from inside the box broke the spell.

Lucas frowned as if he had completely forgotten what he was carrying. 'Er...aren't we supposed to rub butter on its paws or something?' he asked.

'I think that's just an old wives' tale,' Molly said. 'I'm sure if we show him around first he'll soon work out his territory. I don't suppose you happen to have a pet door?'

He gave her a speaking look. 'No.'

'Oh, well, he'll soon let you know when he wants to go in or out. Maybe you could leave a window open.'

'No.'

Molly pursed her lips in thought. 'How about a kitty litter box? Then you wouldn't have to worry about him getting locked inside while you're at work.'

'Read my lips,' he said, eyeballing her over the top of the box. 'I am *not* keeping this cat. This is an interim thing until you find a pet-friendly place to stay.'

'Fine.' She opened the folded over lid of the box. Mittens immediately popped his head up and mewed at her. 'Isn't he cute?'

'Adorable.'

Molly glanced up at him but he wasn't looking at the cat. 'Um...I brought some food with me,' she said, and rummaged in her handbag for the sample packs the vet had given her.

Mittens wound himself around Lucas's ankles, purring like an engine as his little cast bumped along the floor.

'I think he likes you,' Molly said.

Lucas glowered at her. 'If he puts one paw out of place, it will be off to the cat shelter.'

She scooped the cat up into her arms, stroking his soft, velvety little head as she looked up into Lucas's stern features. 'I'll just feed him and give him his medication and get out of your hair,' she said.

'The kitchen is this way,' he said, and led the way.

Molly stood back to watch as Mittens tucked into the saucer of food she had placed on the floor. 'He's been wormed and vaccinated,' she said.

'Desexed?'

'That too,' she said. 'He might still be a bit tender down there.'

'My heart bleeds.'

Molly picked up her handbag and slung it across her shoulder. 'He'll need to use the bathroom once he's finished eating. Do you know you can actually train a cat to use a human toilet? I saw it on the internet.'

He didn't look in the least impressed. 'How fascinating.'

'Right, well, then,' she said, and made a move for the door. 'I'll leave you to it.'

'What are you doing for dinner?' Lucas suddenly asked.

Molly blinked. 'Pardon?'

His mouth twisted self-deprecatingly. 'Am I that out of practice?'

'What do you mean?'

'I haven't asked anyone to stay to dinner in a while,' he said. 'I like to keep myself to myself once I get home. But since you're here you might as well stay and share a meal with me. That is if you've got nothing better to do.'

'You're not worried what people will think about us socialising out of hours?' she asked.

'Who's going to know?' he said. 'My private life is private.'

Molly felt tempted to stay, more than tempted. She told herself it was to make sure Mittens was settled in, but if she was honest, it had far more to do with her craving a little more of Lucas's company. It wasn't just that he was from back home either. She felt drawn to his aloofness; his don't-come-too-close-I-might-bite aura was strangely attractive. His accidental touch earlier had awoken her senses. She could still feel the tingling of her skin where his fingers had brushed against hers.

'I haven't got anything planned,' she said. 'Simon's going to the theatre with his friend. There wasn't a spare ticket.' She saw his brows lift cynically and hastily added, 'I didn't want to see it anyway.'

Lucas moved across the room to open the French doors that led out to the garden. He turned on the outside light, which cast a glow over the neatly clipped hedges that made up the formal part of the garden. A fountain trickled in the middle of a pebbled area and a wrought-iron French provincial setting was against one wall where a row of espaliered ornamental trees was growing. Mittens bumped his way over and went out to explore his new domain. He stopped to play with a moth that had fluttered around the light Lucas had switched on.

'It's a lovely garden,' Molly said. 'Was it like that when you bought it?'

'It had been a bit neglected,' he said. 'I've done a bit of work on the house too.'

'You always were good with your hands,' she said, and then blushed. 'I mean, with doing things about the farm.'

His lips gave a vague sort of movement that could not on anyone's terms be described as a smile. 'Would you like a glass of wine?' he asked.

'Sure, why not?' Molly said. *Anything to make her relax and stop making a fool of herself,* she thought.

He placed a glass of white wine in front of her. 'I have red if you prefer.'

'No, white is fine,' she said. 'Red always gives me a headache.'

Lucas went about preparing the meal. Molly watched as he deftly chopped vegetables and meat for the stir-fry he was making. He worked as if on autopilot but she could see he was frowning slightly. Was he regretting asking her to stay for dinner? He wasn't exactly full of conversation. But, then, she was feeling a little tongue-tied herself.

'So why an intensivist?' he asked after a long silence. 'I thought you always wanted to be a teacher.'

'My teacher stage only lasted until I was ten,' Molly said. 'I've wanted to be lots of things since then. I decided on medicine in my final year at school. And I chose intensive care because I liked the idea of helping to save lives.'

'Yeah, well, it sure beats the hell out of destroying them.'

Molly met his gaze over the island bench. 'How long are you going to keep punishing yourself? It's not going to bring him back.'

His eyes hardened. 'You think I don't know that?'

Molly watched him slice some celery as if it was a mortal enemy. His jaw was pulsing with tension as he worked. She let out an uneven sigh and put her wine down. 'Maybe it wasn't such a good idea for me to stay and have dinner,' she said as she slid off the stool she had perched on. 'You don't seem in the mood for company. I'll see myself out.'

He caught her at the door. His long, strong fingers met around her wrist, sending sparks of awareness right up to her armpit and beyond. She looked into his eyes and felt her heart slip sideways. Pain was etched in those green and brown depths—pain and something else that made her blood kick-start in her veins like a shot of pure adrenalin. 'Don't go,' he said in a low, gruff tone.

Molly's gaze drifted to his mouth. She felt her insides shift, a little clench of longing that was slowly but surely moving through her body.

His body was closer than it had ever been. She felt the warmth of it, the bone-melting temptation of it. She sensed the stirring of his response to her. She couldn't feel it but she could see it in his eyes as they held hers. It sent an arrow of lust through her. She wanted to feel him against her, to feel his blood surging in response to her closeness. She took a half a step to close the gap between their bodies but he dropped her wrist as if it had suddenly caught fire.

'I'm sorry,' he said, raking that same hand through his thick hair, leaving crooked finger-width pathways in its wake.

'It's fine,' Molly said, aiming for light and airy but falling miserably short. 'No harm done.'

'I don't want you to get the wrong idea, Molly,' he

said, frowning heavily. 'Any…connection between us is inadvisable.'

'Because you don't mix work with play?'

His eyes were hard and intractable as they clashed with hers. 'Because I don't mix emotion with sex.'

'Who said anything about sex?' Molly asked.

His worldly look said it all.

'Right, well…I'm not very good at this, as you can probably tell,' she said, tucking a strand of hair back behind her ear. 'I try to be sophisticated and modern about it all but I guess deep down inside I'm just an old-fashioned girl who wants the fairy-tale.'

'You're no different from most women—and most men, for that matter,' he said. 'It's not wrong to want to be happy.'

'Are *you* happy, Lucas?' Molly asked, searching his tightly set features.

His eyes moved away from hers as he moved back to the kitchen. 'I need to put on the rice,' he said. 'You'd better keep an eye on your cat.'

Molly went outside to find Mittens. He wasn't too happy about being brought back inside, but she lured him back in with a thread she found hanging off her coat. She closed the door once he was inside and went back to where Lucas was washing the rice for the rice cooker. 'What can I do to help?' she said. 'Shall I set the table in the dining room?'

'I don't use the dining room,' he said. 'I usually eat in here.'

'Seems a shame to have such a lovely dining room and never use it,' Molly said. 'Don't you ever have friends over for dinner parties?'

He gave a shrug and pressed the start button on the cooker. 'Not my scene, I'm afraid.'

'Do you have a housekeeper?'

'A woman comes once a week to clean,' he said. 'I don't make much mess, or at least I try not to. I wouldn't have bothered getting anyone but Gina needed the work. Her husband left her to bring up a couple of kids on her own. She's reliable and trustworthy.'

Molly cradled her wine in her hands. 'Do you have a current girlfriend?'

He was silent for a moment. 'I'm between appointments, so to speak.'

She angled her head at him. 'What sort of women do you usually date?'

His eyes collided with hers. 'Why do you ask?'

Molly gave a little shrug. 'Just wondering.'

'I'm not a prize date, by any means,' he said after another long moment. 'I hate socialising. I hate parties. I don't drink more than one glass of alcohol.'

'Not every woman wants to party hard,' she pointed out.

He studied her unwaveringly for a moment. 'Not very many women just want to have sex and leave it at that.'

Molly felt a wave of heat rise up in her body. 'Is that all you want from a partner?' she asked. 'Just sex and nothing else?'

Had she imagined his eyes looking hungrily at her mouth for a microsecond? Desire clenched tight in her core as his gaze tethered hers in a sensually charged lock. 'It's a primal need like food and shelter,' he said. 'It's programmed into our genes.'

Molly was more aware of her primal needs than she

had ever been. Her body was screaming with them, and had been from the moment she had laid eyes on him on the street the other day. It still was a shock to her that she was reacting so intensely to him. She had never thought herself a particularly passionate person. But when she was around him she felt stirrings and longings that were so fervent they felt like they would override any other consideration.

'We're surely far more evolved and civilised than to respond solely to our basest needs?' she said.

His eyes grazed her mouth. 'Some of us, perhaps.'

The atmosphere tightened another notch.

'So how do you get your primal needs met?' Molly asked with a brazen daring she could hardly believe she possessed. 'Do you drag women back here by the hair and have your wicked way with them?'

This time his gaze went to her hair. She felt every strand of it lift away from her scalp like a Mexican wave. Hot tingles of longing raced along her backbone. She felt a stirring in her breasts; a subtle tightening that made her aware of the lace that supported them. Her heart picked up its pace, a tippity-tap-tap beat that reverberated in her feminine core.

His eyes came back to hers, holding them, searing them, penetrating them. 'I'm not going to have my wicked way with you, Molly,' he said.

'But you want to.' *Oh, dear God, had she really just said that?* Molly thought.

'I'd have to be comatose not to want you,' he said. 'But I'm not going to act on it. Not in this lifetime.'

Molly felt an acute sense of disappointment but tried to cover it by playing it light. 'Glad we got that out of the way,' she said, and picked up her wine. 'You're not really my type in any case.'

A short silence passed.

'Aren't you going to ask what my type *is*?' she asked. 'Oh, no, wait. I remember. You already have an opinion on that, don't you?'

'You want someone strong and dependable, loyal and faithful,' he said. 'Someone who'll stick by you no matter what. Someone who'll want kids and has good moral values in order to raise them.'

Molly raised her brows in mock surprise. 'Not such a bad guess. I didn't know you knew me so well.'

'You're like an open book, Molly.'

She dropped her gaze from his. He was seeing far too much as it was. 'I need to use the bathroom,' she said.

'The guest bathroom is just along from the library.'

As Molly came back from the bathroom she took a quick peek at the library. It was a reader's dream of a room with floor-to-ceiling bookshelves stacked with old editions of the classics with a good selection of modern titles. The scent of books and furniture polish gave the room a homely, comfortable feel. She ran her fingers along the leather-bound spines as if reacquainting herself with old friends.

She thought of Lucas in his big private home with only books for company. Did he miss his family? Did he miss the wide, open spaces of the outback? Did he ever long to go home and breathe in the scent of eucalyptus and that wonderful fresh smell of the dusty earth soaking up a shower of rain?

Molly turned from the bookshelves and her gaze

came upon a collection of photographs in traditional frames on the leather-topped antique desk. She picked up the first one—it was one of Lucas with his family at Christmas when he'd been a boy of about fifteen. His parents stood proudly either side of their boys. Lucas stood between his brothers, a hand on each young shoulder as if keeping them in place. All of them were smiling; their tanned young faces were so full of life and promise.

Within two years it would be a very different family that faced the camera. The local press had hounded the Bannings after the accident. And then the coroner's inquiry a few months later had brought the national press to their door. Sensation-hungry journalists had conducted tell-all interviews with the locals. Even though the coroner had finally concluded it had been an accident and Lucas was not in any way to blame for Matt's death, the press had painted a very different picture from the gossip and hearsay they had gleaned locally. They had portrayed Lucas as a wild boy from the bush who had taken his parents' farm vehicle without permission and taken his best friend for a joyride that had ended in his friend's death. Jane and Bill Banning had visibly aged overnight, Lucas even more so. He had gone from a fresh-faced teenager of seventeen to a man twice that age, who looked like the world had just landed on his shoulders.

Molly reached for the other photo on the desk. Her heart gave a tight spasm as she saw Matt's freckled face grinning widely as he sat astride his motocross bike, his blue eyes glinting with his usual mischief.

The last time she had seen her brother he hadn't

been smiling. He had been furious with her for going into his room and finding his stash of contraband cigarettes. She had told their parents and as a result he had been grounded.

For every one of the seventeen years since that terrible day Molly had wished she had never told their parents. If Matt hadn't been grounded he might not have slipped out with Lucas that night behind their parents' backs. Matt had hated being confined. He'd got claustrophobic and antsy when restrictions had been placed on him. It was one of the reasons he had been thrown from the vehicle. He hadn't been wearing a seat belt.

'I thought you might be in here,' Lucas said from the doorway.

Molly put the photo back down on the desk. 'I hadn't seen that picture before,' she said, and picked up another one of Ian and Neil with their current partners. 'Neil's been going out with Hannah Pritchard for quite a while now, hasn't he? Are they planning on getting married?'

'I think it's been discussed once or twice,' he said.

She put the photo down and looked at him. 'Would you go home for the wedding?'

His expression visibly tightened. 'Dinner's ready,' he said. 'We'll have to make it short. I have to go back to the hospital to check on a patient.'

Molly followed him back to the kitchen, where he had set up two places, one at each end of the long table. He seemed distracted as they ate. He barely spoke and he didn't touch his wine. She got the feeling he had only eaten because his body needed food. He seemed relieved when she pushed her plate away and said she was full.

'I'll walk you home on the way,' he said, and reached for his coat.

'You're not going to drive?'

His eyes shifted away from hers as he slipped his hospital lanyard over his neck. 'It's only a few blocks,' he said. 'I like the exercise.'

They walked in silence until they came to the front door of Molly's bedsit. 'I'll let you know as soon as I find another place to rent,' she said. 'I hope it won't be more than a few days.'

'Fine.'

'Thanks for dinner,' she said after a tight little silence. 'I'll have to return the favour some time.'

'You're not obliged to,' he said, and glanced impatiently at his watch. 'I'd better get going.'

'Bye.' Molly lifted her hand in a little wave but he had already turned his back and left.

CHAPTER THREE

Lucas didn't leave the hospital until close to three a.m. and the streets were deserted as he trudged home. The chilly wind drove ice-pick holes through his chest in spite of his thick woollen coat and scarf. He shoved his hands deep into his pockets and wondered what it was like back home at Carboola Creek. He loathed February in London. It was so bleak and miserable. If the sun did manage to break through the thick wad of clouds it was usually weak and watery, and while the snow was beautiful when it first fell, it all too soon turned to slippery brown slush.

He thought longingly of Bannington Homestead. If he closed his eyes he could almost smell the rain-soaked red dust of the plains. It seemed a lifetime ago since he had felt the bright hot sun on his face.

He opened the door of his house and a piteous meow sounded. 'Damn you, Molly,' he muttered as the little cat came limping towards him with its big possum-like eyes shining in welcome. 'Don't get too comfortable,' he addressed it in a gruff tone. 'You're not staying long.'

The cat meowed again and ribboned itself around his ankles before moving way to play with the fringe of the Persian carpet. Lucas caught a faint whiff of Molly's perfume in the air as he moved through the house. It was strongest in the library, or maybe that was just his imagination. He breathed in deeply. The hint of jasmine and sweet peas teased his nostrils, reminding him of hot summer evenings sitting out on the veranda at the homestead.

He let out a long weary sigh and picked up the photograph of his family. His parents were in their sixties now. They were still working the land alongside Neil. Ian was the other side of town on another property. His parents had come over to London for visits a few times. He had loved having them here but it made it so much harder when they left. His mother always cried. Even his stoic father had a catch in his voice and moisture in his eyes. Lucas had come to dread the airport goodbyes. He hated seeing them so distraught. He had not encouraged them to return and always made some excuse about being too busy to entertain visitors.

Lucas wondered if they missed him even half as much as he missed them. But it was the price he had to pay. He put the photo back down and looked at Matt's photo. He saw echoes of his mate's face in the pretty features of Molly. That dusting of freckles, the same uptilted nose, the same light brown hair with its sun-bleached highlights.

Was that why he felt so drawn to her?

Not entirely.

She was all woman now, a beautiful young woman with the whole world at her feet. He saw the way the male staff and patients looked at her. It was the same way *he* looked at her. He had been so close to pulling her into his arms and kissing her. He had wanted to press his mouth to the soft bow of hers to see if it felt as soft and sweet as it looked.

But he could just imagine how her parents would react if he laid a finger on their precious daughter. He thought of what *his* parents would feel. They wouldn't say anything out loud, but he knew they would find it hard to accept Molly. It wasn't her fault, but any involvement with her would make moving on from the past that much more difficult for them and for him. Did he want her so badly because he knew he couldn't have her? Or was it just that she was everything he had always wanted for himself but didn't feel he deserved?

When Molly got to work the next morning Su Ling, one of the registrars, pulled her over and said in an undertone, 'Keep away from the boss. He's in a foul mood. We had a death overnight—David Hyland in Bed Four. He went into organ failure and Lucas was here until the wee hours with him and the family.'

Molly glanced at the empty bed and felt a sinking feeling assail her. David Hyland had only been forty-two with a wife and two young children. He'd developed complications after routine gall-bladder surgery and Molly had only spoken to his wife the day before about how hopeful they were that he would pull through.

Deaths in ICU were part of the job. Not everyone made it. It was a fact of life. Miracles happened occasionally but there was only so much medicine and critical care could do. She wondered if every death on the unit brought home to Lucas the death that haunted him most.

'Don't you have anything better to do than to stand there staring into space?' Lucas barked from behind her.

Molly swung around to face him. 'I was just—'

'There are two families waiting in the counselling rooms for updates on their loved ones,' he said in a clipped, businesslike tone. 'I would appreciate it if you got your mind on the job.'

'My mind is on the job,' she said. 'I was on my way to speak to the Mitchell family now. Do you have any further updates on Claire that I should make them aware of?'

His eyes looked bloodshot as if he hadn't slept the night before. 'Claire is stable,' he said. 'I can't give them anything other than that. We'll try and wean her off the sedation again tomorrow. We'll repeat the scans then as well.'

Molly watched as he strode away, barking out orders as he went. Megan, one of the nurses, caught her eye and raised her brows meaningfully as she walked past with a catheter bag. 'He obviously didn't get laid last night.'

Molly hoped her face wasn't looking as hot as if felt. 'Obviously not,' she said, and headed off to the counselling room.

Molly was waiting for a coffee at the kiosk later that day when Simon breezed in. 'Hello, gorgeous,' he said, throwing an arm around her shoulders and planting a smacking kiss on her mouth. 'How's tricks?'

Molly tried to wriggle out of his embrace. 'Stop it, Simon. People are watching.'

'Don't be such a cold fish,' he chided as he tried to land another kiss. 'Are you still angry with me for blowing you off last night? I told you the theatre was booked out.'

'I believe Dr Drummond told you to stop.'

Molly felt a shiver run down her spine at that strong, commanding voice. She turned to see Lucas eyeballing Simon the way a Doberman did a small, annoying terrier.

'Who's this?' Simon asked, with a pugnacious curl of his lip.

'This is my boss,' Molly said, blushing in spite of every attempt not to. 'Lucas Banning, head of ICU.'

Simon's lip curled even further. 'Aiming a bit higher, are we?' he said.

Molly wished the floor would open up and swallow her whole. She glanced at Lucas but his expression gave little away apart from a glint of derision in his eyes. She turned back to Simon. 'I'm not sure what you're implying but I would rather you—'

'You won't put out for me but I bet you'll put out for him if he promises to fast-track your career,' Simon said with his sneer still in place.

Molly was desperate to get away before any more people joined the audience. As it was, she could see one of the nurses dilly-dallying over the sweeteners as she shamelessly eavesdropped. 'I think you've got the wrong idea about our friendship, Simon,' she said. 'I'll call you later.'

'You do that,' he said, throwing Lucas a death stare before looking back at her. 'You have some explaining to do.'

Molly walked out of the kiosk without collecting her coffee. She had only gone three or four strides when

Lucas caught up with her. 'Are you out of your mind?' he asked. 'What are you *thinking,* dating that jerk?'

She kept walking with her head held high. 'It's none of your business who I date.'

'I beg to differ,' he said. 'He's distracting you from your work.'

Molly rolled her eyes. 'He's doing no such thing.'

'He's totally wrong for you,' he said. 'I can't believe you can't see it.'

She stopped and glared at him. 'My private life has absolutely nothing to do with you.'

His gaze held hers for a long tense moment and she saw a pulse beating at the edge of his mouth. 'You're right,' he said. 'Go and break your own heart. See if I care.'

Molly frowned as he strode ahead of her down the corridor. She could be mistaken but she could almost swear that was jealousy she had seen glittering in his eyes.

Lucas put some kitten biscuits in the saucer on the floor. Mittens crunched his way through a little pile before lifting his head and giving a soft purring meow of appreciation.

'You're welcome,' Lucas said. 'But don't think for a moment that I'm warming to you because I'm not.'

The doorbell sounded. For a moment he thought he had imagined it. But then it sounded again. He wasn't expecting visitors, he never had them. Even the most fervent religious proselytisers had given up on him.

He opened his front door to find Molly standing there with a shopping bag in one hand. She looked tiny, standing there in the cold. Her coat looked too big for her and her hat and scarf framed her heart-shaped face, giving her an elfin look that was unbelievably cute. 'I've brought more supplies for Mittens,' she said. 'I hope you don't mind me calling in without notice. I was worried you might be running out of food for him.'

'I picked up some more at the corner store on the way home,' he said.

She handed him the bag. 'I won't come in. I'm busy.'

'Going out with lover boy?' Lucas said as he took the bag.

Her eyes clashed with his. 'What's it to you?'

'Nothing,' he said, wishing it was true. 'I just wouldn't like to see you get hurt. He's a player. I heard a rumour he's got his eyes on Prof Hubert's daughter. As career fast tracks go, you can't get much better than that.'

She gave him a cold look and took a step backwards. 'I'd better get going. I'd hate to take advantage of your warm hospitality.'

'Aren't you going to say hello to your cat?' Lucas asked.

She raised her chin. 'I wasn't sure if I was welcome,' she said. 'The way you spoke to me today in ICU was deplorable.'

He leaned a hand on the doorjamb. 'You want me to apologise? Sorry, but I'm not that sort of boss. If you can't suck it up then you'd better find some other job where you can get your ego stroked all day.'

'You were out of line,' she said, shooting him a little glare. 'You know you were. You were taking out your frustration on your staff. That's not how to run a department like ICU.'

'Are you telling me how to do my job?' he asked.

She held his challenging look. 'I'm telling you I won't be bullied and harassed by you just because you had a bad day.'

'Did you happen to speak to David Hyland's wife and family?' Lucas asked. 'They were expecting him to make it. *I* was expecting him to make it. Do you know what it felt like to go out there and tell them he had died while we were trying to resus him?'

'I know what that feels like. I've had to—'

'His wife looked at me as if I had just stabbed her in the heart,' he said. 'The kids looked at me in bewilderment. Those are the faces that keep me awake at night. Not the bureaucrats who insist on reducing admission times whilst contributing nothing to the running of the hospital other than sipping double-shot caramel lattes and shuffling a bit of paperwork around their desks. Not the CEO who hasn't got a clue what it feels like to be up all night, worrying about a desperately ill patient. It's the families that come back to haunt me. They want me—*they expect me*—to make it all better, to fix things. But I can't always do that.'

'I'm sorry,' she said, nibbling at her lip, her eyes losing their defensive glare. 'A death is hard on everyone.'

Lucas blew out a breath and held open the door for her. 'I should warn you that I'm not good company right now.'

'Maybe I'm not looking for good company.'

He closed the door and turned and faced her. 'What are you looking for?'

She gave a little shrug of one of her slim shoulders. 'I'm not sure…just any company, I guess…'

Lucas kept a wide berth even though he wanted to reach for her and hold her close. He wanted to block out the hellish day he'd had with a bit of mindless sex. But sweet little Molly Drummond wasn't the right candidate. He had a feeling it wouldn't be mindless sex with her. Those soft little tender hands of hers would not just unravel him physically. They would reach inside him and unpick the lock on the vault of his soul. 'Would you like a drink or something?' he asked.

'I'm fine,' she said. 'I won't stay long. I just wanted to check on Mittens. Oh, you got him a litter tray.' She turned and smiled up at him disarmingly. It was like a ray of sunshine after a wet week. It seemed to light up the foyer, or maybe that was just his imagination.

'Yeah, well, he kept me awake half the night howling to be let out,' he said, keeping his voice gruff in case she had noticed his guard slipping momentarily. 'I don't mind tossing and turning over patients but I draw the line at stray cats.'

'Do you think he's settling in?'

'I don't think there's any doubt of that,' he said wryly. 'He's taken up residence on the end of my bed. I tried to shoo him off but he was back within minutes.'

She was still smiling at him. 'You big softie,' she said.

Lucas glowered at her. 'Have you found alternative accommodation yet?'

Her smile faded and her shoulders went down in a little slump of defeat. 'I've rung heaps of agencies but there's nothing close to the hospital, or at least none than I can afford. And no one wants to rent a place for just three months. I don't know what else to do. Simon offered to share his place with me but I'm not sure I want to do that.'

Lucas felt as if each and every one of his spare rooms had suddenly developed eyes and was staring at him pointedly. His thoughts zigzagged in his brain. It wasn't as if she would be in the way. He would probably never even run into her. It was a big house. Too big really, but he'd liked the thought of working on something in his spare time. He'd *needed* something to distract himself. He really should have sold it by now and bought some other rundown place to renovate. It seemed a shame that no one but him got to see how comfortable and convenient it was before he moved on. Molly had already hinted at his lack of hospitality. What would it hurt to have a houseguest for a week or two?

'You could always stay here until something becomes available.' He hadn't realised he had said it out loud until he saw the surprised look on her face.

'Here?' she said. 'With you?'

'In one of the spare rooms,' he said. 'I'd charge you rent and expenses. I'm not running a charity.'

'Are you sure?'

Lucas wasn't one bit sure. He still didn't know why he had uttered those words. But he had and he couldn't unsay them. Besides, he was already looking after her wretched cat. Better that she moved in and took charge of its feeding and toileting. It could sleep on her bed, not his. And he would willingly suffer the invasion of his private domain for a week or two rather than see her move in with Simon-up-himself Westbury.

'I'd expect you to do your share of the cooking while you're here,' he said. 'And I would prefer it if you entertained your men friends off site.'

'It's a very generous offer…' Her perfect white teeth nibbled at her lower lip. 'But what if people think we're actually living together as in *living* together…you know, as a couple?'

Lucas couldn't stop a vision of her lying naked in his bed taking over his mind. He wondered what it would be like, waking up beside her each morning. Seeing her sunny smile, feeling her arms around him, smelling the scent of her on his skin, his body sated from long, passionate hours of lovemaking. He pushed the thoughts aside like a row of books toppling off a mantelpiece. 'I don't waste time worrying what other people think,' he said. 'What I do outside the hospital is no one's business but my own.'

'What about our families?' she asked.

He gave her a grim look. 'Don't you mean *your* family?'

'I don't think my mother will have a problem with it,' she said, frowning a little. 'My father is another story.'

'Isn't it time you lived your own life?' he asked. 'You're twenty-seven years old. You shouldn't have to justify your actions to him or anyone.'

'I know,' she said. 'That's one of the reasons I came to London. I wanted to break free. I think my father still sees me as a little girl who needs protecting.'

'Yeah, well, given your choice in men so far, I'm inclined to agree with him,' Lucas said.

'I know Simon gave you the wrong impression,' she

said. 'He's not usually so…possessive. I think it was all show, to tell you the truth.'

'He's a prize jerk,' Lucas said. 'I thought you had much better taste than that.'

Her grey-blue eyes flashed. 'Perhaps I should have you assess every potential partner to see if they meet your exacting standards,' she said. 'Would that satisfy you?'

Lucas had a feeling he wasn't going to be satisfied by anything other than having her to himself, but he wasn't going to admit that to her. She wasn't his to have. He had to remember that. She was his best mate's little sister. Any chance of a future together had died along with Matt. 'Do you need a hand moving your things across?' he asked. 'I have an hour free now.'

His offer to help appeared to mollify her. 'That would be very helpful,' she said. 'Thank you.'

Molly put the last of her things in the spare room furthest away from Lucas's master suite. She still couldn't quite believe he had made her the offer of temporary accommodation, although she suspected it had more to do with discouraging her from moving in with Simon. It was very dog in the manger of him, given he'd made it clear he wasn't going to pursue her himself. Perhaps he wanted to prove to himself that he could keep his hands off her. Lucas's house was certainly big enough for them to avoid intimate contact. They didn't even have to share a bathroom. There were six to choose from as well as his en suite.

But even sharing a space as large as this had its complications. There was her attraction to him, for one thing. She couldn't seem to control it. Every time he looked at her she felt a stirring of longing deep inside. She *ached* to feel his mouth on hers. It was almost an obsession now. She didn't think she would rest until she had tasted him. And then there was his body: that strong, tall body that was so lean and fit and in its prime. She wanted to explore its carved muscles, smooth her hands over the satin-wrapped steel of his back and shoulders, hold him in her hand, feel the throb of his blood against her palm. Her body got moist thinking about it. Her nerves got twitchy and restless, the contraction-like pulse deep and relentless in her core.

She gave herself a mental shake. She was probably only fixated on him because he had said he wasn't interested in acting on his attraction to her. It was the contrariness of human nature—wanting something you knew you couldn't have.

Molly took Mittens with her downstairs and placed him on the floor near his kitten milk and biscuits. It was raining outside; the droplets of water were rolling like diamonds down the glass of the windows and French doors. It was hard not to think of home when the weather was so dismal. The cold seemed to seep right into her bones. The bedsit had felt like an icebox, but at least Lucas's house was warm, even if his manner towards her was not.

She heard his firm tread behind her as he came into the room. 'Are you all settled in?' he asked.

'Yes, thank you,' Molly said, turning to face him. 'It's a lovely room and so spacious. Much nicer than the bedsit, I can assure you.'

He gave her one of his brisk, businesslike nods. 'I'm

going out for a while,' he said. 'I have some paperwork to see to at the hospital.'

'You work too hard,' she said.

'I get paid to work hard.'

'Surely not this hard,' Molly said. 'You look like you didn't sleep at all last night. Why do you drive yourself so relentlessly? No, don't tell me. I already know.'

His mouth flattened grimly. 'I would prefer it if you kept your opinions to yourself. You might currently share my house but that's all you're going to share. I don't need you to take on the role of a caring partner. Do I make myself clear?'

'When was the last time you had a partner?' Molly asked.

It was a moment or two before he spoke. She wondered if he was trying to remember. 'I can assure you I'm no monk,' he said.

'Tell me the last time you had sex.'

His brows snapped together. 'What *is* this? Do you really think I'm going to give you a blow-by-blow account of my sex life?'

'You've felt at perfect liberty to comment on mine,' Molly pointed out.

'That's because you were conducting it in the hospital cafeteria.'

'That is not true!' she said.

'You'd better keep a lid on your public displays of affection if you want to keep your job,' he said.

Molly felt her back come up. 'Are you threatening me?'

His eyes warred with hers. 'Not personally, but I think I should inform you the current CEO is a stickler for professional behaviour at all times,' he said. 'Patients come to St Patrick's for health care, not to witness a cheesy soap-opera love scene in the middle of the corridor. If a patient complains to him it would be one look at the CCTV and you'd be fired on the spot.'

'And I bet you'd be the first to be glad to see me go,' she said with a resentful look.

'So far I've heard nothing but good reports about you from patients and staff alike,' he said. 'I would hate to see all that come undone by behaviour that would be considered puerile in a high school, let alone in a professional setting.'

Molly set her mouth tightly. 'I can assure you it won't happen again.'

'Make sure that it doesn't,' he said, and strode out.

When Molly came downstairs in the morning Lucas had already left for work. His housekeeper was in the kitchen, unloading the dishwasher. She smiled and straightened as Molly came in. 'I'm Gina,' she said. 'Dr Banning told me you and the little cat are staying for a few days.'

'Yes,' Molly said. 'I hope that's not going to make extra work for you?'

'Not at all,' Gina said. 'It will be good for Dr Banning to have some company in this big old house of his. You're from his home town in Australia, yes?'

'Is my accent that obvious?' Molly asked with a self-deprecating smile.

'Not your accent,' Gina said. 'Your looks.'

'My...looks?'

'The photo in the library,' Gina said. 'You're Matthew Drummond's sister, yes?'

Molly frowned. 'You know about Matt?'

Gina nodded solemnly. 'Dr Banning's mother told me when they visited a few years ago. Very sad. Such a tragic accident.'

'Yes…yes, it was.'

'It is good that you are still friends,' Gina said.

Friends? Molly thought. Is that what she and Lucas were? 'Um…yes,' she said. 'Our parents were neighbours for years and years. We sort of all grew up together, same school, same teachers even.'

'He is a very kind man,' Gina said. 'But he works too hard. I tell him he needs to find a nice girl, get married and have some kids. It would help him to have something other than work to occupy his mind, yes?'

'Um…he does seem very career driven,' Molly said.

'He uses work to forget,' Gina said. 'He saves lots of lives but he can never bring back the one he wanted to save the most.' She shook her head. 'Sad, very sad.'

Molly gave the housekeeper a pained smile. 'I have to get going,' she said. 'It was lovely meeting you.'

'I hope you're still here when I come next week, yes?' Gina said with a twinkle in her chocolate-brown eyes.

'Oh, no,' Molly said hurriedly. 'I hope to find another flat well before then.'

'Have you found another flat?' Jacqui asked in the staff tearoom a couple of days later.

Molly closed the newspaper rental guide with a dispirited sigh. 'I've looked at five so far but none of them allow pets,' she said. 'The ones I've looked at that do allow them are not fit for an animal, let alone a human. I swear the last one I looked at, even the vermin have packed up and left in disgust.'

'So how's it working out at Lucas's place?' Jacqui asked.

Molly trained her gaze on her mug of tea rather than meet the ward clerk's eyes. She had hoped to keep her temporary living arrangements a secret but apparently someone from the hospital had seen her walking out of Lucas's front door a couple of mornings ago. It had been all over the hospital by the time she'd got to work. If Lucas was bothered about his private life being a topic of public speculation, he hadn't mentioned it, but, then, she hadn't seen him other than in passing, and bringing up the topic at work, even in the privacy of his office, wasn't something she was keen to do. She suspected he was avoiding her but, then, she could hardly talk. She had kept well out of his way too.

'It's fine,' she said. 'I don't see much of him. I see more of him here, to be honest.'

'You could've knocked me down with a feather when I heard you were shacking up with him,' Jacqui said. 'As far as I know, no one from here has even stepped inside his place.'

'I'm not "shacking up" with him,' Molly said, trying not to blush. 'He very kindly offered me a room for a few days.'

'Has he made a move on you?'

Molly pushed her chair back and took her teacup to the sink. 'We don't have that sort of relationship,' she said. 'We're just…housemates.'

Jacqui angled her head at her speculatively. 'You'd

make a nice couple, you know. It's kind of sweet you grew up in the bush together. Kind of a friends-to-lovers thing.'

'I'm a bit over men at the moment,' Molly said. She'd been keeping her distance from Simon over the last couple of days. After his altercation with Lucas in the cafeteria he had increased his pressure on her to move in with him, but she didn't like being used as a pawn in a game of one-upmanship.

'I thought you were seeing someone—Simon what's his name? The plastics registrar.'

'Simon Westbury,' Molly said. 'Yes, well, I've been trying to get out of that relationship for a while now. I shouldn't have got into it in the first place.'

Jacqui tapped her lips thoughtfully. 'Mmm, I can definitely see it.'

'See what?'

'You and Lucas,' Jacqui said. 'I think you two would be a perfect match.'

'Not going to happen,' Molly said flatly. 'Dr Banning is not interested in me. Quite frankly, he can't wait to see the back of me. He hates it that I came here. He thinks I only came to cause trouble for him.'

'Yes, I've been picking up on that vibe,' Jacqui said. 'But why would he think that?'

Molly blew out a breath and pushed open the door to leave. 'Never mind,' she said. 'I have to get back. I'll see you down there.'

CHAPTER FOUR

LUCAS WAS IN his office, writing up some notes, when he got a call from Alistair Brentwood in Accident and Emergency. He'd had hundreds of calls over the years from various doctors in A and E, but something about this one made the hairs on the back of his neck stand up as soon as Alistair gave him the rundown on the incoming patient.

It was like hearing his and Matt's accident replayed back to him. The names and ages had changed but it was so similar he felt like he had been swept up in a time warp. The horror of that night came back to him in hammer blows of dread. He felt them pound through his blood as he listened to his colleague's description.

'Lucas, we've got a male, twenty-one, with a serious head injury,' Alistair said. 'Blunt chest trauma and haemodynamically stable. I can see a bit of lung contusion on his chest CT, abdo is OK, but his brain scan looks like global contusions and oedema. His GCS was three at the scene but picked up to six in here. One pupil fixed and dilated, the other sluggish. Pretty serious closed head injury. You got a bed for him up there?'

'Thanks,' Lucas said, mentally gearing up to face the shattered family. He would have to deal with them on a daily basis, helping them come to terms with the severity of their loved one's injuries. 'We're right to take him. Have the neurosurgeons assessed him yet?'

'Yes, they'll put in an ICP monitor when he's settled in the unit. If he survives it's going to be a long haul,' Alistair said matter-of-factly. 'Name's Tim Merrick, he was the passenger. The driver got off very lightly—a Hamish Fisher. He's going to the ward for obs.'

Lucas felt a cold hand press hard against his sternum. *Two shattered families*, he thought. Lives that just hours ago had been normal would now never be normal again. He wondered if Hamish Fisher had any idea of what lay ahead for him—the guilt, the despair, and the what-ifs and if-onlys that would haunt his days and nights for the rest of his life. 'OK. I'll come down now if he's ready,' he said.

'Yeah, he's fine to go.'

'Dr Drummond, this is Tim Merrick, twenty-one-year-old male from a MVA,' Lucas said with his usual clinical calm as the patient was transferred to ICU. *Just another patient*, he kept saying inside his head, but it wasn't working as it normally did. This was somebody's son, someone's brother.

Someone's best friend.

A cold, sick feeling curdled his stomach. Bile rose in his throat. His chest felt as if it was being compressed by an industrial vice. He was having trouble breathing. He could feel sweat beading between his shoulder blades. His temples pounded.

Scenes from seventeen years ago kept flashing through his mind on rapid replay. Matt's parents looking ashen and gutted as they came in to where their son's broken and bloodied body lay on a hospital gurney. Molly standing there, holding her mother's hand, her grey-blue eyes wide with fear and dread, her little face as white as milk but for the nutmeg-like dusting of her freckles. Lucas's parents looking shocked. Their faces seeming to age in front of him as he falteringly tried to explain what had happened.

The doctors with their calm clinical voices and the police with their detached demeanours as they took down his statement and asked questions he could barely answer for the ropey knot of anguish that had risen in his throat.

Lucas blinked a couple of times and brought himself back to the moment. 'He's got a severe closed head injury, but not much else. Neurosurgery are coming up in twenty minutes to put in an ICP monitor. Can you set him up on the ventilator?'

'Sure,' Molly said.

'I'm going to start mannitol and steroids, and do the paperwork,' he said. 'Some relatives have just arrived. I'll go and talk with them. We're going to pull out every stop here to give him a chance of recovery.'

'I'll run the CO_2 slightly up and put in a central line, and get the ICP monitor set up ready to connect,' Molly said.

'Good,' Lucas said. 'He's got right pulmonary contusion, and I've just got the official CT report. He's also got a small pneumothorax on the right.'

'Good that was picked up,' Molly said. 'We could've blown that up overnight on the ventilator. I'll put in a right chest drain after I've set the ventilator.'

'Thanks.' He drew in a heavy breath that felt like it had a handful of thumbtacks attached. 'I'll talk to the relatives. He's got a severe head injury, but he could recover. He's only young. He's got to be given the maximum chance.'

Once Molly had put in Tim Merrick's chest drain she went back to the central office where Aleem Pashar was going through the patient notes that had come up from A and E.

'Not sure why the boss is insisting pulling out all the stops,' Aleem said. 'The CT scan's not looking good. Look.'

Molly took the report and read through it with a sinking heart. A positive outcome was very unlikely. What had Lucas been thinking? Surely he of all people knew the data on severe brain injuries? It wasn't fair to give the family unrealistic expectations. They needed to be gently prepared for the imminent loss of their loved one. It might be days, or weeks, sometimes even months, but someone as badly injured as Tim Merrick might not leave ICU alive, or if he did, he would be severely compromised.

'I sure wouldn't want to be the one who was driving,' Aleem said as he leaned back against the desk. 'Can you imagine living with that for the rest of your life?'

Molly frowned as she looked at the registrar. 'Pardon?'

'Tim Merrick's mate,' he said. 'He was the one driving. All he got was a fractured patella.'

Molly bit her lip. Was that why Lucas was doing everything he could to keep Tim alive? He was reliving his own nightmare through the driver. He would be feeling the anguish of the young man, having been through it himself. Keeping Tim Merrick on life support indefinitely was his way of giving the young driver time to come to terms with what had happened. But while she understood Lucas's motives, she wasn't sure she agreed with giving the family false hope. They could end up suffering more in the long run.

'No alcohol involved, which is one thing to be grateful for, I suppose,' Aleem said. 'Apparently he swerved to avoid a kid on a bike. Missed the kid but as good as wrote off his best mate. Can you imagine having that on your conscience? I'd never get behind the wheel again.'

Molly put down the CT report. 'I think I'll have a word with Tim's parents. Dr Banning should be finished with them now.' She turned at the door. 'Can you ring the orthopaedic ward and find out the driver's name? I think I'll visit him before I go home.'

'Will do,' Aleem said, and reached for the phone.

'Mr and Mrs Merrick?' Molly gently addressed the middle-aged couple who were still sitting huddled together in the counselling room.

There was no sign of Lucas, although Molly could pick up a faint trace of his light aftershave in the small room, suggesting he had not long ago left. A pile of used tissues was on the table beside the wife and she had another one screwed up in her hand. The husband was dry-eyed but his Adam's apple was going up and down like a piston.

'I'm Dr Drummond,' Molly said. 'I've been looking after your son in ICU. He's on the ventilator now and comfortable.'

'Can we see him?' the wife asked, absently tearing the tissue in her hand into shreds.

'Yes, of course,' Molly said. 'But first…I think I should warn you that ICU can be an upsetting place. There are lots of machines making all sorts of noises. You are free to come and go as you like but we have a strict hygiene policy to reduce the risk of infection. Did Dr Banning go through all this with you?'

The wife nodded. 'He said Tim's stable for the time being. He said we should talk to him as much as possible…that it might help bring him round.'

'It will certainly do no harm to sit with him and talk to him,' Molly said. 'Has Dr Banning been through Tim's scans with you?'

'He said it's too early to be certain what's going on,' the husband said. 'There's a lot of swelling and bleeding. He said he'd like to wait till that settles before giving a more definitive diagnosis.'

Molly could see the sense in what Lucas had told the Merricks but she wondered if he was just buying time. She had seen the scans. Bleeding and swelling notwithstanding, Tim was critically injured and nothing short of a miracle could turn things around.

She took the parents to their son's bedside and watched as they spoke to him and touched him. It was heart-wrenching to think that in a few days they might lose him for ever.

It was impossible not to think about her brother's death at times like this, how that night in A and E had been such a surreal nightmare. Her parents had done the same as the Merricks. They had touched and stroked Matt, talking to him even though they had already been told he had gone. Molly had seen Lucas on their way out of the hospital. He had been standing with his parents, his face so stricken it had been like looking at someone else entirely. Matt had lost his life, but in a way so too had Lucas. Nothing would ever be the same for him again.

'Dr Drummond?' Mrs Merrick's voice interrupted Molly's reverie. 'Can I talk to you for a minute?'

'Sure,' Molly said.

Mrs Merrick looked at her son again, tears rolling down her face. She brushed at them with her hand and turned back to Molly. 'Tim would hate to be left an invalid. He wouldn't cope with it. We talked about it only recently. A relative—his cousin—had a serious accident at work and was left a quadriplegic. He's totally dependent on carers for everything now.

'Tim said it would destroy him to be left like that. That he would rather die. He insisted on drawing up an end-of-life directive. We tried to talk him out of it. We thought only old or terminally ill people signed them but he was adamant. I suppose what I'm saying is…I want to know what we're dealing with here. I want to do the right thing by my son. I want to be…' She glanced at her husband and continued, '*We* want to be prepared for whatever is ahead.'

'I understand,' Molly said. 'We'll keep you well informed on Tim's progress. There are protocols to go through in regard to end-of-life directives. I'll speak to Dr Banning about it.'

'There's one other thing,' Mr Merrick said as he

came and stood by his wife. 'I want to be clear on this. We don't blame Hamish for what happened to Tim. This is an accident—a terrible, tragic accident. It could've been the other way round. We're devastated for Hamish as well as ourselves.'

Molly felt a lump come up in her throat. She could remember all too well the dreadful words her father had shouted at Lucas and his parents in A and E all those years ago. Everyone had known it had been the raw grief talking but it hadn't made it any easier to witness. If only her father had demonstrated even a fraction of the dignity and grace of the Merricks. 'I'm going to see Hamish now,' she said. 'I'll tell him you're thinking of him.'

Molly went to the orthopaedic ward where Hamish Fisher was spending the night prior to having his knee repaired the following morning. She found him lying in a four-bed ward with the curtains drawn around his bed. Curled up there with his back to the room, he looked a lot younger than twenty-one. Her heart ached for him. He looked so alone and broken. From this day forward his life would never be the same. She wondered if in seventeen years' time he would be just as locked away and lonely as Lucas.

'Hamish?' she said. 'I'm one of the ICU doctors, Molly Drummond.'

Hamish opened his reddened eyes. 'He's dead, isn't he?' he said in a bleak tone.

'No,' she said, taking the chair beside the bed. 'He's on a ventilator and at this point he's stable.'

The young man's chin shook as he fought to control

his emotion. 'But he's going to die, isn't he?' he said. 'I heard the ER doctors talking.'

'No one can say for sure at this stage,' Molly said.

He swallowed convulsively. 'I swerved to avoid a kid on a bike,' he said. 'It all happened so quickly. I saw this little kid coming out of nowhere and I hit the brakes but there must have been oil on the road. I lost control…'

Molly put her hand on his where it was gripping the sheet with white-knuckled force. 'Tim's parents don't blame you,' she said. 'They're with Tim now but I'm sure they'll come down to see you when they get the chance. Do you have anyone here with you? Your parents?'

He shook his head. 'I haven't got a dad. My mum is on her way. She's been on a cruise with friends: She'd saved up for years to go… She's flying home tonight.'

'It's important you have people around to support you,' Molly said. 'I can organise for the hospital chaplain to visit you. It helps to talk to someone at a time like this.'

'Talking isn't going to turn back the clock, is it?' Hamish said.

She gave his hand another squeeze. 'Just try and take it one day at a time.'

Molly didn't see Lucas again until later that night. He came in just before midnight, his face looking drawn and his eyes hollow, as if two fingers had pushed them right back into his head.

'Are you OK?' she asked, rising from the sofa where she had been flicking through a home renovating magazine without managing to remember a word of what she had read.

He scraped a hand through his hair. 'Yeah,' he said. 'Why wouldn't I be? It was just another day at the office.'

'It was hardly that,' Molly said.

He dismissed her with a look and turned to leave. 'I'm going to bed.'

'Lucas?'

His back looked concrete tight with tension in that infinitesimal moment before he turned to look at her. 'I've handled hundreds of critically ill trauma patients,' he said. 'This is just another case.'

She came over to where he was standing. 'It's not just another case,' she said. 'It's like you and Matt all over again.'

A stone mask covered his features. 'Leave it, Molly.'

'I think we should talk about it,' she said. 'I think my parents should've talked to you about it long ago. It was wrong to blame you the way they did. Tim's parents are obviously shattered by what's happened but at least they're not blaming Hamish.'

'That will come later,' he said grimly.

'I don't think so,' she said. 'I think they realise it could just have easily been Tim behind that wheel. It's devastating for them to face the prospect of losing their son but—'

'They are *not* going to lose their son,' Lucas said with implacable force.

Molly frowned at him. 'Lucas, you can't possibly think he's going to survive more than a few days or a week or two at the most.'

A thread of steel stitched his mouth into a flat, de-termined line. 'I've seen plenty of critically injured pa-tients come off ventilators. He deserves every chance to make it. I'm not withdrawing support.'

'But what if that's not what Tim would've wanted?'

'We'll find out what he wants when he wakes up,' he said.

'What if he doesn't wake up?' Molly asked. 'You saw the scans. It's not looking good right now.'

'Early scans can be misleading,' he said. 'You know that. There's bleeding and swelling everywhere. It can take days or even weeks to get a clear idea of what's going on.'

'I don't think it's fair to give his family false hope,' she said. 'I think they're the sort of people who need to know what they're up against right from the get-go. They want to be prepared.'

His eyes were hard as they clashed with hers. 'I hate to pull rank here but I have a lot more clinical experi-ence than you,' he said. 'His parents are still in shock. This is not the time to be dumping unnecessary and distressing information on them.'

'Tim Merrick signed an end-of-life directive,' Molly said. 'His mother told me. They all did it a couple of years ago after a relative was made a quadriplegic in a workplace accident.'

Lucas drew in a short breath and then slowly re-leased it. 'So?'

'So his wishes should be acknowledged,' Molly said. 'He didn't want to be left languishing in some care fa-cility for the rest of his life. Evidently he was quite adamant about it. He couldn't bear the thought of being dependent on others for everything.'

He moved to the other side of the room, his gait stiff and jerky as if his inner turmoil was manifested in his body. He rubbed the back of his neck. The sound of his hand moving over his skin was amplified in the silence.

'He would want the ventilator turned off, Lucas.'

'It's too early to decide that.'

'There might be a time when it's too late to decide,' Molly pointed out. 'What will you say to him then? "Sorry, we disregarded your directive because we thought you were going to wake up and be back to normal"?'

He cut his gaze to hers. 'I've seen patients with much worse injuries walk out of ICU,' he said.

Molly gave him an incredulous look. 'You think Tim Merrick is going to walk when he can't even *breathe* on his own? Come on, Lucas, surely you haven't abandoned the science you were trained to respect and rely on? He's not going to walk again. He's probably not going to do anything for himself again. And you're prolonging his and his family's agony by insisting on keeping him hooked up to that ventilator.'

'What about Hamish Fisher?' he asked, nailing her with a look.

Molly released a little breath. 'Lucas, it's not Hamish Fisher lying in that bed.'

'No,' he said. 'But he's the one who's going to spend the rest of his life wishing to hell it had been.'

Molly felt the anguish behind his statement. She saw the agony of it on his face. For all these years he would have given anything to trade places with her brother.

But that's not how fate had decided things would be. 'I know this is difficult for you,' she said. 'But you have to keep your clinical hat on. You can't let what happened to you all those years ago influence your decision in managing Tim Merrick's care.'

He looked at her for a long, tense moment. 'Just give him some time,' he said. 'Surely he deserves that?'

'Are we talking about Tim or Hamish?' Molly asked.

He walked to the other side of the room and looked out of the window at the blizzard-like conditions outside. Molly saw his shoulders rise and fall as he let out a long, jagged sigh. She wanted to go to him, to wrap her arms around him and hold him close. But just as she took the first step towards him he turned and looked at her.

'I had a patient a few months back,' he said, 'a young girl of nineteen who'd fallen from a balcony at a party. She fell five metres onto concrete. It was a miracle she survived the fall. She had multiple fractures, including a base-of-skull fracture. She was in a coma for a month. Just when she was showing signs of waking up she got meningitis. The scans looked as if things were going downhill. Every other doctor and specialist involved with her care was ready to give up. I refused to do so. In my view, she just needed more time. I was right. She was young and fit and her other injuries were healing well. After another week she started to improve. It was slow but sure. She's back at university now, doing a fine arts degree. She comes in now and again and brings cupcakes for us all.'

'I'm glad it worked out that way for you and for her,'

Molly said. 'But there are just as many cases where it doesn't.'

He held her look for a long moment. 'The day she walked out of hospital with her parents I went to my office and closed the door and cried like a baby.'

Molly could picture him doing it. He had depths to his character that could so easily go unnoticed in a brief encounter. He was dedicated and professional at all times and yet he was as human as the next person. It was perhaps his humanity that made him such a wonderful ICU doctor. He didn't want anyone to suffer as he had suffered. He worked tirelessly to give his patients the best possible chance of recovery.

His own personal tragedy had moulded him into the man he was today—strong, driven and determined. He was a leader, not a follower. He expected a lot from his staff but he didn't ask anything of them he wasn't prepared to do himself. She could not think of a more wonderful ally in the fight for a patient's life. But she wondered if it all took its toll on him personally. Was that why he was all work and no play? He simply had nothing left to given anyone outside work.

'It must have been an amazing moment to see her walk out of hospital,' she said.

'It was,' he said. 'I know doctors are meant to keep a clinical distance. You can't make sound judgements when your emotions are involved. But once the patient is in the clear, sometimes the relief is overwhelming. I've had staff go on stress leave after a patient leaves. It's those sorts of miracles that make our jobs so rewarding and yet so utterly demanding.'

'How do you deal with the stress?' she asked.

'I fix stuff.'

'Fix stuff?'

He wafted a hand at their surroundings. 'There's nothing quite like tearing down a wall or painting or replastering or refitting a kitchen or bathroom,' he said. 'I'm thinking of selling in the spring. I've just about run out of things to do.'

'But this is such a fabulous house,' Molly said.

He gave a shrug. 'It's just a roof and four walls.'

'It's much more than that, surely?' she said. 'You've put so much work into it. It seems a shame not to get the benefit of it for a while.'

'Don't worry,' he said as he hooked his jacket over one shoulder. 'I'll give you plenty of notice before I let the realtor bring potential buyers through.'

Molly bit her lip. 'I'm having trouble finding anywhere else to live so far.'

'There's no hurry. You can stay here as long as you need to.'

'But not for the whole three months.'

He held her look for a beat. 'I can't imagine that you'd want to. I'm not the most genial host.'

'I think it's best if I keep looking,' she said. 'I'm having a hard time convincing everyone we're not a couple.'

'And that embarrasses you?'

Molly found his green and brown gaze mesmerising. 'No, not at all,' she said. 'Does it embarrass you?'

His eyes moved over her face, as if he was committing her features to memory. The silence throbbed with a backbeat of electric tension. She felt it echoing in her blood and wondered if he could feel it too. His eyes dropped to her mouth, pausing there for an infinitesimal moment. 'In another life I would've kissed you the other night,' he said in a gravel-rough tone. 'I probably would've taken you to bed as well.'

Molly looked at his mouth. She could see the tiny vertical lines of his lower lip and the slight dryness that she knew would cling to her softer one like sandpaper does to silk. 'Why not in this life?' she asked softly.

He reached out and brushed her lower lip with the pad of his index finger. His touch was as light as a moth's wing but it set off a thousand bubbly, tingly sensations beneath her skin. 'I think you know why not,' he said, and stepped back from her.

Molly felt like the floor of her stomach had dropped right out of her as he turned and left the room. She put her hand to her mouth, touching where his finger had so briefly been...

CHAPTER FIVE

LUCAS LOOKED AT the bedside clock and groaned. Another hour had gone by and he still couldn't sleep. His body felt restless, too wired to relax enough to drift off. He wondered if Molly was faring any better. But of course that was his problem—thinking about Molly.

He couldn't *stop* thinking about her. About how soft her plump lower lip had felt against the soft press of his fingertip. How luminous her grey-blue eyes had been when she had looked at him. How husky and sexy her voice had sounded. How he had wanted to pull her into his arms and kiss her, to taste her, to feel her respond to him.

He groaned again and threw off the bedcovers. Having her under the same roof was a form of self-torture. What had he been thinking, inviting her to stay with him? The house had changed since she'd moved in. And it wasn't just her little cat, who right at this moment was curled up on the foot of his bed, purring like an engine.

Molly made his big empty house seem warm and inviting. It was subtle things, like the way she had brought a bunch of flowers home and put them on the kitchen table in a jam jar because he hadn't ever thought to buy a vase. It was the fragrance of her perfume that lingered in the rooms she had wandered into. It was seeing the little array of girly things in the guest bathroom she was using—the lotions and potions, the hairdryer and straightening iron. And it was the not-so-subtle things, like her sexy black wisp of lace knickers hanging to dry over the clotheshorse in the laundry.

It wasn't just the house that had changed since she'd moved in. *He* had changed. He no longer came home wanting to be alone. He came home and looked forward to seeing her, hearing her, being with her. It wasn't enough to see her at work. He wanted more. He wanted to talk to her and to have her talk to him. He wanted to see her smile, hear her laugh.

He wanted her.

But he couldn't have her without the past overshadowing everything. How long before her parents—either singularly or jointly—expressed their misgivings? Such antagonism would poison any alliance between them as a couple. But it wasn't just the family stuff that gave him pause. How could he make her happy when he had nothing to offer her? He was used to being alone. He didn't know how to live any other way. He would end up hurting her, just like he hurt everyone who dared to care about him.

Molly was out of his league, out of bounds, forbidden.

But he still wanted her.

Molly woke to the sound of mewing outside her door. She threw off the bedcovers and padded over to let Mittens in. 'So now you want to sleep in my room, do you, you traitorous feline?' she said.

The little cat blinked up at her guilelessly and mewed again.

'Don't just sit there looking at me like that,' Molly said. 'Are you coming in or not?'

Mittens wound his body around her ankles and then padded off towards the stairs, stopping every now and again to look back at her as if to tell her to follow him.

Molly shook her head in defeat and reached for a wrap. She followed the cat to the kitchen downstairs, where she poured some cat biscuits into the dish on the floor and watched as he munched and crunched his way through them. 'You'd better not make a habit of this,' she muttered. 'I can't see Lucas waiting on you whisker and paw for nocturnal top-ups.'

There was a sound behind her and Molly turned and saw Lucas standing there dressed in nothing but a pair of long black silk pyjama trousers that were loose around his lean hips. Her eyes drank in the sight of his broad muscular chest. The satin skin with its natural tan, the carved pectoral muscles, the tiny pebbles of his flat male nipples, the ripped line of his abdomen and the dark hair that trailed beyond the waistband of the trousers. 'Um…I was just feeding Mittens,' she said, waving a hand at the cat, who was now licking his paws and wiping them over his face in a grooming session.

'So I see,' Lucas said.

'I hope I didn't wake you, nattering away to him,' Molly said.

'I wasn't asleep.'

She looked at his drawn features—the bloodshot eyes, the deep grooves that ran each side of his mouth. *Don't stare at his mouth!* She brought her gaze back up to his eyes and felt a tremor of want roll through her. He was so arrantly sexy with his dark stubbly regrowth and his hair all tousled.

'Can I make you a hot drink or something?' she asked, and started bustling about the kitchen to stop herself from reaching for him. 'I bought some chocolate buttons the other day. They're my weakness. That's why I put them on the top shelf, so they're not in my face and tempting me all the time.' She reached up on tiptoe in the pantry but she couldn't quite reach the packet in her bare feet.

Lucas's arm reached past her and took the packet of chocolate buttons off the shelf. 'Here you go,' he said.

He was *incredibly* close in the tight space. Molly could smell his warm male smell. She could see the individual points of his raspy regrowth along his jaw. She could see the dark flare of his pupils as he held her gaze in a lock that had distinctly erotic undertones. Her fingers touched his as she went to take the packet from him but he didn't release it. She gave it a little tug but still he held firm. She nervously sent the tip of her tongue out over her lips and gave the packet another little tug.

She felt the faintest loosening of his hold, but just as she was about to claim victory, his fingers wrapped around hers. The electricity of his touch sent a shockwave through her senses.

He gently tugged her towards her him until she was flush against his pelvis, her stomach doing a complete flip turn when she encountered the ridge of his growing erection. She lowered her lashes as his mouth came down, down, down as if in slow motion.

As soon as Molly felt the imprint of his mouth on

hers, a rush of sensation spiralled through her. His kiss was light at first, experimental almost, a slow, measured discovery of the landscape of her lips. He gradually increased the pressure but he didn't deepen the kiss. But somehow it was all the more intimate for that.

He cupped her face in his hands, his lean, long fingers gentle on her cheeks. It was a tender gesture that made her insides melt. She felt the rasp of his unshaven jaw against her chin as he shifted position. It was a spine-tingling reminder of all the essential differences between them: smooth and rough, hard and soft, male and female.

He gently stroked his tongue along the seam of her mouth. It wasn't a command for entry but a tempting lure to make her come in search of him. She pushed the tip of her tongue forward, her whole body quivering when it came into contact with his—male against female. It made fireworks explode inside her body. It unleashed something needy and urgent inside her. She gave a little whimper as his tongue touched hers again, a stab and retreat that had an unmistakably sexual intent about it.

Molly pressed herself closer, her insides clenching with desire as she felt his erection so hot and hard against her belly. His tongue glided against hers, calling it into a circling, whirling dance that made her senses spin like a top.

Had she ever been kissed like this?

Not in this lifetime.

He increased the pressure of his mouth on hers, interspersed with gentle but sexy thrusts and glides of his tongue. His hands slid up into her hair, his fingers splaying out over her scalp where every hair shaft was shivering and quaking in delight.

He broke the kiss to pull at her lips with his mouth, teasing little tugs that made her belly flip and then flop. Then he caressed her lips with a slow, drugging sweep of his tongue before covering her mouth again in a kiss that had a hint of desperation to it.

Molly felt her bones turn to liquid as his mouth worked its mesmerising magic on hers. She had never felt so turned on by a kiss. Hot darts of need pierced her. Her breasts felt tight and sensitive where they were pressing against his chest. Her inner core was moist and aching with that hollow feeling of want that nothing but sex could assuage. She moved her lower body against him, loving the feel of him responding to her so powerfully.

He took a deep breath and pulled back, holding her with his hands on her upper arms. 'We need to stop,' he said, breathing raggedly. '*I* need to stop.'

'Right…of course…good idea. We definitely should stop,' Molly said, suddenly embarrassed at how passionately she had responded to him. Would he think her too easy? Too forward? That was ironic as she was quite possibly the most conservative lover on the planet. But somehow he had unlocked a part of her she hadn't known existed.

He dropped his hold and rubbed at his face with both of his hands. 'I knew this was going to happen. I'm sorry. It's my fault. I was the one who crossed the line. It won't happen again.'

'We kissed,' she said, trying to be all modern and laid back about it. 'What's the big deal?'

His expression tightened. 'This is not just about a kiss and you damn well know it.' He moved to the other side of the kitchen. 'I don't need this right now.'

'Maybe this is just what you need,' Molly said. 'You're too focussed on work. That's why you can't sleep. You haven't got an off button.'

'Don't tell me how to live my life.'

'You're not living your life, though, are you?' she said.

His brows snapped together. 'What's that supposed to mean?'

'You have no life,' Molly said. 'You work ninety-to a hundred-hour weeks. You bite people's heads off. You push people away. You can't even remember the last time you got close to someone.'

'I had sex three months ago.'

Molly arched her brow. 'On your own or with someone?'

He rolled his eyes. 'With a woman I met at a conference.'

'Did you see her more than once?'

'There was no point,' he said. 'The chemistry wasn't right.'

'So it was a one-night stand.'

'There's nothing wrong with a one-night stand as long as it's safe.'

'And you like to be safe, don't you, Lucas?' Molly said. 'Safe from feeling anything for anyone. Safe from having anyone feel anything for you.'

She could see the tension in him. It was in every line and contour of his face. It was in the set of his shoulders and the tight clench of his fists. She could even feel it in the air. It made the atmosphere crackle like scrunched-up baking paper. 'What are you trying to do, Molly?' he asked. 'Push me until I lose control?'

She stepped up to within an inch of his body. His nostrils flared like those of a wild stallion as her scent came to him. Her breasts almost touched his chest. He held himself rigid, every muscle on his face set in stone, his body a marble statue. 'This is what you're frightened of, isn't it, Lucas?' she said as she placed a hand on his chest where his heart was thumping. 'Wanting someone. *Needing* them.'

He covered her hand with his and pulled it off his chest, the strength and grip of his fingers making her wince. 'I want you out of here by the end of the week,' he said, dropping her hand as if it was poisonous.

'Why?' she asked. 'Because you don't like letting someone see how incredibly lonely you are when you haven't got work to distract you?'

His jaw looked like it had been set in concrete. 'If you're not careful I'll throw you out tonight.'

'I don't think you mean that,' Molly said.

'You want to put it to the test?' he asked.

She looked at the steely glint in his eyes and backed down. 'Not particularly.'

'Wise of you,' he said.

'I'm only doing it because of Mittens,' she said. 'If it wasn't for him, I would've left before this.'

'You shouldn't have come in the first place.'

'You invited me!'

'I meant to London,' he said. 'You should have known it would cause trouble. But that's probably why you came. You could destroy my reputation with a word to the right person and you damn well know it.'

Molly frowned as she looked at him. 'I didn't realise you had such an appalling opinion of me. Do you really think that's why I'm here?'

'I've paid for what happened to your brother,' he said. 'Every day of my life since I have paid for that error of judgement. I can't bring him back. I can't undo what's done. I just want to be left to get on with my life. Is that too much to ask?'

'But you're not getting on with your life,' Molly said. 'You're stuck. Just like I'm stuck. Matt haunts us both. We both feel guilty.'

'You have no need to feel guilty,' he said. 'You weren't driving the car that killed him.'

'Why did you go out that night?'

He closed his eyes as if trying to block out the memory. 'I didn't want to go,' he said. 'Matt was pretty wired. He was in one of those moods he got into from time to time. I didn't find out until later that he'd been grounded, otherwise I wouldn't have agreed to go. But he always wanted to push the boundaries. He wanted the adrenalin rush. That's why I insisted on getting back behind the wheel. I thought he was being reckless. I didn't mind going for a drive to hang out, but doing tailspins and doughnuts wasn't my thing. I didn't see the kangaroo until it was too late. If I'd had more experience or if we'd been in a later model car, I would probably have handled it better. I lost control on the gravel. I didn't even realise he hadn't done up his seat belt until I saw him hit the windscreen.'

'Matt wouldn't have gone out at all if it hadn't been for me,' Molly said.

'What do you mean?' he asked.

'I found his stash of cigarettes and told my parents,' she said. 'That's why they grounded him. He was upset with me about it. I've always blamed myself for what happened. I wish I'd kept my mouth shut.'

Lucas frowned. 'You were just a little kid,' he said. 'You did the right thing. Matt shouldn't have been smoking, especially as he had asthma. He stole those cigarettes from Hagley's store. I was furious with him about it. But he was always pulling pranks like that.'

Molly let her shoulders drop on a sigh. 'I can't help blaming myself. Not just about Matt, but about my parents. Once he was gone…I wasn't enough for them. I couldn't make them happy. I couldn't keep our family together no matter how hard I tried.'

He came over to her and placed a gentle hand on her shoulder. 'Your parents were having trouble well before Matt's death,' he said. 'He told me about it heaps of times. You might not have noticed, being so much younger. Young kids tend to see what they want to see. Matt was sure your parents were heading for a breakup. His death probably just postponed it for a few years.'

Molly looked up into his face. His eyes were kind, his touch so gentle it made her melt all over again. 'I've never really talked to anyone about this before,' she said. 'Everybody always clammed up as soon as I came into the room. It was like the mere mention of Matt's name would damage me in some way. I guess they thought they were protecting me, but in the long run it made it so much harder. I had no one to talk to about him, about how much I missed him, about how guilty I felt. It must have been like that for you too.'

His expression spasmed in pain as he dropped his hand from her shoulder. 'It was one of the worst things about the whole tragedy,' he said. 'I lost my best mate and then no one would ever talk to me about him. My parents did their best but they didn't want to upset me. My brothers didn't know how to handle it. It was as if Matt had never existed.'

'I don't think Matt would want us to keep punishing ourselves for what happened,' Molly said. 'He would want us to be happy—to get on with our lives. Can't you see that?'

'I'm not going to take advantage of you,' he said, his mouth flattening in resolve. 'You're a long way from home. You're way out of your depth. You're uncertain about your relationship with Simon whatever his name is. I'm not going to add to your confusion by conducting an affair with you that will only end in tears.'

'It doesn't have to end in tears,' she said. 'We could have a great relationship. We have a lot in common. We have the same values. We have the same background.'

He gave her a bleak look. 'How long do you think a relationship between us would last?' he asked. 'Your parents would be up in arms about it. It would devastate them. It would devastate my own parents. Do you think they haven't suffered enough? They've paid a high price for my mistake. I won't have them suffer anything else.'

'You're wrong, Lucas,' Molly said. 'It wouldn't devastate them. It might actually help them, and my parents too. Can't you see that? It would help them to realise life goes on. We could help them heal.'

'I can't do it,' he said. 'I *won't* do it. You're not thinking straight. You're caught up with the nostalgic notion of me being your brother's best friend. That's all it is, Molly. You're not attracted to me for any other reason.'

'This is not about Matt,' Molly said. 'This is about us.'

'There is no us without Matt,' he said. 'Can't you see that? He's a shadow that will always be over us. You will always see me as the person who was responsible for his death. I get that. I totally understand and accept it because it's true. But I don't want to spend the rest of my life being reminded of it. Every time I look at you I see Matt. Every time you look at me you see the man who tore your family apart. How long do you think a relationship with that sort of backstory will last?'

'There is such a thing as moving on,' Molly said. 'We can't change the past but we can move on from it.'

'I'm sorry, Molly,' he said. 'You're a sweet girl. You're exactly the sort of girl I used to think I would one day settle down with. But that was then, this is now. I don't want to complicate my life with emotional entanglements.'

'There will come a day when work won't be enough any more,' she said. 'What will you do then?'

He gave her a wry look. 'I'll get myself a cat.'

'Funny.'

'That's me,' he said. 'A laugh a minute.'

'You're never going to allow yourself to be happy, are you?' Molly said. 'This is the hair shirt you've chosen—to live the rest of your life without love and connection. But it's not going to bring Matt back. It's not going to do anything but make you and the people who love you miserable. I feel sorry for you. You're like a tiger in a paper cage. You're the only one who can free yourself but you're too stubborn to do it.'

'Why are you so interested in my happiness?' he asked. 'You're the last person who should be worrying about how I feel.'

'You're not a bad person, Lucas,' Molly said. 'You just had a bad thing happen to you. You need to forgive yourself for being human.'

He touched her on the cheek with a slow stroke of his finger. 'Sweet, caring little Molly,' he said. 'You've always had a soft little heart. Always rescuing lame ducks and hopeless cases and getting yourself hurt in the process.'

She looked into his hazel eyes as tears welled in her own. 'I don't know how to live any other way.'

He leaned down and pressed a soft kiss to the middle of her forehead as if she were ten years old. 'Go back to bed,' he said. 'I'll see you in the morning.'

Molly slipped out of the room but it was a long time before she heard him make his way upstairs.

CHAPTER SIX

LUCAS WAS RECALIBRATING Tim Merrick's respirator the following morning and talking Catriona, one of the more junior nurses, through it. 'The pressure has gone up, which indicates pulmonary oedema,' he said. 'This means the lungs are stiff, and the ventilator pressure has to be turned up to inflate the lungs and get enough oxygen on board to give the brain the best chance of recovery. If the oxygen level in the blood drops, the brain damage will worsen instead of improve.'

'Is he likely to recover?' Catriona asked with a concerned look.

'We're doing all we can to make sure he does,' he said. *Don't die. Don't die. Don't die.* It was like a chant he couldn't get out of his head.

He had visited young Hamish on the ward first thing this morning. It was like looking at himself seventeen years ago. Hamish had the same hollow look of anguish in his eyes, the same shocked, this-can't-be-happening expression on his face. It was gut-wrenching to witness. It brought back his own anguish and guilt in great swamping waves.

Lucas turned to the nurse again. 'Can you run some blood gases through the analyser? I've got inflation pressure up another notch and oxygen is on one hundred per cent. I'm going to administer some frusemide to increase urine output to try and dry out the lungs a bit.'

A few minutes later Catriona called the readings out to Lucas.

'Damn,' he said. 'He's getting respiratory acidosis and we still haven't got the O2 up.'

'The X-ray's here for his chest film, Lucas,' Molly said as she came over.

'Maybe that will show something reversible,' he said. 'If we can't get that oxygen level up then the chance of recovery is going to slip away. Hypoxia and cerebral oedema is a bad combination.'

They looked at the images on the screen. 'You still think he's going to make it?' she asked.

Lucas stripped off his gloves, tossed them in the bin and walked over to the lightbox. 'It's still too early to say with any certainty,' he said. 'It might be a couple of weeks or more before that swelling goes down.'

'He's got a decerebrate posture—the clawed hands,' Molly said. 'I can't imagine how his parents must be feeling, to see him like that.'

'Emma Wingfield looked as bad at this stage, if not worse,' he said. 'Young brains have a knack of beating the odds and recovering. By the time people are admitted here with a tube in every orifice even their relatives don't recognise them. A few months later they'll walk in here with a box of chocolates—you'd never have guessed it was them under all that technology.' *He just hoped Tim was going to another one of them.*

'He's got a big effusion on the right,' Molly said.

'Yeah,' he said, looking at it. 'That's definitely worth draining. Might significantly improve lung function.'

Su Ling came across. 'Dr Banning?' she said. 'We've got a response from Claire Mitchell.'

Lucas called to Aleem, who was coming in with blood reports. 'Can you get set up here for me to do a drain?' To Molly he said, 'Come with me. It'll take half an hour for him to set up. I could use you over here.'

'What's happened?' he asked, when they got to Claire's bed.

'She's opened her eyes and she's fighting the ventilator,' Su Ling said.

It was the best news Lucas had had all day, maybe all year. 'Talk to her, Molly, while I look at the pressure.'

'Claire, can you hear me? It's Dr Drummond,' Molly said gently. 'You've had an accident and you're in Intensive Care. You're going to be all right. We've got you on a machine to help you breathe.'

'Her intracranial pressure's through the roof,' Lucas said. 'It's good she's responding but we're going to have to sedate her to get the pressure down. We need a few more days to wean her off the supports.'

'I'll give ten IV diazepam and up the sedation for twenty-four hours,' Molly said.

'Good,' he said. 'Another twenty-four hours and we'll turn down the sedation, see if she's less agitated and the IC pressure doesn't go up so much. I'll go and have a word with her parents. Are they here?'

'They left just half an hour ago to grab a coffee,' Su Ling said. 'They won't be long.'

'Right,' he said. 'I'll do that drain first.'

'I can do the drain,' Molly said, swinging her gaze to his. 'You can't do everything all at once.'

She had a point but Lucas wasn't going to let her know it. 'Call me if you have any difficulties,' he said, and left to find Claire's parents.

'Dr Drummond,' Jacqui said as Molly came into the office after a break later that day. 'This is Emma Wingfield. She's a previous inmate of ours. Emma, this is Dr Drummond. She's from Australia, like Dr Banning.'

'Hello,' Molly said with a smile. 'I've been hearing wonderful things about you. Dr Banning told me you were one of his star patients.'

Emma blushed, making her look far younger than nineteen. 'I owe him my life. He's the most amazing man.' She held out a plastic container. 'I've made him brownies. They're his favourite. Is he here? I'd love a quick word with him.'

'I don't think he's back from a meeting with the CEO,' Jacqui said, glancing up at the clock. 'It's been a pretty crazy day around here. He was late leaving so the meeting will probably run overtime.'

'That's OK,' Emma said. 'I'll wait. That is if I'm not in the way?'

'Not at all,' Jacqui said. 'Why don't you take a seat in one of the counselling rooms and I'll get him to come to you as soon as he gets back?'

Emma tucked the brownie container under one arm and left with another shy smile.

Jacqui turned and looked at Molly. 'I didn't have the heart to tell her you were living with Lucas,' she said. 'Her first real crush. Don't you just ache for her?'

Molly felt a blush steal over her cheeks not unlike the one young Emma had just experienced. 'I told you I'm not involved with him. I'm just sharing his house temporarily.'

'Yeah, but I've got two eyes in my head,' Jacqui said. 'He can barely take his eyes off you and you blush every time he walks into the room. So what gives? What's the deal with you guys? Did you have a fling in the past or something?'

'No, of course not,' Molly said. 'I was just a kid when he left to come over here.'

Jacqui tapped her finger against her lips. 'But there's something between you, isn't there?'

Molly gave a little sigh. 'He and my older brother were best friends,' she said, hoping to fob her off.

'Ah, now I get it,' Jacqui said. 'Lucas thinks your brother wouldn't approve of him making a move on his kid sister. That's typical of him, ever the gentleman. So what does your brother do? Is he a doctor too?'

'Um…no.' She paused for a moment before continuing, 'He died a while back. A car accident.'

'I'm so sorry,' Jacqui said. 'How dreadful for you and your family. And for Lucas too, to lose a best mate.'

'Yes…yes, it was dreadful,' Molly said. 'But it was an accident. It wasn't anyone's fault. It was just one of those things.'

Jacqui looked past Molly's left shoulder. 'Ah, here he is now,' she said as Lucas came in. 'You have a visitor—Emma Wingfield. She's waiting in one of the counselling rooms. She's brought you brownies.'

'Right.' Lucas gave a brisk nod and walked back out again.

Jacqui rolled her eyes. 'One of us should probably tell him,' she said. 'You know what men are like. You have to hit them over the head with something before they see it.'

Molly chewed at her lip. 'I'll have a word with him later.'

Molly found him in his office, going through some journals at the end of the day. 'Can I have a quick word?' she asked from the door.

'Sure,' he said, placing the journal he'd been reading to one side. 'What's up?'

She rolled her lips together to moisten them. 'Um... it's about Emma.'

He frowned. 'Emma?'

'Emma Wingfield.'

'What about her?'

Molly shifted her weight from foot to foot, feeling a little out of her depth and uncertain. Maybe she should have got Jacqui to say something. Would he misread her motives for bringing Emma's infatuation to his attention? 'I may be speaking out of turn but I couldn't help noticing she's rather attached to you,' she said.

His eyes held hers steady. 'And your point is?'

She felt her cheeks fire up. 'She's very young. You should be careful you don't give her the wrong idea. She could get very hurt.'

'I was her doctor, for God's sake,' he said. 'Anyway, she's just a kid.'

'She's nineteen, almost twenty,' Molly said. 'That's old enough to have a relationship with a man who is technically no longer her doctor.'

'I'm not having a relationship with her,' he said. 'She comes in from time to time to say hi to all the staff who looked after her. I told you that the other day.'

'She only wanted to see you today,' Molly said. 'She barely said a word to anyone else. I think she fancies herself in love with you.'

'That's rubbish,' he said. 'Why would she be in love with me?'

'You're handsome and kind and you saved her life,' Molly said. 'That's just for starters. I'm sure there are a hundred reasons why she has a crush on you. Just about every single woman at St Patrick's fancies you like crazy so why should she be any different?'

His eyes measured hers for a pulsing moment. 'Why indeed?'

Molly knew her cheeks were bright red but carried on regardless. 'I think you need to let her down gently. She's young and vulnerable. She's been through a traumatic experience and is still finding her way.'

'Emma wants to do something for the unit,' he said. 'Some fundraising. That's why she wanted to meet with me as unit director. I said I'd help her do something. I'm not sure what. We're still at the brainstorming stage. Maybe you could offer some suggestions. I haven't got a clue about that sort of thing.'

'I'd be happy to help,' Molly said. 'I was involved in a dinner dance for our unit back home. It was a great success. Everyone talked about it for months afterwards.'

'I'll arrange a meeting between the two of you to get things rolling,' he said.

'I still think you should be careful in handling Emma,' Molly said. 'I'm sure her reasons for the fundraising are very noble, but you still have to keep in mind she could be actively seeking time alone with you.'

'Thanks for the tip-off,' he said. 'But I'm sure you're mistaken. Anyway, I think she already has a boyfriend.'

'Yes, well, that doesn't always signify,' Molly said.

His brow came up in an arc. 'Are you speaking from experience?'

'Not necessarily.'

'How is Simon what's-his-name?' he asked. 'I saw him chatting up one of the young midwives in the cafeteria this afternoon. He sure gets around, doesn't he?'

'He's a free agent,' Molly said. 'He can chat up whoever he likes.'

'So you're no longer an item?'

'We weren't really one in the first place,' she said, blowing out a breath. 'I was what you'd call a rebound fill-in for him. I was feeling a bit lonely at the time but now I wish I'd never let him cry on my shoulder. I can see why his ex left him. He's quite narcissistic and controlling.'

'And possessive.'

'That too.'

There was a little silence.

'I might be a bit late coming home this evening,' Molly said. 'I'm going to a movie night with Kate Harrison's group. I was…um, wondering if you'd like to come too.'

'Why would I want to do that?' he asked.

'It would be good for you,' she said, 'to take your mind off work for a change. Things have been pretty stressful what with Tim Merrick and all. I thought it'd be nice to get out and socialise a bit so—'

'I already have an engagement this evening.'

'Doing what?'

'Do you really want me to spell it out for you?' he asked with a sardonic quirk of his brow.

Molly blushed. 'Oh, right… Sorry, I didn't mean to embarrass you or anything…'

He picked up his journal again. 'Close the door on the way out, will you?'

CHAPTER SEVEN

MOLLY WAS DISTRACTED all the way through the movie. She couldn't stop thinking about what Lucas was up to and who he might be with tonight. Who was it? She didn't think it was anyone from the hospital. She felt agitated at the thought of him bringing someone back to his house.

What if his lady friend spent the night? She herself would no doubt encounter her in the morning. It would be beyond embarrassing. It would be heart-breaking to see him with someone else. She couldn't handle it. She didn't want to handle it. She hated the thought of some woman coming back just to sleep with him. Would they be interested in who he was as a person? Would they take the time to get to know him? To understand what had made him the quiet, reserved man he was?

Of course not.

He wouldn't allow them to. He had let no one into his private world of pain. He shouldered his guilt and anguish with dogged determination. He had no joy in his life, or at least none that she could see. He was isolated and deeply lonely but he wouldn't allow anyone to get close to him.

Molly didn't join the others for drinks after the

movie. She caught a cab back to Lucas's house and went inside with an ear out for the sound of voices, but it was as silent as a tomb. She checked the sitting room but it didn't look like anyone had even been in there. The cushions on the sofa were all still neatly arranged. The coffee table was neat with its glossy book of iconic photographs from around the world centred just so. There were no condensation rings from drinks or crumbs from nibbles.

Maybe he'd decided to stay at his date's place, or maybe he'd booked a hotel room, she thought in stomach-plummeting despair. She didn't want him to make love to someone who didn't know him, who didn't care for him...*who didn't love him.*

Molly was about to head upstairs after feeding and playing with Mittens when the front door opened and Lucas came in, bringing a waft of chilly air with him.

'How was your date?' she asked.

'I had to take a rain-check,' he said as he shrugged himself out of his jacket. 'I got a call from the hospital. Tim Merrick's temperature suddenly skyrocketed. He started leaking CSF from one ear.'

'Oh, no...' Molly frowned in concern. Leaking cerebrospinal fluid and a fever probably meant meningitis had occurred. The damage to his brain could increase if it wasn't quickly controlled.

'It's a setback,' he said. 'But I hope we've caught it in time.'

Molly watched as he rubbed a hand across the back of his neck. He grimaced as if his muscles were in knots. 'You look tired,' she said.

'Yeah, well, eighteen-hour days do that.'

'I could massage your neck for you if you like,' she offered.

'You'd break your fingers working on my golf balls of tension,' he said. 'I'll be fine. I just need a couple of hours' sleep.'

'I'd like to do it for you,' Molly said. 'It won't take long. I'm pretty good at it. I used to do my dad's neck and shoulders all the time.'

He looked at her for a long moment. 'You sure you want to get that close to me?' he asked.

'Will you bite if I do?' she asked with an arch look.

'Guess there's only one way to find out,' he said.

A few minutes later Molly had him sitting on one of the sofas in the sitting room. She stood behind him and started kneading his neck through his shirt. His muscles felt like concrete and his shirt wasn't helping matters as it kept bunching up. 'I think you'd better take your shirt off,' she said. 'I can't get into those muscles the way I want to.'

'It's been a while since a woman's asked me to strip for her,' he said as he unbuttoned his shirt.

'Ha ha,' Molly said. 'Now, stay put while I get some massage oil.'

When she came back with some perfumed oil he was sitting bare chested on the sofa. She drank in the sight of his broad tanned shoulders and the leanness of his corded muscles. She poured some oil into her hand and emulsified it before placing her hands on his shoulder.

'I'm sorry if my hands are cold,' she said. 'It won't take long to warm them up.'

'They're fine,' he said with a little groan. 'Perfect.'

'You're so tense.'

'You should feel it from my side.'

Molly smiled and kept massaging. She loved the feel of his warm male skin underneath her hands. After a while he started to relax. She worked on his neck muscles right up to his scalp, turning his head to the right and then to the left to loosen the tension.

'You missed your calling,' he said.

'When was the last time you had a massage?' she asked as she worked on his scalp with her fingertips.

'Can't remember.'

Molly kept stroking and gliding her hands over his shoulders. Over time the movements of her hands became less vigorous and more like caresses. She breathed in the musky scent of him as she worked her way down over his pectoral muscles. She heard him draw in a breath as her fingers skated over the top of his abdomen. It was daring and brazen of her but she couldn't leave it at that. She inched her way down, taking her time, stroking each horizontal ridge of toned male flesh.

The air became loaded with sensual intent as she found the cave of his belly button surrounded by its nest of coarse masculine hair.

He suddenly captured her hand and stilled it against the rock-hard wall of his stomach. 'Molly.' His voice was as rusty as an old hinge.

'Yes?'

He pushed her hand away and got to his feet, turning to face her across the sofa, his eyes dark and full of glittering desire. 'What the hell are you playing at?' he asked.

'I was massaging you.'

'The hell you were,' he said. 'Do you have any idea

how hard this is for me? Do you think I don't want you? Of course I do. I can't think of a time when I've wanted someone more.'

'Then why are you fighting it?'

He flicked his eyes upwards as he turned away. 'For God's sake, you know why.'

Molly came from behind the sofa to stand in front of him. 'No, I don't know why,' she said. 'We're both adults. There's no reason we can't have a relationship. This has nothing to do with anyone else but us.'

He dragged a hand over his face in a weary fashion. 'I can't promise you a future because of the past. The past *I'm* responsible for.'

'We can make the future *in spite* of the past,' Molly countered. 'Haven't we both suffered enough? Why should we spend the rest of our lives grieving over what we've lost instead of celebrating what we still have?'

'It will always be there between us,' he said. 'It won't go away. It will fester in the background until one day it will blow up in our faces. I can't risk that.'

'Life is full of risks,' she said. 'You can't protect yourself from every one of them. Loving and losing are part of what a rich human life entails.'

'I lost everything when Matt died,' he said heavily. 'I lost my best mate. I lost my family. My community. The future I'd envisaged for myself. It was all gone in the blink of an eye.'

'So you're going to punish yourself for the rest of your life because you don't feel you deserve to be happy?' Molly asked. 'But what about my happiness?'

He closed his eyes briefly. 'I can't make you happy.'

'You're not even prepared to give it a try, are you?' she asked. 'You've made up your mind. You're going to live a life of self-sacrifice. But it won't achieve anything. All it will do is make you end up lonely and isolated. Pretty much as you are now. You're jammed on replay. Lonely, lonely, lonely.'

He gave her an irritated look. 'I'm not lonely. I like being alone. I don't need people around me all the time.'

Molly rolled her eyes and turned away. 'Good luck with that.'

He snagged her arm and turned her back to face him. 'What's that supposed to mean?'

She gave him a direct look. 'Why did you ask me to stay here with you?'

'You needed a place to stay in a hurry,' he said. 'I couldn't see you tossed out on the street. I wasn't brought up that way.'

'I think you asked me to stay with you because deep down you're tired of being alone,' Molly said. 'You're sick of rattling around in this big old house with no one to talk to. The occasional dates and one-night stands aren't cutting it any more. You're yearning for something more meaningful.'

'You're wrong,' he said, snatching up his shirt and shoving his arms through the sleeves.

'Am I?'

'I don't need to be rescued, Molly,' he said, glowering at her. 'I'm not going to be another one of your lame-duck projects. Find someone else to rehabilitate.' He turned and strode out of the room, closing the door with a snap behind him.

* * *

Over the next few days Molly only saw Lucas at work. He barely seemed to spend any time at home at all. He left in the morning before she got up and he came back when she was already tucked up in bed. She didn't know when he ate or slept. She found herself listening out for him at all hours of the night, not really settling until she heard him come up the stairs and close his bedroom door. He drove himself relentlessly. She wondered how long he could keep doing it. The job was demanding at the best of times, but he had taken on extra shifts as if work was all he wanted to do.

Molly had the weekend off and spent it shopping and sightseeing. But on Sunday night she felt at a loose end. She hadn't seen Lucas all weekend, although she had noticed he had fed Mittens and cleaned his litter tray.

After watching a movie she wasn't really interested in, Molly took a long soak in the bath before preparing for bed. She spent a couple of hours trying to relax enough to go to sleep but she kept jolting awake when she thought she heard Lucas's key in the lock.

Finally, at three in the morning, she gave up and came back downstairs for a drink. On her way back up she noticed there was a light on in the library. It seemed she wasn't the only one having trouble sleeping. She padded to the door, which was ajar, and gently pushed it open. Lucas was sitting on the comfortable sofa in the middle of the room with his head resting against the back, his long legs stretched out in front of him, crossed at the ankles. His book was lying open on his lap and his eyes were closed, as if he had fallen asleep in mid-sentence.

He looked much younger in sleep. His features were less harshly drawn and the normally grim set of his mouth was relaxed. His hair was tousled as if his hands had been moving through it, and his shirt was crumpled and the first three buttons undone, showing a glimpse of his sternum.

She walked over to him but still he didn't stir. She watched his chest rise and fall on each slow and even breath. After a moment she carefully took the book from his lap and placed it on the nearby side table.

Still he slept.

Molly reached out with her hand and ever so gently brushed a lock of hair off his forehead. His eyelids flickered momentarily but didn't open. He made a small murmuring noise and let out another long exhalation.

She picked up the throw rug that was draped over the end of the sofa and gently spread it over him.

He didn't stir.

She touched his face with her fingertips. His stubble caught on her soft skin like silk on coarse-grade sandpaper. She sent her fingertip on an even more daring journey to trace over his top lip and then his bottom one. His lips were dry and warm and so very, very tempting...

She hesitated for a moment before she leaned down and pressed a soft-as-air kiss to his mouth. His much dryer lips clung to hers as she gently pulled back. But then he gave a little start and opened his eyes, his hands wrapping around hers like a snare captured a rabbit.

'I was just...making sure you were warm enough,' she said.

For a moment he said nothing. Did nothing. Just sat

there with his eyes meshed with hers, his warm strong hands holding hers captive.

The silence swelled with sensual promise.

'I didn't mean to wake you…' Molly said. 'You looked so…peaceful.'

He gave her hands a gentle little tug to bring her down beside him on the sofa. 'Why aren't you in bed?' he asked.

'I couldn't sleep.'

His eyes moved over her face as if he was memorising every tiny detail. He paused longest on her mouth. 'Isn't it the handsome prince who's supposed to kiss Sleeping Beauty to get her to wake up?' he asked.

Molly moistened her lips with a quick dart of the tip of her tongue. 'Yes, but I'm already awake so what would be the point?'

His eyes smouldered as they came back to hers. 'This thing between us…it's not going to go away, is it?'

'Not in this lifetime.'

A corner of his mouth lifted.

'Hey, you almost smiled,' she said, touching his lip with her finger.

He captured her finger with his mouth and sucked on it erotically while his gaze held hers. Molly felt her stomach drop. The sexy graze of his teeth and the rasp of his tongue made her shiver with delight. He tugged her closer, a gentle but determined tug that had a primal element to it. His eyes were dark with desire as he pressed her down against the cushioned sofa, his long lean body a delicious, tantalising weight on her.

His eyes made love with hers for endless seconds. 'I told myself I wasn't going to do this,' he said.

Molly looped her arms around his neck. 'I want you to do this,' she said. 'And I'm pretty sure you want to do this too.'

His mouth tilted wryly. 'I guess I can't really deny that right now, can I?'

She moved against the hard press of his erection. 'Not a chance.'

He brought his mouth down and covered hers in a hungry kiss. It was a kiss of longing and desperation, a kiss that spoke of deep yearnings that hadn't been satisfied for a long, long time. His tongue stroked the seam of her mouth to gain access, thrusting between her lips to meet her tongue in a sexy tangle. Molly clasped his head in her hands, her fingers threading through his hair as he worked his sensual magic on her mouth. Her breasts were tingling against the hard wall of his chest, her pelvis on fire where his erection probed her boldly.

One of his hands lifted her hips to bring her even harder against him. She gave a little gasp of pleasure as his other hand cupped her breast through her wrap. But it wasn't enough for him. He tugged open the wrap and went in search of her naked flesh. She shivered as he bent his head to suckle on her. Her nipple was sensitive and tightly budded but he seemed to know exactly what pressure to subject it to. He swirled his tongue around her areole before moving to the exquisitely reactive underside of her breast. He kissed and stroked and suckled in turn, until she was almost breathless with want.

Molly pushed his shirt back off his shoulders, smoothing her hands over the muscled planes of his chest, delighting in the feel of him, so hard and warm and male. He groaned as she slid her hands down over his taut abdomen, his kiss becoming more and more urgent against her mouth. She wriggled out of her wrap and then set to work on the waistband of his trousers. She finally uncovered him, stroking and cupping him until he was breathing as hard as she was. He was gloriously aroused, thick and swollen, hot to her touch, already moist at the tip. She rubbed the pad of her thumb over him, her insides quivering when he gave a low, deep groan of pleasure.

After a moment or two he pulled her hand away and pressed her harder back against the sofa cushions. He kissed his way down her body, lingering over her breasts, down to her belly button, dipping in there with his tongue before moving to the feminine heart of her.

Molly drew in a sharp breath as his warm breath skated over her sensitive folds. She clutched at his head, her fingers digging in for purchase when his tongue gently separated her. 'I don't usually do this…' she said. 'Can we just…? Oh…*oh*…' She closed her eyes as the delicious sensations barrelled through her like a set of turbulent waves. Once it had subsided she opened her eyes and looked at Lucas, suddenly feeling shy. 'That was…amazing… I've never let anyone do that before.'

He leaned his weight on his elbows as he looked down at her. 'You haven't?'

She shook her head. 'I've always felt a bit uncomfortable about it. I know this sounds ridiculous but it always seemed a bit too intimate.'

He brushed back her hair from her forehead. 'You probably weren't with the right partner,' he said. 'Trust is just as important as lust.'

'Speaking of lust…' She stroked her fingers over his erection. 'Don't you want to…?'

'I haven't got a condom on me right now,' he said.

'Do you have any upstairs?' she asked.

'A couple maybe.'

Molly caressed his lean jaw with her fingers. She was used to men who were *always* prepared. 'Let's go upstairs,' she whispered softly.

Lucas carried her in his arms, stopping now and again to kiss her deeply and passionately. Finally he laid her on his bed and came down over her, his weight balanced on his arms so as not to crush her. Molly lifted her hips towards his, her whole body aching and yearning for his deep possession.

He kissed her lingeringly, moving from her mouth to her breasts and back again until she was whimpering and writhing. She clawed at him with her hands, digging her fingers into his buttocks to hold him close to the pulsing heat of her body.

He paused for a moment to apply a condom, and came back over her, his strong thighs imprisoning hers. His first thrust was gentle, almost tentative, as if he was uncertain of whether or not to proceed. But her body gripped him hungrily and with a deep groan of pleasure he surged forward, again and again and again. Molly clung to him as the delicious friction sent her nerves into a frenzy of excitement. He went deeper, his breathing harsh against her neck as he fought for control, his lean, athletic body taut as a bow with the build-up of tension. She caressed his back and shoulders with her hands, feeling the gravel of goose-bumps break out along his skin as he responded to her touch.

He slipped a hand between their rocking bodies to find her most pleasurable point as he continued his rhythmic thrusts. The touch of his fingers, so gentle, so intuitive, triggered her orgasm within seconds. It was like a tumultuous wave that tossed and turned her over and over and over until she was gasping and sobbing with the aftershocks. She had never felt such powerful, all-consuming sensations before. Her body reverberated with them as he laboured towards his own release. She held him tightly against her as he finally let go. She felt every deep pumping action inside her, heard his desperate groan, a primal sound that made her shiver all over in feminine response.

Molly held him to her, unwilling to break the intimate connection. To lie there with his body still encased in hers, to have his arms hold her close, to feel the rise and fall of his chest against hers as his breathing gradually slowed, was too precious, too special to sever just yet.

'I'm sorry if I rushed you,' he said against her neck where his head was resting.

She toyed with his hair with her fingers. 'You didn't,' she said. 'It was perfect.'

He lifted himself up on one elbow to mesh his gaze with hers. It was hard to know what he was thinking. His expression wasn't shuttered but neither was it totally open. 'I guess I should let you get to bed and get some sleep,' he said.

Molly felt a little frown pucker her forehead. 'You don't want me to stay here with you?'

He eased himself away and dealt with the disposal of

the condom, his eyes not meeting hers. 'I'm a restless sleeper,' he said. 'I'll disturb you too much.'

She watched him as he shrugged on a bathrobe, but the thick terry towelling fabric was not the only barrier he had put up. A mask had slipped over his face as well.

'I guess I'd better get out of your hair, then,' Molly said, and got off the bed, taking the top sheet with her to cover her nakedness. Hurt coursed through her like a poison. How could he dismiss her like that? As if she was a call girl who had served her purpose and now he wanted her gone. She had expected more—*wanted* more—from him. Tears prickled and burned behind her eyes as she shuffled to the door in her makeshift covering, almost tripping over the fringe of the Persian rug.

'Molly.'

She held herself stiffly, with her arms wrapped around her middle as she faced him. 'I can see why your sex life has been experiencing a bit of a downturn,' she said. 'Your bedside manner definitely needs some work.'

He put a hand through his hair, a frown carving deep in his forehead. 'I'm sorry,' he said. 'It wasn't my intention to hurt you.' He dropped his hand back by his side. 'Tonight was…perfect. I mean that, Molly. *You* were perfect.'

She let out a long, exasperated sigh. 'Then why are you pushing me away?'

He held her look for a long moment. 'This is all I can give you,' he said. 'You have to understand and accept that. I know it's not what you want in a relationship but it's all I can give right now.'

'Just…sex?' she asked.

A tiny knot of tension flicked on and off in his jaw. 'Not just sex.'

'But not love and commitment,' she said.

He exhaled a long breath. 'You're only here for three months. It wouldn't be fair to make promises neither of us might be able to keep. Besides, you might feel very differently about things once your parents hear we're involved.'

Molly knew that was going to be a tricky hurdle to cross. For so long she had striven for her father's approval and becoming involved with Lucas was going to destroy any hope of ever achieving that. 'I'm hoping both my parents will put my happiness before any misgivings they might have,' she said. 'Isn't that what most parents want—their kids to be happy?'

'Most, I imagine,' he said.

'How will your parents handle it?'

A shadow passed through his eyes. 'I'm not planning on telling them any time soon.'

Molly couldn't help feeling a little crushed. Did that mean he didn't think they would be involved long enough for his parents to find out? Was he ashamed of his attraction towards her? She bit down on her lip, torn between her pride and her passion for him. Why did it have to be so hard to be happy? Was her life always going to be one of compromise? Of never feeling quite good enough?

Lucas closed the distance between them, tipping up her chin to bring her gaze in line with his. 'I've upset you,' he said.

'Why would you think that?' Molly asked. 'You had sex with me and as soon as it was over you told me to leave. You don't want anyone to know about us being involved. And you can't see us having any sort of future. Why on earth would I be upset?'

He brushed his thumb over her bottom lip, his gaze rueful as it held hers. 'You deserve much better than I could ever give you.'

'But what if I only want you?' she said trying not to cry.

He gathered her close, resting his chin on the top of her head, his warm breath moving through the strands of her hair. 'I have this amazing habit of hurting everyone I care about,' he said.

Molly looked up at him. 'You care about me?'

He held her gaze for an infinitesimal moment. 'Are you going to give my sheet back?' he asked.

'You want it back?'

'Only if you come with it.'

'You'll have to fight me for it,' she said with a coquettish smile.

His eyes smouldered as he reached for the edge of the sheet. 'Game on,' he said, and stripped it from her.

CHAPTER EIGHT

LUCAS WOKE TO find one of Molly's arms flung across his chest, her head snuggled against his side and her slim legs entwined with his. He couldn't remember the last time he had woken up beside someone in his bed. His sexual encounters were normally brief and purely functional. As soon as they were over he forgot about them.

But waking up beside Molly was not going to be something he could so easily dismiss from his memory. The way she had responded to him had been one of the most deeply moving things he had ever experienced. He felt like he was her first lover. In a way she had felt like his. Had he ever felt so fully satiated? So in tune with someone that he forgot where his body ended and hers began? His senses had screamed with delight and they were still humming now hours later. The scent of her perfume was on his skin. Her taste was in his mouth. His hunger for her was stirring his blood all over again.

She moved against him and slowly opened her eyes. 'Hello,' she said with a shy smile.

'Hello to you,' he said as he brushed an imaginary hair off her face.

She traced one of her fingertips over his top lip. 'Last night was wonderful,' She said. '*You* were wonderful.

I've never felt like that before. I've always thought it was my fault, you know, that I wasn't very good at sex. But now I can see what I've been missing out on.'

He caught her hand and kissed the end of her finger. 'It was wonderful for me, too,' he said.

She trailed her fingers over his sternum, her grey-blue eyes lowered from his. 'I guess it's pretty much the same for men, no matter who they have sex with,' she said.

He brought her chin up. 'Not always,' he said. 'I agree that it's often more of a physical thing for men than for women, but caring about someone does make a difference.'

Her eyes shone as she put her arms around his neck. 'Is it time to get up yet?' she asked.

He rolled her beneath him and pinned her with his body. 'Not yet,' he said, and covered her mouth with his.

Molly came downstairs after her shower to find Lucas had already left for the hospital. There was a short note on the kitchen counter to say he would catch up with her later at work. She put the note down and sighed. They hadn't really had time to discuss how they were going to manage their relationship in public.

Was it a relationship? Or had she done the same thing she had done with Simon—drifted into something that didn't have a name?

She knew Lucas was keen to keep his private life separate but she couldn't see how they would be able to stop people finding out they were intimately involved unless he planned to be all formal and distant with her at work. It wasn't that she wanted her private life out on show, but neither did she want to hide her relationship with Lucas away as if she was somehow ashamed of it.

She still couldn't believe how amazing he made her feel. Her body was still tingling from his passionate lovemaking. Every time she moved her body she felt where he had been. Holding him tightly within her as he had come had surpassed anything she had ever experienced before. She had felt so deeply connected to him and had felt every one of his deep shudders of pleasure reverberating through her flesh.

She hoped it had been much more than just a physical release for him. She knew it had been a while since he'd been intimate with anyone but, even so, it had felt like he had truly cared about her. He had made sure she'd been comfortable and at ease with him and had made sure she'd experienced pleasure before he'd taken his own. He'd coached her without coercing her to do bolder things. Had been passionate and yet achingly tender with her. How would she be able to pretend he was just her boss at work? Wouldn't everyone guess as soon as they saw her?

When she got to work Kate Harrison and Megan Brent were in the change room, putting their things in the lockers. 'Looks like the boss has got himself a new girlfriend,' Kate said as she hung up her coat and scarf.

Molly kept her gaze averted as she unlocked a locker. Was it somehow written on her face? Had she given off some clue? Could people actually tell she had spent the night in Lucas's arms? 'What makes you say that?' she asked.

'He actually smiled at us as he walked past,' Kate

said. 'Can you believe that? He never smiles. We reckon he got laid last night. Don't we, Megan?'

'Sure of it,' Megan said. 'I wonder who it is?'

Molly stashed her things inside the locker. She could see her cheeks were rosy red in the reflection in the little mirror hanging on the inside of the door. How soon before they put two and two together? Everyone knew she was sharing his house. It wasn't much of a step to sharing his bed as well, or so most people would assume.

How would Lucas deal with everyone talking about them? How would *she* deal with it? She didn't want anything to spoil her relationship with him. It was all too new and precious to her. She wanted time to feel her way with him, to help him see how wonderful being together could be. If a gossip-fest started he might bring things to an abrupt end. He put work before relationships and if their relationship threatened to jeopardise his career, she knew which he would choose.

'I don't think it'd be anyone from the hospital,' Kate said. 'He has a bit of a thing about staff hooking up with each other. He told off one of the residents for getting it on with a nurse in one of the storage rooms. We all thought he was going to have him fired.'

'Do you know who it is?' Megan asked Molly.

'Um…' Molly felt flustered. Should she say something? Oh, why hadn't they talked about this earlier? What was she supposed to do? Deny it? Broadcast it? Lie about it?

'You're renting a room at his place,' Kate said. 'Surely you'd be the first to know if he brought someone home. Who is it? Did you get a good look at her? What's she like?'

Molly turned to close her locker door before she faced the two women again. 'I don't think Dr Banning would appreciate me discussing his private life,' she said. 'I know I wouldn't appreciate him discussing mine.'

Kate lifted her brows as she exchanged a look with Megan. 'Right,' she said. 'Fair enough.'

Molly slipped her lanyard over her neck. 'I'd better get going,' she said, and hurriedly left.

Lucas headed back to ICU after speaking to the infectious diseases doctor about Tim Merrick's antibiotic cover. He hadn't seen Molly since he had left her in the shower that morning. He had intended to talk to her about how they were going to handle their relationship at work but he'd got a call about Tim's rising temperature and had had to rush to the hospital.

He wondered if she would feel uncomfortable about separating their private lives from their work ones. He was good at switching off his emotions but he had a feeling she might not find it as easy. She was the type to wear her heart on her sleeve. She was open and honest to a fault. He, on the other hand, preferred to play his cards close to his chest. He didn't want to be the subject of gossip and loathed people speculating about his private life. The thought of everyone picking apart his relationship with Molly was anathema to him. He didn't want to be ribbed about his involvement with her. He didn't want to be the butt of jokes or on the receiving end of teasing comments.

He wondered how long it would be before the news was out. It was more or less common knowledge that she was rooming at his place. How soon before people assumed they were sleeping together?

Being involved with Molly was an emotional minefield. She was only here for a short time. He wasn't sure how he was going to navigate the next few weeks. A short-term affair sounded good in theory, but how would it play out in practice? What if he didn't want her to leave when her time was up? What if she didn't want to go? His mind swirled with a torrent of thoughts. How would she face her parents if she chose to be with him? How would he face his? Their relationship would cause even more heartache. How could it not?

He was the last person her parents would want her to be with. He had torn apart their family. He couldn't undo the damage of that one moment in time. There was no way he could atone for the death of Matt. He had given years of his life to serving others, to saving others, but it still didn't make an iota of difference.

He could not bring Matt back.

Even if by some miracle her parents and his were OK about him being with Molly, there were still his own doubts over whether he could make her or anyone happy. He had spent so long on his own he wasn't sure he could handle the emotional intimacy of a long-term relationship. He had never been half of a couple before. His relationships—hook-ups was probably a more accurate term—had never involved the sharing of feelings, hopes, dreams, values and goals. He didn't know how to be emotionally available to a partner. He didn't know how to be emotionally available to *anyone*.

He kept that part of himself tightly locked down. His parents and brothers had all but given up on trying to draw him out. He didn't want anyone to see the bottomless black hole of despair deep inside him. He had concreted it over with work and responsibilities that would have burnt out a weaker man. He knew it wasn't healthy, he knew it wasn't going to make him happy either, but he had long ago resigned himself to a life lived without the contentment and fulfilment other people took for granted.

His hope was that Molly would finally come to see he was not worth the effort.

Molly was at Claire Mitchell's bedside as Lucas came into ICU. She had worked tirelessly with Claire each day and he had been impressed by her dedication and patience. Claire had a long road ahead of her and would have to spend months in a rehab facility, learning to walk and talk again. But at least she was going to make it. Her parents would still have their daughter, even if she wasn't quite as physically able as she had been.

Tim Merrick, on the other hand, was an ongoing nightmare. The CSF leak from his ear had increased overnight. The base-of-skull fracture had entered the middle-ear cavity and opened up a potential entry point of bacteria. Lucas had repeated an EEG but there was still little brain activity. The transplant team had contacted him earlier that morning but he had refused to enter into a discussion about harvesting Tim's organs. He was treating Tim hour by hour, refusing to give up hope, even though a part of him was seriously starting to doubt there would be any chance of him recovering. He kept thinking of Hamish Fisher, how shattered he had looked that morning as he had been discharged from hospital. Lucas remembered it all too well—the day he had walked out of the hospital, with his best mate lying cold and lifeless in the morgue.

At least Tim was still alive—for now.

'Claire, can you hear me?' Molly was saying. 'Open your eyes. Lift your arm. Wriggle your toes.'

'Is she responding?' Lucas asked.

'Yes, she opened her eyes a couple of times,' she said. 'She's fighting the ventilator. Her intracranial pressure and all other obs are stable. I think it's time to start weaning her off the ventilator and sedation. I've asked the nurse to let me know if her stats drop. How is Tim Merrick doing? I heard things got worse overnight.'

He gave her a grim look. 'I've started high-dose imipenem and gentamicin and I've just spoken to the ID doctor about recommendations for antibiotic cover. If we don't get on top of this quickly, his chance of a recovery is going to disappear. The next forty-eight hours are going to be critical.'

'Jacqui told me the transplant team called,' Molly said, giving him a pained look.

Lucas drew in a tight breath. 'Yes, but I'm not going to make any decision until we repeat the EEG a couple of times at least.'

'His parents seem resigned—'

'His parents are shocked and upset,' he said. 'They need more time to come to terms with their son's injuries. It's too early to say how things will pan out. Trust me, Molly. I know what I'm doing.'

She caught her lower lip with her teeth. 'I was wondering if you had a minute to talk…in private, I mean.'

'I'll be in my office in about twenty minutes,' he said. 'I have a couple more charts to write up first.'

Molly knocked on Lucas's open office door but he was on the phone and gestured to her to come in and sit down. She closed the door and came over to the chair opposite his desk, not sitting down but waiting for him to finish his call.

'Sorry about that,' he said, and placed his phone on the desk. 'It's been one of those mornings. Everyone wants everything yesterday.'

'Yes…'

He studied her for a moment. 'Are you OK?' he asked.

Molly let out a little breath. 'I was wondering how we're going to handle this…um, situation between us. A couple of the nurses were talking in the change room when I came in this morning. I didn't know what to say.'

'There's nothing *to* say,' he said.

'It's not that simple,' she said. 'I think people are going to put two and two together pretty quickly. I'm not sure how to deal with it. We didn't get a chance to talk about it this morning.'

He blew out an impatient breath. 'Personally I can't see why it's anyone's business. I don't go around asking staff members who they're sleeping with, do you?'

'No, of course not.'

He raked a hand through his hair as he leaned back forcefully in his chair. 'What do they want us to do? Release a press statement or something? *God*. Why don't these people have lives of their own instead of speculating about everyone else's?'

'If you'd rather not have people know about us then I'll deny any rumours.'

He leaned forward again and dropped his hand back down on the desk with a little thump. 'These things have a habit of fizzling out after a week or two,' he said. 'It's best just to ignore the speculation.'

'I'm sorry…'

He gave her a wry look. 'Why are *you* apologising?'

Molly dropped her shoulders. 'I seem to have made your life even more complicated.'

'Yes, well, it's not as if it's going to be that way for ever,' he said, making a business of shuffling the papers on his desk.

'You can come right out and say it, you know,' she said, hurt at how he seemed to have filed her away too, as if she was something temporary he had to deal with. 'You don't have to spare my feelings or anything. I understand this is just a fling between us.'

His expression tightened as his gaze met hers. 'The one thing you can't accuse me of is not being honest with you,' he said. 'This is all I can give you.'

'Fine,' Molly said in a perverse attempt to act all modern and casual about it. 'We'll have our fling and once it's time for me to leave, I'll just kiss you goodbye and get on with my life and you'll get on with yours. Does that sound like a plan?'

His jaw worked for a moment. 'As long as we both know where we stand.'

'But of course,' she said. 'If anyone asks, I'll just say we're housemates with benefits. How does that sound?'

His forehead was deeply grooved with a brooding

frown. 'Couldn't you think of a better way to put it than that?' he asked.

'Get with the times, Lucas,' Molly said as she gave him a cheery fingertip wave from the door.

Lucas came back from helping the registrars with a new patient when Jacqui pulled him to one side. 'What's going on between you and Molly Drummond?' she asked.

Here we go, he thought with a roll of his eyes. This would be the first of no doubt many comments he was going to get. 'Why do you ask?' he said.

'Everyone's saying you're a couple now,' she said, her eyes bright with interest. 'Is it true? Are you officially together?'

Lucas was still trying to get his head around Molly's term for their relationship. Call him old-fashioned, but he didn't like the sound of housemates with benefits. It sounded like he was taking advantage of her. He hadn't invited her to stay in his house so he could sleep with her. That had just…happened. OK, well, sure, he'd *wanted* it to happen. He *still* wanted it to happen, but it couldn't happen for ever.

He wasn't a for ever type of guy.

'You know I never discuss my private life at work,' he said as he continued briskly on his way.

Jacqui kept pace with him like a little Chihuahua snapping at his heels. 'Come on, Lucas,' she said. 'What would it hurt to get it out in the open? She's such a sweetheart and it's so cool that you've known each other for years and years. I bet your parents and hers will be thrilled to bits. It's so romantic.'

He threw her a hard look. 'Don't you have work to do?'

'You make such a lovely couple,' she said. 'I bet you'll make gorgeous babies together. Will you invite me to the wedding? I've always wanted to go to Australia. That's where you'll have it, won't you?'

Lucas dismissed her with a look. 'There's not going to be a wedding,' he said, pushing open his office door. 'Excuse me. Some of us around here have work to do.'

Molly was home first and spent some time playing with Mittens before she started cooking dinner. She wondered if she was doing the right thing in setting candles and flowers on the table, but she just couldn't get her head around being *that* casual about things. Somehow waiting naked in bed for him wasn't quite her. She wanted to read his mood first, see what sort of day he'd had. Help him relax and put work stresses aside. She wanted to show she cared about him as a person, not just as someone she was having a fling with. She put on some romantic music on the sophisticated sound system that was wired through the house and opened a bottle of wine she had bought on the way home.

Glancing at her watch a couple of times, she wondered when Lucas would be home. She hadn't seen him since their conversation in his office. She had been busy with a new admission and he had been called to a meeting with the family of an elderly patient who wasn't expected to make it through the night.

He came in just after nine p.m. Molly got off the sofa in the sitting room where she had been whiling away the time with a glass of wine and met him in the foyer. 'Hard day?' she asked when she saw his heavy frown.

'You could say that,' he said, shrugging off his coat.

'I made dinner for you,' she said.

His frown deepened as he hung up his coat. 'You shouldn't have bothered.'

'It was no bother,' Molly said. 'I love cooking. I set up the dining room. It looks fabulous.'

He turned from the coat stand, his frown even darker on his brow. 'What for?' he asked.

'Because it's a beautiful room that's just crying out to be used,' she said. 'What's your problem? You won't eat out. I thought this would be the next best thing. Kind of like a date at home.'

He moved past her on his way to the stairs. 'I'm not hungry.'

Molly felt her spirits plummet. 'What's wrong?' she asked. 'Have I upset you?'

His hands gripped the balustrade so tightly his knuckles whitened beneath the skin. 'Why would you think that?' he asked.

She folded her lips together, feeling horribly uncertain and unsophisticated. 'I was so looking forward to you coming home,' she said. 'I thought you would be looking forward to it, too. I guess I was wrong. You'd obviously rather be alone.' She swung away to the kitchen, determined not to cry.

'Molly.'

'It's all right, I quite understand,' she said, turning back to face him. 'We obviously have different expectations about how this is going to work. I'm afraid I haven't read the latest edition of the *Having A Fling* handbook. Maybe you could give me a few tips. Clearly soft music and candles are out. Perhaps I should've just draped myself over your bed instead.'

He shoved a hand through his hair and blew out a weary sigh. 'I'm sorry,' he said. 'I'm in a rotten mood. It's wrong to take it out on you. Forgive me?'

Molly gave him a huffy look.

'Come here,' he commanded gently but firmly.

She angled her body slightly away from him, her chin up and her arms across her middle. 'I'm not that much of a pushover, you know.'

He moved to where she was standing and gently un-peeled her arms from around her body and gathered her close against him. 'I'm sorry for being a such a bear,' he said. 'I've got a lot on my mind just now. I'm used to coming home and being alone with my thoughts.'

Molly looked up at him with a little pleat of worry on her brow. 'Do you want me to move out?'

He smoothed her frown away with the pad of his thumb. 'That's the very last thing I want you to do,' he said. 'The house feels different with you here. It's warmer, more like a home.'

'I should've checked with you first about dinner,' she said as she toyed with one of the buttons on his shirt. 'I didn't think...I'm sorry.'

'It's fine, Molly,' he said. 'Really.'

'I know it's been awkward for you today with every-one talking about us...'

'They'll stop in a day or two when they realise it's business as usual,' he said. 'I'm usually pretty good at ignoring that sort of thing.'

Molly looked up at him again. 'Are you really not hungry?' she asked.

His eyes smouldered as they held hers. 'My appetite is being stimulated as we speak.'

'I hope I've prepared enough to satisfy you,' she said with a little smile.

He scooped her up in his arms. 'Let's go and find out, shall we?'

CHAPTER NINE

LUCAS WOKE FROM a deep sleep to answer what he thought was his phone. He reached across Molly, who was still soundly asleep, and picked up the phone from the bedside table. 'Lucas Banning,' he said.

There was a shocked gasp and then silence from the other end.

Molly shifted sleepily against him. 'Who is it?' she asked.

He handed her the phone. 'I think it's for you,' he said. 'I thought it was my phone. Sorry.'

She sat up and pushed the tousled hair out of her eyes. 'Hello?'

Lucas heard Molly's mother on the other end. 'I think I called you at a bad time. Do you want me to call back when you're alone?'

Molly glanced at Lucas. 'No, it's fine, Mum… Um, how are you?'

Lucas got off the bed and went to the bathroom to give her some privacy. When he came out again she had hung up was sitting on the edge of the bed with a strained look on her face. 'That was my mother,' she said.

'So I gathered.'

'She was a bit shocked that you answered my phone.'

'I gathered that, too,' he said.

She nibbled at her bottom lip for a moment. 'It's not that she doesn't approve of me getting involved with you...'

'You don't have to pull your punches, Molly,' he said. 'I realise I'm not her top pick as a partner for you.'

'She'll be fine about it once she gets her head around it,' she said. 'It was a shock to find out like that, that's all. I should've called her and told her.'

'I guess it'll be your father calling you next to tear strips off you,' Lucas said, snatching up his trousers and shaking out the creases before he put them on.

She got off the bed and came over and put her arms around his waist. 'I can handle my father,' she said. '*We* are the only people in this relationship. It's got nothing to do with anyone else. Not at work or back at home in Australia. This is about us, here and now.'

Lucas let out a long exhalation and gathered her close. The here and the now wasn't his greatest worry. It was what happened next that had him lying awake at night. Within a few weeks she would be heading home. He couldn't ask her to stay with him, to give up her life back home, all her friends and family, all that was familiar and dear to her. How could he ask it of her? He could more or less cope with the parental opposition but he couldn't cope with hurting her by not being good enough for her. How could he ever be good enough when he had caused her more hurt than anyone?

He kissed the top of her head and put her from him. 'I have to get moving,' he said. 'I have a couple of meetings this morning and another one after work. I'm not sure what time I'll be home.'

'I thought I'd touch base with Emma Wingfield about the fundraising dinner,' she said. 'Would you be agreeable to having it here? It would cut down the costs of hiring a venue. I understand if you don't want to. I know it's a lot to ask.'

Lucas saw the little spark of enthusiasm in her eyes. What would it hurt to let her go to town with the dinner? It would be something to look back on once she had gone. 'Sure,' he said. 'Why not? Let me know what you need. I'll get Gina to give you a hand.'

She stood up on tiptoe and kissed him on the lips. 'Thank you,' she said. 'I'll make sure it's a night to remember.'

Molly hadn't long got home from work that evening when her father called.

'What the hell do you think you're doing?' he said without preamble.

'Hi, Dad,' she said. 'I'm fine, and you?'

'Of all the people in London you could hook up with,' he went on, 'why him? I had to drag it out of your mother. She wasn't going to tell me but I knew something was up as soon as I spoke to her. When were you going to tell me you're sleeping with the enemy?'

Molly rolled her eyes. 'I'm not going to discuss my love life with you, Dad. Lucas and I are seeing each other and that's all I'm prepared to say.'

'He'll break your heart,' he said. 'You just see. It's what he does best. He'll use you and then walk away. He just wants his conscience eased. I reckon he thinks a little fling with you will fool everyone into thinking we've all moved on. But I'll never forgive him. Do you hear me? I will not allow that man to come within a bull's roar of me or any of my family.'

'How is your new family?' Molly asked.

'Don't use that tone with me, young lady,' her father said. 'I'm telling you right now, if you continue to see him I will never speak to you again. Do you hear me? It's him or me. Make your choice.'

'Dad, you're being ridiculous,' she said. 'Isn't it time to move on? Matt would be appalled by your attitude. You know he would.'

'I mean it, Molly. I'll disown you. You see if I won't.'

Molly fought to contain her temper. There was so much she wanted to throw at her father. All the times he had let her and her mother down. All the times he had criticised her for not being as good as Matt at things. All the times she had felt unloved and undervalued by him. It bubbled up inside her like a cauldron of caustic soda. 'You know, that's exactly the sort of thing I've come to expect from you,' she said. 'When things don't go your way, you have a tantrum or throw in the towel, just like you did with Mum. I'm not giving up Lucas just to appease you. If you want to disown me then go right ahead. It's your choice.'

'You're the one making the choice,' her father said. 'Once I hang up this phone, that's it. I won't be calling again, not unless I hear you've ended things with Lucas Banning.'

The line went dead.

Molly pressed the off button on her phone just as the front door opened and Lucas stepped in.

His brows moved together. 'Your father?'

'Yes,' she said with a little slump of her shoulders.

He came over and put a gentle hand on the nape of her neck. 'Hey.'

Molly looked up at him through moist eyes. 'I've never been able to please him,' she said. 'It wouldn't matter who I was seeing, he wouldn't approve. He doesn't love me, not like a father should love his daughter. If he loved me he'd be happy for me.'

He drew her close against his chest, his hand rhythmically stroking her head where it rested against him. 'He does love you, Molly,' he said. 'He's just afraid to lose you. It colours everything he does. I would be the same in his place.'

She gave a heavy sigh and began to fiddle with his loosened tie with her fingers. 'I thought you weren't coming home early,' she said.

'We got through the agenda of the meeting in record time,' he said. 'I thought we could go out to dinner.'

She blinked at him in surprise. 'Dinner? As in out somewhere? In a restaurant? In public?'

He gave her a rueful half-smile. 'I really am dreadfully out of practice, aren't I?' he said. 'Yes, out in public in a fancy restaurant.'

Molly smiled as she flung her arms around his neck. 'I would love to.'

Lucas was putting on his jacket at the foot of the staircase when Molly came down half an hour later. Her perfume preceded her—a fresh, flowery fragrance with a hint of something exotic underneath. He turned to look at her, his mouth almost dropping open when he took in her appearance. She was classy and sexy, modern and yet conservative, sweet and sultry. Her mid-thigh-length black velvet dress clung to her figure like a glove. Her high heels showcased her racehorse-slim ankles and calves, and she had styled her hair in a teased messy ponytail at the back of her head, giving her a wild-child look. Her lips were shiny with lip gloss, her eyes smoky with eye shadow and eyeliner.

It was a knockout combination and he wondered how she had managed to get to the age of twenty-seven without some guy snapping her up and carting her off to be his wife and the mother of his children.

He tried to ignore the pang he felt at the thought of her ripe with someone else's child. He didn't want to think about another man taking her in his arms and making love to her. He didn't want to imagine another man's mouth pressed against those soft, sweet lips.

He wanted her to himself, but how could he have her with the past like a stain lying between them? It would always be there. It would seep into and discolour every aspect of their lives. If they married and had children, he would one day have to explain to them what had happened to their uncle. How would any child look at its father knowing he was responsible for the death of another human being? There had been a time when he had envisaged himself with a family similar to the one he had grown up in. He'd had great role models in his parents. They were strict but fair, loving and supportive, committed to their children and to each other. He had seen them weather some of life's toughest dramas and yet they had never faltered in their devotion to each other and their boys. He had assumed he would have a similar relationship but, of course, that's not how things had panned out.

It was different now.

It had to be.

'You look beautiful,' Lucas said.

Her eyes shone as they met his. 'You look pretty hot yourself.'

He tucked her arm underneath his. 'Shall we go?'

The restaurant Lucas had booked was a fifteen-minute drive from his house. He barely spoke on the journey, other than to point out places of interest like a jaded tour guide.

Molly glanced at him surreptitiously from time to time, but each time she looked at him his brow was lined with a frown as if he was chewing over something mentally taxing. Was he regretting issuing his invitation to have dinner? All her insecurities came out to play. Maybe he was having second thoughts about their involvement.

After all, she had been the one who had made the first move when she had found him sleeping in the library the other night. If it hadn't been for her bending down to kiss him they might not have become involved at all. They might still be just housemates, two ships passing in the night as they went about their busy working lives. Did he regret their involvement? Did he want to put a time limit on it?

What was going to happen when it was time for her to leave? Would he sever the connection or expect her to? They had by tacit agreement avoided mentioning the future. But it was still something that lurked in the background. Molly could even sense the ticking clock on their relationship. She had been here almost three weeks. That left only nine to go. Each day was another day closer to the time she would be leaving. Would he ask her to stay? Or would he be relieved when she got on that plane back to Australia?

'Are you OK?' Molly asked after a long stretch of silence.

He glanced at her distractedly. 'Pardon?'

'You seem a bit preoccupied. You've hardly said a word since you pointed out the Houses of Parliament.'

He reached out and took her hand and brought it up to his mouth and kissed it. 'Sorry,' he said. 'I have a lot on my mind just now. Work stuff. Brian Yates had got a bit behind with some paperwork. It's a nightmare sorting it all out.'

'When was the last time you took a holiday?' she asked.

'I went to a conference in Manchester three months ago.'

She looked at him askance. 'The one where you had the one-night stand?'

His expression tightened. 'Yes.'

'That's hardly what I'd call a holiday,' Molly said. 'I meant a proper holiday. Lying on the beach somewhere, drinking cocktails. That sort of thing.'

He lifted one shoulder. 'I'm not big on cocktails. And I've seen enough people dying with melanomas to put me off lying in the sun for life.'

'All the same, you can't expect to work all the time without a break,' she said. 'It's not good for your health.

People in their early thirties can still get heart attacks, you know.'

'I know,' he said. 'That's why I go to the gym. I go to a twenty-four-hour one a couple of blocks from home. I have a couple of guest passes if you want to try it out some time.'

'I'm not much of a gym bunny,' Molly confessed. 'I prefer long walks in the fresh air.'

'Fair enough,' he said.

Lucas parked the car and came around to open her door. Molly loved it that he had those old-fashioned good manners. He had been brought up to treat women with respect and consideration. She felt feminine and protected as he helped her out of the car with a light hand at her elbow.

Once inside the restaurant they were shown to a cosy table in a candlelit corner. Soft ambient music was playing, making the atmosphere romantic and intimate. 'Have you been here before?' she asked once the waiter had left them to study the menu.

'Not for a long time,' Lucas said. 'I think it's changed hands a couple of times since then but it got a good write-up recently.'

The waiter took their order and left them with their drinks. Molly was conscious of the silence stretching between them. 'I had the meeting with Emma today,' she said. 'She was really excited about the dinner dance at your house. We've marked a tentative date for the first Saturday in May. We're thinking about fifty or sixty couples. The more exclusive it is the better. People don't mind paying top dollar for something that's really special.'

'Sounds like a good plan.'

'And we also thought we might have a theme,' she said.

He gave her a forbidding look. 'Don't ask me to dress up in a ridiculous costume.'

Molly gave him a teasing smile. 'Where's your sense of fun?' she asked. 'I think you'd look fabulous in a Superman costume.'

'No way,' he said, glowering at her. 'Don't even think about it. It's not going to happen.'

'It's all right,' she said, still smiling at him. 'We thought we'd have a black and white theme. Everyone has to wear either black or white or both. We'll decorate the ballroom the same. It'll be very glam.'

'I think I can manage to rustle up a tuxedo,' he said. 'But I should warn you I'm not much of a dancer. I have two left feet.'

'I can help you with that,' she said. 'Mum sent me to debutante school. It won't take me long to teach you to burn up the dance floor.'

He gave a noncommittal grunt as the waiter came over with their meals.

It was raining when they came out of the restaurant. Lucas took off his jacket and used it like an umbrella over Molly. 'Aren't you freezing?' she asked as they made a dash for the car.

'I'm used to it,' he said. 'Mind your step. The pavement's uneven in places.'

It was a quiet drive home but Molly thought Lucas had lost some of his earlier tension. He had started to relax a little after the entrée and had even smiled at one of her work anecdotes. For a while she had felt like they were any other couple having a meal out together. But every now and again she would look across at him and find him with a frown between his eyes.

'I enjoyed tonight,' she said as they walked into the house a short time later.

'I did too,' he said.

'Our first date.'

'Pardon?'

Molly looked at him. 'That was our first proper date.'

'So how did it measure up?' he asked.

'I don't know,' she said. 'It's not over yet.'

A half-smile lurked around the edges of his mouth. 'You seem pretty sure about that.'

She stepped up to him and placed her arms around his neck. 'I want to dance with you.'

'Right now?'

She pushed his thigh back with one of hers. 'Right now.'

A gleam came into his eyes as he started to move with her along the floor. 'I think I could get used to this dancing thing,' he said. 'How am I doing?'

She smiled as he brought her up close to his aroused body. 'You're a natural. You have all the right moves.'

He stopped dancing, his eyes burning as they held hers. 'I want to make love with you. Now.'

Molly shivered as he gripped her hips and held her harder against him. 'Right now?' she asked.

'Right now.'

He swooped down and captured her mouth beneath his in a sizzling hot kiss, his tongue driving through to find hers in a sexy lust-driven tango. Molly felt her senses career out of control as his aroused body probed the softness of hers. Desire was hot and wet between her thighs as he moved her backwards along the foyer in a blind dance of passion until her back was against the wall.

Her hands went to his shirt, tugging and pulling until it was out of his trousers and unbuttoned. She slid her hands all over his chest, caressing, stroking until she came to the fastener on his waistband. She worked on it blindly as his mouth masterfully commandeered hers. Electricity pulsed like a powerful current through her body as his hands shaped her breasts through her clothes. Her nipples felt achingly tight, her breasts full and sensitive.

Her insides quivered as he deepened his kiss, his tongue stabbing and stroking, thrusting and gliding until she was mindless with need. She could feel it building in her body. All the sensitive nerves stretching and straining to reach the pinnacle of pleasure she craved. It was centred low and deep in her body, the feminine core of her alive and aching for the intimate invasion of his body.

Finally she freed him from his trousers. He was thick and full and like satin wrapped steel in her fingers. She caressed him with increasing pressure and speed, delighting in the low deep grunts of approval he was giving. Spurred on by his reaction, she dropped to her knees in front of him and brought him to her mouth.

He gripped the sides of her head. 'No, you don't have to do that,' he said.

'I want to do it,' Molly said. 'I want to taste you like you tasted me.'

He gave a muttered curse as she closed her lips over him. She felt him shudder against the walls of her mouth as he fought to control his response. It thrilled her to have such feminine power over him. He was so thick and so strong and yet he was at the mercy of her touch.

After a few moments he pulled out with a gasping groan. 'No more.' He hauled her to her feet and roughly pulled up her dress until it was bunched around her waist.

She clung to him with one hand as the other peeled away her tights and knickers. Excitement raced along the network of her veins like rocket fuel. She was breathless with it, impatient with it, hungry for every deliciously erotic thing he had in store.

He positioned her against the wall and thrust into her with a deep primal groan that lifted every hair on her head. Her sensitised flesh gripped him tightly, drawing him in, holding him, squeezing him, tormenting him. He rocked against her almost savagely. She held onto his hips, with him all the way, wanting more speed, more pressure, more of that tantalising friction. She was getting closer and closer to the point of no return. She could feel every nerve preparing itself for the free-fall into paradise.

And then she was there, falling, spinning, falling, spinning, delicious contraction after delicious contraction moving like an earthquake through her flesh. She gasped and cried as her body shook and shuddered against his, her hands digging into his taut buttocks as he finally emptied himself.

Molly held him tightly against her as her breathing calmed. She could feel the stickiness of his essence between her legs. It was so incredibly intimate to be that close to him. She had never felt so close to someone.

It was not just the physical experience. There was something much deeper and elemental in how she responded to him and he to her. It was like they were meant to be together—two halves that made a complete whole. She felt a connection with him that went beyond their similar upbringings. It was as if he was the only person who could love her the way she wanted and needed to be loved—with his whole being, his body, his mind and his soul. What woman didn't want a love like that?

Molly knew he was capable of that sort of love. What she didn't know was if he would allow himself to be free of the past in order to act on it.

Lucas brushed her hair away from her face, his eyes dark and serious now the passion had abated. 'I wasn't too rough with you, was I?' he asked.

Molly was touched that he was concerned. 'You were amazing,' she said, looking up at him. '*We* are amazing together. I never thought it could be this good. It keeps getting better and better.'

He tucked some of her hair behind one of her ears, his gaze becoming shadowed, his expression twisted with ruefulness. 'We are amazing together...'

'But,' she said. 'That's what you were going to say, wasn't it? There's always a but with you, isn't there?'

A mask slipped over his features. He drew in a breath and slowly released it. 'Molly...'

'There doesn't have to be a but,' Molly said. 'We can be amazing together for always. You know we can.'

He put his hands on her wrists and unlocked her

hold from around his neck. 'We've already talked about this,' he said. 'I told you what I can give you. There's no point going over it all the time in the hope that I'll somehow change my mind. This is the way it is. You have to accept it.'

Molly blinked back burning tears, her chest feeling as if hard fists were pummelling against her heart. 'Are you really going to just end our relationship when it's time for me to leave?' she asked. 'Have you already circled the calendar or marked it your diary? Have you've written, "*Finish things with Molly*"?'

His features were pulled tight. 'Think about it, Molly,' he said. 'You'd gain me but you'd lose your family. Your father will cut you off. He's probably already threatened to do so. Yes, I thought so. Your mother will make an effort but every time she sees me she'll think of the son she lost. And then, if we were ever to have children…' His throat rose and fell and his voice came out hoarse as he continued, 'What will you tell them when they ask about their uncle? Will you tell them their father *killed* him?'

Molly swallowed the knot of anguish clogging her throat. How could she get him to change his mind? Could they have a chance in spite of everything that had happened? Surely other people overcame tragic circumstances. Why couldn't they? Was it because he didn't love her? He hadn't said anything, but, then, neither had she. He didn't seem the type to be saying 'I love you' at the drop of a hat. But, then, she had never told anyone other than her parents that she loved them. But she sensed that Lucas cared very deeply for her. He showed it in so many little ways.

Was that why he refused to promise her a future? He wanted her to be free to move on from the tragedy of the past and he believed she couldn't do that if she was with him. He was determined their relationship had a strict time limit.

Molly suddenly realised what it must be like for couples during times of war and separation. Of having to live in the moment, of not being sure of what the future would hold, clinging to one another, grateful for every tiny chance to be together. Not making plans but living and loving while they could. It was the same for long-term married couples or even younger couples where one partner was facing the imminent death of the other due to a terminal illness. She had seen them time and time again in ICU. The clock ticking down, each moment more and more precious as it could very well be the last.

How did people do it? How would *she* do it? She wanted fifty, sixty, seventy years—a lifetime to love Lucas, not just a matter of weeks.

Molly couldn't think of a time when she hadn't loved him. When she had been a little kid she had loved him, but that had been more of a hero-worship thing. He had been her older brother's best friend, someone she'd admired from afar. He had always treated her well. He had been far kinder to her than her own brother. Growing up without sisters had made him particularly mindful of the feelings and sensibilities of little girls. He had always treated her with respect and, to some degree, affectionate indulgence. How could she not fall in love with him as an adult? He was the same kind, gentle man—a man who gave up so much of his life for others. Matt's death hadn't caused that other focused part of his personality, rather it had just enhanced it.

But loving Lucas came with a hefty price tag. Her father had already made it clear that he wanted nothing more to do with her if she continued to be involved with Lucas. After the initial shock her mother seemed more accepting, but how long before she too worried that Molly was being short-changed emotionally? No mother wanted to see her daughter with a man who wasn't capable of loving her.

And then there was the issue of children. She wanted a family. She had wanted to be a mother since she had been a little kid. She had nursed every baby animal she had been able to get her hands on, adopting every stray she could in her effort to nurture them.

Lucas was the only man she could imagine as the father of her children. She wanted to feel his baby moving inside her womb. She wanted to feel the march of the contractions through her abdomen that would bring their baby into the world and she wanted to see his face as she gave birth. She wanted to see him hold their baby in his strong arms, to cradle it against his broad chest, to protect and love it as tenderly as he had been loved and nurtured.

But now all those hopes and dreams she had stored in her heart for all this time would never be realised. It was so bitter-sweet to know he loved her but was prepared to give her up because he felt that was best for her.

He was wrong.

He *had* to be wrong.

She would be miserable without him. She would be heartbroken without him in her life. She would be totally devastated to have loved and lost him. She wanted him to live life with her, to share the highs and lows and all the little bits in between: the happy bits; the sad bits; the angry bits; and the funny bits—all the things that enriched a couple's life together.

Surely he would see that eventually? It might take more than the nine weeks left, but surely he would come to realise that it was better to be together than apart? How could she *make* him see it? Would she have to take a gamble on it? To spend the next few weeks in the hope that he would not be able let her go at the end?

Molly looked up at him through misty eyes. 'Can we not talk about this any more?' she said. 'I just want to pretend we are just like any other couple in a new relationship. Can we do that, please?'

He brushed her quivering bottom lip with the pad of his thumb. 'Of course,' he said, and bending his head he softly covered her mouth with his.

CHAPTER TEN

MOLLY WAS AT work a few days later, supervising Claire Mitchell's transfer to the rehabilitation unit. Claire was not fully mobile but she was completely conscious and responding to commands. Her tracheotomy tube had been removed and the hole taped closed, but it would take up to two weeks for the wound to heal over completely. Claire could speak in a whisper but her words were still slurred and a little jumbled and she still had some short-term memory problems. Her parents were relieved but clearly a little daunted at the long road ahead for their only child.

Claire would probably spend months in the rehab centre and was unlikely to regain the full use of her legs. It was a heartbreaking thought that a young woman who had been so fit and athletic, who before the accident had been at the top of her game in equestrian events, was now no longer able to take even a few paces, let alone vault up into a saddle and ride her beloved horse.

Jacqui walked back with Molly to the ICU office once the orderly had left with Claire and her parents. 'For a while there I thought that poor girl wasn't going to make it at all,' she said. 'You should have seen her when she first came in. A bit like our Tim, poor chap.

You just never know how they're going to end up, do you?'

'No, you don't.' Molly glanced to where Tim's parents were by his bedside in ICU, keeping their lonely vigil. They came in each day, spending hours in his cubicle, talking to him, playing his favourite music on an MP3 player, stroking him and praying over him with the hospital chaplain.

Lucas was still treating him hour by hour, stubbornly refusing to give up hope of a recovery. The CSF leak had stopped once they'd got control of the infection, and while a subsequent scan had shown a little brain activity, it was still not as positive as everyone had hoped.

Hamish Fisher had been in just about every day. Molly had watched on one of his first visits as Lucas had taken him aside and talked to him in his quiet, supportive way. It had been particularly moving to see Tim's parents hug Hamish by their son's bedside. There were lots of tears but no harsh words or accusations— so different from her father, who after all this time was still so antagonistic towards Lucas.

'Lucas still thinks there's a chance with Tim Merrick,' Jacqui said, following the line of Molly's gaze. 'He's getting a bit of flak from some of his colleagues, though.'

'Yes, I know,' Molly said, thinking of some of the angry exchanges she'd either witnessed or heard when Lucas had been on the phone. Lucas had given Tim mannitol a couple of times to reduce brain swelling and he had stopped the steroids. This was considered controversial by some as high-dose steroids were commonly used to reduce brain swelling, with mannitol generally only used in the acute situation, straight after the occurrence of an injury. But Lucas was concerned the steroids might suppress Tim's resistance to infection so he had stopped them and closely monitored intracranial pressure.

'So how are things going between you two?' Jacqui asked with a twinkling look. 'Lucas won't tell me a thing, damn him.'

'Things are fine,' Molly answered evasively. She didn't want to talk about her relationship with Lucas. It was precious and private. Their workplace relationship was friendly but professional. She was careful not to overstep the mark in any way. But there were times when she caught his eye and a secret message would pass between them. She would hum with longing all day until she got home. Sometimes she would barely get in the door before he reached for her. Other times he took his time, torturing her with long drawn-out foreplay that had her begging for mercy.

But not a day went past when she didn't long that they were indeed like any other young couple starting out together, without the past casting its dark shadow over them. Over the last few days she had found herself thinking wistfully of an engagement ring and a wedding gown. She had even wandered past a high street wedding designer on one of her walks. She had stood for long minutes in the freezing cold, wishing she was like the young bride in there with her mother, excitedly trying on gowns. She had turned away with a sinkhole of sadness inside her stomach. How would she ever be a bride if she couldn't be with Lucas? She didn't want anyone else. She couldn't think of being with anyone else. She was wired to love him and only him.

'Have you thought of staying on?' Jacqui asked. 'Your time with us is racing away. It'll be over before you know it.'

Tell me about it, Molly thought with a spasm of pain near her heart. 'I have a job lined up at home,' she said. 'It's at a big city teaching hospital close to where my mother lives. They held the post open for me while I came here. I'd feel bad if I didn't show up. Anyway, isn't the person I'm filling in for over here coming back from maternity leave?'

'Yes, but I thought Lucas, being director, might be able to wangle a position for you,' Jacqui said. 'It reeks of nepotism but who cares about that?'

'I don't think Lucas would do anything that wasn't fair and above board,' Molly said. 'Anyway, I wouldn't want him to.'

'You're good for him,' Jacqui said. 'He still works too damn hard but he seems a lot happier in himself since you've been here. I've been quite worried about him, to tell you the truth. I've never met a more driven doctor. I keep telling him he'll drive himself into an early grave if he doesn't let up a bit. He hasn't taken a holiday in I don't know how long.'

'I've been saying much the same thing,' Molly said.

'Maybe he'll take some time off and visit you back in the home country,' Jacqui said. 'Nothing like absence to make the heart grow fonder.'

Molly stretched her mouth in a brief pretence of a smile. 'Let's hope so.'

'You love him, don't you?' Jacqui's expression was full of mother-hen concern.

Molly sighed as she straightened some notes on the desk. 'I'll get over it.'

'Will you?'

Molly looked at the ward clerk's concerned expression. 'I'll have to, won't I?' she said. 'This is just for here and now.'

'But you want the whole package.' It was a statement, not a question. And it was the truth.

'Don't most women?' Molly asked.

'But he's not talking marriage and babies, is he?' Jacqui said. 'He told me point-blank there wasn't going to be a wedding when I asked him about it the other day. It doesn't make sense. Why wouldn't he want to marry you? He's old school right to his backbone. He's not one of these playboys who want their cake and eat it too. He doesn't say much, but anyone can see he's a family man at heart.'

Molly looked at the stack of papers on the desk again, absently flicking through the top right-hand corners of the pages with a fingertip. 'It's complicated...'

'It's because of your brother, isn't it?' Jacqui said. 'I've been watching him with Tim and that young friend of his Hamish, the one who was driving. That's why Lucas is so hell bent on keeping Tim alive. He was driving when your brother was killed, wasn't he?'

'It was an accident,' Molly said, looking at her again. 'It wasn't his fault. A kangaroo jumped out just as he came around the bend. There was nothing he could do. He didn't see it in time.'

'How sad,' Jacqui said. 'I've always wondered why

he's so hard on himself. He works harder than any other doctor I know. Poor Lucas. And poor you.'

'It was a long time ago,' Molly said. 'I'd prefer it if you kept this to yourself. We're all trying to move on from it.'

'But you haven't moved on from it, or at least Lucas hasn't,' Jacqui said. 'But, then, one doesn't move on from something like that. I guess you just have to learn to live with it.'

'I don't think Lucas sees it quite that way,' Molly said. 'He's punishing himself. He's been punishing himself for the last seventeen years. I hate seeing him do that to himself. Matt wouldn't have wanted him to do that to himself. It's all such a mess and there's nothing I can do to fix it.'

Jacqui gave Molly's arm a gentle squeeze. 'Your job is to love him, not to fix him,' she said. 'The rest is up to fate or destiny.'

If only fate and destiny weren't so damned capricious, Molly thought in despair as she walked back to ICU.

Lucas looked at the most recent scans of Tim Merrick's brain with Harry Clark, one of the more senior neurologists on staff.

'There's some activity but not much,' Harry said. 'I've seen a couple of cases where the patient has recovered after scans like this but it's not the norm.' He turned and looked at Lucas with a grim expression. 'He might not thank you for keeping him alive if he has to spend the rest of his days sitting slumped and drooling in a chair. Nor might his parents if it comes to that.'

Lucas tried to ignore the prickle of apprehension that had been curdling his stomach for days. Claire Mitchell had been moved to the rehab unit, which was a positive outcome considering how bleak things had looked when she had first been admitted. But she was going to have a very different life from the one she had known before. He had seen many patients and their families just like her struggle with what life had dished up.

But he didn't want to see Hamish Fisher go through the living hell he had gone through—*was still* going through. He wanted a miracle. He wanted it so badly, not just for Tim and his devoted parents. He wanted it for Hamish and he wanted it for himself. Tim might not have the life he'd had before, but he would still be alive. That was all that mattered.

'Wouldn't most parents want their kid to stay alive, no matter what?' Lucas asked.

Harry let out a long breath. 'Some do, some don't,' he said. 'I've had parents divided over a child's treatment. We had a case a few years back, a kid with severe epilepsy. He'd had one too many seizures and suffered oxygen deprivation. He was virtually vegetative. The father wanted to withdraw treatment. He was adamant about it. He didn't want to see his kid suffer any more. He'd spent fifteen years watching his boy suffer. The mother... Well, I guess that's what us men will never truly understand—the mother bond. She wanted her boy alive, no matter what state he was in.'

'What happened?'

'The parents divorced,' Harry said. 'The mother looked after that kid on her own for a couple of years and then one night he died in his sleep. I've often wondered if the father regretted not being there, helping her.'

'The kid could have lived for another twenty years,' Lucas pointed out.

'Yes,' Harry said with gravely. 'But would he have wanted to?'

Molly was late getting home after sending off the last of the invitations to the dinner dance. Everyone was getting excited about the event. It was the topic of every conversation at the hospital. The exclusivity element had created a furore, which she and Emma had milked for all it was worth. They had kept twenty-five double tickets back and had put them up for bidding on the hospital website.

The money they were raising was beyond anything they had imagined and it was thrilling to think people were so keen to be involved. Even the caterers had offered their services free of charge, and the string quartet—one of whom was a neurosurgical registrar at the hospital—had also offered to perform without charging a fee.

Molly couldn't wait to tell Lucas. She knew he would be pleased that so much money would be raised for the unit. Hospitals had to work so hard to meet their budgets and there was rarely money left over for any extras. With the money she and Emma were raising, new monitoring equipment could be purchased so patients like Emma would benefit in the future.

Mittens came over to Molly with a plaintive meow as soon as she walked through the front door. She bent down to stroke him and noticed he was wearing a new collar with a tinkling bell attached. 'My, oh, my, don't you look smart?' she said. 'Has Daddy been spoiling you?'

Lucas appeared in the doorway of the sitting room. 'He brought in a bird,' he said with a brooding glower.

'Oh... What type?'

'What does it matter what type?' he asked.

'Well,' she said as she hung up her coat, 'if it was a nightingale or a cuckoo I would probably be a little upset. But if it was a sparrow or a starling I wouldn't be as concerned.'

'We need to talk about what you plan to do with him when you leave,' he said. 'Are you planning to take him with you?'

Molly rolled her lips together for a moment. She could sense Lucas was in a tense mood. She wondered if he too was thinking of how quickly her time with him was passing. He hadn't said anything, but she had sensed the increased urgency in his lovemaking over the last few days. Was he thinking of how much he would miss her when she left? 'I hadn't really thought that far ahead...'

'Then you need to,' he said with a jarring brusqueness. 'I didn't sign up for cat ownership. I said I'd babysit him. I've done that. That's all I'm prepared to do.'

'So you'll kick him out when you kick me out, will you?'

His brows snapped together. 'I'm not kicking you out. You're here for a set time. We've both known that from the outset.'

Molly moved past him with a rolled-eye look. 'Whatever.'

'We've talked about this, Molly,' he said. 'You know the terms. I've never hidden them from you.'

She turned to face him. 'Why are you being so prickly this evening?' she asked. 'I came home all excited to tell you stuff about the dinner and you've done nothing but bite my head off since I walked through the door. Sometimes I think you don't really like having me here. I bet you're secretly counting the days until I leave.'

A long tense moment passed as his gaze tussled with hers. But then he expelled a breath and lifted a hand to rub the back of his neck. 'I'm sorry,' he said. 'I didn't mean to rain on your parade.' He dropped his hand back by his side. 'Tell me about your exciting news.'

Molly wasn't going to be won over that easily. 'You probably won't even find it exciting,' she said with a little pout. 'It's not like you really want a bunch of people—most of whom you won't know—wining and dining and dancing in your precious house. You probably only agreed to it to get me off your back.'

'I'm fine about it,' he said.

She gave him a cynical look.

'OK,' he conceded. 'It's not my idea of a fun night at home. But it's obviously important to you so I'm happy to go along with it.'

Molly gave him a haughty look and went to move up the stairs, but he stopped her with a hand on her wrist. 'Do you mind?' she said. 'I'm going upstairs to have a shower.'

His fingers tightened like a handcuff, and his eyes went dark, *very* dark as they locked on hers. 'Have one with me,' he said.

Molly felt a little shiver roll down her spine like a red-hot firecracker. Sparks of awareness prickled over her skin. Her breasts tightened beneath her clothes. Her legs trembled in anticipation of being thrust apart by his commanding possession. But some little demon of defiance pushed up her chin and ignited her eyes. 'What if I don't want to have one with you?' she said. 'What if I want to be on my own right now and sulk and brood and be in a rotten mood?'

He tugged her against him, thigh to thigh, hard male arousal to soft but insistent female need. 'Then I'll have to think of ways to convince you,' he said, and lowered his mouth to the sensitive skin of her neck.

Molly shivered again as she felt his teeth on her skin. It was a playful bite—the primal tug of an alpha male showing his selected mate that he meant business. She tilted her head as he moved down her neck to her left clavicle, his tongue moving over the tightly stretched skin, licking, laving and teasing. Her breasts tingled behind her bra as she felt his warm breath skate over her décolletage.

Sensual excitement sent her heart rate soaring as he pushed his hands up under her top to cup her breasts. His mouth sucked on the upper curve of her right breast pushed up by his hands. She snatched in a breath as she felt his teeth graze her flesh. He went lower, taking her lace-covered nipple in his mouth and sucking on it. It made her all the more desperate to feel his lips and tongue on her bare flesh.

She moved sinuously against him, rolling her hips against the proud jut of his erection, tantalising him with her body, wanting him to be as desperate for her as she was for him.

And he was.

He growled against her mouth as he finally covered it with his, thrusting his tongue through her parted lips to mate with hers in a heart-stopping tango. His hands worked at her clothes methodically but no less hastily. Molly did the same with his, but perhaps with a little less consideration for buttons and seams.

She had only just got him free of his trousers and underwear when he lowered her to the floor. The Persian rug tickled the skin of her back as she felt his weight come down over her. She gasped as he speared her with his body, a deep, bone-melting thrust that made her insides turn to molten lava. It was a frenzied coupling—rough, urgent, desperate and deliciously exciting. Her nerves shrieked in delight, twitching and tensing, contracting and convulsing as each deep thrust drove into her.

She started to climb to the summit. Up and up she went, her body stretching and stretching to reach that blissful goal. He increased his pace as if he had sensed her need for more friction. And then he brought his fingers into play against the swollen heart of her, tipping her over the edge into a tumultuous sea of mind-blowing sensations.

It went on and on, rolling waves coursing through her, each one sending another cataclysmic reaction through her body. She dug her fingers into his back, her teeth sinking into the skin of his shoulder as the riot of sensations shook and shuddered through her until she was finally spent. Still she hung onto him as he reached his own pinnacle of pleasure. She felt it power through her, an explosive release that had him slump against her once it was over.

Lucas eased himself away and offered her a hand to help her to her feet. 'About that shower,' he said. 'Have I convinced you to share it with me yet?'

Molly gave him a playful smile, her body still tingling from his passionate lovemaking. 'I don't know. What's in it for me?'

His eyes ran over her tousled form, leaving a trail of hot longing in their wake. 'You can't guess?'

Her insides fluttered with excitement. 'You're in a dangerous mood tonight, Dr Banning,' she said.

His mouth tilted upwards in a sexy half-smile, his eyes smouldering like hot coals. 'You'd better believe it, Dr Drummond,' he said, and scooped her up in his arms and carried her upstairs.

Molly was in a dangerous mood herself by the time Lucas had turned on the shower. She stepped into the cubicle with him, pushing against his chest with the flat of her hand until his back was up against the marbled wall of the shower. 'Stay,' she said, giving him a sultry look before she slithered down his body.

He gave a groan as she took him in her mouth. She felt his legs buckle and he thrust out a hand to brace himself as she worked on him. It was the most erotic thing she had ever done. She tasted the essence of him on her tongue as she swirled it over and around the head of his erection. He groaned again and she heard his breathing rate escalate. She felt the tension building in him; she could feel the blood surging through his veins, filling him, extending him to capacity and she drove him on relentlessly.

He tried to pull her away but she refused to budge. She drew on him, again and again, using the moistness of her mouth to lubricate him. She used her tongue again to tantalise him, to tease him, to take that final plunge. She felt the intimate explosion, felt the warm spill of his release, heard the raggedness of his breathing, felt the sag of his limbs as the pleasure flowed through him.

Molly got to her feet and rinsed her mouth under the flowing water before trailing her hands over his chest. 'Good?' she asked.

'Where the hell did you learn to do that?' he asked in a husky rasp.

'Instinct,' she said. 'You bring out the wild woman in me.'

He put his hands on her hips and brought her against him. 'You're incredible,' he said.

She turned in his arms and wiggled her behind against him. 'Scrub my back for me?'

He pumped a handful of shower gel from the dispenser on the wall and smoothed it over her back and shoulders. He used slow, stroking movements, caressing all the way down to the dip in her spine. She shuddered in pleasure as he trailed a finger down the crease of her bottom. She shifted her legs apart to give him better access and shuddered again when he found the swollen, pulsing heart of her. She gasped as he played with her, teasing her, taking her to the brink before backing off.

'Please…' Molly leant her weight against the shower wall in front of her. '*Oh, please…*'

'You like that?' he said as he brushed against her from behind.

She shivered as she felt his erection between her legs, every pore of her skin intensely aware of him. 'Yes, oh, yes,' she said.

He guided himself between her parted thighs, rubbing against her, letting her know he was about to mount her but letting her have full control. The sensation of him entering her from behind was wildly, wickedly erotic. There was a primitive aspect to it as he finally possessed her, his groin flush against her buttocks, his thighs braced around hers as he started thrusting, gently at first but slowly building momentum.

Molly was lost within seconds. She tumbled head-first into a whirlpool of such intense pleasure she was gasping and sobbing with it as it rumbled through her. The tight convulsions of her body triggered his release. She felt him pump himself empty, his hands holding her hips with a tight, almost fiercely possessive hold.

His whole body gave a shiver, and then he slowly turned her round and pushed her wet hair back off her face, his eyes dark and intense as they met hers. 'Still want to be on your own to sulk and brood?' he asked.

Molly put her hands on his chest and raised her mouth for his kiss. 'What do you think?'

CHAPTER ELEVEN

MOLLY DIDN'T KNOW if it was because she was so busy with work and organising the dinner dance that time felt like it was set on fast forward, but suddenly it was the day of the dance and she had only three weeks left of her post at St Patrick's.

She had taken the day before the event off to be at Lucas's house to help Gina with the final clean and polish before the flowers and decorations were delivered. The ballroom looked amazing by the time Saturday evening came around.

When Emma dropped by with the after-dinner chocolates a London chocolatier had donated, she gasped in wonderment when Molly led her in to see her handiwork. 'It's like something out of a fairy-tale,' she said turning around to look at the black and white helium-filled balloons festooned in giant bunches with satin ribbons dangling in curling tails.

'Uh-oh,' Molly said as Mittens made a grab for one of the ribbon tails. She scooped him up out of harm's way and hugged him close to her chest.

'Isn't he adorable?' Emma said, reaching to give him a pat.

'He's a little mischief maker, that's what he is,' Molly said. 'He's been unstoppable since he got his cast off.'

'Are you going to take him back with you to Sydney when you go?' Emma asked.

Molly felt the all too familiar pang seize her at the thought of leaving. She took Mittens to the entrance of the ballroom and closed the door to keep him out before she answered. 'I was hoping Lucas might keep him. But nothing's been decided as yet.'

Emma began to chew at her lower lip with her teeth. 'I was kind of hoping you and Lucas were going to stay together...' She looked at Molly and blushed. 'To be honest, I didn't feel like that at the beginning. I feel embarrassed about it now, but I think I was a bit in love with him myself. I suppose it was more of a crush really. But, then, I think a lot a patients fall in love with their doctors. My mum said she fell in love with her obstetrician, her GP *and* her dentist. I think falling in love with the dentist was taking it a bit far but anyway...'

Molly smiled wryly. 'I've had a few crushes over the years myself.'

'The thing is...' Emma continued. 'Dr Banning needs someone like you. You understand the stress and strain he's under because you experience it yourself. You probably think it's none of my business and I shouldn't be so impertinent to comment on your and his private life, but these last few weeks I feel I've got to know you. You love him, don't you?'

Molly gave her a bitter-sweet smile. 'Of course I do,' she said. 'But sometimes loving someone is not enough.'

'How can it not be enough?' Emma asked. 'Love is supposed to conquer all.'

'Lucas isn't ready to commit to a relationship,' Molly said. 'I can't force him to be ready. He has to do that in his own time.' *If he ever does*, she thought with a crippling pain around her heart.

'But he loves you,' Emma said. 'I know he does. It's so obvious. His eyes light up when you walk into the room. And he actually smiles now. He never used to do that before. It must be love.'

Molly wanted to believe her, but Emma was like a lot of young girls caught up in the romantic fantasy of seeing what she wanted to see.

Did Lucas love her?

She had thought so, but if he truly did why wouldn't he promise her the future with him she wanted so much?

Lucas had planned to help Molly with the preparations for the dinner dance but a new patient had come in with severe pancreatitis. He had been caught up with putting in a central line to the forty-eight-year-old man and managing his treatment. Time had slipped away, which it had a rather frightening habit of doing just lately.

As each day came to a close he felt a sickening feeling assail him. He would lie awake for hours with Molly asleep beside him, wondering how he was going to find the strength to let her go. He had thought about it from every angle but he always came to the same conclusion—she was better off without him.

He was concerned that she hadn't spoken to her father since that phone call when Jack Drummond had issued an ultimatum. He knew how much it distressed her to have to choose between him and her family. He had seen relatives torn apart with guilt when an estranged loved one was suddenly taken ill or, even worse, died without being reunited with their family. He couldn't bear to think of Molly having to live the rest of her life estranged from either one of her parents because of her involvement with him.

Her loyalty to him astounded him. And yet he couldn't quite shake the feeling that he didn't deserve it. He kept telling himself she would be better off with someone who didn't have a road train of baggage dragging behind, but every time he thought of her with someone else he felt like a lead boot was stomping on his chest.

Only that day one of the senior surgeons had playfully elbowed him in the ribs and told him to put a ring on Molly's finger before someone else did. Lucas had shrugged it off with an indifferent smile, but inside he'd been so knotted up he had scarcely been able to breathe.

How would he bear it? He'd already started to torture himself with how it might play out. He imagined how he would hear from one of his brothers that Molly had met some other guy—maybe another doctor—and was setting up a home and family with him. Maybe they would even send him photos of her wedding.

Dear God, how was he supposed to cope with that? His life had been pretty bleak before, but that would be taking it to a whole new level of misery.

He imagined the years passing... Molly would have a couple of kids, a little scrubby-kneed boy just like Matt and a gorgeous little sunny-faced princess like herself.

The children *he* wanted to have with her.

He swallowed against the prickly tide of despair that filled his throat. Why did life have to be so hard, *so cruel*? Hadn't he suffered enough, without life dumping more misery on his shoulders? He wanted to be normal again. How long ago that seemed! He had once been a normal kid with the same dreams and aspirations others had. Then fate had cut him from the herd and set him aside, marking him as different.

There was no chance of a normal life now. It would *never* be normal. He had to make the most of what he had and be grateful he had it, because so many—just like Matt—didn't even get the chance.

By the time Lucas came home from the hospital Molly was about to head upstairs to shower and dress for the dinner. He wished he could have spent the evening on his own with her rather than share her with a hundred or so people, but she was terribly excited about the money she and Emma were raising. He was proud of her. She had such a heart for people and the way she had mentored and supported Emma was a credit to her generous and giving nature.

'Sorry I'm so late,' Lucas said as he bent down to brush her lips with a kiss. 'I would've been back ages ago but I had trouble putting in a central line on my last patient. Anything I can do to help?'

She gave him a smile but he noticed it was a little shaky around the edges. 'No, it's all under control.' She crossed her fingers. 'I think.'

He suddenly realised she was nervous about this evening. 'Hey,' he said, tipping up her face. 'You've done a wonderful job. The house looks amazing. Tonight will be fabulous. Everyone is going to be super-impressed with your ability to put on a party to remember.'

Her grey-blue eyes looked misty all of a sudden. 'Lucas…' She blinked a couple of times and bit her lip and began to turn away. 'Never mind…'

He stalled her with a hand on her arm. 'No, tell me, what's worrying you?' he asked.

She looked up at him with a little frown pleating her forehead. 'I want this to be a wonderful night for you too,' she said. 'I want you to enjoy it, not just to endure it for my sake.'

Lucas cupped her face and looked deep into her gaze. 'If I can have the first and last dance and all the other ones in between with you then I will enjoy every single minute,' he said. 'Is it a deal?'

She smiled a smile that was like a blast of sunshine with just a few clouds floating around the edges. 'It's a deal.'

'Great party, Lucas,' Jacqui Hunter said as she scooped up a glass of fizzing champagne from a passing waiter. 'Your house is amazing. You really are a dark horse, aren't you? I didn't know you were such a DIY expert.'

Lucas gave a loose shrug as he took a sip of his soda water. 'It fills in the time.'

She waggled her brows at him. 'Seems to me you might need to find yourself another big old run-down mansion to spruce up in a few weeks,' she said. 'You could end up with a lot of time on your hands.'

He tried to ignore the jab of pain around his heart. 'Yeah, well, I've been looking around,' he said.

'Find anything?'

'Not much.'

'Didn't think so,' Jacqui said, glancing to where

Molly was smiling up at one of the single anaesthetists. 'A house like this is a once-in-a-lifetime sort of find, don't you think?'

Lucas put his glass down on a side table. 'Excuse me,' he said. 'I think someone's cutting in on my next dance.'

Molly smiled at him he approached. 'I thought you were going to stand me up,' she said. 'Tristan was going to fill in for you.'

Lucas gathered her up close and spun her away from the clot of other dancers. 'Yes, well, he can get to the back of the queue,' he said.

She gave him a teasing look. 'Are you jealous?'

He pretended to glower at her. 'When is this party going to be over?' he asked.

She gave him a crestfallen look. 'You're not enjoying it, are you?'

He tapped her on the end of the nose with his finger. 'I'm enjoying seeing you enjoy yourself,' he said. 'It's a great party, not that I'm any judge. I can't remember the last time I went to one.'

She touched his face with the velvet soft caress of her palm. 'Maybe when it's over we can have a party of our own,' she said.

Lucas turned her out of the way of a rather enthusiastic couple who hadn't quite figured out the timing on the waltz they were doing. 'Sounds like a good plan,' he said. 'Do I need to bring anything?'

She stepped up on tiptoe and brushed his ear with the soft vibration of her lips. 'Just you.'

Molly got the phone call just before coffee was served. She wouldn't have heard her phone at all if it hadn't been for Emma needing a sticky plaster for a blister she'd got while dancing with one of the handsome young residents from the hospital. She took Emma upstairs to the main bathroom and she heard her phone ringing in Lucas's room on her way back.

She told Emma to go on without her, and quickly picked up the phone, with the intention of ignoring the call if it wasn't the hospital or anyone important, but then she saw it was her mother. 'Mum? You're calling at an odd hour,' she said. 'Is everything all right?'

'Oh, darling,' her mother said. 'I have some terrible news.'

Molly felt an icy hand grasp at her heart. 'What's happened?'

'It's your father,' Margaret Drummond said. 'He and Crystal have been in an accident. He's OK apart from a broken ankle but Crystal has a ruptured placenta and—'

'Oh, God,' Molly gasped. 'What about the baby?'

Her mother was trying to talk through sobs. 'They had to do an emergency Caesarean. The baby's in the neonatal unit. They're not sure if he's going to make it. The priest has been in to christen him. Poor Crystal… it's just so awful. I don't know what to do.'

'Is she all right?' Molly asked. 'I mean physically?'

'They had to do a transfusion but, yes, she's out of danger now,' Margaret said. 'Your father is beside himself. Can you come home? I know I shouldn't ask you but I can't bear for you to be away at a time like this. Your father needs you right now. We all need you.'

'Of course I'll come,' Molly said, already rushing to her previous room where her suitcase was stored in one of the built-in wardrobes. 'I'll book a flight tonight. Try not to panic. I'll be there as soon as I can.'

Lucas appeared in the doorway a few minutes later just as Molly had turned on her laptop. 'What are you doing, checking emails now?' he said. 'I thought you promised me the last dance and then a private party?'

She clutched at her face with both hands. 'Oh, Lucas, I have to go home. I have to go right now.'

His brows came together. 'Whatever for?'

'My father and his wife were in an accident,' she said. 'Their baby had to be born via Caesarean, but he's so premature he might not make it. I have to go to help them. I can't be away from them at a time like this.'

'Of course you must go,' he said. 'Here, let me make the flight booking for you. You start packing. Just take the minimum. I'll send the rest of your stuff on later.'

Molly moved away from the computer and quickly changed into a travelling outfit. She started to pack, but she had barely tossed a change of clothes in the bag when she turned and looked at him. 'Please come with me,' she said. 'Take some leave from the hospital and come with me.'

Another frown—deeper this time—appeared between his brows. 'I can't leave.'

'Yes, you can,' Molly said. 'What if you were ill or something? They'd find someone else. I want you to come with me. I *need* you to come with me.'

He got up from the computer. 'I can't come with you, Molly,' he said.

Tears blurred her vision. 'That's because you don't *want* to come with me,' she said. 'You don't want to be with me—period. That's why you jumped at the chance to book my flight. You can't wait until I walk out that door for the very last time, can you?'

He went white with tension. 'That's not true,' he said. 'I'm merely trying to keep calm here. You're upset and not thinking straight.'

'Of course I'm upset!' Molly said. 'My father could've died tonight or tomorrow or whatever time it is there. Oh, God. I'll never forgive myself. I should've called him back. I shouldn't have been so stubborn. Now I might never get to meet my little brother.'

'Darling,' he said, and reached for her but she backed away.

'How can you call me that?' she asked. 'I'm not your darling. I'm just a fill-in, just like I was with Simon.'

'Now you really are talking rubbish,' he said in a steely tone.

'Am I?' she asked, challenging him with her gaze. 'Then come with me. Drop everything and come with me.'

A muscle beat like a maniacal hammer in his jaw. 'I will not be issued with ultimatums,' he said. 'That is no way to conduct a relationship.'

'Is that what we have—a relationship?' she asked. 'What we have is an arrangement. A housemates-with-benefits arrangement.'

'You know it's much more than that,' he said with a brooding look.

Molly gave a scornful snort as she flung another couple of things in her bag. 'Sure it is,' she said. 'That's why my stuff is still in this room instead of in your room with yours. And that's why you're not packing a bag right this minute and coming with me.'

'For God's sake, Molly, we have a hundred people downstairs,' he said through tight lips. 'Do you really expect me to drop everything and fly halfway around the world with less than five minutes' notice?'

Molly tried to see it from his perspective. It was a lot to ask at short notice. It was wrong to expect him to drop everything. She wouldn't like him to ask it of her if the tables were changed.

'You're right,' she said, releasing a breath. 'I'm sorry. I'm just all over the place with this.' She pinched the bridge of her nose, trying to keep her emotions under some semblance of control. 'What about in a few days' time?' She dropped her hand from her face to look at him again. 'Will you come then?'

His frown was heavy and forbidding. 'Molly...'

'What about early next week or the week after?' she asked. 'It will give you time to clear your diary, find a locum or someone to step in for you.' *Please, just say you'll try*, she silently begged.

His eyes moved away from hers. 'It's not that simple, Molly. I have patients, responsibilities. I have people depending on me.'

'But what about me?' Molly asked, trying to hold back tears. 'Aren't I important enough for you to put those responsibilities aside for just a few days to be with me when I need you most?'

He looked back at her again, but his expression was masked. 'Your flight leaves in a couple of hours,' he said. 'I've put you in business class so you can sleep.'

'But I can't afford to fly business class.'

'I've paid it for you.'

'I'll send you the money when I get home,' she said.

'Consider it a gift.'

Molly gave him a cynical look. 'A parting gift, Lucas?'

He thrust his hands in his trouser pockets, his expression still as blank as a brick wall. 'Are you coming back for the rest of your term?' he asked.

Molly closed her bag with a click that sounded like a punctuation mark being typed at the end of a sentence. 'You'll have to find someone else,' she said. 'I'll send you a formal resignation as soon as I get home.'

He gave a businesslike nod. 'Would you like me to drive you to the airport?'

I'd like you to tell me you love me, Molly thought as her heart gave a tight spasm. *I'd like you to tell me you can't bear the thought of me leaving. Tell me you love me. Tell me you can't live without me.* 'No, thank you,' she said. 'It'll be quicker if I just leave. I'm sorry to leave you with Mittens. I'll try and sort something out. I'm not sure what the quarantine arrangements are if I were to ship him home. It might be too stressful for him. Cats are funny like that. Maybe one of the nurses at the hospital will take him.'

'It's fine,' he said. 'He might get confused if he was taken somewhere else. This is his home now.'

'Right…well, I'd best get going, then,' Molly said. 'Will you give my apologies to everyone? I'm sure they'll understand it's an emergency.'

'Of course.' He looked at her then, his eyes dark and unreadable. 'Goodbye, Molly.'

Molly came up to him and going on tiptoe gently placed a soft kiss on his lean cologne-scented jaw. 'Goodbye, Lucas,' she said, and then she turned and walked out the door.

* * *

Lucas closed the front door as the last of the guests left. He looked at the emptiness of his house now that the party was over. It was like a big ship after a luxury cruise had ended or a kid's birthday party room after all the children had gone.

Empty.

Even the decorations looked exhausted. Some of the balloons looked as if they had let out a sigh of disappointment now that everyone had stopped playfully punching them about the dance floor. A black balloon bounced listlessly across the floor towards his foot. He gave it a half-hearted kick and let out a string of curses his mother would have washed his mouth out for when he was a kid.

Mittens came mewing through the house. He had stayed away while the party was in full swing. He gave Lucas a quizzical look and peered around as if looking for Molly.

'She's gone,' Lucas said, bending down to pick him up. He held him against his chest and stroked his velvety head.

'Prrrput?' Mittens said, and head-bumped his hand.

Lucas blinked to clear his vision but still the tears kept coming as if a tap had been turned on somewhere deep inside him. 'You're right,' he said. 'This place sucks without her.'

CHAPTER TWELVE

'YOU'RE *ACTUALLY GOING on leave?*' Jacqui asked, swinging round to face Lucas in the office a week later.

Lucas took off his stethoscope and dropped it on the desk. 'Why are you so surprised?' he asked. 'I'm entitled to some time off, aren't I?'

'Well, yes, of course, but you haven't even taken sick leave in I don't know how long,' she said. 'Where are you going?'

'Nowhere special.'

Jacqui folded her arms as she leaned her hips back against the desk. 'So it's finally happened.'

He shot her a quick sideways look as he straightened the papers on the desk. 'What's finally happened?'

'You're finally ready to go home.'

Was he ready?

No, not really. It was a hurdle he had to face—a bridge to cross. He wasn't sure of his reception on the other side but he couldn't waste another moment worrying about it. He wanted to be where Molly was, tell her how much he loved her, how he couldn't bear the thought of the rest of his life without her in it, making him smile, making him feel loved, making him *live* again.

How had he thought he could survive without her? This past week had been one of the loneliest weeks of his life. Even Mittens had joined him in his misery by moping about as if the sun was never going to come out again.

Molly was his sunshine, his only light in the darkness of what his life had become.

She was his second chance, his *only* chance.

'I have a little favour to ask you,' Lucas said.

'Sure,' Jacqui said, eyes twinkling. 'What is it?'

'Do you know anything about cats?'

'He's beautiful,' Molly said as she looked at little baby Oliver Matthew Drummond lying in the neonatal crib.

Jack Drummond brushed at his eyes with his hand, carefully juggling his crutches to do so. 'Yeah, he is,' he said. 'You were too. You were the prettiest baby in the nursery. I felt so proud. Scared out of my wits, though.'

Molly gave him a quizzical look. 'Scared? Why?'

'There weren't a lot of females about the place while I was growing up,' he said. 'Your gran died when I was twelve. Dad had to do things pretty rough and ready, bringing up four boys on his own. Having a daughter terrified me. I guess that's why I left a lot of it up to your mother. I knew how to handle a son because I'd been one myself and I'd had little brothers to help rear. But a little girl dressed in pink? Well, I guess I didn't always get it right with you, did I?'

Molly was still not ready to forgive him. 'No, you didn't.'

He cleared his throat, looking exactly what he was—a rough-and-tumble country man, out of his depth with showing emotion or even witnessing it in others. 'Thanks for coming, love. I reckon the little tyke held on just so he could meet his big sister. The doctors reckon he's out of danger now.'

'I'm happy for you and Crystal,' she said. 'I really am.'

He cleared his throat again. 'Yeah, well, I wanted to talk to you about things.' He let out a long breath. 'I'm a stubborn old goat. Your mother will tell you that— Crystal too, if it comes to that. I wish I'd handled things differently. Not just with the divorce but just…things…'

'You were wrong about Lucas,' she said, looking at the sleeping baby again. 'You were *so* wrong.'

'I know,' he said. 'I've been wanting to talk to you about that all week.'

Molly turned and looked at him again with tears springing into her eyes. 'I love him, Dad. I'm not going to apologise for it. He's the most wonderful man I've ever met. He's suffered so much for what happened with Matt. It wasn't his fault. You know it wasn't. I can't bear to think of him over there all alone. He just works, that's all he does. He works and works and works. He has no life. I *want* him to have a life. I want a life with him. I know it will be hard for you, but I can't live without him. I don't want to live without him.'

'I never really thought of how it was for him until I saw that car suddenly veer in front of me,' Jack said. 'It must have been like that for him when he rounded that bend and that roo jumped out in front of him. In that split second you don't have time to think. You just react. He was a young, inexperienced driver. He did what any young driver would do. It wasn't his fault.'

'Do you really mean that?' she asked.

He looked at Molly with red-rimmed eyes, his throat moving up and down like a tractor piston. 'It wasn't his fault. I want to tell him that. I know it's seventeen years too late, but I want to call him and tell him that. Do you have his number?'

Molly couldn't control the wobble of her chin. Her eyes were streaming and her throat felt raw with emotion but she thought she had never loved her father more than at that point. 'Of course I have his number,' she said. 'Let's go to the relatives' room so it'll be more private.'

Jack handed back her phone a few minutes later. 'He's not answering,' he said. 'I would've left a message but I'd rather speak to him person to person.'

Molly checked her watch. 'He's probably still at the hospital. He works the most ridiculous hours. I told you he was a workaholic.' She looked up at her father and frowned when she saw his expression. 'What?'

Jack gave a crooked smile. 'I wouldn't want him to come anywhere near my little girl if he wasn't dedicated and responsible. He saves lives, Molly. What could be more important than that?'

Molly blew out a breath. 'I'll try the hospital,' she said, and scrolled down for the number. 'If he's not there then I haven't got a clue where else he would be.'

She hung up the phone half a minute later. 'He's on leave.'

'Where?'

'No one knows,' she said. 'He didn't say but, then, he wouldn't. He never tells anyone anything.'

'I'd better get back to Crystal,' Jack said. 'You'll let me know if you hear from him?'

Molly's shoulders dropped on a sigh. 'Yes, but don't hold your breath.'

Lucas breathed in a lungful of hot air as he walked out of Mascot airport. He couldn't get over the Australian accents surrounding him. Even the airport announcements had sounded exaggerated, as if the person on the loudspeaker was pretending to be an Aussie. He hadn't realised his accent had changed until he'd jumped in a taxi and the guy had asked him if it was his first time visiting the country. His brothers had been ribbing him about it for years but now he realised he was one of those ex-pats who didn't really know where they belonged any more.

He checked through his messages as he headed to the taxi rank. There were dozens from the hospital but that wasn't unusual. It was probably hard for the staff to get it into their heads that he was actually on leave.

There was one message he was particularly thrilled about, however. Tim's latest scan had shown some definite activity and his mother had felt his fingers curl around hers when she spoke to him. It was just the sort of response he had been hoping for. The recovery might be slow but he was hopeful it would be like Emma's.

There was a missed call from Molly's phone but no message. He wasn't sure what to make of that. Maybe she had just wanted to let him know she had got home safely.

He headed straight to the private hospital in the eastern suburbs. He had done a quick phone around to track down Molly and her family. It really helped, being part of the medical profession. One of the guys he'd worked with at St Patrick's was now a neonatal specialist at Sydney Metropolitan. He had given Lucas an update on Molly's little half-brother. The little guy was out of danger now. That was great news but Lucas still wasn't sure how he would be received, turning up in the middle of a family crisis. But he couldn't stay away. He wanted to be with Molly, not just now but always. How could he have thought otherwise? His life without her was like his house without a party or a cruise ship without passengers.

Empty.

It was weird, walking into a hospital from the other side of the counter, so to speak. He was just a visitor here, not one of the top specialists. An officious nurse gave him directions to the neonatal ward. Lucas assumed Molly would be somewhere near her little brother.

And he was right.

He saw her from a way off. She was standing outside the unit, looking in through the glass window.

But she wasn't alone.

Lucas stopped in his tracks. He didn't want to cause a scene in the middle of the neonatal unit. But neither did he want to slink away as if he was scared to stand up to Jack Drummond. But before he could take a step forwards or backwards Jack turned and saw him.

'Lucas?'

Molly swung around and her mouth dropped open. *'Lucas?'*

'Did you call me?' Lucas said. It was the first thing

that came into his head. There were a thousand things
that he should have said instead but it was all he could
think of at the time. It was so good to see her. She
looked gorgeous. Tired, but gorgeous. She was dressed
in tight-fitting jeans and a loose jersey top that had
slipped off one of her shoulders. He wanted to crush
her to him, feel that soft little body against his hard one
and never let her go.

'What are you doing here?' Molly asked.

'I came to see you,' he said. 'To tell you I love you.'

Her eyes widened to the size of dinner plates. 'You
came all that way to tell me that?' she said. 'Why didn't
you tell me the night of the party?'

'I was an idiot that night,' Lucas said. 'I was caught
off guard. I'd worked myself up to you leaving in another three weeks. I wasn't prepared for you to just up
and go like that.'

'Can I say something here?' Jack stepped forward.
'*Dad.*'

'No, let me speak,' Jack said. He turned to Lucas. 'I
was wrong to blame you for Matt's death. I don't expect you to forgive me. I'll never forgive myself. You
were like another son to Margie and me. I can't believe I
treated you the way I did. For all these years I've blamed
you for something that was never your fault.

'I just want you to know that I'm sorry. It's too late to
undo the damage I did to Margie. How she still speaks
to me is testament to the sort of person she is. But I
don't want Molly to suffer any more. She's just like
her mother—loving and generous to a fault. I want her
to be happy. I think you're the only person who can
make her so.'

'Can I have a word with you in private?' Lucas said to Jack. 'There's something I want to ask you.'

Molly put her hands on her hips. 'Excuse me?' she said. 'Hello? Don't I have some say in this?'

Jack grinned from ear to ear as he slapped Lucas on the shoulder. 'She's all yours, mate,' he said. 'She'll drive you nuts and make you tear your hair out at times, but she'll stick with you through thick and thin. She's a good girl. I'm proud of her. I'm proud of you, too. You're a good man. I'll be proud as punch to call you my son-in-law.'

Molly glowered at her father. 'Dad, you're jumping the gun here. He hasn't even asked me.'

'I'm getting to it,' Lucas said with a melting look. 'But you know me, darling, I don't like being rushed.'

Molly felt her heart give a little flip like a pancake, but she still wasn't going to capitulate without a show of spirit. 'You're assuming, of course, that I will say yes?' she said with a pouting, you-hurt-me-and-I'm-not-quite-ready-to-forgive-you look. 'I've been crying myself to sleep for the past week. You didn't even send me a text.'

'I know,' Lucas said. 'I just couldn't say what I wanted to say in a text. I wanted to see you.' He brought her up close, his arms wrapping around her securely. 'Will you marry me, Molly? I want you to be my wife. I want you to be the mother of my babies. I want to spend the rest of my life with you. I want to love you, laugh with you, fight with you, celebrate and commiserate with you. I even want to party with you. I want to live life with you no matter what it dishes up. I just want to be with you.'

'For God's sake, Molly, put the poor man out of his misery,' Jack said.

Molly smiled as she flung her arms around Lucas's neck. 'Yes,' she said. 'Yes, yes, yes, a thousand million squillion times yes.'

Lucas laughed as he swung her around in his arms. It was the first time he had laughed since he'd been a teenager. It felt good. It felt really good.

It felt right.

* * * * *

AN INESCAPABLE
TEMPTATION

SCARLET WILSON

My family are so lucky to have been blessed with three beautiful babies in the last year.

Welcome to the world, Taylor Jennifer Hyndman, Oliver Edward Nyack and Noah Alexander Dickson.

Wishing you lives filled with love, health and happiness.

Scarlet Wilson wrote her first story aged eight and has never stopped. She's worked in the health service for twenty years, trained as a nurse and a health visitor. Scarlet now works in public health and lives on the West Coast of Scotland with her fiancé and their two sons. Writing medical romances and contemporary romances is a dream come true for her.

CHAPTER ONE

'Help!'

Gabriel turned his head, trying to figure out where the cry had come from amongst the bustling bodies at the port side. The Venezia Passegeri was packed—mainly with crew and harbour staff. Carts packed with passengers' luggage and an obscene amount of fresh food were being piled aboard the cruise ship in front of him, all blocking his view.

'Help! Over here. Someone help!'

The cry rippled through the crowd as heads turned and focused towards the shout. It only took Gabriel a few seconds to realise the cry was coming from the edge of the quay. He dropped his bag and pushed his way through the crowd. A woman was standing near the edge, her face pale, her breathing coming in rapid, shallow breaths. Her trembling hand was pointing towards the water.

Gabriel's eyes followed her finger. There, in the water, was a child—a teenager—struggling in the waves that already seemed to have a grip of him. He must have only just fallen in, but this part of the marina was right on the outskirts of Venice, nearest the sea, and the waves were picking him up and down as he coughed and spluttered, pulling him out to sea.

Gabriel didn't even think. He just dived in. Straight into the murky waters of Venice.

By now a few crew members had noticed the commotion and were shouting in rapid Italian. Gabriel swam quickly towards the boy. It only took a few seconds to wish he'd taken the time to remove his shoes and dress uniform jacket. They weighed him down almost instantly. His white uniform would never look the same again.

The boy kept sinking before his eyes, the waves sweeping over his head as he struggled for breath. Gabriel powered forward, anxious to reach him before he disappeared from sight again.

He got there in less than a minute but the boy had sunk under the waves. Gabriel took a deep breath and dived underwater, reaching down into the darkness. It was amazing how the strong Italian sun penetrated so little through the murky waters. Venice was renowned for its dirty canals. The cruise ship terminal was situated on the outskirts near the edge of the Adriatic Sea, where the deep-keeled ships could dock. And although the waters were marginally better here, they still looked nothing like the clear blue seas depicted in the travel brochures. His fingers brushed against something and he tried fruitlessly to grasp it. Nothing.

Frustration swept over him. His face broke the surface of the water and he gasped for air, trying to fill his lungs. Beneath the waves he shucked one foot against the other. It was a move he did every night in the comfort of his penthouse flat while sitting on the sofa, but struggling to stay afloat it was so much more awkward. Finally he felt a release as the five-hundred-euro hand-made leather shoes floated down into the murky depths. Now he would find the boy.

He dived beneath the waves again, reaching out, trying to circle the area beneath him. This time he felt something bump against his hand and he grabbed tightly before kicking his burning legs to the surface. The two of them burst above the waves, the teenager's flailing legs and arms landing a panicked punch on the side of Gabriel's head.

He flinched. His brain switching into gear. The woman at the quayside had shouted in English.

'Stay still,' he hissed at the boy. The sun was temporarily blinding him as the water streamed down his face.

He could see the jetty. Figures shouted towards him but he couldn't hear a word. The current was strong here and he could hardly believe how quickly they'd moved away from the quay.

The glistening hull of the luxury cruise ship seemed so far away. He'd been standing before it only a few minutes earlier.

He put both hands around the boy's chest and pulled him backwards against his own chest, trying to swim for both of them in his version of the classic lifesaving manoeuvre.

But the boy couldn't stop panicking. The waves were fierce, the water still sweeping over the top of them, causing the boy to writhe in Gabriel's arms as he struggled for breath. A shadow loomed behind them.

His arms were aching as he fought to keep their heads above the water. How on earth was he going to get them back to the quay? Again he could hear the boy coughing and spluttering, choking on the waves that kept crashing over their heads.

He'd never done a sea rescue before. Last time he'd seen one he'd been watching TV. It had all looked so much easier then. Didn't the lifeguards on TV always put people on their backs and pull them towards shore? It didn't seem to be working for him. And they had that strange red plastic thing to help them. Where were the lifebelts here? Shouldn't every port have them?

What on earth was he doing? This was madness. Being a cruise ship doctor was supposed to be easy. It wasn't supposed to kill you the first day on the job.

The irony of this wasn't lost on him. He'd known this job was a bad idea right from the start. A cruise ship doctor was hardly the ideal role for a paediatrician.

But family came first.

And this had been the first job he'd been able to find at short notice. Close enough to Venice to be here when needed but far enough away not to attract any unwanted media attention.

His father's health was slowly but surely deteriorating. And the call to the family business—the one he'd never wanted to be part of—was getting louder and louder. Being a fourteen-hour flight away was no longer feasible. Then again, finding a position locally in his specialist field hadn't been feasible, either.

Timing was everything. If he'd applied for a paediatric post six months previously, with his background and experience he could almost have guaranteed his success. But all the desirable posts had been filled and it would be another six months before slots were available again.

This was a compromise. Only the compromise wasn't meant to kill him.

He saw a small boat in the distance. It seemed to be moving very slowly, creeping around the huge hull of the cruise ship as if it was crawling towards them like a tortoise. Every muscle in his body was starting to burn. His arms were like blocks of lead. The figures on the jetty were still shouting towards them and the shadow appeared again.

Gabriel struggled to turn his head as the brick wall loomed above them. All at once the danger became apparent. The sweeping current was taking them straight towards it and with Gabriel's hands caught tightly around the teenager's chest there was no opportunity to lift his hands and protect his head.

So much for being here to support his family.

And then everything went black.

Francesca was bored. Bored witless. Her mother's favourite British expression.

She smiled and nodded as someone walked past, shifting uncomfortably in the dress uniform. This was the one part of her job she hated. All the staff hated it. So much so, they drew straws each time the captain insisted one of the medical staff stand near the check-in desks in the terminal.

Standing in front of a pull-up banner of the *Silver Whisper* was not her idea of fun. The captain thought it made the medical staff look 'accessible'. She was going to have to talk to him about that.

She watched the passengers wandering in and looking in awe at the side view of the ship. As soon as they appeared the crew entertainment staff were all over them, thrusting brochures of trips the cruise ran at every port they stopped at. Francesca sighed and looked at her watch. This was going to be long day.

She glanced over her shoulder. None of the other senior staff were around. Who would notice if she slipped out for a few minutes? A smile danced across her lips. She crossed the terminal building in long strides, slipping out through a side door that took her down to the dock where the ship was moored.

The dock was jammed with suitcases and sweating crewmen struggling to load them on board. Her brain automatically switched into work mode—ticking off in her head who hadn't attended for their required medicals. She was going to have to crack the whip with the crew. Huge delivery crates of food were being wheeled up one of the gangways. It was amazing the amount of fresh food that was loaded at every port.

She wandered along the walkway, nodding greetings at several of the familiar crewmen, relishing the feel of the sun on her skin. Today, as every day, she'd applied sunscreen. But her Mediterranean skin rarely burned and the slightest touch of sun just seemed to enhance her glow.

This was the life. Working on a cruise ship had sounded like a dream at the time and a good sideways move. A chance to use all the skills she'd learned working in Coronary Care and A and E, along with the ability to use her advanced nurse practitioner status, and all in a relatively calm and safe environment.

But the long hours and constant nights on call were starting to wear her down. Thankfully she had a good supportive team to work with. A team that was slowly but surely helping her rebuild her confidence. The ship was a safe place to try and learn to trust her nursing instincts again. She'd once thought those instincts were good, but personal experience had taught her differently. It was time to start over and the ship seemed a good—if a little boring—place to start.

At the end of the day this was only supposed to be a temporary arrangement while she waited for her work visa for Australia to come through. But there had been delay after delay, with two months turning into three and then four. It seemed as if she'd been waiting for ever for the chance to spread her wings and go further afield. A chance to escape the memories of home.

'Nurse! Nurse!'

She turned swiftly towards the shout. It was at the end of the dock where a small crowd was gathered, pointing and looking out towards the sea. Francesca started running towards the shouts—one of the crew had obviously recognised her.

She could feel the adrenaline start to course through her veins. When had been the last time she'd dealt with an emergency? Would she be able to deal with one again? She'd started her staffing in a coronary care unit where cardiac arrests had been a daily occurrence. Then she'd moved to A and E to increase her skills. Expect the unexpected. That's what the sister she'd worked with had told her.

And she'd been right. From toddlers with a variety of household objects stuffed up their noses to RTA victims, she'd never known what would come through the door. Up until now she'd enjoyed the relative calm of the cruise ship. It could be a little mundane at times, dispensing seasickness tablets, dealing with upset stomachs and advising on sunburn. Maybe things were about to liven up?

She reached the edge of the dock and followed the pointing fingers to the two figures in the water. One looked like a child. She felt her stomach sink. The last thing she wanted was an injured child. A motorboat was approaching them and not before time. She winced as she watched the strong waves barrel them both into the port wall. Even though it was hundreds of yards away she could almost hear the crack.

The boat was almost on top of them and she watched

as they dragged the child on board then struggled to reach the man, who had slipped beneath the waves. One crewman jumped into the water to help. Her heart thudded in her chest. Were they going to find him? The child was older than she'd first thought—probably a teenager—but the man?

Yes! They'd found him.

Oh, no. He was dressed from top to toe in white—an officer's uniform—and they were dragging his lifeless body out of the waves.

She started pushing the others aside. 'Let me through.' The boat was heading towards them. She turned to one of the crewmen, 'Go on board to the medical centre. Tell Dr Marsh I need some help. Tell them to bring a trolley and some resus equipment.' The crewman nodded and ran off.

Francesca noticed a woman sobbing near her and elbowed her way through the crowd. 'Are you okay?' she asked.

'My son Ryan. He was running along the walkway and he slipped. I got such a fright.' She gestured around about her. 'I couldn't find anything to throw to him. I couldn't find any lifebelts. And he can barely swim. Only a few lengths in a pool.' She shook her head furiously. 'Never in the sea.'

Francesca nodded, trying to take in all she'd heard. 'Who's the man?' she asked gingerly, dreading the answer she was about to hear.

The woman shook her head again. 'I've no idea. He appeared out of nowhere and dived straight in. Ryan was swept away so quickly, then he disappeared under the waves.' She was starting to sound frantic again. 'That man had to dive a few times before he finally found him.' The woman turned to face Francesca, her voice trembling. 'But

what if he hadn't? What if he hadn't found my son…?'
Her voice drifted off and her legs were starting to shake.

Francesca put a firm arm around her shoulders. 'Just
hold on for a few minutes longer. Your son will probably be
in shock when the boat reaches us. The sun may be shining but the water out there is pretty cold. How old is he?'

'He's thirteen.'

Francesca's brain was rapidly calculating the drugs she
might need for an adolescent. It was always tricky to cal-
culate for kids—everything was generally based on their
weight as children came in all different shapes and sizes.
And from her experience, at a time of emergency the last
thing a parent remembered was their child's weight. It
didn't matter. It was worth a try.

'Do you know how much Ryan weighs?'

The woman shook her head. Just as she'd suspected.
If necessary, she'd have to make an educated guess when
she saw him. Hopefully by then the rest of the team would
have arrived.

Please don't let her have to resuscitate a child. She'd
done it a few times in A and E and had been haunted by
every occasion.

The motorboat was getting closer. Francesca recognised a few crewmen who must have commandeered some
poor unsuspecting local's boat. Fear crept through her. The
teenager was sitting at one side, a blanket flung around his
shoulders, his face pale and water dripping from his hair.
But the officer lay unmoving in the bottom of the boat—
never a good sign. One of the other crewmen was leaning
over him, so she couldn't see clearly what was going on.

The boat bobbed alongside them and she leapt over the
gap to the other craft. She took a few seconds to check
Ryan over. He was conscious, he was breathing and his

pulse was strong. How he looked was another matter entirely. 'Get him onshore and get one of the medical team to assess him,' she instructed, before pushing the others out of her way to get to the man.

She glanced at his face and noted the three gold stripes on his shoulders. Not only an officer—but a senior officer. The uniform was familiar but the face wasn't. Maybe he wasn't one of theirs?

She was on autopilot now, the adrenaline bringing back all the things she'd thought she'd forgotten. She knelt by him, putting her head down next to his, her eyes level with his chest looking for the rise and fall that was distinctly lacking. Her fingers went to the side of his neck, checking for a carotid pulse. Nothing. She tipped his head back and had a quick check of his airway. Clear.

She didn't hesitate. She could do this in her sleep. On some occasions she almost *had* done this in her sleep. Some skills were never forgotten.

She took two deep breaths, forming a tight seal around his mouth with her own, and breathed into him, watching for the rise of his chest. She pulled at the white jacket, ripping down the front, and gold buttons pinged off and scattered around the bottom of the boat, revealing a plain white T-shirt underneath. She wasn't going to waste time trying to remove it. The firm muscles of his chest were clearly outlined and she had all the definition she needed.

She positioned her hands on his chest and started cardiac massage, counting in her head as she went. She was frantically trying to remember everything she could about drowning victims—an area she had little experience in. It seemed almost absurd when she was working on a cruise ship—but most passengers never came into contact with the sea. Didn't they have quite a good chance of survival if they were found quickly enough? She knew that there had been newspaper stories about children with hypothermia being pulled from frozen lakes and resuscitated successfully. But although this man's skin was cold, he wasn't hypothermic. There wasn't going to be any amazing news story here.

She kept going, conscious of voices behind her and shouted instructions. There was a thud as the boat rocked and a pair of black shiny shoes landed next to her. Her heart gave a sigh of relief. David Marsh was here to help her but she didn't stop what she was doing, leaning over and giving two long breaths again.

'Throw me over a defib and a bag and mask,' came the shout next to her.

Francesca kept going, the muscles in her arms straining as she started cardiac massage again. David was more than capable of organising everything around them.

She was counting again in her head. Twenty-two, twenty-three, twenty-four... *Come on.* She willed him to show some sign of recovery.

The handsome Italian features weren't lost on her. The dark brown hair, long eyelashes, strong chin, wide-framed body and muscled limbs. This man could be very impressive—if he was standing up.

David was pulling up the T-shirt that had been underneath his officer's jacket. 'I don't recognise him.' He squinted. 'Who on earth is he?'

She shook her head, 'I have no idea. Somehow I think I would have remembered this one.'

He slapped the pads on the muscular brown chest that Francesca was desperately trying not to notice and turned to switch on the machine. Then, before her eyes, the lean stomach muscles twitched. 'Wait!' she shouted.

She held her breath for a few seconds and then he did it again. Twitched. And then coughed and spluttered everywhere. The Venetian water erupted from his lungs all over the deck around them and she hurried to help him on his side.

The monitor kicked into life, picking up his heart rate. His breathing was laboured and shallow. David read her thoughts and handed her over a cylinder of oxygen with a mask as he slipped a pulse oximeter on the man's finger.

Francesca bent over the man, blocking out the bright sunlight and shading his face from the nosy bystanders. She spoke in a low, calm voice. 'I'm holding an oxygen mask next to your face to help your breathing,' she said, praying he would understand because right now she had no idea if he spoke English. He opened his eyes. They were brown. Deep dark brown.

Wow.

But she must think purely as a professional. She must ignore everything about the Italian hunk they'd just pulled from the water. All the little things that would normally have sent shivers skittering down her spine.

She pulled her penlight from her pocket. This man probably had a head injury. She'd seen him being bounced off the port wall. She lifted his groggy eyelids and shone the light first in one eye and then the other. He gave the smallest flinch.

Pupils equal and reactive. She turned to David. 'We need to start proper neuro obs on this guy.'

He nodded. 'What happened?'

'He went in to rescue the boy. Once he'd got him the current carried them to the port wall and he was knocked unconscious. I think he was under the water for just over a minute.' Her hand reached around to the back of his head.

His dark brown hair was wet but she could feel some abrasions at the back of his head. She pulled her hand back—blood.

'Can you give me something to patch this before we move him, please, David?'

David nodded and handed her some latex gloves and a dressing pad. 'Stretcher will be here in a minute. We'll get him onto the trolley and see if we can find some ID.'

Francesca hadn't lifted her head. He was still groggy. In all the TV shows she'd ever watched, victims of a near-drowning seemed to get up almost as soon as they were revived and walk off down the beach into the sunset. Usually hand in hand with their rescuer.

The thought of walking off into the sunset with this guy was definitely appealing. Like something out a fairy-tale. If only he would come round.

As a child she'd always loved the childhood fairy-tales Cinderella, Rapunzel, Snow White and Little Red Riding Hood. Her father had read them to her over and over again. Those were some of her fondest memories of him.

She leaned in a little closer to the man. If she really wanted to do a set of neurological observations on this guy then she needed to try and elicit some kind of response from him, a response to a painful stimulus.

'Wake up, Sleeping Beauty,' she whispered.

CHAPTER TWO

GABRIEL was in a dark place. Nothing. Nothingness. Then a sharp pain in his chest and the need to be sick. He coughed and spluttered, conscious that he was being pushed on his side but totally unable to assist. His head was thudding. His lungs felt as if they were burning. He heard a little hissing noise and felt a gentle, cool breeze on his face. What was that?

Someone tugged his eye open and shone a bright light at him. How dared they? Couldn't they see he just wanted to sleep? To be left alone for a few moments in this fuzzy place?

He felt a little pinch on his hand. Then another, more insistent.

'Ouch!' He was annoyed, irritated. Then he heard a soft, lilting voice with the strangest accent he'd heard in a while. 'Wake up, Sleeping Beauty. Are you with us?' Warm, soft breath tickled his cheek.

His eyelids flickered open. The sun was too bright.

Someone was trying to block the sunlight out.

Rats. It must be a dream. She was far too pretty for real life.

She was every guy's dream. A real-life modern-day princess. Mediterranean skin and dark eyes with tumbling brown curls. But something in this fairy-tale still wasn't working.

She spoke again. 'There we go, that's better.'

It was that accent. It didn't fit with his Mediterranean dream princess.

It confused him. Made his brain hurt. No—that wasn't his brain, that was his head.

He blinked again. The smell of the Adriatic Sea assaulting his senses. His skin was prickling. All of a sudden he felt uncomfortable. Something wasn't right. He was wet. Not just damp but soaked all over.

In the space of a few seconds the jigsaw puzzle pieces all fell into place. The young boy drowning, his attempt at saving him and the almighty crack to his head. He pushed himself up.

'Whoa, sailor. Take it easy there. You've had a bump on the head.'

'You can say that again,' he mumbled, squinting in the sunlight. 'And it's Doctor, not sailor.'

The princess's face broke into a wide perfect-toothed smile. 'Actually, I'll correct you there. On board, you're a sailor first, doctor second.'

David Marsh leaned forward, clutching some wet credentials in his hand. He held out his other hand. 'Well, this is an interesting way to meet our new boss. Gabriel Russo, I'm Dr David Marsh, your partner in crime. And this...' he nodded towards Francesca '...is Francesca Cruz, one of our nurse practitioners. But as you've just been mouth to mouth with each other, introductions seem a little late.' He signalled to the nearby crewmen. 'We're just going to get you on this stretcher and take you to the medical centre to check you over.'

Francesca felt a chill go down her spine at the name.

She recognised it but couldn't for the life of her think why. She stared at him again. Was he vaguely familiar? She was sure she'd never met him, and with features like those he wasn't the kind of man you'd forget.

Gabriel looked horrified and shook his head, water flying everywhere. 'No stretcher. I'm fine. I can walk.' He pushed his hands on the bottom of the boat and stood up, standing still for a few seconds to make sure his balance was steady.

His eyes found the thick rope securing the small boat to the quay before he stepped over the gap and back to the safety of solid ground. He spun round to face Francesca. 'How's the boy? Is he all right?' But he'd turned too quickly and he swayed.

She caught hold of his arm and gave him a cautious smile. 'He's on his way to the medical centre to be checked out. He was conscious, breathing but distinctly pale when he arrived. Now, how about I get you a wheelchair?'

'I don't do wheelchairs.'

She signalled over his shoulder. 'I can be very bossy when I want to be.'

Dr Marsh cut in, 'I can testify to that. Particularly if you think you're going to get the last chocolate. I should warn you in advance that's criminal activity in the medical centre.'

Gabriel felt pressure at the back of his legs as he thudded down into a wheelchair that had appeared out of thin air. 'I said I don't do chairs,' he growled.

'Let's argue about that later,' said Francesca as she swept the wheelchair along the dock.

The hairs on his arms were standing on end and he started to shiver—an involuntary action—a sign of shock.

A few seconds later a space blanket was placed around his shoulders.

He grudgingly pulled it around him, noting the efficiency of his new staff and the easy rapport and teamwork—all good signs. Within a few seconds his nurse appeared to have walked the hundreds of yards along the dock and was pushing him up the gangway.

This was a nightmare. The worst way possible to meet your new staff. Yet another reason he should never have taken this job.

She seemed to turn automatically to her left, heading toward the service elevators. Gabriel felt mild panic start to build in his chest. Could this day get any worse?

Then she quickly veered off to the right. 'Where are we going?' he growled.

'To the medical centre. We're already on Deck Four so it will only take a couple of minutes.' If she was annoyed by his tone there was no sign.

Gabriel heaved a sigh of relief and settled back in the chair. He'd be fine once he got something for this headache and was out of these wet clothes. Then he could get started.

The chair turned sharply into the modern medical centre. Consulting rooms, treatment rooms, in-patient beds and state-of-the-art diagnostics and emergency equipment. He knew the spec for this place off by heart—it was impressive, even by his exacting standards.

She wheeled him through to one of the rooms and pulled the curtains around the bed, pushing the brake on the wheelchair. She disappeared for a second and came back with a towel and set of scrubs.

Francesca's brain was whirring. Gabriel Russo. Why was that name so familiar? Then it hit her like a ton of bricks falling from the sky. She *had* seen him before. Only last time he'd been wearing a pair of white designer swimming trunks and been perched on the edge of a multi-million-pound yacht, his arm lazily flung around the shoulders of her bikini-clad friend Jill.

The Italian stallion, Jill had called him and that picture had adorned her flatmate's bedside cabinet until one night when a sobbing Jill had phoned Francesca at 3:00 a.m. to come and pick her up.

Francesca would never forget the sight of Jill in her sodden green designer gown, her hair plastered around her face and tears running like rivulets down her cheeks after Gabriel had flung her out of his penthouse flat.

Jill had been broken-hearted over his treatment of her and had taken a good few weeks to get over him—a long time for Jill.

And Francesca had waited a long time, too—to tell this man exactly what she thought of him. He was alive. He was breathing. His heart rate was sound. After a few general observations for head injuries he should be fine. There was a determined edge to her chin; it would be criminal to waste this opportunity. And she had absolutely no intention of doing so.

Something was wrong. Something had changed. He could sense it immediately; the tension in the air was palpable. Right now, all he wanted to do was climb into that pristine white bed, close his eyes and lose this thumping headache.

But the soft side of his Mediterranean princess had vanished and she was staring at him as if he were something she'd just trodden on.

Or maybe he was imagining it? Maybe the resuscitation and head knock had affected him more than he'd thought?

'You're Gabriel Russo.'

Gabriel's pounding head jerked in response to the sharp tone in her voice. He wasn't imagining it. 'I thought we had established that.'

'No, you're Gabriel Russo, *Italian stallion*.' She lifted her fingers in the air, making the quotation mark signs, wrinkled her nose and then continued, 'Stinking love rat. You used to date my friend Jill—until you threw her out of your apartment in London at 3:00 a.m. in the pouring rain.'

'No one's ever called me Italian stallion to my face before.' He felt almost amused. The nickname had been plastered across the press often enough. He wasn't used to being blindsided. Then again, he wasn't used to being resuscitated.

Jill. The name flickered through his brain. He'd certainly dated more than his fair share of beautiful women and he'd worked all over the world. Something fell into place. London. No. Let's hope she wasn't talking about *that* Jill. Just what he needed—a misguided, loyal friend. If his head wasn't thumping so much this could almost be funny. Not only that—Ms Misguided was a knockout. A beautiful work colleague would never be a problem. But an angry, venomous one would be. This was a small team. They had to work together. It could be badly affected by two people who didn't get on.

She wasn't finished. 'But I bet plenty of women have called you a heartbreaker before.'

'Have we met?' His eyes ran up and down her body and she felt a prickle of disgust—he'd almost mirrored her thoughts from earlier. 'I think I'd remember.'

A few minutes before she'd had nice thoughts drifting about her head about their new doctor. She'd thought he was handsome. She'd thought he was fit. She'd even thought... No. She hadn't. She couldn't possibly have.

He frowned. 'Jill? Who was she again? Remind me.'

Francesca felt rage build inside her. Arrogant so-and-so. The palm of her hand itched—she wanted it to come into contact with his perfect cheek.

'Six years ago. London. Blonde model. You took her on your yacht for the weekend.'

'Oh, *that* Jill.' His frown deepened, puckering little lines around his eyes. He turned away, pulling his muddied jacket and T-shirt over his head, and she sensed it was on purpose. She tossed the scrubs and towel onto the bed beside him.

'Yes, *that* Jill.' The volume of her voice increased in proportion to her rage. 'The one you dumped in the middle of the night in the pouring rain outside your flat. What kind of a man does that?'

He whipped around, the muddied jacket and T-shirt clenched in his fists, leaving his wide brown chest right in front of her eyes. The fury in her voice couldn't match the venom in his eyes. 'What kind of a man does that?' he growled.

She gulped. He was half-dressed, his shoulder muscles tense, his bare abdomen rigid. If they were shooting an action movie right now he would be the perfect poster-boy hero.

All of a sudden the room felt much smaller. Maybe it was the six-foot-four presence. All trembling muscle and eyes shooting fireballs in her direction.

She could feel every hair on her body stand on end. And she hated it.

Because amongst the repulsion there was something

else she was feeling—something more—and it went against every principle she had.

She pushed all those thoughts aside. If she ignored them then they weren't actually *there*.

He still hadn't answered. Probably because he was incoherent with rage.

'What are you doing here anyway? Aren't you supposed to be some billionaire-type doctor? You don't actually have to work for a living, do you? Why on earth would you be working on a cruise ship?'

He shook his head, almost imperceptibly. What a surprise. All the usual assumptions, misunderstandings and wrong conclusions. All the things he went to pains to shake off. Normally he wouldn't care what some stranger thought of him. But this stranger was part of his team *and* she was going to have to learn who was boss around here—hardly an ideal start. 'Some things you wouldn't understand.' He leaned against the side of the bed, and could feel the pressure inside his head increase.

'Try me.'

Something flashed across his face. He took a deep breath. 'How well do you know Jill?'

'She is my friend. She was my flatmate in London. We lived together for six months.'

'Six years ago?' There was an edge to his voice—almost as if he couldn't believe someone had been friends with Jill that long.

'Yes. We don't live together any more but we keep in touch.' She scanned her brain, trying to think of the last time she'd heard from Jill—maybe a week or more?

'And how many times did you have to pick her up heartbroken in the middle of the night?'

'Once.' Not strictly true. But he was beginning to look

too smug. There was a lot not to like. He was too hand-some and too sure of himself. And she didn't like that look on his face—as if he knew something she didn't.

'Jill is a really good friend of mine. She helped me when I needed it most. Make no mistake about where my loy-alty lies, Gabriel.'

Those words didn't even touch what Jill had done for her. When her father had died, Jill had dropped everything and flown straight up from London to Glasgow. She'd or-ganised the funeral, dealt with the post-mortem, sorted out the insurance and the contents of the house—all things that Francesca couldn't possibly have dealt with. Jill had been her rock.

In the past their relationship had always felt uneven, as if Francesca was constantly running after Jill and taking care of her. But when the chips had been down Jill had more than risen to the challenge. Francesca couldn't have got through it without her.

'How long are you here for?'

'I haven't even done my first shift and you're trying to get rid of me?'

She shrugged.

'As long as I want. I took this job at short notice—someone had broken their contract—so I was pretty much offered what I wanted. It's up to me to decide how long I want to stay.'

Great. Who knew how long she would be stuck with him? 'You didn't answer the original question. Why would a billionaire doc like you want to be working on a cruise ship?'

He waved his hand dismissively. 'Family stuff.'

It was the first interesting thing he'd said.

Yip. The walls in the room were definitely closing in

on her. This was her worst nightmare. Working with this man every day was going to play havoc with her senses and her principles. She hated the fact that under other circumstances she might like him. She hated the fact she'd almost flirted with him.

'I know you'll have some clean uniforms in your quarters but how about putting these on right now?' She pointed to the scrubs. She wrinkled her nose at the ruined jacket and T-shirt, still in his hand. 'I don't care how good the laundry staff are here, they're not going to be able to save *those*.'

Gabriel stood up, his legs feeling firmer than before. He hadn't even considered his appearance. The pristine white uniform he was holding was covered in remnants of brown sludge. His body hadn't fared much better. From the port wall perhaps? She was right, no matter what the TV adverts pretended to show, no washing powder on the planet could sort this out.

He grabbed the towel to rub his hair, momentarily forgetting the reason he was there and wincing as the edge of the towel caught his wound.

'Easy, tiger.' Francesca pushed him down onto the edge of the bed. 'Let me do that.' She took the towel from his hands and gently dried around the edges.

'Stop fussing,' he muttered, trying to swat her hand away. 'I need a shower.'

Francesca was doing her best to push her anger aside. She had a job to do. Whether she liked him or not, he was a patient—one she'd just resuscitated and with a head injury. She was a good nurse. This was straightforward. She could do this. 'Right now I'm in charge—not you. You can go in the shower when I say so.' She stuck a tympanic thermometer in his ear. 'I'm going to do a full set of neurological observations on you, then clean that head wound and either glue or stitch it.' She glanced at the reading on the thermometer. 'You're still cold. We're going to heat you up a bit first.' She pulled a blanket from one of the nearby cupboards.

Gabriel sighed. At least she was an efficient nurse, even if she was smart-mouthed and hated his guts. 'Where's Dr Marsh?'

She peered around the edge of the door. 'He and Katherine are dealing with the teenager. Children get priority. I'm sure you'd agree with that.'

The child, of course. What was he thinking? There was a child to be attended to. 'I should go and check him over.' He tried to push his blanket off, but she laid her hand firmly on his shoulder.

The constricting feeling across his chest was almost instant. Paediatrics—children were his whole reason for being a doctor. There was no way he'd watch a child suffer. He couldn't stand the thought that there was a child in the next room requiring attention while he was being pushed onto a bed.

It made him feel useless. It pushed him into dark places imprinted on his mind. Memories of long ago. Of a child with a scream that sent shivers down his spine. Feelings he'd spent his whole professional career trying to avert.

He pushed himself off the bed again.

'Gabriel.'

Her face was right in front of his, her large brown eyes looking him straight on and her voice firm.

'Ryan is fine. David Marsh is more than capable of looking after a shocked teenager. Maybe—just maybe—if we were resuscitating him, like we did with you, I might let you go and assist. But this isn't an emergency situation. You're not needed. You're not even officially on duty. Right now you're a patient, not a doctor. And a cranky one at that. You'd better hope that your head injury is making you cranky because if that's your normal temperament you won't last five minutes in here.

She was right. The rational part of his brain that was still functioning *knew* she was right. But his heart was ruling his head. He was cursing himself for not paying more attention to the port wall. He shouldn't have dived straight in, he should have taken a few more seconds to get his bearings. Then maybe he could have protected Ryan and stopped him from slipping from his arms.

They could hear rapid chatter next door. She obviously didn't realise his background in paediatrics. It was hardly surprising. Six years ago he'd been just about to pick his speciality and he'd dumped Jill before he'd made his final choice.

'You should stay where you are. I'm going to attach you to a monitor for a few hours. You, sir, are going to do exactly as I say—whether you like it or not.' She pulled the wires from the nearby monitor. 'I'm not the pushover Jill was,' she murmured.

Gabriel felt a weight settle on his chest again. For a second he'd seen a little glimpse of humour from her. For a second he'd thought maybe she didn't hate him quite as much as it seemed. This was the last thing he needed— some smart-mouthed nurse with a load of preconceived ideas him. How close was she to Jill? Hopefully she didn't have any of the same tendencies—that could be disastrous.

Every part of his body was beginning to ache and if he didn't get something for this headache soon he was going to erupt.

It was almost as if she'd read his mind. 'I'll give you

something for your headache in a few moments. I want to have a clear baseline set of neuro obs and I can't give you anything too strong—I don't want to dull your senses.' There was a hint of humour in her voice, the implication that his senses were already dulled crystal clear.

It was just about as much as he could take.

'Enough about me. What about you?' he snapped. 'What's with the accent? Where are you from?'

The unexpected question caught her unawares and she jolted. She put the unattached wires down and her brow wrinkled. She bent to shine her penlight in his eyes again, satisfying herself that his pupils were equal and reactive.

'I'm from Scotland.' She straightened up.

'You don't look like you're from Scotland,' he mumbled as he dropped the towel he'd been using to dry himself, revealing the taut abdominal muscles, and pulled the scrub top over his head. 'You look like a native. And what were you doing in London?'

'I could be offended by that,' she said quickly, placing one hand on her hip as she tried to drag her eyes away from his stomach. Was this his natural response? Was he normally so blunt? Or was this an altered response that she should be concerned about? She had no background knowledge on which to base a judgment. Should she just take for granted that he could be quite rude?

He'd paused, half-dressed, and was watching her. Watching the way her eyes were looking at his taut abdomen. She felt the colour flooding into her cheeks. There was no point averting her eyes, she'd been well and truly caught. She could be cheeky, too.

'Put those away. You'll give a girl a complex. And they'll need to go, too.' She pointed at his muddied underwear and handed him the scrub bottoms, averting her eyes for a few seconds to allow him some privacy. She slid her hand up inside his scrub top to attach the leads to his chest. His brown, muscled chest.

Time to change the subject. 'My parents were from Trapetto, a fishing village in Sicily. But I was brought up in Scotland. I'm a Glasgow girl through and through.' She waved her hand. 'And don't even try to speak to me in Italian. I'm not fluent at all—I know enough for emergencies and how to order dinner but that's it.'

'Didn't you speak Italian at home?'

His voice brought her back to reality. 'Rarely. There wasn't much call for it in Glasgow.'

Her eyelids had lowered, as if this wasn't a conversation she wanted to get into. Why was that?

Francesca picked up his dirty clothes. 'I take it you're okay if I dump these?'

He nodded and shifted on the bed, frowning at his attached leads. 'So what are you doing here, Francesca?'

She froze, a little shocked by the bluntness of the question. This guy was going to take a bit of getting used to.

She frowned at him, knowing her brow was wrinkled and it wasn't the most flattering of looks. 'What on earth are you talking about?'

There it was again, that little hint of something—but not quite obvious.

'I would have thought that was obvious. I'm here working as an ANP. Maybe I should check that head knock of yours again.'

His eyebrows lifted. 'I'm curious what a young, well-qualified nurse like you is doing here.' His hand swept outwards to the surrounding area.

She felt a little shiver steal down her spine. Nosy parker.

She kept her voice steady. 'You mean here...' she spread

her arms out and spun round '…in this state-of-the-art medical complex, in the middle of the Mediterranean, with a different port every day and a chance to see the world?'

She planted her hands on her hips and looked at him as defiantly as she could. She was stating the obvious. The thing that any website would quote for prospective job-seekers. It was a cop-out and she knew it. But she didn't like the way he'd asked the question. It was as if he'd already peered deep inside her and knew things she didn't want anyone else to know.

'I'm just curious. Your family is in Glasgow. And yet, you're here…' His voice tailed off. Almost as if he was contemplating the thought himself.

Something inside her snapped. Were all Italians as old-fashioned as him?

'My family isn't in Glasgow any more. Get a life, Gabriel. Isn't a girl allowed to spread her wings and get a job elsewhere? Maybe I'm trying to connect with my roots in Sicily. Maybe I was just bored in Glasgow. Maybe I want to see the world. Or it could just be that I'm killing time until I get my visa to Australia. I thought cruise ships would be fun. Truth be told, so far I've found it all a bit boring.' The words were out before she'd thought about it. Out before she had a chance to take them back.

She cringed. He was her boss. He was her *brand-new* boss, who had no idea about her skills, experience and competency level—probably the only things that could be her saving grace right now. How to win friends and influence people. Not.

She pushed the dirty clothes inside a plastic disposal bag, 'I'll get rid of these,' she muttered as she turned to leave.

This was going to be nightmare. This ship was huge.

Big enough for two thousand, six hundred passengers and five hundred staff. But this medical centre? Not so big. And the staff worked very closely together. Some days the medical centre felt positively crowded.

And the last thing she needed was to be stuck with some playboy doc. A pain shot through her chest. The last time she'd been distracted by a playboy doc it had had a devastating effect on her family life, causing irreparable damage. She could *not* allow that to happen again, no matter what the circumstances.

Every part of her body was buzzing. She hadn't even had a chance to think about what had happened today. She'd resuscitated someone.

Someone who could, potentially, have died if she hadn't taken those actions.

The thought of dealing with a death again horrified her. It didn't matter that she was a nurse. Her circumstances had changed. Everything had changed.

Deaths weren't supposed to happen on cruise ships. Working here was part of her safety net—keeping her away from the aspects of her job she couldn't deal with any more.

And now him.

On top of everything else.

She leaned back against the wall. There was no two ways about it.

This ship wasn't big enough for the two of them.

CHAPTER THREE

FRANCESCA'S fingers thumped furiously on the keyboard.

Hey babe!
You'll never believe who I'm working with right now—
Gabriel Russo. Yes, the very one. And he's every bit the
conceited billionaire boy that he was six years ago. It took
me a few minutes to work out who he was—probably because I had to resuscitate him first—but needless to say,
once I'd reminded him I was your flatmate you could cut
the atmosphere in here with a knife.

Cruise ships might look huge in real life but the reality is, when you can't stand to be around someone, they
seem very small.

Haven't seen you in a while, so hope you're doing well.
In the meantime living in hope he'll fall overboard,
Fran xx

'Busy?'

The voice, cutting through the dark medical centre in
the dead of night, made her jump. Couldn't she get any
peace from this man?

She could barely tolerate being in the same room as
him. What's more, he constantly appeared at her shoulder,

checking over what she'd done. And for someone whose confidence was already at rock bottom it was more than a little irritating.

There were always two crew members on call at night— one for the passengers and one for the crew. One week had passed and this was Gabriel's first official night on call and Francesca had drawn the short straw of babysitting him.

She spun around in her chair to face him. He had his black medical bag in his hand. 'I'm waiting for one of the crew members to meet me,' she said. 'She's complaining of abdominal pain.'

'Need a hand?'

Francesca bit her tongue to stop her saying the words that were dancing around her head right now. *Over my dead body* probably wouldn't go down that well with her boss.

'No, I'm fine, thanks.' She pasted a smile on her face and gestured towards his bag. 'You look busy enough anyway. Lots of passenger callouts?'

He nodded, rubbing his hand across his eyes. 'Three in the last hour. All for really ridiculous things. Please tell me this isn't a normal night.'

Francesca smiled. If it had been anyone else she would have told him about the 'cougar list' currently taped inside one of the cupboard doors in the treatment room.

The list of well-known passengers—mainly women in their forties and fifties—who developed symptoms requiring a cabin call whenever a new, young doctor came on board. She could bet in the last hour Gabriel had seen a lot of skin and satin negligees.

Not all the passengers changed every week or every fortnight. A certain select group seemed to spend a large part of their life cruising. It was not unusual to have the same passengers on board for four to six weeks at a time. Sometimes they swapped to another ship for a month and then came back to the *Silver Whisper* again.

The 'cougar list' had been started by Kevin, one of the nurses, after he'd noticed a sharp rise in callouts whenever a new doctor started. It was really just a warning list to give the person on call the opportunity to decide if they wanted to take the other crew member on duty with them. She would tell him about the list—really, she would—just not yet.

Francesca was sure that Gabriel could handle a few coy looks. After all, hadn't he spent his life chasing women, collecting them like trophies and then unceremoniously dumping them? This should be a breeze for him.

'Here, have a look at this.' She handed him the communiqué she'd been given requesting details about the rescue at Venezia Passegeri. Apparently the media were keen to run a story. 'They're a little late but maybe they were short of news.'

A dark shadow passed over his face as his eyes flew over the page. 'Absolutely not. No names. I don't want to talk about last week. Make sure the communications officer understands.'

She shrugged, a little surprised by his reaction. 'The cruise line probably wants the publicity,' she suggested. 'What's the problem? You're used to being in the news.'

'No!' He looked furious. He crumpled the piece of paper in his hand and threw it deftly into the wastepaper bin. She smirked. *Message received, loud and clear.*

Was this man temperamental? Maybe his snappiness after his head injury hadn't been the result of the accident. His questions to her had been a little blunt. He certainly wasn't exhibiting all the traits Jill had told her about of the flirtatious, playboy doctor. Gabriel Russo seemed to be a wolf in doctor's clothing. And the thought intrigued her.

Katherine had complained bitterly last week that Gabriel wasn't the best of patients—apparently she'd had to practically pin him to the bed to monitor his neuro obs overnight after his head injury. He'd been furious when Dr Marsh had insisted he be monitored overnight and it had been a relief to them all when he'd been given a clean bill of health the following morning and allowed to take on normal duties.

His pager sounded again and he sighed, picking up his medical bag and heading for the door. 'If I'm not back in an hour page me.' He hesitated for a second, his brown eyes connecting with hers. 'Please.'

Francesca couldn't help but smile. Maybe he was finally catching onto the cougar brigade.

She turned back to the computer and pulled up the file for the crew member she was about to meet.

The notes were limited. Elena Portiss, twenty-seven, from Spain, working on board as a bartender, with a declared past medical history of endometriosis.

She'd phoned ten minutes earlier saying her abdominal pain was worse than usual—bad abdominal pain was not uncommon in a woman with a history of endometriosis.

There was a noise behind her and Francesca stood up and flicked the switch, lighting up the medical unit.

'Elena?'

The young woman nodded.

Francesca was immediately struck by how pale the girl was. Her pale blue eyes were dull and lifeless, her normally tanned skin pallid and slightly waxy.

'Come in here.' Francesca walked into the nearby room and gestured Elena towards one of the examination trolleys. She worked quickly, checking her temperature, blood pressure and pulse. 'You have endometriosis?' Francesca spoke slowly, taking care in case there was any difficulty in language.

Elena nodded. Francesca noted that her hands were positioned carefully over her stomach, obviously trying to keep her pain in check. 'It was diagnosed last year after I had very painful periods.' She lifted her shirt and pointed to a little scar next to her belly button. 'I had a camera in there.'

Francesca nodded. If Elena had had a laparoscopy done and the diagnosis confirmed then it was likely that her symptoms were related to her endometriosis.

'Do you normally use painkillers?' Elena nodded and fumbled in her bag, pulling out a battered box with the name written in Spanish. Francesca took the box, looking at it and writing the name down in the notes. It was a commonly used non-steroidal anti-inflammatory drug that was effective in treating endometriosis.

'We will be able to give you something similar,' she reassured Elena, 'but the box may look a little different. Have you tried anything else?'

Elena pulled a second, slightly more battered cardboard box from her bag. 'I stopped taking these,' she said, 'as they made me feel unwell.' As she didn't recognise the name on the box Francesca opened it and pulled out the foil strip with the twenty-eight tablets enclosed. Around half were missing and she realised immediately what they were. Oral contraceptives were commonly used to treat endometriosis in women who weren't trying to start a family. They worked by regulating the hormone levels to stop the production of oestrogen in the body. Without exposure to oestrogen, the endometrial tissue could be reduced and this helped to ease symptoms.

'Do you remember when your last period was?' Francesca asked.

'I'm not sure. I had some bleeding yesterday and a little this morning, but it wasn't much.'

'I'm so sorry, but I'm going to have to get a urine specimen from you. Do you think you can manage to go to the toilet for me?'

Elena grimaced as Francesca helped her to the toilet. It only took a few minutes before she was back on the couch and Francesca reattached her to the blood-pressure cuff. BP was ninety over sixty. Hypotensive. Colour poor. Alarm bells started to go off inside Francesca's head.

The amount of pain that Elena was exhibiting was more than would be expected. Elena nodded, still clutching her stomach.

Francesca's spider sense was tingling. Her instinct—the thing she'd thought she'd lost.

This wasn't right. This didn't *feel* right. Elena's pain seemed too severe and too localised to be endometriosis. Francesca knew that endometriosis was a painful condition in which the endometrial cells that would normally be present within the lining of the womb could be deposited in other areas around the body. These cells were still influenced by the female hormones and could cause pain in various areas, particularly around the pelvis.

And she knew how painful it could be—one of her friends spent a few days every month doubled up in bed. But this just didn't add up.

She checked the urine sample for infection and it was clear. Francesca opened the nearby cupboard and pulled out another test. It was only a hunch and she could be wrong. Using a little pipette she dropped a few drops of urine onto the test and checked her watch. A little line appeared.

Her heart gave a flutter in her chest. She hadn't been wrong and for a second she felt almost elated. Then common sense pulled her back to reality.

She needed help. And no matter how much he irritated her, she knew who to call.

The pager sounded again.

Gabriel was annoyed. What would be the reason for this ridiculous callout? A stubbed toe? A grazed elbow? He was going to have serious words with the team in the morning if this was what they normally dealt with.

He glanced at the number on the pager. The medical centre. Francesca. Now, that *was* a surprise. She'd looked as if she'd rather set her hair on fire than ask him for help earlier.

And as for the media request...

It made his blood boil. His family were constantly in the paper—particularly in Italy. With the words 'tragic' usually appearing in the second sentence. Twenty-five years ago the media had been all over them and their 'tragic' loss. Every time they were mentioned in the press it was all raked over again.

The last thing they needed was more painful reminders.

Didn't they get that the loss of Dante was imprinted on them for life, seared on their very souls?

Gabriel had never once given an interview to a journalist.

Correction. Gabriel had never *knowingly* given an interview to a journalist. The ugly remnants of a faked past relationship by an aspiring reporter burned hard. That, and his experience with Jill and a few others like her, told him that women weren't to be trusted. Under any circumstances.

It only took him a few moments to reach the medical centre.

'What's wrong?'

Francesca was waiting at the door for him, some notes in her hands and a worried expression on her face.

She thrust the notes towards him. 'Elena Portiss, twenty-seven, severe abdominal pain, past history of endometriosis.'

'Have you given her some analgesics?'

'Not yet.'

'Why not?'

She hesitated just for a second. 'Because she's pregnant and she doesn't know it. I think it may be an ectopic pregnancy,' she said tentatively.

Gabriel's eyes skimmed over the notes in front of him. He'd no idea why she looked like a deer currently caught in the headlights. She'd done everything he would have expected. 'Let's find out.'

Francesca caught his arm as he walked past her. 'I haven't given her any indication about what I think may be wrong.' Gabriel caught the worried expression in her eyes. He understood completely. Endometriosis was frequently associated with infertility. To tell the patient that she was pregnant but that the pregnancy was ectopic would be a devastating blow. He strode through to the treatment room and spoke to Elena, who was lying on the examination couch, her face still racked in pain.

'Hello, Elena,' he said confidently, 'my name is Dr Russo. I'm one of the ship's doctors. Nurse Cruz has asked that I take a little look at you.' He shook Elena's trembling hand. As he placed his hands very gently on her stomach he noticed her visibly flinching. 'I promise you, I will be very gentle.'

He moved lightly across her abdomen, pressing gently with his fingertips from one side to the other. 'Where is the pain worse? Here? Here?'

Elena shook her head tensely, and then grimaced again in pain as his fingers reached her right side. The clinical signs were all present. She was pale, hypotensive, with lower abdominal tenderness and distension. That, together with a positive pregnancy test, gave an almost conclusive picture.

Francesca watched him from the corner of the room. Had she been wrong to mention her tentative diagnosis? Other doctors might have thought she was stepping on their toes to make such a suggestion.

But Gabriel hadn't even blinked. He didn't seem offended or annoyed with her suggestion. His only concern seemed to be for the patient.

Given the hostility between them it could have been a perfect opportunity for him to take her to task.

But apparently not. This man wasn't exactly how she'd imagined him to be.

'Okay, that's me finished.' He took his hands from Elena's abdomen and stood next to her.

'Do you know the date of your last period, Elena?'

She shook her head miserably. 'I have been bleeding on and off for several months. I can't say for sure. I was taking the Pill, too, but it made me feel unwell, so I stopped. Then I had some light bleeding yesterday. I'm not sure when my last period was.'

Gabriel nodded, 'That's okay'. He turned to Francesca. 'Can you check her BP and pulse again for me, please, and draw some bloods? I'll need her urea and electrolytes, but more importantly a full blood count, please.'

Francesca nodded and set the monitor to retake Elena's blood pressure while she opened the nearby drawer to find the blood bottles. Once the blood pressure had been recorded she removed the cuff and replaced it with a tourniquet to facilite taking some blood. It only took her a matter of seconds to locate a vein. 'Just a little prick,' she said to Elena as she gently slid the needle into the vein and attached the bottle to collect the blood samples. Francesca released the clip on the tourniquet, letting it spring apart, relieving the pressure on Elena's arm. She placed the needle in the nearby sharps box and gave Gabriel a quick glance as she left the room. 'I'll phone Kevin and get him to do the blood results for us.'

She wondered if he realised how quickly her heart was beating in her chest. Elena's blood count would be a good indicator of whether her diagnosis was correct or not.

It could also prove that her instincts were still completely off.

The medical centre was equipped with a wide range of laboratory equipment that allowed the staff to carry out many diagnostic tests that were essential to diagnosing and treating patients. Kevin arrived a few minutes later, hair mussed, took the blood samples and prepared them for testing. When she returned to the room Gabriel was sitting next to the examination trolley, talking to Elena. Francesca could see the serious expression on his face and watched as he gently took Elena's hand to explain her condition. Gabriel was surprising her. He was taking time to talk to Elena, to hold her hand and explain clearly what was happening. For some reason she found it almost the opposite of what she'd expected. This was a man who'd flung her friend out on the street at three o'clock in the morning yet here he was as a doctor, doing everything he should and showing empathy for his patient. In her head that just didn't fit. Her curiosity was piqued.

She listened quietly in the background.

'Elena,' he said gently, 'I think it is likely that you're having an ectopic pregnancy.' He noticed the complete confusion on her face, and realised she hadn't really understood. 'Your urine test shows that you are pregnant—but this is not a normal pregnancy.'

'But I can't be pregnant—I have endometriosis—it's not possible for me to be pregnant.' Her face was filled with shock.

'It is possible,' Gabriel continued carefully. 'Have you had sex in the last six weeks?'

Elena nodded numbly.

'Although your condition makes it difficult to conceive, it is not impossible. It is likely that because you were taking the contraceptive pill you've become unclear about when your next period was due. Your urine test is definitely positive. However, the pain and discomfort that you are feeling makes it likely that, instead of implanting in the womb, the fertilised egg has implanted in your Fallopian tube.' He picked up a nearby book with pictures of the female reproductive system and pointed to the various areas, showing her where the fertilised ovum had likely reached.

The medical staff often used these clear diagrammatic books to explain conditions to crew members of different nationalities. 'The embryo can't develop within this confined space and causes bleeding and pain. Sometimes the tube can rupture and that can be very serious. But in all cases the pregnancy can't continue.'

He waited for a moment, until he could tell that Elena

had processed the information he had given her. Elena started sobbing uncontrollably. Gabriel had been right. The news of a pregnancy, followed by the news that it was ectopic and couldn't produce a baby, had devastated her.

'What happens now?' she asked.

Gabriel stood up from the chair. 'We have to watch you very closely so we are going to admit you to our intensive care unit. I'll put up some fluids and give you some pain relief. One of our nurses will come and take some more bloods from you in the next few hours. I will have to arrange for you to go to hospital at the next port.'

Kevin appeared and handed Gabriel the blood results. Haemoglobin eight point seven. Gabriel glanced in Francesca's direction. No words were needed. They both knew that was much lower than normal for a woman of her age and more than likely an indicator of some internal bleeding.

Francesca felt the flush of relief rush through her system. She'd been right. For once her instincts had been good. If things weren't so serious for their patient right now she would run outside and breathe a big sigh of relief.

When had been the last time she'd felt like this? The last time she'd had real confidence in her abilities as a nurse?

After her initial meeting with Gabriel, she couldn't have blamed him if he'd ignored her instincts at all. But he hadn't.

He hadn't even really questioned her. He'd taken her at her word and just moved on. He hadn't even *doubted* her. Why?

This virtual stranger had more faith in her than she had in herself. Maybe there was more to him than met the eye.

Sure enough, they'd been mouth to mouth before, but he couldn't remember any of that—could he?

Francesca administered the analgesia and then moved through to the intensive care unit to set up the bed and equipment that would be needed.

Gabriel came over and placed a hand on her shoulder, his forefinger touching the delicate skin at the side of her neck. She felt herself flinch but not in displeasure, just at the electricity of his warm touch. The tingles running down her spine were making her lose her concentration. He leaned towards her with a wide smile, showing his perfect teeth. 'That was an impressive call, Francesca,' he praised. 'Not one that everyone would have recognised—and that includes medical staff. Her initial symptoms could easily have been written off as her ongoing endometriosis.' He nodded his head in appreciation. 'What made you think twice?'

'Instinct,' came the immediate reply, followed by a loose shrug of the shoulders. 'It just didn't seem right.' *Instinct.* The word had come to her lips so easily. Almost automatically. Too bad she hadn't always trusted her instincts. Maybe then she would still be in Glasgow.

Maybe then she would still have some of her family left.

Something else stirred inside her. He was praising her. He was giving her the credit for the diagnosis. And it spread a warm feeling through her insides. Maybe she should be more confident about herself—the way she used to be.

'I've spoken to the captain. We are due to dock in Piraeus tomorrow at nine. He's told me that if there are problems he will probably be able to arrange a quicker dock time, as long as we give him some notice. He could alter the speed accordingly as the actual physical sea miles could be covered more quickly if it was necessary. Who will be looking after the patient?'

'I will.' There was no way she wanted anyone else to look after Elena. She wanted to see this through.

The next port was in Athens, Greece, and although the actual distance between Venice and Athens was not huge, they often spent full days at sea. This gave passengers time to adjust to the feel of the ocean and a chance to find their way around the boat. They'd already circled the Med once and were repeating the journey again.

Kevin appeared at the door. 'She's complaining of shoulder-tip pain now, Dr Russo.' Gabriel crossed the room quickly. Shoulder-tip pain could be a serious sign. It could mean that there was internal bleeding into the abdominal cavity that was irritating the diaphragm. This was usually a sign that the ectopic pregnancy had ruptured and would require surgery—something they were not equipped to do at sea. He spent a few more moments examining Elena, while Francesca rechecked her pulse and blood pressure.

'Pulse one-ten, BP eighty-five over fifty.' Her hand reached automatically towards the intravenous fluids that were hanging next to the bed. 'Do you want these increased?' He nodded and she automatically adjusted the controls on the machine. It was clear from her symptoms that Elena's ectopic pregnancy had ruptured and she was bleeding internally. Her pulse had risen and blood pressure dropped, which meant she was going into hypovolaemic shock. Increasing her intravenous fluids would only be a minor stopgap in trying to treat her. She really needed surgery.

Gabriel stood up swiftly. 'I'm going to notify the captain and arrange an emergency evac.'

Francesca watched his retreating back. She was impressed by how calm he was. She hadn't been able to ascertain whether Gabriel had much experience of being at sea, but on more than one occasion she had seen other doctors panic at the thought of dealing with a surgical emergency on board. Most doctors were used to working in large general hospitals that had all the services they needed at their fingertips. Working at sea was entirely different. Making a wrong decision could cost a patient their life, but Gabriel appeared to be taking it all in his stride.

There was the tiniest flutter in her stomach. If, for any reason, they couldn't get Elena off the ship there was a possibility she could die.

Francesca pushed the thought from her mind. She couldn't even contemplate anything like that. She couldn't bear the thought of having to deal with the death of a patient. Not now.

She watched as he pressed the button on the phone to end his first call and start another. 'The captain will go with my decision. We can't wait to get to the port. I'm phoning the Medevac agency to arrange a suitable rendezvous point for the helicopter.'

'I'll get the Medevac checklist.'

Francesca started completing the essential checklist that would give the Medevac team all the vital information they needed to know about the patient. By the time she had finished Gabriel had put down the phone. He quickly checked Elena again, noting her BP and pulse and checking her IV fluids.

'Have you told her yet?' he asked.

Francesca shook her head. 'I wanted to wait until you had confirmed it with the captain. Do you want me to tell her now?'

Gabriel shook his head. 'Let me,' he said.

There it was again. Compassion for his patient. This from a man who had thrown her friend out on the street in the middle of the night. Some things just didn't add up. How long would it take Jill to answer that email?

He walked over to where Elena was lying and took her hand again. 'Elena? It's Dr Russo. I need to speak to you again.'

Her eyes flickered open at the sound of his voice. She was obviously still in pain.

'Elena, I think that the ectopic pregnancy has probably ruptured and caused bleeding into your abdomen. That's why you are feeling so unwell.' He pointed to the IV fluids hanging next to her. 'These can only help for a limited amount of time. You really need to have surgery to stop the bleeding.'

'But how can I?'

'We've made arrangements for you to be airlifted off the ship and taken to a nearby hospital. The helicopter will be here soon, we just need to make sure you are ready to be moved.'

She looked shocked at the prospect and twisted uncomfortably on the bed, her face still racked with pain. 'But where will it land?'

Gabriel spoke reassuringly. 'Deck Sixteen—the sports deck has room for the helicopter to land next to the jogging track. We'll arrange to take you up there once we have word they will be arriving.'

The phone rang in the nearby office and Gabriel came out. 'The closest largest town with medical facilities is Amaliada. They have a large general hospital that can deal with this. We're around ninety miles off the coast from Amaliada right now. That was the captain. He's cleared the landing site and ETA is in the next ten minutes. We better get a move on.'

Francesca produced some thick woollen blankets to

protect Elena from the wind and tucked them round her. Gabriel finished casting his eye over the Medevac checklist and signed it. He grabbed the nearest luminescent jacket and pulled it over his uniform; Francesca and Kevin were already wearing theirs. 'Are we good to go?' he checked, and when they nodded in agreement he released the brake on the trolley and started pushing it out of the door.

His hand and forearm were next to Francesca's and she glanced up at him, wondering if he realised his hand was touching hers. His head was down and he seemed totally focused on his task, then, out of the blue, he gave her hand a little squeeze and shot her a quick grin. Two other crew members were waiting in the corridor for them to clear the path to the nearest lift. Francesca watched Elena carefully. Her BP was still low and colour poor, but she could already hear the hum of the approaching helicopter so it wouldn't be long now.

The doors of the lift opened at Deck Sixteen and they were immediately met by the biting wind caused by the hovering helicopter. The noise was deafening.

'Let's stay in here until the helicopter lands,' shouted Gabriel. They watched as four crewman wearing luminescent jackets like their own, and carrying paddles, signalled the helicopter it was safe to land.

The helicopter touched down and they ran forward, pulling the trolley between them and keeping their heads down low. A Medevac team member opened the side door of the helicopter and jumped out.

'Dr Russo?' he shouted above the din of the rotating blades. Gabriel nodded and helped move Elena onto the helicopter's own trolley, which could be easily lifted inside. He bent his head next to the Medevac team member, handing over the checklist and shouting some extra instructions.

Francesca and Kevin pulled the medical centre trolley back towards the lift, moving out of the way of the crewmen who were ready to signal the helicopter to lift off.

Gabriel ran over to join them next to the lift and in a matter of seconds the door banged shut and the helicopter took off into the sky with a small wave from the Medevac team member. They watched as the noise dissipated and the whirring blades became a blur in the distance.

Silence fell over them. All that was left was the steady sound of the ship's engines, purring away in the dark of the night.

'Well,' said Gabriel, the serious expression leaving his face and a wicked glint in his brown eyes as he turned towards Francesca. He gave her a wink. 'A near drowning, a resuscitation and an ectopic pregnancy all in the space of one week. Who said this job was boring!'

CHAPTER FOUR

'DID you know about this?'

Gabriel looked distinctly unimpressed. He was holding the pink piece of paper containing the 'cougar list' in his hand. The tape was still stuck to the top of the page and the cupboard door was lying open.

She smiled. 'Oops. Did I forget to mention that?'

'Yes. You did.'

For a second she almost felt guilty. But it didn't last long. He was scowling at her again. The thrill and adrenaline from last night was gone and they were back to the routine of her hating him and him watching her every move. This would be a long day.

He was still growling at her. 'Any reason you didn't tell me about it?'

Because I think you're a snake and you deserved a bit of your own medicine.

The words danced around her brain. She bit her lip to stop herself from saying them out loud. Why did he look so mad? Offended almost?

Was he currently reading her less than complimentary thoughts?

She tried to change the subject quickly. 'It's probably going to be quiet today—most of the passengers will dis-

embark at Piraeus to go on the sightseeing tours of Athens.'
Francesca picked up a crew list. 'Katherine is working too
this morning so it would probably be best if we tried to
cover as many of the crew medicals as possible.'

Gabriel glanced over the list, underlining a few names
in red. 'These are the ones I want to see.'

Francesca felt her lips tighten. The role of the advanced
nurse practitioner was one that some doctors struggled to
understand. Her job included most of the extended skills
that general nurses could do—cannulation, suturing,
venepuncture. But she also had advanced skills in reading X-rays, prescribing some general medications and diagnostic skills more equated with those of a junior doctor.

On a day-to-day basis these weren't always needed.
Most patients attended with minor illnesses, respiratory
and gastrointestinal infections, minor skin complaints and
fractures and accidental injuries that happened either on
board or ashore.

But the crew medicals could involve more intensive
work-ups and regular reviews of ongoing chronic conditions, and Francesca enjoyed doing them. Gabriel had just
underlined some of the patients that she normally reviewed
herself and it irked her.

'I normally see these patients.' She pointed to the few
he'd marked on the list.

His brow narrowed. 'And today I'm going to see them.'

Was he just being pig-headed? Did he think this a role
that only a doctor could fulfil? Or was he just doing this
to annoy her?

'But I've seen these patients on a regular basis. I understand them, and how they deal with their conditions. Surely
it would be best if they were reviewed by someone familiar
with their set of circumstances?' She was determined to

keep the annoyance out of her voice. She wanted to sound professional. She wanted to sound completely rational.

Gabriel seemed unmoved. 'Like I said, today I'm going to see them.' He picked up the list and started walking to his room. 'Sometimes it takes a fresh pair of eyes to look over a case to decide on the best plan of treatment for a patient.'

She could feel the hackles at the back of her neck rise.

She wanted to shout. She wanted to tell him he was condescending. She wanted to tell him to stop trying to find fault with her. Did he really think she was going to fall for that lame excuse?

She knew he was going to look over all her patient consult notes to see if he could find a reason to get rid of her. Did he have to be so obvious?

She turned and smiled sweetly, pasting a smile so sickly on to her face he would have no doubt what she was thinking. 'Whatever you think, Dr Russo.' She picked up her copy of the list and headed into the next room, sitting down in front of one of the computers and tapping furiously.

Her mind whirred. *I hate him. He's a superficial, condescending git. He has more money than sense. He flung Jill onto the street at 3:00 a.m. Who does that? How dared he? Does he think he can treat all women like that?*

'So what's with you and our hunky new Italian doctor? You can't keep your eyes off him.' Katherine had perched on the edge of the desk next to her.

'What?'

She smiled at Francesca and folded her arms. 'But I can't quite get what's going on between you two. When I say you can't keep your eyes off him—it's not in a good way. You look at him as if you're plotting fifty different ways to kill him and hide the body.' She shook her head knowingly. 'Now, that isn't the sweet-natured Francesca I know and love.' She bent across the desk, closing the space between them both and propping her chin on one hand. 'So what gives? Are you a lover scorned? Did you meet in a past life? Were you secret childhood sweethearts—?'

'Have you completely lost your mind?'

Katherine's face broke into a wide smile. She nodded her head, 'See? I knew it. I *knew* there was something there.' She couldn't hide the self-satisfied look from her face. 'So why do you hate him so much? Because, to be honest, after that one hellish night doing his neuro obs I've found him quite charming. And so has everyone else. And have you seen him with kids? The guy is *seriously* good with them.'

Francesca shook her head. She couldn't believe this. She couldn't believe the rest of the staff was fooled by his good looks and killer abs. She finished the notes she was inputting and turned to face Katherine.

'I think he's conceited. I feel as if he's constantly looking over my shoulder, trying to find fault.'

Katherine sighed. 'He's only been here just over a week. How can you possibly think that?'

Francesca held up the list. 'Look at this. He's taken all my usual crew members for review. He's checking up on me. He's trying to find fault.'

'Or maybe he's the new guy and he's trying to work out how we do things around here?'

Her words hung in the air. Francesca didn't like them. It made her look as if *she* was trying to find fault with him. Not the other way about.

'You honestly find him charming?'

Katherine nodded slowly, her gaze disappearing off into the distance. 'Yeah, he is kind of charming. And those dark brown eyes are just to die for. And his teeth…' She turned back to face Francesca. 'He's got a set of teeth that could appear in a television commercial. When I was doing his neuro obs in the middle of the night he got up for a shower. Now, that really was an eyeful.' She was off again, into her daydream-like state.

Francesca cringed. All the things that she'd noticed first about Gabriel. The kind of superficial things that shouldn't really matter. Looks were only skin deep. Words that she'd repeated over and over again to Jill.

And yet she'd done it herself. She'd seen him lying on the bottom of that boat and for a second had thought, Wow. Totally unprofessional. Thank goodness hearing his name had brought her back to her senses.

'Don't be fooled by his looks, Katherine. It's what's inside that counts. And I have it on good authority that his handsome looks don't penetrate beneath the surface.'

Katherine looked shocked. 'What does that mean?'

'He used to date one of my friends. And he didn't treat her particularly well.'

'Why, what happened?'

Francesca waved her hand. 'I don't want to get into it. Needless to say, the feelings are mutual. I'm not impressed to be working with him and he's not impressed to be working with me.' Francesca shook her head. 'And anyway, is it the handsome looks that are the attraction or is it the fact the man is practically dripping with diamonds?'

Katherine's pretty face turned into a frown. 'Now I really have no idea what you're talking about.'

'Gabriel Russo? Member of one of the richest families in Venice?'

Katherine shook her head. The name obviously meant nothing to her.

Francesca sighed and turned back to the computer, tapping into one of the internet search engines. 'I hadn't heard of him, either. But after he treated my friend so badly I looked him up. See?' She turned the screen to face Katherine.

Katherine leaned forward. 'Oh, wow!' Headline after headline. All about the Russo family and how they were one of the first printing families in Venice. Image after image appeared on the screen. Francesca drew in a sharp breath.

'What is it? Is it that one?' Katherine pointed to a brown, muscled, very well-endowed picture of Gabriel perched on the edge of a brilliant yacht in a pair of white swimming trunks. The picture left nothing to the imagination. It could have adorned the walls of teenage girls up and down the country.

'What? Yes... I mean, no.' Francesca sighed. 'That's my friend.' She pointed to a figure in the background of the picture, a young blonde in a turquoise bikini. 'I just didn't expect to see her online.'

Katherine read a few more of the headlines. 'It seems our new resident doc is dripping with diamonds. So what's he doing here?'

'It's a good question and I've no idea. I just know I won't be joining his fan club.'

'Look at that.'

'What?' Francesca really didn't want to look at another picture of Gabriel in his swim shorts. But Katherine was pointing at some professional journal articles, all with Gabriel's name attached, and all on paediatrics. So he specialised in paediatrics. The penny dropped. That explained his actions the other day. That was why he was so good with kids. How come he hadn't mentioned it?

Katherine pursed her lips. 'So what's he like?'

'What do you mean—what's he like? It wasn't me who used to date him.'

'No, I mean as a doctor. You worked with him last night—and I heard you didn't tell him about the cougar list, by the way, naughty, naughty.' She waggled her finger at Francesca. 'Was he any good?'

Francesca almost felt the words stick in her throat. Last night *had* bothered her. Whilst she knew someone who was a rat in real life could be professionally good at their job, it was more than that. She'd seen the compassion in Gabriel's eyes when he'd spoken to their patient. He'd been more than calm and competent in a situation in which others might have panicked. Especially when he was new on board. Especially now that she knew his speciality was paediatrics. He could have felt totally out of his depth and how much help would she have given him?

'He was fine.' Struck by the realisation of how well he'd performed the night before, it was as much as she could manage.

The look on Katherine's face said it all as she slid off the desk. 'He was fine? He diagnosed an ectopic pregnancy and organised an emergency airlift—probably saving a life on his first night on call. All from a guy who specialises in paediatrics, and "he was fine"?' She nodded her head sarcastically and disappeared out of the room.

Francesca felt overwhelmed. So much had happened in the last few days. She couldn't make sense of most of it. Most of the time she couldn't stand to be around Gabriel. But even that confused her. Everyone else thought he was charming, so why couldn't she?

It would be easy to say it was her extended knowledge of him. But there was something else. Something she hated.

The way she found her eyes following him around the room.

The way she believed the compassion in his eyes the night before had been real.

The admiration she'd felt for his skill while treating Elena.

The fact that if this was another life, another set of circumstances, she might actually be attracted to him.

A sense of loneliness swept over her, coupled with the feelings of inadequacy creeping up out of nowhere. The feeling of being under a microscope, her every move examined. Completely exposed.

She thought back to last night—automatically falling into self-preservation mode. She'd been right about Elena's condition. She'd made the right call. A new feeling of determination swept over her. Her mind was telling her one thing but her churning stomach telling her another. Why did she feel so unsure?

Katherine's words echoed in her brain. *He diagnosed an ectopic pregnancy and organised an emergency airlift—probably saving a life on his first night on call.*

Francesca was left staring at her screen. 'I diagnosed the ectopic pregnancy,' she whispered to the empty room.

Gabriel was furious. He'd gone back to raise a query with Francesca about a patient's medication and he'd caught the words 'dripping with diamonds'. They'd sent an icy chill down his spine.

He hadn't listened to much more—he didn't need to. Once more he'd been judged and valued on his bank balance rather than his clinical expertise.

He hated internet search engines with a passion. Wasn't a person allowed a modicum of privacy any more?

So now he was being judged on his money once again. His family name. How long before they found the word 'tragedy' attached to something and started to tiptoe round about him?

It was the overwhelming reason he'd chosen to work overseas—away from Italy and its close-knit gentry. Away from others who were aware of his family background.

It was bad enough that she hadn't told him about the cougar list. Yet another person sitting in judgement of him and believing the gossip.

For a second—just for a second last night—he'd seen a glimmer of hope in Francesca. She'd seemed an able and competent nurse. More than that, she'd shown good instincts. Even if she hadn't been sure of them herself, they had still been there. It would have been so easy for her not to ask for a consultation on their patient.

Some medical staff would have been content with the endometriosis diagnosis and assumed that some of the cells had spread, causing more pain and inflammation. Most would probably have given a stronger painkiller with instructions to come back if there was no improvement.

Might he have done that?

Last night he'd had respect for his prickly nurse—despite her poor choice of friend. Respect because she'd earned it.

Today she was back in the doldrums of disgust. Francesca had already told him she knew who he was and questioned his need to work. To earn his own salary.

But she knew nothing about his attempts to distance himself from the family business. About the general chaos he'd created as a teenager when he'd announced his intentions not to move into the well-paid position created for him but to follow the career of his heart. The one imprinted into his being years before.

He was the last remaining son—his father had been devastated by his decision. But Gabriel had been determined—nothing would change his mind. And his strong, intelligent and often overlooked sister was more than ready to step into his shoes, with a passion, drive and commitment to the family business that Gabriel could never have equalled.

Francesca knew none of this and probably would never understand. Not if she had the same mindset as her friend. One that could never look underneath the surface.

Jill had been horrified when she'd been caught with Gabriel's twenty-thousand-pound watch stuffed in her bag. He might have even believed the feeble story she'd started to spout if he hadn't seen her deliberately take it and hide it in the inside pocket. She was lucky he'd only flung her out on the street instead of calling the police.

Why did Francesca feel the need to tell all her colleagues about his wealth? He'd hoped to be part of a team that would judge him on his clinical competence, not the fact he was 'dripping with diamonds'.

How could he trust anyone now? Rich kids learned quickly that wealth attracted all sorts of insincere friends. It had never really been an issue at work before.

And now Francesca had made it an issue by gossiping.

He gritted his teeth. He wanted to hate her—he really did.

But he'd noticed something. Her happy, bubbly exterior with her colleagues was just that—an exterior. Scratch the surface and who knew what he might find? There had been a wistfulness in her eyes that had looked as if it reached down into her very soul. She genuinely hadn't trusted her instincts last night and he had to wonder why. She was a good nurse. She should have confidence in her abilities. Had something or someone taken her confidence away?

Whether he liked it or not, she was part of this team.

He wanted to work with competent, confident individuals. He liked to know their strengths—and their weaknesses—to get the best possible results for the patients they were serving. Here things would be no different.

It was why he'd taken some of her patients today. She seemed an able and competent nurse but he wanted to dig a little deeper.

So far, he'd found nothing to concern him. All the patients she'd seen had been well cared for. Her decision-making was sound. In fact, what he'd seen had given him even more confidence in her abilities.

Not that she'd ever know. She'd looked as if she was going to bite him when he'd said he wanted to check over her patients.

As a doctor he nearly always had staff to mentor, opportunities to increase their learning experience and instil confidence in their abilities. He just hadn't expected to find it here on a cruise ship. He'd almost expected the rest of the staff to be running circles around about him based on their longer experience. But it wasn't the case with Francesca. And whether he liked her or not, he was determined to find out why.

CHAPTER FIVE

ONE week later Francesca felt as if she was still fighting to see her own patients. Gabriel had reviewed practically every staff member she'd ever seen. And for a man who'd spent the last six years in paediatrics he was a meticulous adult practitioner who missed nothing.

If she hadn't been so busy she would have been nervous. What if he did find something wrong? What if she'd mismanaged a patient?

Working with Gabriel was like walking a tightrope. Constantly teetering on the high wire, with him waiting to see her fall. There was no doubt he wouldn't be there to catch her. It was almost a certainty that he'd watch her splat on the ground like some fly on a windscreen.

He was constantly looking over her shoulder, asking her seemingly inane work-related questions. She was sure he was trying to catch her out and she felt like an amoeba under a microscope.

She almost wished he'd just come out and tell her that, rather than pussyfoot round about her. She preferred the direct approach rather than the wolf in sheep's clothing.

Everyone else around him was well and truly smitten. With the rest of the staff and the passengers, his Italian charm served him well. But the air between the two of them still crackled with animosity.

Francesca hated to admit it but there was something really intimidating about an insanely handsome man hating the ground you walked on. Sometimes she caught him looking at her with a strange expression on her face, as if he was trying to get the measure of her. She'd no idea why.

He could the see the practical examples of her work all over the ship. He could audit her written and electronic records until he was blue in the face. She was almost sure there was nothing for him to find.

But it was that little touch of uncertainty that made her nervous. No matter how well she performed there was almost always a tiny part of her wondering if she'd missed something. Wondering if she was about to make a mistake that would affect someone's life.

Before her father's death it had never been there. She'd been confident at her work and in her abilities. But no matter how hard she tried, she felt as if that confidence would never return.

It was always going to be there—that little voice in her head, telling her to guard herself and walk carefully. Questioning her abilities. Just the way Gabriel was constantly doing.

And worse still it was all her own fault.

There was nobody else to blame.

She'd allowed herself to be swept off her feet by a playboy doc just like Gabriel. A man with the attention span of a goldfish and the staying power of an ice cream on a sunny day.

But for a few months she'd been smitten. More important, she'd been distracted.

She'd spent less time with her father, too busy being swept from one date to the next by Dr Wonderful. Except he wasn't.

If only she'd paid attention. If only she'd spotted the signs of what her father had been planning. But she hadn't.

Now she had to live with the consequences. And Dr Wonderful? All the more reason to stay away from men like Gabriel. Turned out he hadn't been so wonderful after all. He'd dropped her like a hot brick when her father had died. Thank goodness for Jill.

How long could she work in this environment?

And what had happened to her Australian visa?

She looked down at the two lists in front of her—one for crew, one for passengers. Finally, a patient of her own to review. For a second she almost felt relief that he wasn't checking up on her today, then a glance at the passenger list made her realise that four children were waiting to be seen.

Gabriel always wanted to see the children himself. It was natural—he was a paediatrician after all. But he was almost a little too fastidious about it. To the point of being slightly obsessional. He'd even asked David Marsh to page him, whether he was on duty or not, to see any children requiring treatment.

Maybe the man was just a control freak. But she hadn't noticed it in anything else that he did. And it hadn't been on the list of complaints from Jill, either.

Jill. She still hadn't emailed Francesca back yet and Francesca was curious to know what her response would be. She couldn't quite decide whether Jill would send a rant about what a louse Gabriel was or a request for new pictures of her unrequited love. You could never tell with that girl.

Francesca gave a sigh and picked up the crew list. It was time to do some work. The waiting room already had a few customers.

'Roberto Franc, please.' Francesca smiled and ushered him into a nearby consulting room.

Roberto Franc was a twenty-year-old busboy on the ship. He had been diagnosed with diabetes mellitus a few weeks before and was struggling to control his condition. Diabetes mellitus was usually diagnosed in childhood and Roberto was older than the average new patient but Francesca was confident she could help him cope.

He settled into the chair opposite Francesca, pushing his diary across the desk towards her.

'How are you?' she asked.

'Not bad,' he muttered. She took the diary from him and glanced at its contents. Newly diagnosed diabetics were taught to monitor their blood-sugar results regularly and record them in a diary. It helped give an accurate picture of how they were coping on insulin injections, and if the injections were controlling their blood sugars accordingly.

'I can see you've been testing frequently,' Francesca said. 'Sometimes six times a day—how are your fingers?'

'Sore.' He lifted his hands and placed them palms upward on the desk in front of her.

She could see the little marks on his fingertips where the tiny lancet had pierced his fingers. The little dots appeared all over his fingertips, with some fingers looking slightly swollen. 'I think we can help with that,' she said. 'What type of meter do you have?'

He pulled a black package from the back pocket of his trousers. It was little bigger than a wallet, but when opened contained his testing strips, blood glucose meter and lancet holder. Francesca smiled, recognising the type of meter. She pulled the instruction card from inside the front pocket. 'I know it's hard initially, but until we have your blood sugars completely under control it is important that you keep testing. There are other sites you can take blood from—it doesn't always have to be from your fingertips.' She showed him on the instruction leaflet. 'You could try the forearm.'

He nodded slowly. 'I hadn't really thought of that.'

'It would give your fingers a few days to recover—you might find it useful to try.' She was still studying his diary carefully. 'I think we need to adjust some of your insulin doses,' she continued slowly. 'Your injection that you take at night—the long-lasting insulin that gives you a backdrop throughout the day—it needs to go up a little.' She pointed at the diary 'For the last week your blood-sugar levels have been quite high in the mornings when you wake up, that tells us we need to adjust the insulin you take last thing at night. We will put it up by two units initially and review it again in another week.'

He nodded thoughtfully. 'What about the dinnertime dose?'

'I notice that you've had a few hypoglycaemic attacks around 7:00 p.m. When have you been having lunch?'

'About three o'clock, after all the passengers have finished.' Francesca was aware that as a busboy Roberto would be expected to be on duty during lunch and dinner service times. It made it more difficult to control his own eating times. He wouldn't be having lunch till three and dinner till around nine. Hypos—or hypoglycaemic attacks—happened when a person's blood sugar fell too low. It didn't just affect people with diabetes. Lots of people could become tired, lack concentration or become cranky if they didn't eat for a while and, as a result, their blood sugar became low. For Roberto however, it was more serious. Diabetics' blood-sugar levels could fall so low that they could lose consciousness.

'How did you feel when you had the hypos? Did you have any warning signs?'

Roberto raised his hands and shrugged his shoulders. 'On a few occasions I was trembling and sweaty, and at those times I knew to sit down and have something to eat. On other occasions I haven't noticed so much, especially when it's busy during service. I dropped some plates the other night and one of the other busboys came and told me to sit down as I was a terrible colour. I checked my blood sugar then and it was low.'

'Okay.' Francesca nodded reassuringly. 'It takes time to recognise the signs of a hypoglycaemic attack—and they can be different in every person with diabetes. I realise it's even more difficult if you're busy and thinking about other things. It's good that your colleagues know what is wrong with you and can point out if you're not looking so good.'

His face twisted in frustration. 'But I hate that. I want to be able to control this myself.'

'I know all about how frustrating diabetes is. My dad was diabetic for years. Sometimes he struggled to control it, too. You've just been diagnosed and you need to give it a little time.' She patted his hand. 'We will get this under control. I think you need to reduce the insulin dose you're taking at three o'clock when you're having your lunch. It's a short-acting insulin and could be contributing to the hypos you've been having around 7:00 p.m. It could still be lasting in your body, particularly if you haven't eaten enough, or if your physical activity levels have been raised.

'We'll reduce it just by a few units, two would be best. I would also suggest that you need to have a think about how long you go between meals. I think you should have an extra snack around six. It's a long time until nine when you actually eat your evening meal.'

'But that's right when service starts for evening meals so we're really busy then.'

'I know that. But if you eat just before the doors open at six o'clock, then you'll probably be fine throughout service. I can speak to the dining room manager if it helps.'

'Thanks, you'll probably have to. I don't want him to think I'm shirking off.'

Francesca made a little note in his file. 'That's no problem. I'll speak to him today. Keep doing your blood-sugar readings and make the adjustments to your insulin as we've discussed. I've written a little note of them inside your diary. I'll give you an appointment for the same time next week and we'll see how you're doing.'

Roberto stood up from his chair and put his diary and meter back in his pockets. 'That's great, thanks, Nurse Cruz.'

'My pleasure.'

She showed him out to the door, and then headed back to put some more notes in his file and record his appointment in the book for next week.

Gabriel was standing at the doorway, his arms folded across his chest, watching her intently. He'd obviously finished seeing his four children in record time.

'That's quite a gift you've got.'

Her head snapped up from the appointment book. She realised that he must have been listening to her from the consulting-room door. She had been so focused on her patient that she hadn't noticed. A pink tinge of embarrassment flushed her cheeks. 'What do you mean?'

'You dealt with him like a real expert—as if you really understood.'

She could feel the adrenaline cursing through her veins.

Fight or flight syndrome. Gabriel was being nice to her—should she be suspicious right now or not? 'I do.'

'So I gathered. How long was your dad diabetic?'

'From around the same age. He was actually really well controlled, but I grew up recognising any signs of hypo in him and knew how to deal with it. Later in life, when things were a little more difficult for him, I helped adjust his insulin when he needed it.'

'It must have been a distinct advantage, having a daughter who was a nurse.'

Francesca shook her head and he could almost see her cringe. 'To be honest, most of the things I learned about diabetes I already knew before I started my nursing. But it made it easier for me when looking after patients with diabetes, and for dealing with the families.'

'You seemed to cover everything. Even how he must be feeling and coping with his fears and anxieties. You're good.'

It was a compliment but as soon as he'd said the words a shadow passed over her face. 'Not that good.' The words were quiet, almost whispered.

'What?'

He sensed her take a deep breath and saw her straighten, pushing her shoulders back. 'All nurses are supposed to practice holistic care,' she said, as if she was quoting straight from a textbook. 'But don't kid yourself. I'm not a mental health nurse. Experience has taught me I'm not good at any of that kind of stuff.'

Gabriel stopped his mouth from automatically opening in response. It would be so easy to pursue this. It would be so easy to ask her exactly what she meant by that. But Gabriel didn't pry. If she wanted to tell him she would. Was this the reason she had no confidence at work?

She tried to change the subject quickly to deflect what was obviously on his mind. 'I guess you could say diabetes was one of my "babies". We all have them. What's yours?'

'Paediatrics. It was the only reason I came into medicine. I always wanted to work with children.'

She tilted her head to the side. 'But yet you don't have any of your own. Makes me wonder about you, Gabriel. Too much playboy, not enough family man. Maybe it's time for you to settle down.' He had no idea how relieved she was right now to have moved the conversation away from her dad. The one person she didn't want to talk about. Not to anyone.

But Gabriel didn't look too happy now. His relaxed expression had disappeared. 'Having children has never been high on my agenda. Taking care of children has.'

There was finality in his words. Determination.

She wanted to reply, *But you've ended up on a cruise ship,* but the words stuck in her throat. Something told her not to respond that way. Not right now.

Katherine appeared at the door, her face pale and her hands on her stomach. It broke the instant tension in the room. He walked straight over and put his arm around her shoulders. 'What's wrong?'

'I'm not feeling so good.' She glanced between them. 'Do either of you mind if I go and lie down for a few hours?'

Francesca shook her head and Gabriel guided Katherine towards the door. 'Of course not. The clinics are finished for this morning and it's only emergency callouts this afternoon. Francesca and I can manage those. Go and lie down. And give me a page if you need anything.' He nodded at Francesca, who smiled in response.

'Thanks, you two. See you later.' Katherine practically bolted out the door.

Francesca bit her lip. 'Please let this be just an upset stomach. The last thing we need is a Norovirus outbreak.'

Gabriel's brow wrinkled as the realisation of her words hit him. There had been several cruise ships last year that had been affected by Norovirus. Cruises had had to be stopped and vessels berthed and deep-cleaned or sanitised before any new trips were started. It had been a nightmare for both crew and passengers.

He groaned. 'I hadn't even thought of that.' He shot her a quick smile as he leaned back in his chair. 'A Medevac, a near drowning and now a possible outbreak. I'm turning into the bad-luck fairy, aren't I?'

Francesca shook her head. 'There are always a few people aboard that become unwell. Katherine could just be unlucky. The next few hours will tell us if we need to put our public health hats on. Let's cross our fingers that we don't.'

She walked over to the side of the room, her eyes resting on a calendar in front of her. A tight fist was clenched around her heart as she realised the date. She felt physically sick. Almost instantly tears formed in her eyes. Was it the seventeenth already? How could she not have noticed?

She turned quickly to Gabriel. 'If you don't need me, I'm going up on deck to catch a little sun.' Before he had a chance to answer, she was gone.

Gabriel leaned back in his chair. For once the medical centre was empty.

He felt frustrated. Just when he thought he might have had an opportunity to talk to Francesca. To try and dig a little deeper, to try and find out what was going on in her head. But she'd dashed out of here like a startled rabbit.

He was sure she'd brushed a tear from her face as she'd left out the room. What on earth was wrong with her?

Should he go after her?

He looked around him, trying to figure out why. What on earth could have made her cry?

Nothing stood out. The conversation about Norovirus had been totally work related and entirely unremarkable. There was no reason for her reaction.

He was torn. The last thing he wanted to do was unintentionally upset another member of staff, even if the atmosphere between them had been prickly. Even if her actions at times had annoyed him.

He'd tried to brush aside the playboy comments. He didn't want to go down that road. What was the point in finding a wife and settling down? He'd seen what happened to families. There were some things that you could never recover from.

And although he'd never courted the media, being labelled a playboy wasn't so bad. It meant that most women had no illusions about him. No expectations.

His father had been furious at his decision to become a doctor. The printing business was their legacy, their mark on the world. Who was going to continue that now?

The reminder that Gabriel was the last remaining male was clear and it had stung. He could still picture his father's face—red with anger and glistening with sweat.

But even as a teenager Gabriel had been clear that saving lives was more important than a family business. Saving lives like Dante's. Surely his father had to be rational? Had to see the reasoning behind Gabriel's decision?

He'd dismissed him with the wave of a hand. And Gabriel had been furious with his father—at his lack of acknowledgement of Dante's lost life. At the way he'd focused on his work instead of his family, causing Gabriel to step into his shoes at far too young an age.

And now, with his increased frailty, it was happening again.

He looked over at the clock, calculating the time difference between Greece and Italy. He had an ideal opportunity to sort out of some of his father's day-to-day work duties. He could put this time to good use and maybe even fit in a phone call to find out how his father was feeling.

Whatever was wrong with Francesca would have to wait—even though it did leave his stomach churning.

He really didn't have time to waste on some nurse.

CHAPTER SIX

FRANCESCA was feeling sick and it was nothing to do with a bug. She dashed along the corridor to her cabin. How could she not have noticed the date?

Eighteen months ago today. Eighteen months since her father had committed suicide and she'd found his body sitting in the armchair in his house, with a letter for her and a bottle of pills next to it.

It didn't matter where she was, or what she was doing. The seventeenth of the month was always a day where she felt in the doldrums. It was always a day she needed to clear her head.

It was also a day that was usually imprinted on her brain. What had happened to her?

She threw off her uniform and pulled on her swimming costume and matching red sarong. She needed to be out in the fresh air as the walls seemed to be closing in on her.

A few minutes later she reached the adults-only part of the ship. Away from the frantic swimming pools and happy families crowded onto sun loungers.

Up here in the adults-only section there were wicker pod sun loungers, the cocooned structures designed to give a little more comfort and a little shelter from the sun's rays. She flopped down into one and pulled her book from her bag.

There was a fantastic view of the sea from here. The beautiful blue sea that stretched on for miles and miles. The sun's rays licked at her toes and she could feel the cooling sea breezes through her hair. She always escaped up here when she needed to. The ship was huge, but still a confined environment, and it was often hard to get some time and space on your own.

She stared out ahead. The tears already prickling at her eyes. Why hadn't she noticed? Why hadn't she realised just how bad her dad had been feeling?

He'd taken the loss of her mum really hard. But that had been five years before and after a dark spell of depression he'd seemed to be making improvements. He'd started to go out more, eat a little better and socialise with friends again.

It was probably why she'd felt safe enough to allow distractions. To listen to the insincere words of flattery from the playboy doc and be fooled by them.

Her father's suicide had been like an absolute bolt from the blue.

And his handwritten letter had just broken her heart.

He couldn't face life any more without his beloved wife. And as much as he loved Francesca, he felt as if he was holding her back. It was time to go.

Did he think she'd found someone to love?

She'd taken a job back in Glasgow after her mum had died as she hadn't wanted to leave her dad on his own. The truth was, she *had* turned down other job opportunities so she could stay in Glasgow with her dad, but she'd never mentioned them. And after he was gone she'd flitted from job to job, gaining experience and building her portfolio.

But nowhere had felt like home. Nowhere had removed the ache of loneliness she always felt.

She closed her eyes. The padding inside the pod was wonderfully comfortable. The quiet sound of the sea was calming. The book slipped from her hands.

'So this is where you've been hiding. There's good news and there's bad news. What do you want first?'

There was a jolt as the weight of someone sitting at the entrance of her pod made the whole structure move. Gabriel's voice broke into her dream. A dream of her father reading her favourite bedtime stories, Rapunzel, Cinderella.

For an instant she wanted to be angry with him. But the truth was she was getting used to him. Gabriel Russo wasn't turning out to be the man she'd thought he was. The more she saw of him the less deplorable he became.

She groaned. 'You've just ruined my dream.'

He leaned forward, his body entering into the pod. It seemed like an intimate gesture and she pushed herself further back into the cushions.

'Was it a good dream?'

'It was perfect.'

'Was I in it?' He'd switched on his million-dollar smile. There was no way she was going to be affected by it.

'Not a chance.'

Other women would love this. A sheltered pod on a huge cruise ship with a handsome man. His face was only inches away from hers, his body seemed even closer. Whilst her red swimming costume and sarong were normal attire for most of the passengers, she automatically wanted to cover herself up. He had a pair of beach shorts on and those killer abs were visible again. Why couldn't he put them away around her?

She pushed herself up a little, moving her legs closer to

the pod entrance, the only route of escape. 'If you'd been in it Prince Charming would have turned into a slimy frog.'

'Ouch.' He sat up next to her at the pod entrance. 'What are you doing here?'

'I would have thought that was obvious. I'm being extremely lazy and lying here, reading a book.'

'What are you reading? Something pink and fluffy?'

She raised her eyebrows at him.

'Or something, dark, dangerous and mysterious?'

'What do you care?'

'I'm interested. I like to know what people read.' He picked up her book and looked at the title, flipping it over and starting to read the back cover blurb.

A smile crept across her face as she waited and watched for the penny to drop. Any second now his face would go scarlet and he would drop the book as if it were on fire.

But no. Nothing. Just the tiniest twitch of his leg. He turned and handed it back to her.

She knew exactly what part of the body a blurb like that would have an effect on.

His face remained calm. 'So, hot and sexy, then?'

She nodded, 'Yeah, definitely hot and sexy.' She raised an eyebrow at him. 'A girl can dream, right?'

What was she doing? She'd just flirted with him. The man she hated. The man who was watching her every move. Was she mad?

Gabriel's dark brown eyes were getting even darker. He sat up straighter. 'About tonight…' he started.

'What about tonight? I'm off duty.'

'Yeah, I know.' He shrugged his shoulders. 'But Katherine's feeling really bad. She wondered if you'd mind covering for her.'

'Is that the good news or the bad news?'

'It depends entirely what you think of the next bit. Katherine was supposed to be on dining-room duty tonight, eating with some of the passengers.'

Francesca nodded. 'Yeah, that's fine. What else?' All officers on the ship had to take a turn in dining with the passengers.

Gabriel smiled. 'I'm on that duty, too.'

Francesca groaned and flopped back inside the pod. 'Am I ever going to get rid of you?'

The words were there but the atmosphere between them had changed. There wasn't the same tension. There wasn't the same angst. It was almost as if they'd reached a mutual plateau.

'You owe me.'

She narrowed her eyes at him. 'What?'

He shook his head at her. 'You know well that after the dinner we're supposed to go and watch the entertainment—be a visible presence amongst the passengers without officially being on duty.'

'And so?' The cogs in her brain were starting to turn. Dining-room duty was easy—eat dinner, make general conversation with the passengers.

After that she would be free to have a few drinks. She wouldn't be expected to respond to any patient queries—Kevin and David were on duty for those—so she could let her hair down. Try and forget about this bad day.

'There's no way I'm going out there alone. You'll have to watch the entertainment with me. You can rescue me from any cougars that may be about. You know—the ones you forgot to tell me about.'

She started to laugh and pushed herself up from the entrance to the pod. 'But you deserved that.' She lifted her book and pressed it close to her chest. 'As a professional courtesy I might agree to stay in your company.' She rolled her eyes' at him. 'I'd hate it if our ship's doctor got caught in a compromising position.'

She turned to leave. 'But in that case it will cost you. I'm planning on having a few drinks tonight—and you're buying. See ya.' Francesca sashayed her way across the desk. She could almost feel his eyes burning a hole into her spine. One sentence at the forefront of her brain.

What on earth are you doing, Fran?

Francesca had managed to smile and nod her way through the eight p.m. dinner even though she hadn't been able to eat a bite. Her eyes had watched every minute tick past on the clock in the dining room.

Gabriel had been seated with a family at the table next to hers. Her eyes had kept straying in his direction and she'd watch him read *The Cat in the Hat* to one of the young kids as the adults ate their dinner.

He'd seemed totally at ease and relaxed sitting amongst the family. She'd even heard him laugh. Was that possible for Gabriel?

It was obvious why he was a paediatrician. He was great with kids, had a real affinity with them. It made her wonder why he didn't have any of his own.

This afternoon had been the most relaxed she'd seen him since he'd got here. He hadn't been staring at her with those disapproving eyes.

Maybe they were both tiring of the constant prickliness between them. The jagged edges that had been clashing together were finally being worn down. To be replaced by…what?

Because there was still something that crackled in the air between them. The animosity had been replaced by something else. An underlying current that had been there since they'd first met. That neither of them had acknowledged or acted on. Until now.

The tension had built inside her so much that it was a relief when dinner finally finished at nine p.m. and she was able to make her excuses and rush back to her cabin.

Her laptop pinged behind her and she pressed the button. An email.

From Jill.

Her hand hesitated over the keyboard. What did she want this email to say? That she was furious that Gabriel was there, and rant about how badly he'd treated her? Or something else entirely? The *do I have a chance of getting back in there* type email. You could never tell which way Jill was going to go.

She pressed the button, her eyes automatically skimming the page.

Hi honey!
Gabriel Russo—well there's a blast from the past! Is he still as dashing and gorgeous than ever? No, don't answer that. I might be tempted again.

What on earth happened? Why did you have to resuscitate him? Can't imagine someone as fit as Gabriel falling overboard, so there must be more to it than that. Do tell.

I'd love the thought of being trapped in an enclosed space with him. I'm sure I could find a way to while away the hours with Dr Delicious. Tell him hi from me.

Have to go. Meeting Ferdinand for lunch. He's a duke or something.

Try not to fall out with Gabriel on my account—he was really just another notch on my bedpost. Send me some pictures of him if you can. And remember to tell me all the details!

Love Jill xx

Francesca didn't know whether to breathe a sigh of relief or throw up her hands in frustration. *'Tell him hi from me.'* What was that supposed to mean? And if Jill wasn't in the least perturbed at her working with Gabriel, why was she so bothered?

She slammed the laptop shut. It had taken Jill over two weeks to answer her email. She could wait for a response.

She wrinkled her nose. What exactly had Jill told her about Gabriel? Now she thought back to that night, not a lot. Was there a chance she might have misjudged Gabriel? Maybe she should lower her defences—just a little—and give him a chance to be friends?

Her fingers were trembling as she unfastened her dress uniform and hung it carelessly back in the cupboard. She grabbed the nearest dress, navy blue, stared at it and then flung it back. For some reason she didn't want something boring and dull. Gabriel was a gorgeous man. She didn't want people to glance over thinking, *What's he doing with her?*

Something had changed in her brain. She pulled out a red dress that she'd bought for New Year; it was cut with a generous V-neckline to reveal her cleavage, and skirted just above her knees to show off her long legs. It sparkled with randomly placed sequins that added a little glamour to the colour of the dress. Francesca knew this dress showed off her curves well. Fashion rules said that you either revealed cleavage or legs but this dress made its own rules and showed a little of both—giving just a hint of what was underneath.

She picked up the gold filigree necklace she had bought in Venice a few months ago. It was the most expensive piece of jewellery that she owned—a gift to herself one year after her dad's funeral. He'd left her a little nest egg along with another amount that had instructions to buy something she would love for ever. So she'd wanted to buy something precious, something she could keep and remember him by.

She'd never really embraced her origins so an Italian necklace had seemed entirely appropriate. And somehow she knew he would approve. Especially today.

With its tiny beads of red murano glass it would go perfectly. She fastened the clasp around her neck. No other jewellery was necessary; the necklace was more than enough. She finished off her outfit with gold sandals and ran a quick brush through her chestnut locks. A flick of mascara and some ruby-coloured lipstick and she was ready. A glimpse out of the corner of her eye confirmed it was ten o'clock. A final squirt of perfume and she picked up her cabin card and left.

Gabriel was waiting in the Atlantis Bar. His brain was not entirely sure what he was doing there. Being one of the ship's doctors meant additional roles and responsibilities and he understood that. He'd invited Francesca merely as a means of self-protection. And if he kept telling himself that, he might actually grow to believe it. He eyed his watch nervously—what if she changed her mind and didn't come? The cougars were already circulating.

He looked at the drinks sitting on the bar. He had no idea what she drank, hadn't even thought to ask her beforehand, so he had thrown caution to the wind and decided to order something frivolous.

Seconds later he caught the scent of her perfume. He

was standing facing the main entrance, but she must have came in via the side entrance and crept up behind him. His head swam with the sensual fusion of woody, amber and floral essences with hints of orange blossom. He turned swiftly to find her standing directly behind him.

'Is this mine?' She picked up one of the cocktail glasses sitting on the bar and without waiting for an answer put her lips to the edge of the glass and took a sip. Gabriel stood transfixed, moving his gaze from her deep brown eyes to her ruby-coloured lips sipping from the glass, finally catching a sparkle of the intricate gold creation around her neck.

'Gabriel?'

Her face had broken into a wild smile. 'Don't tell me I've just stolen someone else's drink from the bar?'

He snapped out of his daze. 'Yes. Of course it's yours— I just wasn't sure what to order.'

But it was the gold filigree necklace that attracted his attention most. He recognised the design and the work-manship of the piece.

The necklace was a piece of art. A piece of art that he knew the value of. He was more than a little curious about who'd bought it for her.

Another little mystery about the woman who spoke so little about herself.

That afternoon he'd actually started to quite like her. He'd thought they might manage to have a working rela-tionship. The tension between them seemed to have disin-tegrated and things had seemed almost manageable.

The sight of Francesca in her red swimsuit and sarong had sent blood rushing to parts of his body. As for her taste in books…

He felt as if he was finally getting to know her a little. Finally scratching beneath her prickly surface.

But what now?

Another thought started to creep into his brain. Francesca hadn't mentioned a lover or a boyfriend. She didn't wear any rings. Did she have some sugar daddy who had given her such an expensive present?

'Gabriel, what's wrong?'

She was standing directly under his nose. Her cocktail glass already empty, her dark brown eyes staring up at him. 'You've got the permanent frown on your face again.' She shot a beaming smile at a passenger who said hello on the way past. 'Can't you lighten up a bit?' she muttered. 'This is going to be a long evening.' She waved her cocktail glass at him. 'And I'm going to need another of these. What is it anyway?'

She was positioned right under his nose. And as he looked downwards his eyes were drawn directly to her deep cleavage. She was a knockout in that dress. Not that he hadn't noticed she was a knockout anyway but he'd been too busy disapproving of her to step back and take a good look.

But she seemed on edge, jittery almost. She'd drunk that cocktail in two minutes flat. What was her story? The other team members were open about their home lives, sharing photos and tales of their families and friends. But Francesca remained tight-lipped. He hardly knew a thing about her. What made her tick?

Her nursing skills were impeccable. He'd reviewed every case she'd worked on, observed her, spoken to staff and crew alike—Francesca didn't have a thing to worry about. So why was she nervous?

The intricate goldwork and highly polished murano

glass of her necklace were shimmering under the neon lights of the Atlantis Bar. When she turned in certain directions the reflected light shone back on her face. And she was certainly attracting attention. If Gabriel had felt under scrutiny from the cougars earlier, it was nothing compared to the male reaction in the room to Francesca.

And she hadn't noticed. She flung back her head and laughed at something the man next to her said, her dark lustrous curls tossed over her shoulder. Her clingy red dress hugged her figure to perfection and the man had certainly noticed.

Gabriel was annoyed. He was *more* than annoyed. That guy should back off. Didn't he see that she was here with him?

He reached over and touched the necklace, circling his fingers around the droplet of red murano glass that skirted her cleavage. It might be a little forward but, hopefully, it would get rid of the man on the right.

'This is beautiful, Francesca. Where did you get it? Did a secret admirer buy it for you?'

Everything stopped. She'd been acutely conscious of standing next to him but not quite touching. Aware of his tall, broad frame and penetrating dark eyes. With his permanently knotted brow it was obvious that something was bothering him. He ought to be careful—if the wind changed his face could stay that way for ever. After watching him in the dining room tonight, she was beginning to think his frown was reserved solely for her.

Her eyes flickered up and down his body. He had changed from his dress uniform into dark trousers, a pale blue shirt and dark Italian shoes. It looked simple enough but was obviously expensive. Her eyes caught the several dark curled hairs revealed at the base of his throat. His

Mediterranean skin was bronzed and alluring and his obvious muscled and well-proportioned body seemed to be attracting the attention of much of the female company in the room.

But he was with her.

And she'd been desperately trying to put that out of her mind.

And then he'd touched her, those fingertips unexpectedly brushing the swell of her breasts. Francesca froze. His fingers were fastened around the biggest piece of glass on her necklace and he was watching her. Waiting for an answer. Why couldn't she speak?

She shifted her weight on her feet. Right now she felt like a starstruck teenager. But why? She didn't even like this man so why on earth was he having this effect on her?

Maybe it was the email from Jill. It was strange that she hadn't made any derogatory comments about him. She hadn't been outraged at all. More interested in the details. All of it sent tiny alarm bells ringing in Francesca's head.

Maybe she had misjudged him? What would Gabriel say if she told him? Would he get that disapproving look on his face at the mention of Jill's name? Why was that? He was the one in the wrong.

Her stomach twisted, loyalty to Jill unsettling her.

His dark brown eyes were still staring at her. Watching every expression on her face. Did he know what she was thinking?

She really didn't want to explain about the necklace. She didn't want to tell him that her dad had left her money—that would take the conversation down a road she wasn't prepared to go.

He'd ask her how her father had died. It was only natural. And she didn't want to tell him about the suicide, particularly today—it was just too hard.

Then she'd have to admit she'd missed the signs and that if she'd paid more attention her beloved father might still be here.

Tonight her ambition was to drink herself into oblivion. And these strawberry-type cocktails were a good start. She had to steer this conversation away from the necklace as quickly as possible.

She gulped, struggling to find some words. 'Not so much a secret admirer,' she finally managed.

'No?'

His hand pulled her a little closer, the full length of her body coming into contact with his. What was he doing? She couldn't concentrate. 'I picked it myself. But it was a gift—to remind me of someone very dear to me.'

'Someone special?'

'More than you know.' She lowered her eyelids so he wouldn't see the tears threatening to pool there. Gabriel was a colleague, nothing more, nothing less. He wasn't interested in her. She would place bets he could have any woman in this room.

He'd ordered more drinks so she lifted her glass towards his. 'What is this? You didn't tell me.'

His eyes flitted from her necklace to her dress—was he looking at her cleavage?—and then back to her drink. 'A strawberry daiquiri.'

'Cheers,' she said, taking a long sip from the straw. 'It's almost as if you guessed what I'd be wearing.' She smiled as she tasted the strawberry daiquiri. 'Red to match my dress, and rum, my favourite flavour. Keep this up and I'll be expecting big things from the night ahead.'

She was holding her breath, hoping he wouldn't realise

she'd deflected the conversation. Hoping he'd just accept her answer and move on.

It seemed to take for ever for him to answer. He glanced at his watch. 'The show will start soon. Do you still want to go?'

Her face broke into a beaming smile. 'Absolutely—I've never seen it.'

'Why not? You've been on this boat for months.'

'I'm usually too tired to go and see a show that doesn't start until ten-thirty,' she admitted. 'But tonight I will make an exception, on the proviso, of course, that my boss doesn't give me trouble tomorrow for yawning while on duty!'

They walked along the corridor towards the Whisper Theatre. It was crowded with passengers who had all come to see the popular ten-thirty show. The theatre seated over eight hundred people and, although situated within the ship, its breadth and width covered three internal decks. Francesca and Gabriel filed into the nearest row of seats and sat in the velvet-covered chairs. The lights quickly dimmed and the audience immediately quietened. In the darkened theatre a juggler appeared at the side of the stage, but instead of the usual balls or skittles he was juggling fire-filled torches, which hissed and spat as he threw them in the air. The audience was mesmerised.

Francesca spent the whole time with her brain spinning. She had no idea what was going on. Whatever had shifted between her and Gabriel was terrifying her. She didn't want to be one of the millions blown away by his good looks and TV-star smile.

In the dark theatre, she was also acutely aware of how close she and Gabriel were sitting. Every time their arms brushed against one another she felt a little frisson of excitement tingle up her spine. When she went to change the position of her legs, her crossed leg touched his trouser-clad one and he turned in the darkness and gave her a brief smile. When the show finally finished and the lights came up slowly, Francesca was almost disappointed at being brought back to reality.

'Did you enjoy it?' Gabriel asked.

'It was wonderful.'

They stood back, waiting for the theatre to empty. As the crowd thinned he placed his arm lightly at her back. 'I'll walk you back to your cabin.' He smiled.

'Okay.' Francesca felt her heart dip in disappointment. He hadn't asked her to go back to the bar for another drink. She glanced at her watch. It wasn't that late—was he trying to get rid of her?

The corridor to her cabin was empty. Most people were either already in their cabins or drinking in one of the bars. She stopped outside her door.

'Thanks, Gabriel, that was lovely.' Her eyes were fixed on the floor. She felt awkward and uncomfortable, the ease and relaxation of earlier in the night having left her. Silence hung in the air and neither of them moved.

'So you gave me mouth to mouth?'

Her head shot upwards. Where had that come from? Was he flirting with her? Was he trying to unnerve her?

There was something there. Something hanging in the air between them. Something that kept bringing a smile to her face.

'I did.'

'I'm sorry I can't remember it.' His voice was low, barely loud enough for her to hear. But she did. And it sent a shiver down her spine. 'Shouldn't you have been wearing a red swimsuit for that?'

Her laugh was instantaneous. He'd obviously been having the same thoughts that she'd had. Funny how one TV show had made such a lasting impression.

'In my rush to do the mouth to mouth I forgot about the red swimsuit,' she quipped. 'But what does it matter? You've already seen it.'

'That I have,' he whispered, stepping forward and closing the gap between them. 'I can't remember if I ever thanked you.'

Then, with the lightest of touches, he bent forward and his hand lightly stroked under her chin. Automatically, she raised her head to meet his. He gave her a slow, sexy smile that sent her pulse racing. His eyes smouldered with fire.

'I can't remember, either,' she whispered. No one else was in the dimly lit corridor. All she could hear was the sound of her heart thudding in her ears. Suddenly he dipped forward and his mouth hovered just millimetres away from hers. She stepped forward as her body reacted unconsciously to his. She felt him hardening against her and as she moved even closer she felt a little groan escape from his lips. She could feel his breath on her cheek, tickling her skin.

Now. Kiss me now.

She closed her eyes. It was inevitable. Any moment now she would feel his lips devouring hers.

Instead his lips brushed against her ear. 'Thank you, Francesca,' he whispered.

He stepped back, his breathing shallow and ragged, his eyes burning.

His breathing slowed. 'Goodnight, *cara.*' His accent stroked across her skin and she watched as his lean, athletic body turned and disappeared down the corridor.

She collapsed back against her door. Wow! Her head was spinning.

She lifted her slightly trembling hand and pushed the cabin card into the slot on her door. The door swung open and she collapsed onto her nearby bed.

He'd almost kissed her but had then walked away. The sparks between them could have set the whole ship alight. She could already imagine the sensations of kissing him. A blow-your-mind, send-you-rocketing-off-into-space, turn-your-legs-to-jelly kind of kiss. She didn't know whether to laugh, cry or chase him along the corridor and drag him back to her room!

Everything was racing through her mind. The man she didn't want to like. The man who had treated her friend so poorly had nearly just kissed her. And she'd let him.

Was she losing her mind?

Gabriel wasn't someone she could ignore. She had to work with him every day. How on earth was she going to deal with this?

Kissing the boss could turn out to be an occupational hazard.

Gabriel stared at his inbox—forty-six emails, all having come in during the last few hours. He glanced at the clock. It was after midnight but he could already tell that sleep was going to elude him tonight. Payroll queries, exporters, poor-quality ink, complaints, late deliveries and a pile of other mundane details. Dealing with the day-to-day enquiries had seemed simple at first but the more he dealt with, the more seemed to come his way. He'd finished one long day and it looked like he'd have an even longer night ahead.

What on earth had he been thinking of? Kissing her. Was he mad?

If she was anything like her friend and money was her motivator then this time tomorrow he could be slapped with a sexual harassment lawsuit.

The thought made his blood run cold.

How well did he really know Francesca?

Not well at all.

Tonight she'd looked beautiful. He'd almost been blown away by how stunning she'd looked in that red dress, with her long hair falling about her shoulders. The few cocktails had certainly relaxed her and made her seem less guarded. Less unapproachable.

But it had been the reaction to his touch that had caught him by surprise. He hadn't been imagining things between them. The slightest brush of skin had electrified them both.

Her stolen glances towards him. The lingering looks between them, lasting just longer than was entirely natural. The way you felt when you couldn't tear your eyes off someone.

And in that darkened corridor, when it had just been the two of them, he'd acted entirely on instinct. And she'd responded, without a doubt.

A single lapse of concentration could result in a huge pile of trouble.

What had he been thinking?

Gabriel banged his hand off the desk. His laptop wobbled, teetering close to the edge of the desk. He pulled it closer, focusing on the unopened emails in front of him.

Work. That's what he would do.

Anything to get his mind off Francesca.

Anything at all.

CHAPTER SEVEN

FRANCESCA starcd at the duty roster and felt her stomach plummet. Gabriel had swapped shifts this morning. The sinking feeling of dread continued as her overactive brain sent a million signals all at once.

He'd only swapped a few hours ago. It was obvious he was trying to avoid her. He must be regretting almost kissing her. She cringed. This was a nightmare.

She was beginning to think it hadn't happened. Maybe it was all just a figment of her overactive imagination? So why did it feel like he was body-swerving her?

There was no way they could avoid each other on a cruise ship and with a medical crew as small as they had.

Talk about out of the frying pan and into the fire. They'd gone from one whole heap of tension between them to another entirely.

She hadn't slept a wink last night. No matter how hard she'd tried. Her brain just hadn't let her. She'd eventually got up and tried to compose an email to Jill but nothing had sounded right.

In fact, everything had sounded exactly the way she felt—guilty.

The first email hadn't mentioned Gabriel at all and had been a dead giveaway as complete avoidance.

The second had been too vague.

The third had been too over the top. Nothing had sounded normal. Nothing had sounded like she'd wanted it to. So she'd eventually given up, made herself a cup of coffee and watched the sun rise from the top deck.

She'd worry about the return email to Jill later.

She glanced over the clinic lists. The ship was due to dock in Ephesus, Turkey today and most of the passengers would probably disembark. Any passenger who needed medical attention would try and attend the medical centre early to avoid missing the coach trips ashore. Sure enough, the list for this morning was busy.

David appeared at her shoulder. 'Morning, Francesca. You okay? You're looking tired. Hope you're not coming down with the same bug as Katherine.'

Francesca shook her head fiercely. 'Just didn't get much sleep last night.'

'You as well?' He raised his eyebrow at her as if she'd just revealed a closely guarded secret.

'What do you mean?'

David shrugged his shoulders. 'Gabriel asked me to swap with him this morning as he didn't sleep last night, either. He said he'd be in around eleven to take over from me.'

'Gabriel didn't sleep, either?' She could barely keep the squeak out of her voice. What did that mean? That he wasn't really avoiding her? That last night had bothered him just as much as it had bothered her? For a second her spirits almost lifted.

David looked up from the chart he was marking. 'Yeah, he was up late into the night, doing some work for his father.'

Her spirits plummeted immediately again. Gabriel

hadn't been thinking about her last night at all. She'd probably been the last thing on his mind. He'd been busy doing other things. 'I didn't know he worked for his father,' she said lightly.

David leaned over and put a few ticks on the clinic list. 'Apparently that's why he came back from America. His dad's health isn't too good and Gabriel is taking over some of the day-to-day running of the company. Trying to ease the strain, so to speak.'

'Wouldn't it make more sense for him to stay in Venice?'

David wagged his finger. 'Aha. You'd think so. But apparently if he's too close to home they'll try and drag him into the family business. Strangely enough, they weren't too keen on him becoming a doctor. All right with you if I see these patients? A few of them are follow-ups from the other day and one is a patient in renal failure I'm familiar with.'

'What? Oh, of course.' She nodded absent-mindedly, lifting the list. Gabriel was helping his father? Why hadn't he mentioned it?

They hadn't wanted him to become a doctor? It seemed almost absurd. Most families would be delighted if their son or daughter became a doctor. What an odd reaction.

She cringed. Of course he hadn't mentioned it—she'd hardly rolled out the red carpet for him. He probably thought it was none of her business.

She looked at the first name on her list. The quicker she started, the quicker she could finish. There were a few crew members who'd managed to avoid their medicals for over a month. She could go and track them down. Thoughts around Gabriel's avoidance tactics would have to wait. And they would probably require another cocktail.

She pasted a smile on her face and walked into the waiting room. 'Eleanor Kennedy, please.'

A few hours later she was nearly finished. Just one child to see: a four-year-old who was feeling generally unwell.

Gabriel had swapped places with David half an hour ago but she hadn't set eyes on him as he'd remained locked in the doctor's office with a notorious staff member who was trying to get out of his duties.

'Carly Glencross, please.'

Carly was sitting on her mother's knee, her eyes red, her face flushed and looking generally miserable.

Carly's mother carried her into the treatment room. 'I'm sure it's nothing,' she said, 'probably just a virus, but she's been like this the last few days. She's been really irritable. Can you just check her over?'

'No problem.' Francesca bent down next to Carly. 'Hi, Carly, I'm Fran, the nurse. Is it okay if I take a little look at you?'

Carly eyed her suspiciously before eventually nodding.

Francesca picked up the tympanic thermometer and demonstrated it to Carly. 'I'm just going to put this in your ear to take your temperature. It only takes a second and I press this little button. Okay?'

Carly nodded again. Francesca got the impression she wasn't going to get a word out of her.

She checked her temperature. High. She knelt in front of Carly and checked her face, neck and chest. Her eyes were red and a little sticky—probably some kind of conjunctivitis. She had a blotchy rash over her chest. The lymph glands in her neck were swollen and so were her hands.

'Have you given her something for her fever?'

Mum nodded. 'I'm giving her paracetamol and ibuprofen alternately. It's not really having much effect and not helping with her other symptoms.'

Francesca made a few notes in the chart. Carly was like a hundred other children she'd seen on the cruise ship or in A and E in her previous role. No specific infection. Just some random virus that spiked a temperature and made the kid miserable for a few days.

'Is she eating anything?'

Mum shook her head. 'I've been feeding her ice lollies to keep her going.'

Francesca nodded. Viruses commonly put kids off their food and it was important to keep them hydrated, particularly when they had a temperature. If ice lollies worked, that was fine.

She was always a little nervous around children. Even though she'd had lots of experience with them in the past, she wasn't specifically trained as a paediatric nurse so she liked to make sure she hadn't missed something.

She walked over to the drawer to pull out a general advice sheet to give to the mother. Her eyes were drawn to Gabriel's door. He normally liked to see all the kids who came to the medical centre. Should she give him a shout?

Carly gave a little cough, so Francesca poured out some water into a cup. 'Do you want to have a little drink?'

Carly nodded, still not speaking, and opened her mouth to take a sip of the water.

Her lips were slightly chapped, with painful cracks at the corners, and her tongue looked slightly swollen.

Francesca took a deep breath. She'd been just about to send this little one away with instructions to come back if there was no improvement in a day or so. But now she wasn't so sure.

Even more than that, she wanted to see how he would

react to her. Would he be embarrassed or act as if nothing at all had happened? Her stomach was clenched in a knot. It was better to get this over and done with.

'If you don't mind, I'm going to get our doctor to take a quick look at Carly. He's a paediatrician, so it's probably best if he sees her, too.'

Just at that Gabriel's door opened. The crew member stormed off and Gabriel's face was like thunder. They'd obviously had words.

It was a shock seeing him after last night. For the first time she noticed every inch of his face—the tiny lines around his eyes, the furrows on his brow and the tense expression when he caught sight of her. It was just as she'd expected. He was dreading the thought of seeing her after last night. He probably had a million lines prepared to try and fob her off. As if she'd give him the chance.

'Dr Russo,' she said briskly, 'could you have a look at Carly Glencross, please?'

Gabriel seemed to snap to attention. He crossed the room in a few steps, the automatic smile appearing on his face at the sight of the little girl and her mother. If only he'd smiled like that for her.

'What have you got?'

Francesca handed over the chart with the notes she'd made. 'Carly's four and has been sick for the last few days. She has a temperature, conjunctivitis and a blotchy rash. The lymph glands are up in her neck. Mum just wondered if there was anything else we could do for her.'

Gabriel knelt down and spoke in a soft voice to Carly. 'Well, hello there, princess.'

Gabriel only took a few minutes to examine Carly carefully, listening to her heart and lungs, looking in her throat and examining her hands.

He ran his fingers across the palms of her hands. They were slightly oedematous with the skin particularly red on the palms and peeling slightly around her nails.

'What are you looking for?' Francesca felt uneasy. What did Gabriel suspect? Some of Carly's symptoms were a little out of the ordinary and for some reason they were now setting off alarm bells in her head.

He'd barely made eye contact with her since he'd left his room. Was this how it was going to be between them now? Avoidance and aloofness?

'Stick your tongue out for me, please, Carly.'

She did, with pleasure, pulling a face at Gabriel.

'Strawberry-coloured tongue. Get me some aspirin please, Francesca.'

'But kids can't have aspirin, Gabriel, it's dangerous for under twelves.' Her words were automatic. Surely, as a paediatrician, he should know that?

Francesca may not have been trained as a paediatric nurse and normally she coped well but right now she was feeling out of her depth. But there were some golden rules that had been drummed into her by the sister of the A and E department where she'd previously worked. Aspirin being dangerous for under twelves was one of them.

He shook his head. 'In these circumstances it's exactly what we need.'

Gabriel stood up and made a few notes. He touched the side of Carly's face and gave her a little smile. 'You have been the best patient I've seen today. Would you like a fairy sticker?'

He pulled some from a roll attached to the wall. 'You pick the one you like best.'

Carly bent over the roll of fairy stickers, examining their colourful dresses. The stickers were used widely for the kids that attended the medical centre—fairies for girls and dinosaurs for boys.

'Could you bring over the ECG machine, please, Francesca?'

An ECG for a kid? Did a child's ECG look different from an adult's? Francesca didn't even know.

Cardiac. He thought it was a cardiac condition. She had a mad flash.

He sat down next to Carly's mum. 'Have you heard of Kawasaki disease?'

The woman almost did a double-take at the strange-sounding disorder. Her face automatically paled and she shook her head. 'No. What on earth is that? Is that what's wrong with Carly?'

Gabriel nodded. 'It's not widely known. It's a kind of autoimmune disorder that causes inflammation, particularly around the blood vessels.' He touched Carly's palms. 'It has a whole set of classic symptoms. The red palms and peeling skin is one of them, as is the strawberry-coloured tongue, persistent temperature and cracked lips.'

Francesca had wheeled the ECG machine over and felt frozen at the bottom of the bed. Kawasaki disease? Oh, no.

She'd just remembered. A kid from one of her days in A and E. Just like this.

A kid where the key indicator had been peeling skin on the soles of his feet.

She automatically walked over to Carly and removed her socks. Sure enough, peeling skin on the soles of her feet.

She held one foot aloft.

'Gabriel?'

He nodded.

She should have caught this. Yes, it was unusual but she'd come across this before.

The sinking feeling in her stomach wasn't going to go away.

She'd done it again. The one thing she'd said she'd never do.

She'd been distracted by Gabriel.

And she'd missed something. She'd missed *this*. Her head had been too full of Gabriel and the night before to concentrate on the patient in front of her.

Distracted by the playboy doc.

It made her feel physically sick. The fallout from the last time had affected her father. The time it could have been a kid.

Gabriel swung Carly's legs up on to the bed and laid her back against the pillows. 'I'm just going to get a little tracing of your heart, Carly.' He held up the leads from the ECG machine. 'I just need to attach these onto your chest.'

It only took him a few seconds and Francesca pressed the buttons. The heart tracing spat out the other side of the machine a few moments later.

'What does this mean for Carly?' Mrs Glencross's voice was becoming higher.

'First, we give her some aspirin. That's the first line of treatment for Kawasaki disease. Carly should really have some bloods taken and a chest X-ray, too. I'm going to phone the local paediatric unit here and talk to their consultant. It might be better for her to have the rest of her tests done there.'

'We need to leave the ship?'

Gabriel nodded. 'Carly will need to be admitted to hospital. Kawasaki disease can cause complications in children.'

'What kind of complications?'

Francesca could see him bite his bottom lip, as if trying to decide how much information to give. 'Some kids can develop inflammation around the blood vessels at the heart. They need to be monitored closely. Carly will need to have a scan of her heart. There's also another drug treatment called gammoglobulin that can be given. But it's a treatment that needs to be administered in hospital.'

Carly's mother sagged back against the wall. 'I thought she just had a bit of a cold, or a virus. I'd no idea it could be anything like this.'

Gabriel reached over and took her hand. 'I'm going to give Carly some aspirin in the meantime. Let me make a call to the local hospital and then I'll tell you what happens next.'

Francesca rechecked Carly's observations and gave her the aspirin that Gabriel had prescribed.

She tried to make herself busy, making tea for Mrs Glencross and phoning her husband to come and join them in the medical unit. They had docked at Ephesus that morning with Kusadasi being the nearest large town. Francesca knew it had two large, well-equipped hospitals—one public and one private—but she had no idea about the paediatric facilities.

She walked into Gabriel's office just as he was replacing the phone.

'What kind of complications can Kawasaki disease cause?' She tried to keep the tremble from her voice. It had been obvious to her that he'd been trying to stick to the basics for Carly's shocked mother. She couldn't remember what had happened to her last patient.

That was the trouble with A and E, the patients came through so quickly with little or no chance of follow-up.

He leaned back in his chair. 'The ambulance will be here in half an hour to transport Carly to the paediatric unit.' His heavy eyelids lifted, meeting her gaze for the first time that day. He watched her for a few seconds before answering. 'The inflammation of the blood vessels can affect the coronary arteries. One in five kids with Kawasaki disease will develop inflammation of the coronary arteries. It can lead to an aneurysm.'

He picked a pencil from his desk, twiddling it through his fingers as if concentrating deeply. 'That's why we give aspirin—to try and reduce the inflammation. Even kids who have been treated can still develop an aneurysm. This is serious stuff. One per cent of kids with this disease die. And it can have lasting impacts. Carly will need to be monitored for the rest of her life.'

An aneurysm. Francesca's head spun around to the treatment room where Carly was sitting with her mum and newly arrived dad. That little girl could have a life-threatening condition. And she'd almost sent her back to her cabin with a basic child-with-a-viral-infection sheet.

She could have sentenced that child to death. All because she'd almost missed something essential.

Her legs felt like jelly underneath her.

'Francesca, are you okay? You're very pale.' Gabriel was standing next to her, his hand touching her shoulder.

She couldn't look at him. She couldn't look him in the eye.

After her earlier thoughts about him avoiding eye contact with her, the irony was that now *she* couldn't look at him.

If she did, he would see it. He would be able to read her like a book. He'd know the mistake she'd almost made.

She couldn't bear to look at him. She couldn't bear to

think she might have based her decision to get Carly a second opinion on the fact she'd wanted to see Gabriel.

It made her feel pathetic. And absolutely useless at her job.

What if she'd sent that child back to her cabin? What if she'd developed an aneurysm that had ruptured at sea?

She'd been so close to doing that. So very close…

'Francesca.' His voice was firm and he had a hand on either shoulder, standing in front of her and looking her square in the eye.

'Can you phone a ship's porter to help the family with their packing and luggage? We don't have a lot of time here.'

She nodded numbly. It was time to go on autopilot. She could do this. She could get through this.

Gabriel was still talking. 'The hospital is going to carry out her blood tests and chest X-ray. We just need to write a transfer.' He glanced over his shoulder. 'And I need to have another word with the parents.'

Francesca nodded again. Phone the porter, instruct him to pack up the cabin. She could do that.

She turned towards the office, ready to make the phone call.

'Good call, Francesca.'

The words stopped her in her tracks. 'What?' It was the last thing she'd expected.

Gabriel was giving her a knowing smile. 'It was a good pick-up. Lots of people would have missed that. You didn't.' He turned and walked back into the treatment room.

Francesca held her breath. He had no idea. No idea at all.

But I almost did miss it.

Her heart was pounding in her chest. It was making

her head swim and sending tingles down her arms—and not in a good way.

This could have held a very different outcome for that little girl. An outcome based on *her* poor instincts. It didn't matter how hard she tried to work at it. Her worst fear had been realised.

She really had lost her nursing instincts. They were dead. Gone.

Or maybe they weren't. Maybe it was all about distraction.

She'd allowed herself to get distracted by Gabriel instead of focusing on the job.

How could she admit the truth to anyone? That the reason she'd asked for a second opinion hadn't been based on the little girl's condition but her own selfish, misplaced desires. What kind of a person did that make her?

Everything about this had been a bad idea. From the second she'd set eyes on Gabriel she'd known he was going to be trouble. As for last night? That had been a joke. Something to push out of her mind and forget about.

She had to concentrate on her work. Concentrate on her duties as a nurse. This couldn't be about her. This had to about her patients.

She picked up the phone and dialled the porter automatically. She grabbed Carly's chart and transferred the written remarks into the electronic record, ready for Gabriel to print out for the transfer.

The porter was going to meet them portside with the family's luggage. There would be no room for it in the ambulance, so it would have to be transported in a taxi. Francesca made another quick call to the cruise company representatives to organise someone to meet the family locally and sort out accommodation for them.

There. That was everything she could do right now. So why were her hands still trembling?

She'd seen this condition with its unusual set of symptoms before. She should have picked it up. And she would have—if she hadn't been so distracted by Gabriel.

She stood up and walked back through to the treatment room. Gabriel had just lifted Carly and seated her in a wheelchair.

There was no getting away from it, the little girl and her family looked frightened. Gabriel was doing his best to put them at ease: he'd managed to find a book for Carly to read and was telling her about his favourite character as he tucked a blanket around her knees.

She still looked unwell, but no more unwell than dozens of other children Francesca had seen in her life as a nurse. How many other kids could she have sent home with this condition?

The thought sent a shiver down her spine and the hairs at the back of her neck tingling.

The phone next to her rang. 'Ambulance is here, Gabriel,' she said as she replaced the receiver. 'I've also spoken to the main office. Marie, a company rep, will meet Mr and Mrs Glencross at the hospital and sort out accommodation for them. The family luggage will be transferred by taxi.'

Gabriel gave her a nod. 'That's great, Francesca, I'd been so busy organising things with the hospital I hadn't considered that.'

He grabbed the handles of the wheelchair and turned to the parents. 'I'll walk you down to the ambulance. You can man the medical centre, can't you, Francesca?'

She nodded and he pushed the chair out the door. His voice drifted along the corridor, 'Dr Demir will be waiting for you, he's fully informed about Carly's condition and will be able to carry out the rest of her tests...'

Francesca sagged against the wall of the treatment room. The rest of the medical centre was empty and it was just as well as she didn't think she could cope with seeing anyone right now.

Tears pooled at the corners of her eyes. She sat down in front of the computer and opened one of the search engines. Kawasaki disease. A mediocre collection of symptoms that she could so easily have missed.

The temperature, rash, joint pains and sore throat and tongue could be attributed to just about any childhood ailment. Irritability, sore eyes, swollen lymph glands, going off food all seemed so run of the mill to her.

But the key indicators of the disease—the strawberry-coloured tongue, red palms and soles of feet and the peeling skin on hands or feet—were often used to help the diagnosis.

She'd missed them.

If she hadn't ever heard of this disease before, she could forgive herself.

But she *had* seen it before. And she couldn't forgive herself for missing it.

A handsome doctor was no excuse.

But Gabriel hadn't. He hadn't missed anything.

Her brain was ticking furiously. Would Katherine have made the same assumption? Would Kevin? Would David Marsh have picked it up? Or was it only the fact that Gabriel was a paediatrician that had gone in Carly's favour?

She couldn't even bear to think about it.

The tears started to trickle down her face.

Gabriel had praised her. He'd looked her straight in the eye and told her she'd done a good job.

But he'd had no idea she'd just wanted to see him. To see what his reaction to her would be.

He'd had no idea she had been wondering if he was as confused about the night before as she was.

She pulled herself up straight.

There was no way she could let this happen again.

She had to forget about Gabriel and just focus on her job.

She couldn't allow the slightest distraction—no matter how handsome.

CHAPTER EIGHT

GABRIEL was relieved to wave the Glencross family off. Dr Demir at the local hospital had sounded confident he could deal with the condition. Carly would be in safe hands.

That was the second time Francesca had surprised him. The second time her instincts had been spot on.

Why was she so unsure of herself? She'd looked like a startled rabbit when he'd told her she'd made a good call.

But maybe that wasn't about her clinical abilities. Maybe it was about him.

In a sense he was relieved. He'd picked up something in a child that others might have missed—something that could have had devastating consequences.

Every time it happened he felt his stomach clench in endless knots at the thought of a child suffering—of something being missed. He was determined it would never happen on his watch.

He'd been there. He'd seen the effect on a family that losing a child could have. He'd experienced it firsthand.

His brother had only been a baby, not even a year old, when he'd died. And Gabriel had never forgotten his mother. She'd known something was wrong. Even when the local doctor had tried to fob her off and tell her Dante would be fine in a few days.

More than anything Gabriel remembered the scream. Dante's high-pitched scream—the scream of a baby with meningitis—had imprinted on him for life.

Once heard, never forgotten.

But by then it had been too late. A hasty trip to the hospital in the dead of night had resulted in some emergency treatment but it had all been in vain.

The day they had buried the little white coffin in the ground at the Isola di San Michele—Venice's cemetery—had haunted him.

For a six-year-old boy it had been hard to understand the impact on the family. He'd only known that nothing would ever be the same again. Over the years his mother had never lost the sadness in her eyes and his father had flung himself into the family business, as if immersing himself would dull the pain.

It hadn't helped that their family's loss had been widely reported in the media by nosy and intrusive reporters.

Dante had been their 'little blessing', their *piccola benedizione*. His mother had thought she couldn't have any more children after the birth of his younger sister, so the arrival of Dante had been greeted with much celebration.

And for years after Dante's death Gabriel and his sister had been afraid to mention his name. They'd kept a photograph of him in a locked cabinet in their room, taking it out and staring at the little smiling face on occasion.

He'd lost most of his childhood after that. His father had barely been in the house—only eating and sleeping there.

It had been obvious his father loved them but the house had held too many painful memories for him. So he'd spent more and more time at work. Long hours, stress and ignoring his physical health over the years had taken its toll.

It was no wonder he was a victim of heart disease—the disease that was slowly killing him.

Even as a child Gabriel had felt all the responsibility for his mother. Was it survivor's guilt? Trying to stick the family back together? Trying to distract her in any way possible to lessen the pain behind her eyes?

The only time he'd ever felt like a child again had been during the long summers they'd spent with his father's cousin and his family in Pisa. It had been the only time he'd ever felt relieved of the burden of family.

And for Gabriel every time a child came before him like this, every time a child with a vague set of symptoms appeared, he reminded himself why he did this job. No child should suffer the way Dante had. And no family should suffer the way they had.

Twenty-five years was a long time, but time didn't lessen the pain. Sometimes it only enhanced it. Only those who truly didn't understand thought that time could be a healer. Those who had suffered a similar loss knew the truth.

One of Gabriel's colleagues had lost a child some years before, and he was the only person Gabriel had ever confided in, sharing his pain as only a fellow sufferer could.

Frank had told him that every year was harder than the one before, particularly as the milestones of life approached. Time to start school, time to leave school, time to have girlfriends, special birthdays, time to make career choices—all things that his son and Gabriel's brother had missed out on.

And Gabriel had noticed little marks on the calendar that his mother kept. It had taken him a few years to work out what they were. Dante's birthday. The day of Dante's death. A star had marked the day he would have been eighteen. A little red triangle the day he would have graduated from school.

Gone but never forgotten.

Families. So much joy, but so much pain. That was why he never objected to the reputation the media had labelled him with. Millionaire playboy. Playboy doc. In a way it was easier for him. Women had fewer expectations of him. None of them were expecting a wedding band and a house with a white picket fence.

He'd made sure of that.

And spent most of his time focused on his work. A job that he usually relished.

But no matter how hard he tried to be relaxed in his role, there were always times it took him back to his childhood. And that's when it was essential for him to be in control.

That's when he got ratty. For some people being a doctor was just a job. But for Gabriel this was a chance for salvation. He might not have been able to save his brother but so far his decisions had probably saved the lives of over a hundred other children. A hundred children who had got to live another day with their families, to run around in the summer sunshine and enjoy a carefree existence instead of being buried in the cold, damp earth.

Precious, precious lives.

He was in charge now. Not some hopeless doctor who'd been more interested in getting back to his bed than caring for Gabriel's sick brother.

He always took the time with patients and their families. He always went that extra mile. No one should suffer the same fate as the Russo family. No one at all.

His phone buzzed in his pocket and he pulled it out to check the message. His father. Again.

Gabriel sighed. No rest for the wicked.

* * *

Katherine had folded her arms across her chest. 'So spill.' She looked serious and she didn't normally take no for an answer.

Francesca tried her best to look innocent as she restocked one of the cupboards. The last thing she wanted to do was talk about Gabriel.

'I don't know what you're talking about.'

'Yes, you do, lady. I heard after the dinner the other night you and Dr Delicious went for drinks. What happened?'

What happened? It was a good question and one that she'd no idea how to answer.

'How did you end up going for drinks with him anyway? I thought you hated him?'

'I do. I mean…I did.'

'Aha.' Katherine slid along the counter towards her. 'Now that definitely sounds interesting.'

Francesca felt cornered. What was she going to say anyway? *I spent all night trying to decide if I liked him or not and then he gave me the most earth-shattering whisper of a kiss and walked away?*

She'd had butterflies in her stomach when he'd kissed her. She'd been too excited—like a pathetic teenager—to think any further ahead.

But the morning after she'd woken up with a terrible feeling in the pit of her stomach. *He'd walked away.*

What did that say about her? He wasn't interested? She wasn't interesting enough? She wasn't sexy enough?

The fact was she'd no idea why he'd walked away or what he was thinking.

Was he planning on doing it again? Or was she just going to have to spend the next few weeks working around him, wondering if anything would happen? Because that wasn't her style. Not at all.

And she'd no intention of being a shrinking violet, hanging around waiting to see if she could get a part of him.

Sure, he was handsome. Sure, he was sexy. Sure, for a few milliseconds she'd actually considered pulling him into her cabin and doing the midnight tango with him.

But he was also her boss.

And she had to work with him every day.

And most days she liked work. Or she used to. Her colleagues were a good team, they were a fun team and she didn't want to do anything to spoil that.

Besides, she was waiting for her visa for Australia, and surely—*surely*—it must be arriving any day now. She'd been repeating this mantra for the last six weeks. The last thing she needed was to have some mad fling with some Italian dreamboat.

Flings weren't her style. Flirting? Well, maybe. That she could control. Then she could decide when to back off and when to proceed.

Maybe things had just gone a little too far?

But she could sort that. She could talk to him. It would be fine.

So why was she talking to herself in her head?

Her eyes met Katherine's. The interrogator hadn't moved and Francesca felt her cheeks start to flush again.

'Nothing happened.'

Katherine raised her perfectly plucked eyebrows. 'Oh, really?' Her voice dripped with good-humoured sarcasm. 'And the band played "Believe it if you like".'

'No. Really, it didn't. We went to watch the show together, had a drink and that was it.'

Katherine nodded her head towards the computer. 'So,

in that case, you wouldn't be interested in anything I'd found online about our resident dreamy Italian?'

Francesca hesitated, just a fraction of a second. She could resist the temptation, couldn't she? She could feign disinterest convincingly.

Nope. She couldn't. Rats.

'What is it?' She crossed the tiny dispensing room in one second flat and sat down at the computer screen.

A gorgeous image of Gabriel in a tux glared back at her. Wow. This photo could rival the Mediterranean white-trunked Adonis that had adorned Jill's bedside cabinet.

But in this one he didn't look happy. And, wow—what about the woman surgically attached to his arm? Hanging on there like some piranha?

Beautiful, blonde, in an emerald-green to-die-for figure-hugging dress. The kind of woman who had the proportions of a Barbie doll, proportions no woman was supposed to obtain naturally. The woman was beautiful, perfectly formed, with exquisite features and wearing a dress that must have cost more than Francesca earned in a month.

Only problem was the ice-cold look on her face.

That face could have sunk the *Titanic*.

'Where on earth is this from?'

Katherine looked smug. 'Oh, so now you're interested, are you?' Her head shot down next to Francesca's, just inches away from her face. 'I thought nothing happened?'

Francesca stared her out, trying her absolute best to keep her face free from anything that might give away the stomach that was currently churning, probably giving her an ulcer as they spoke.

She shrugged her shoulders. 'Let's just say I'm as curious as the rest of the crew about our doctor.'

She read the caption under the photo: *'Heir to the Russo*

printing fortune, Gabriel Russo, with Felice Audair at the annual Venetian charity ball.'

Katherine peered at the screen a little longer. 'Last year's charity ball. I don't think you need to worry,' she said assuredly. 'Look at their faces and their body language.'

'Do I have to?' Francesca's voice was becoming higher pitched by the second.

'Yes,' said Katherine determinedly, 'you do.' She pointed at the screen. 'He might have his arm around her but look at his face, there's no affection there.' She glanced at Francesca. 'And look at her eyes, they're like glass—she isn't really interested in him.' She paused a few seconds then added, 'You've nothing to worry about.'

'Who said I was worried?' Her self-defence mechanism had kicked in.

Francesca's eyes hadn't left the screen. 'Do you think that could be a relative?' she asked half-heartedly, knowing the answer even before she heard the reply. Katherine snorted. 'Not a chance—with those calculating looks I would be more likely to call her a predator than anything else.' She shrugged. 'At least the name matches the looks. She sounds like a prime-time TV villain.'

Francesca sagged back into the chair. She clicked on the links away from the photographs, her eyes scanning the page that came up before her.

It seemed as if at one point Gabriel had been photographed wherever he went. It must have driven him nuts. He seemed permanently surrounded by a bevy of beauties. What did it feel like to have your life examined under a microscope?

She'd no idea how famous he was in Italy. It appeared

he couldn't move without someone reporting it. It seemed almost obvious to her why he'd left.

So why come back?

And just how ill was his father?

Then there were all the listings for paediatric journal articles all with his name attached. Published papers. He was obviously dedicated to his job.

And a whole host of other, older headlines—mainly in Italian. Something about a tragedy. But she didn't have time to read because Katherine had clicked on another link.

She wrinkled her nose. 'I don't get it. He's a millionaire, with a whole host of specialist skills.' She turned to face Francesca. 'I mean, I'm glad that he's here but what *is* he doing here?'

Francesca felt herself bristle. David had mentioned his father being sick but maybe no one else knew. Maybe it was a secret. 'He must have his reasons.'

Katherine had her hand at her mouth. 'I wonder what they are.' She turned to face Francesca. 'Did you find out anything? You're the one who's been for drinks with him.'

Francesca shook her head. 'I was only there as a human shield. Guarding him from the circling bunch of cougars in the Atlantic Bar. He said I owed him after the week before.'

The answer seemed to placate Katherine. She shrugged. 'Yeah, you probably did. Did that family get away okay?'

'What family?'

'The kid, with the Kawa…whatever-it's-called disease, the potential heart condition.'

A chill crept down Francesca's spine. Of course Katherine would have heard about that. The medical unit was small so any unusual cases were always discussed.

'Yeah. She was admitted to the paediatric unit in the

hospital in Kusadasi.' She hesitated, wondering for a second if she should actually say the words. What would Katherine think?

'Did you have a look at the notes?'

Katherine was carrying a pile of boxes of rubber gloves ready to stock in the cupboard. 'Not yet. David said he would look over them later with me—just because it was such an unusual case.'

Francesca took a deep breath. 'Do you think you would have picked up on it?'

Katherine looked surprised. 'The Kawa-whatsit disease? Not a chance.' She shook her head. 'David wasn't sure he would have either. That's why we were going to discuss it later.'

'I almost missed it.' The words were out before she could stop them and the expression on her face must have said it all, because Katherine sat back down opposite her and put her hand on her shoulder.

'But you didn't.'

'But I've seen it before. I should have remembered. The symptoms are so remarkable—the strawberry tongue, cracked lips, peeling skin.'

Katherine stayed silent for a minute. 'How long since you've seen it?'

Francesca trawled her brain. 'A couple of years, in an A and E in Southampton.'

Katherine nodded, obviously choosing her words carefully. 'The symptoms are unusual and I hope I'll remember them. But I can't guarantee it. You've seen hundreds of patients since then. And everything's fine. You asked for a second opinion, that's what matters.' She squeezed Francesca's shoulder. 'And you won't miss it again.'

Francesca bit her tongue. She'd said enough. It wouldn't

do to tell her colleague the rest. That the real reason she'd missed it had been because her mind had been on a man. She couldn't let that happen again.

Francesca tried to appear calm. She gave a little smile and pushed herself up from the chair, away from the computer screen. 'I'm going to go and chase up some of the crew who have missed their medicals. They keep avoiding us, so I'm getting suspicious.'

Katherine nodded. 'Let's go up for a coffee first then I'll give you a hand. One of the engineers has steadily avoided us for over a month.' She gave Francesca a wink. 'I think it might be two-girl job.'

Ten minutes later they had just sat down to a well-deserved cappuccino in the Clipper Lounge when the piercing shrill of Francesca's emergency page sounded. '*Emergency Deck Five, Drake's Dining Room*'.

'Blooming typical.' Francesca sprang from her seat, leaving her steaming coffee untouched.

'Want help?' Katherine yelled after her.

'No, it's fine,' Francesca shouted over her shoulder. 'David or Gabriel will have the other on-call page. One of them will appear.'

She ran to the nearest stairwell and grabbed the emergency bag, which was stowed in a discreet hatch. Deck five was two decks beneath her and the dining room was immediately adjacent to the stairwell. She glanced at her watch as she reached the dining-room doors—ten to six, almost time for the first sitting. The dining room wasn't open yet to the passengers, which meant the incident had to involve a member of the crew. An anxious waiter was waiting to meet her at the doors. 'This way,' he said worriedly. 'I think he's having a seizure.'

Francesca hurried over to where the crewman was lying

on the floor, surrounded by a throng of worried colleagues. She pushed the onlookers out of her way. 'Let me through, please,' she ordered, her voice loud and commanding. They obediently stepped to one side to let her pass and she knelt on the floor next to the patient. Someone had had the good sense to attempt to put him in the recovery position, so he was lying on his side, but was still jerking and twitching, with his colleague's hands trying to steady him.

'Does anyone know what happened?' she asked the sea of surrounding faces. She bent her head over the patient and her heart lurched—it was Roberto Franc.

As soon as she'd identified him, it was obvious what was wrong.

But like any good nurse Francesca started with the obvious—airway, breathing and circulation. His airway was unobstructed and clear. He was definitely breathing, his chest rising and falling rapidly. Her fingers felt the pulse in his wrist, holding it firmly as his limbs continued to twitch intermittently.

'He was disorientated and muttering,' one of the fellow busboys started. 'I kept asking him what was wrong but his eyes were really glazed, it was if he couldn't hear me. Then he just dropped to the floor and started twitching'.

Francesca quickly checked him over. She wouldn't be able to get him to eat or drink anything as his consciousness level was too altered and he would risk choking. He didn't appear to have injured himself in the fall so she pulled the blood-testing meter out of the emergency bag and quickly tested his blood-sugar level. The meter only took five seconds to produce a result. One point four mmol/litre. His reading was way below normal. Francesca knew the average person had a blood glucose ranging between four and seven mmol/litre.

Roberto's blood glucose was so low it had caused him to lose consciousness.

A few seconds later Gabriel appeared at her side. He was obviously out of breath and she could feel the heat emanating from his body as he crouched beside her.

'Where on earth were you?' The medical centre was only one deck below; there was no way he could be so out of breath running up one flight of stairs.

He smiled and shrugged, 'The sports deck.'

'Deck Sixteen? Why didn't you use the lift?'

He gave a fake shudder. 'Too slow. Stops at every floor.' His eyes swept over their patient. 'Isn't this the young man you saw recently?'

She nodded and lifted the glucometer to show him the reading.

'Got any glucagon?'

She opened her nearby emergency bag and pulled out a bright orange box, flipping it open. The glucagon hydrochloride injection was only used in extreme circumstances and would help deliver glucose quickly to the body and bring Roberto out of his hypoglycaemic coma. The same injection was commonly carried by ambulances and used in accident and emergency departments.

'Want me to do that?'

Gabriel found a suitable bit of skin and administered the injection swiftly and waited for it to take effect.

'He's diabetic,' he said to the watching crowd. 'His blood sugar has dropped to a dangerously low level. This injection will bring him round but it takes a few minutes to work.'

'Diabetic? But he looked as if he was having a seizure,' said one of the confused waiters.

Francesca gave a rueful smile. 'It can look like that.

When a diabetic's blood sugar drops, the symptoms can vary from person to person. Some people shake, sweat and become confused, eventually all will lose consciousness, and sometimes their bodies can twitch or shake a little—it doesn't happen to everyone.'

She gave another quick look at Roberto. 'See? His twitching is starting to reduce as the glucose is beginning to take effect.'

'You must have done this a few times,' Gabriel murmured.

Francesca felt herself stiffen. She didn't want to talk about her dad. Her self-defence mechanism went onto autopilot. 'My dad was usually well controlled. He only ever needed glucogon a few times in his life.'

Gabriel looked puzzled for a second, then his face softened and he reached over and touched her hand, his warm skin encompassing hers.

'I wasn't talking about your dad, Fran. I was talking about being a nurse in general.'

Francesca held her breath. Of course. His brown eyes were fixed on hers, a barrage of questions stored in them. She swallowed and looked away quickly. She had a patient to treat and looked up at the staff around them. 'He was supposed to be allowed to take a break to eat before service started. Does anyone know what happened?'

A couple of the busboys shot each other uneasy looks.

Francesca shook her head impatiently. She didn't have time for this. 'Okay, tell me now what happened.'

'Well,' started one reluctantly, 'he asked earlier if he could stop for something, but the dining-room manager wouldn't let him.'

Francesca's face became thunderous. 'What?'

'Get back to work!' The dining-room manager stormed

up behind the crowd of onlookers, having obviously heard the preceding remark. Before the spectators could disperse, another voice cut through the air.

Gabriel was on his feet, his face furious. 'You and I are going to have words, sir.' His voice was louder, commanding, dripping with ice. He cut a path through the crowd of bystanders. He stopped directly in front of the manager. 'Your actions…' he squinted at the badge on his jacket '…Enzo, would make you directly responsible for this young man's condition.'

He pointed to Roberto, who now lay still on the floor. 'It would also make you directly answerable to me,' he continued sternly. 'I know that the medical centre had left strict instructions regarding Mr Franc's condition and the fact he needed extra breaks to allow him to eat.'

Gabriel was now directly face to face with Enzo, his arms folded firmly across his chest. There was no way he was going to allow his authority to be questioned. Enzo's face had turned a beetroot shade of red. 'We were too busy,' he spat. 'I have two members of staff off sick and I can't afford to babysit anybody!'

'When I give advice I expect it to be followed.' Gabriel's voice was low, menacing—the voice of a man getting ready to lose his temper.

Enzo waved his hand dismissively. 'I have a dining room to open and passengers waiting outside to be fed—when will you be ready to move him?' He turned his nose up disparagingly at Roberto.

Francesca could see the rage flaring in Gabriel's eyes. He stepped forward, his nose practically touching the other man's. 'You can open your dining room when *I* say so and not a second before that,' he hissed.

Francesca tugged at his trouser leg, anything to try

and diffuse the conflict. 'Dr Russo, can you give me a hand, please?'

Her words appeared to jolt Gabriel from his concentrated fury. He knelt down next to her. 'How is he?'

'He's going to be fine—but I'm not so sure I can say the same for you.' She was worried about him—he had looked as if he'd been about to erupt. 'I thought it best to distract you before you landed a punch on him.'

'I almost did. Stupid man. Medical orders stand, no matter what else is going on in the ship. He had no right to refuse Roberto time to eat. I'll be taking this up with the captain.'

His anger seemed to dissipate while he was talking to Francesca. She rested her hand on his forearm. 'Now you've calmed down a little, do you think you could give Kevin a call and ask him to bring a wheelchair up? Roberto's starting to come round now and I'd like to get him down to the medical centre.'

Gabriel leaned over Roberto, whose eyes had flickered open. 'What happened?' he groaned, clutching his forehead. He tried to sit up but couldn't quite get his balance. Gabriel put his arm around Roberto's shoulders and helped him straighten up.

'It's all right, Roberto. You had a hypoglycaemic attack. We had to give you a glucose injection to bring you round.'

'Oh, no.' He groaned, leaning forward and putting his head in his hand.

'I'm just going to arrange a wheelchair for you and we'll take you down to the medical centre for a few hours.' He gave Francesca a brief glance before striding off to the nearest phone.

Francesca caught the arm of the nearest waiter. 'Can you

go to the kitchen and get me some sandwiches for Roberto, please?' The waiter gave a quick nod and dashed off.

'How are you feeling, Roberto?'

'Sick. I feel really sick.'

'Unfortunately that's one of the side-effects of the injection we gave you. It can make some people feel nauseous. Once I've got you downstairs I'll start by giving you a cup of tea and see how you feel from there. The injection gives you a boost of glucose, but it would be better if I could get you to eat something.'

Now that Roberto had regained consciousness, some of the dining-room staff had started to disperse to prepare for the influx of passengers. Francesca could hear the voices of the passengers outside the main doors. They were obviously confused about why the dining room hadn't opened yet. A few seconds later she could hear Kevin's voice as he attempted to make his way through the throng. 'Excuse me, folks, can you let me through? We've got a bit of an emergency in the dining room—the sooner you let me through, the sooner I can deal with it.'

Seconds later he emerged red-faced through the dining room doors, pushing a wheelchair. 'Phew!' he said. 'That did the trick. For a minute there I thought they weren't going to move for me.' He parked the wheelchair next to Francesca and Roberto. 'Can I give you a hand?'

Together they helped a still shaky and slightly disorientated Roberto into the chair. 'Where's Gabriel?' asked Kevin as he started to push the wheelchair in the direction of the main doors.

Francesca indicated her head to the side. 'He's on the phone. I take it he's filling the captain in on his displeasure.' She caught hold of the nearest door and swung it open, balancing the plate of sandwiches for Roberto in the other. They were met by an array of anxious faces. 'Excuse me, please,' she said briskly, 'If you would let us past, I'm sure the dining room will be able to open in a few minutes.'

The crowd parted and they made their way over to the nearest lift. In a matter of minutes they were back at the medical centre.

Kevin and Francesca helped Roberto onto one of the nearest beds. 'I'll just start a chart,' said Francesca, lifting one down from above the bed.

'I'll check his blood-glucose level again,' said Kevin. 'What was it originally?'

'One point four.'

Kevin rolled his eyes. 'No wonder he hit the deck.'

The alarm sounded as Kevin checked the blood level. 'Well, it's up a bit. Three point nine. The injection must have started working.'

Roberto was pale and looked exhausted. Having a hypo-glycaemic attack of this level often made patients feel very tired. Francesca knew that Roberto would be best if he was allowed to sleep for a while. She finished writing up his chart. 'I'm just going to get you a cup of tea.' She smiled at him. 'I know you're tired. I'll let you go to sleep once you've had something to eat. We'll keep an eye on your blood-glucose levels over the next few hours. Don't worry if you feel us stabbing your finger while you're sleeping.'

Kevin came and joined her in the nearby consulting room where the kettle was stored. 'Do you want me to do that? I don't mind, I'm due to be on duty anyway.'

'It's okay, Kevin, I don't mind waiting a bit longer. I've got some other patients that I should probably update you on before evening surgery.'

'By the way, there's mail for you.'

He pointed to an official-looking envelope with a tell-tale insignia on one of the worktops.

She drew a sharp breath. Her Australian visa—it had finally arrived. She stuffed the envelope into her pocket. 'Have you mentioned this to anyone?'

He shook his head and shrugged his shoulders. 'Your business, Francesca. No one else's.'

She gave him a smile. 'Thanks, Kevin.'

He gave her a nod and headed back out to Roberto. She finished making the tea and picked up the plate of sandwiches. She knew he was feeling sick but she would have to try and entice him to eat something before he went to sleep.

'Whoa!'

Gabriel let out the cry as Francesca walked out the door and almost crashed straight into him. He caught her hand to stop her spilling the tea.

'I see you're in a better mood. Did you manage to speak to the captain?'

'That's where I've just came from. All medical orders on this ship stand. Enzo will be spoken to this evening.

'I'll take those,' he went on, lifting the plate and mug from her hand. 'I want to speak to Roberto to reassure him that he won't have any more problems in the dining room.' He started walking back towards the door. 'Aren't you off duty now?'

She nodded. There she was being the dutiful nurse again, he thought. She'd handled the emergency situation just as well as he could have. Truth be told, she hadn't really needed him there. Her care and attention to Roberto had obviously been excellent.

It gave him the spur he needed. There was an underlying attraction between them but he still hadn't got to the bottom of what made her tick.

And there still hadn't been the opportunity to talk a little more about her friend. She seemed to get prickly whenever Jill's name was mentioned. Did she really not know what motivated Jill?

He needed to get to know her a little better. Thankfully, she didn't seem to be like her friend at all. And after that night he wanted to see if they could get along together. He wanted her to see the other side of him—away from internet rumours and newspaper headlines.

He needed a chance, outside this environment, to see how she reacted to him. And thanks to Kevin, their colleague, he knew exactly how to do it.

'Francesca?'

She jumped—she'd obviously been daydreaming. She looked at him a little self-consciously and tucked a loose tendril of hair behind her ear. 'Yes?'

'Ever been to Pisa?'

Her head tilted to the side. 'No.' She smiled curiously at him. 'Why do you ask?'

'Because the ship docks at Livorno tomorrow and if you are free I thought you might want to do some sightseeing with me.'

Whoa. Totally sideswiped. Where had this come from?

'Why Pisa?' she asked suspiciously, raising her eyebrows. 'Why not Florence?' Her brain was racing and she was trying her hardest to act as normally as possible. Both cities were accessible from the port of Livorno and it was usually a pretty even split between the passengers over which city they visited.

He crossed the room and put a hand on her waist, bending his head forward to hers. 'Because a little bird told me that you'd never managed to get there so I thought I might have the pleasure of showing you around.'

As his hand touched her waist she sucked in her breath. His movements were so easy, so casual. Almost as if he touched her that way every day. Was all this awkwardness just in her head?

The 'little bird' must have been Kevin as she'd told him the other day that even though she had done this cruise seven times, she had never managed to see Pisa. It was almost as if he'd read her mind.

'I would love to see Pisa.'

'How about we meet for breakfast tomorrow?' he asked. 'Get the day off to a good start?' There was a twinkle in his eye that made her heart flutter. Was he flirting with her? Or was she acting like some crazy hormonal teenager?

'I'll only meet you if you agree to meet at the Poseidon Lounge and not in the dining room. Who knows what Enzo might do to your food in there.'

He rolled his eyes. 'Doesn't even bear thinking about. Eight o'clock?'

'Eight o'clock is fine.' Francesca picked up her bag and headed to the door.

'Francesca?'

She turned back. 'Yes?'

'You won't need to bring your book. I'll keep you entertained.'

CHAPTER NINE

Hi Jill

Sorry for the delay getting back to you. The ship has been busier than I expected.

Gabriel seems to have settled in fine. He's back here because his father isn't keeping too well. He certainly started off with a splash by rescuing a teenage boy who'd fallen into Venice harbour and was being swept out to sea. His first day was nearly his last as he rescued the boy then knocked himself out on the harbour wall. That's why I had to resuscitate him. Though, at the time, if I'd known who he was I doubt I would have bothered.

He hasn't talked about you, even though I told him how I recognised him. He doesn't say much of anything too personal. His doctoring skills, however, are another story and I've seen some impressive paediatric skills in the last few weeks. He caught a really unusual case in a child that could have resulted in her death if it had been missed.

The women seem to love him—all Italian charm, white teeth and Mediterranean skin. Very different from what I'm used to!

Hope things are going well with you. Have sent you a photo as you requested from one of our crew events.

Francesca

SEND. She sighed and leaned back from the computer. Six composed and deleted emails. There was no point in reading this one over and over like the rest of them. Then she'd just start tweaking it again and again.

And against her better judgement she'd sent the snapshot Jill had requested. If she hadn't it would only have resulted in a whole barrage of emails, so it was better to get it over and done with. Kevin had snapped it the other day when they'd been doing a crew training exercise and the photos had been uploaded to the medical centre computer, so it was easy to access without anyone asking difficult questions.

Would this mean that Jill would reply instantly, looking for more information about Gabriel? Because right now, Francesca wasn't sure how to answer any queries. She had no idea what was happening between them. All she knew was that *something* was.

And now she'd agreed to spend the day ashore with him.

The fact of the matter was this man was driving her crazy.

The sun was already streaming through her porthole when Francesca woke up. Her stomach gave a little lurch. A whole day with Gabriel. Half of her was dreading it, the other half…

She felt like a teenager going on a first date. Why?

Was it because he looked like an Italian film star? Or was it because she'd spent the last few weeks getting to know him? She'd seen him charm the most rambunctious child. He was thoughtful and kind with patients and their relatives. And every now and then she caught him looking at her through those hooded lids and it made her heart flutter.

There, she'd said it.

There was a definite attraction between them. One that neither of them seemed prepared to act on.

Ever since that night when he'd walked her back to her cabin and kissed her, she'd felt as if she was just waiting for something to happen. The kiss had been the briefest of touches but it had affected her in a way she'd never expected. How had Gabriel got under her skin?

And now she was going to spend the whole day with him...

Why had he asked her? Did he feel something, too? Maybe she was reading too much into it and he was just being courteous to a colleague, offering to show her around an area he was familiar with.

It wasn't like she'd never been kissed before. Actually, she'd been kissed quite a lot. Just not like *that*—and he hadn't even kissed her on the lips. Even when she'd spent time with the playboy doc he hadn't kissed her like that.

She'd had a number of boyfriends over the years but she'd never been broken-hearted when the relationships had ended. Sometimes she had actually felt relief. The truth was that since her parents had died Francesca had felt totally isolated.

No one had ever filled the gap that they had left. And nowhere had ever felt like home since.

Travelling had been the ideal way for her to try and cope. It gave her convenient blasé answers to difficult questions. *'I don't want to settle down—I want to see the world.'* No one really knew her well enough to ask questions about her family.

Australia was just the next port of call on her long list. After that it would be America—or maybe Hong Kong. Anywhere but Glasgow.

Her heartbeat quickened as she remembered the thick envelope inside her bedside cabinet—currently unopened.

She wasn't quite sure why she hadn't opened it straight away, even though she seemed to have been waiting for it for ever. But once she opened it, it would be time to move on again. And something about the cruise ship was starting to feel like home.

She showered quickly and dressed in white Capri pants, a red cotton blouse and some flat white shoes that would be comfortable to walk in. It only took a few seconds to pull her hair back with a clasp—she didn't want to be hot and uncomfortable today. She tossed sunscreen and lip gloss into her bag before picking it up and heading out the door.

Gabriel was sitting in the sunshine at the Poseidon Lounge, waiting for her. The food was served buffet style inside the lounge, which was surrounded by glass on all sides. Although some tables were inside, the majority were out on the deck, where passengers had the chance to eat breakfast in the early morning sun and watch the waves.

'It's kind of ironic, isn't it?'

'What is?'

Gabriel pointed to the sign above his head. 'That they named one of the restaurants after the greatest US disaster movies of all time.'

Francesca smiled. It was the kind of smile that had captured his attention right from the beginning. The kind that spread across her face and right up into her eyes. The kind she gave when she was relaxed, unguarded.

His eyes ran up and down her body. She looked as gorgeous as ever in her white trousers and red shirt, her chestnut curls swept back with a clip and sunglasses perched on top of her head.

'Somehow I don't think they named the restaurant after

a movie. It think it was named after the Greek god of the sea.'

Gabriel shrugged. 'Greek. I hear he was a bit of a rogue.'

'Poseidon?'

He nodded.

'And Italians aren't?' She raised her eyebrow as if waiting for him to take the bait. 'I think the expression you're looking for is, *It takes one to know one.*'

She had that little sparkle in her eyes. She grabbed his arm. 'Come on, let's eat. I'm starving.'

They walked through to the buffet and he watched while she piled her plate with scrambled eggs, toast and sausages before adding a pot of tea to the tray she was carrying. She turned around and stretched out her hands to add his plates to her tray.

A frown wrinkled her brow. 'What? That's it?'

He handed over his bowl of muesli as he filled up his coffee cup.

'I'm not a big eater in the morning.' His eyes caught her plate again and glinted with amusement. 'Unlike some other people.'

'I have a feeling I will need all the sustenance I can get,' she said with a smile on her face. She walked back out into the sunshine and sat down at the table.

They had arrived at Livorno at 7:00 a.m. This was the port for Florence and Pisa. Even though it was only a little after eight, the port was bustling with activity. Most of the passengers who were travelling to Florence would be leaving soon. The buses had already congregated near the ship and the tour guides were checking lists with passenger names. Gabriel looked at his watch. They still had plenty of time to eat breakfast. Pisa was closer to the port than Florence and the bus journey much shorter.

There it was again—that glint in her eye. She was in a really good mood this morning. Either that or she'd finally loosened up around him and stopped blaming him for what had happened with her friend.

She took a bite of her toast. 'So—just out of interest— think we would have got served in Drake's Dining Room this morning?'

Gabriel choked on his coffee. She was surprising him. Her sense of humour was coming out, the one that she only normally revealed to other people. He shook his head. 'I know the captain read the Riot Act to Enzo yesterday so in principle we should be fine. But in reality? I've no intention of setting foot in that dining room in the near future.' He gave a little fake shudder. 'As you said, who knows what he might do to our food?'

'Just as well we came here, then.' Francesca set her coffee cup down on the table and took in a deep breath of sea air. 'I much prefer it here anyway. There's nothing nicer than eating breakfast out on deck.'

Gabriel gazed out onto the dock. The buses laden with passengers heading for Florence had already started to leave. It would probably be best to get going.

'Have you finished?'

Francesca nodded. 'Do you want to go?'

He gestured his head towards the dock. 'We could catch one of the buses into Pisa. Do you need to get anything from your cabin?'

She shook her head and picked up her bag. 'I'm the kind of girl who travels light. I've got everything I need.'

Just for a second he hesitated, and then he held out his hand towards her. Would she take it? It seemed like the most natural instinct to him, but he didn't want to do anything that made her feel uncomfortable. He wanted to follow her lead.

This was nothing. This was just two colleagues on a day out.

It was harmless. So why was he having thoughts about Francesca that he never had about any other colleague?

Why—every time he closed his eyes—did he relive the feel of her warm body next to his, their lips almost brushing together, the sparks of electricity in the air?

Why did she continually invade his thoughts, no matter what he was doing?

He could see the fleeting expression on her face. As if she was trying to make up her mind.

Then she stretched out her hand and took his, allowing him to pull her up from her seat.

'Ready?'

She was poised right next to his hip. Any other time, any other woman, he would have slid his arm around her waist.

Under any other set of circumstances he would probably have kissed her, too.

But Francesca was different. This was the woman who had spent the first week on board glaring at him. The second week she'd begun to thaw. The third week they'd shared that moment in the corridor. And now? She'd only recently begun to look him in the eye and have normal conversations with him.

He had no idea how she felt. Was she trying to fight the natural attraction between them?

Because he wasn't imagining the chemistry between them. There was definitely something there. They'd both felt it. Especially that night in the Atlantis Bar when he'd walked her back to her cabin.

Those big brown eyes and plump red lips had almost

been the death of him. Not to mention the figure-hugging red dress.

The only thing that had stopped him had been the consequences. That—and the tiny niggling question at the back of his mind about her necklace.

Maybe this was nothing to do with Francesca. Maybe this was about the poor choices he'd made in the past when it came to women. Jill, the would-be reporter, and a number of others all more interested in Gabriel Russo the heir to the Russo fortune than Gabriel Russo the person. Every gold-digger under the sun, it seemed, had tried her hand with him. Maybe he should just get over it.

Because in the last few weeks he'd seen or heard nothing to make him suspicious of Francesca. Maybe she was just naturally quite reserved. Closed off to those she didn't know well. Maybe if he could get to the bottom of her lack of confidence at work, he could get to know her a little better. Maybe even enough to…

Time to get the day started. Gabriel grabbed her hand in his and pulled her towards the gangway. He spoke to one of the cruise stewards who pointed them in the direction of the next bus due to leave for Pisa. It was almost full and they grabbed the last two seats together moments before the doors closed. The bus set off and Gabriel turned to face her. 'So what do want to do in Pisa?'

'What do you think?'

He groaned and shook his head. 'No. I am *not* taking a photograph of you pretending to hold up the Leaning Tower!'

She folded her arms across her chest. 'Then I'm not getting out of this bus.'

'You're such a tourist.'

'I know. But that's why I've came here today. I've never

seen the Leaning Tower and I hear you can climb up it now, so I definitely want to do that. I don't care how many times you have done it before—you're doing it again today.'

'The Leaning Tower was closed for a spell when I was younger but it's been open for the last few years. We used to spend our summers in Pisa so I've been up it more times than I can count.'

'So, are you going to be a tourist, too, and climb the tower with me? Or are you just going to sit at one of the nearby cafés and wave from down below?'

'Anything else for us to do?'

She leaned back in her seat watching everything speed past. 'No, I just want to be a tourist today. Absolutely no medical dramas. No shopping. But definitely eating. You will buy me lunch today.'

He gave her a mysterious look. 'Ah, I've already made plans for that. But I won't need to buy you lunch.'

She looked at him in surprise. 'Don't even try to pass me off with a cruise-ship sandwich.'

He shook his head. 'No need. My father's cousin has a restaurant near the Piazza Dei Miracoli. Lunch is on him.'

Francesca felt her stomach lurch. 'So I get to meet a member of your family? No wonder they call it the Field of Miracles.'

'What do you mean by that?' He looked bewildered.

'Because no one knows that much about you. You don't give much away. You're a bit of an enigma, to be honest.'

'You mean you haven't read all about me on the internet?'

Her cheeks gave the hint of a flush and she had the good grace to look embarrassed. Part of him felt disappointed. 'Never mind.'

The bus pulled up in a large asphalt car park. The passengers disembarked and the tour guides started to put them into groups. 'Come on,' said Gabriel, 'we don't need to wait for this.'

He clasped her hand again and walked her along next to a high wall. The sun was already beating down and the heat could almost be seen rising from the ground. They walked a few hundred yards before they reached a large archway in the wall. They turned to walk through and Francesca stopped dead. 'Wow!'

There before them stood the Field of Miracles. On the left-hand side were the three white monuments. The sun was reflecting off the white marble, making it glisten in the bright light. The effect was startling.

Gabriel watched Francesca's face in amusement. He had wondered what she would think when she first saw this. Many people were taken aback by the initial glare coming off the buildings. That, along with the fact they were hidden behind the large wall and seemed to appear out of nowhere, made the sight all the more startling.

Gabriel could remember the first time he and his sister had come here. They had fallen in love instantly with the monuments and, because they had family here, had spent many hours playing on the grass in front. He gave her arm a little tug. 'You're blocking people's view,' he whispered as he pulled her to one side.

'Sorry.' She stepped to the left-hand side, nearest to the Baptistery.

'It's just astonishing.' Her eyes were alight with excitement. 'I honestly didn't expect that when we walked around the corner.' She watched the crooked smile that was bending up one corner of his mouth. 'You knew, didn't you?'

'Most people get a surprise when they turn the corner. I wondered what you'd say.'

She fumbled around in her bag to find her camera. 'Let's take some pictures.'

'Let's go and admire the monuments first,' said Gabriel. He stopped in front of one the cafés that lined the right-hand side of the square. 'And let's grab a coffee while we do it.'

'Just a coffee?' quipped Francesca. 'Or do you really plan on feeding me all day?'

He shot her a quick smile and came out of the café two minutes later with two steaming paper cups in his hands. He passed one over to her. 'Here you go, cappuccino with extra chocolate on top.'

'How did you know?'

He tapped the side of his nose. 'I know everything.' He handed over something else, a bag containing a pink box tied with a ribbon. 'Italian chocolates—but save them for later.'

They walked towards the Leaning Tower. 'I guess you want to admire this first,' he said, sweeping his hand towards the impressive structure in front of them.

'No,' she said determinedly. 'I don't just want to admire it, I want to *climb* it. Come on, let's go.' She turned him round and pushed him towards the bell tower. 'Now how many steps are there?'

Gabriel looked at the imposing tower. 'It depends which set of stairs you climb. The south-facing staircase has two hundred and ninety-six; the north-facing staircase has two hundred and ninety-four.'

Francesca gulped. She stood underneath and looked straight upwards at the tower. It really did look as if it could topple over at any moment. She had seen dozens of pictures and news reports about the Leaning Tower but here, seeing it in the flesh, so to speak, was entirely different.

She felt as if she could walk over and give it a push with her little finger. 'I should probably know this, but I've forgotten. What made it tilt like this?'

'Shallow foundations, set in weak, unstable subsoil. They tried many ways to stabilise it. They had tons of lead counterweights on the raised end of the base before finally removing soil from underneath. It's supposed to be stable now for at least two hundred years.'

'So it's safe enough to climb?'

'Definitely. Most people book in advance, though. You're usually given a scheduled time to climb the tower.'

Her face fell instantly. 'You're joking, right? Why didn't you tell me this before? You must have known about it.'

There it was again—that vulnerability about her. She looked like a child who had just had her sweeties snatched out of her hand. How could any man resist that?

She was making him see Pisa through a tourist's eyes. She was reminding him how much he used to love being here. Seeing her face as they'd walked through the archway in the wall had made him appreciate his surroundings all the more. What would she think when they reached the top of the Leaning Tower?

Time to find out.

'Because I came prepared.' He pulled two tickets from the back pocket of his jeans as they reached the entrance and stood at the bottom of the winding staircases.

She let out a squeal. 'You rat bag!' And swatted her hands at him. 'Right, that's it.' She put her hand on her hip and looked upwards. 'Tell you what, let's have a race.'

'What?'

'You climb one staircase and I'll climb the other. I'll race you to the top. Loser has to pay a forfeit.'

'What kind of forfeit?'

'Whatever the winner decides.'

'I like that,' he said. 'I'm sure I could think of something.'

Francesca took their paper cups to throw in the nearby rubbish bin. In an instant Gabriel had turned and started sprinting up the steps. Francesca was caught off guard by his quick getaway and dashed to keep up. She had been an excellent sprinter at school and was sure she could outrun him. Her heart was racing as she pounded up the uneven stairs, her legs thumping. She darted to one side to avoid some sightseers who had stopped on the third floor. She heard a yell from the other side of the tower and grinned to herself as she realised Gabriel must have run into some people.

Starting to pant for breath, she continued to charge up the steps, hearing the muttered apologies from the other side of the tower. Her legs were feeling heavy; running up stairs was definitely harder work than sprinting around a racetrack. By the time she reached the seventh floor she could feel the sweat trickling down her back in the warm air. Her face was flushed and her breathing ragged.

With a final spurt she dashed out towards the balcony that looked over the square. Gabriel was standing with his back to her, pretending to be nonchalant, as if he had been waiting for her for a while. She gasped her way over towards him, thudding her hands on the balcony. Although he looked incredibly sexy in his jeans and T-shirt, the small beads of perspiration on his forehead gave away his recent exertions.

'How on earth did you manage to beat me?' she panted. 'I can't believe it'.

He gave her a wide grin. 'What took you so long?'

She slapped his arm in frustration. 'I heard you banging into people on the way up. I was sure I was ahead of you.'

Her heart was thudding rapidly in her chest, but her breathing had started to slow. Gabriel leaned across and pulled her over to one side.

They stood together, looking out over the Field of Miracles. A welcome gentle wind was rippling against them. She leaned forward, looking down at the people in the square. 'This is a beautiful place, Gabriel. You were so lucky getting to spend time here as a child.' She wrinkled her nose, 'Rainy summers in Glasgow weren't quite the same.'

His arm brushed against hers as he leaned next to her. 'I don't think I appreciated it at the time. Everything about it seemed so ordinary. I thought all families did this. It's not till you go away and see the world from another perspective that you realise the importance of what's still at home.'

The words seemed so straightforward but there was a weight beneath them. What did he mean? She turned to face him, leaning back against the railing. 'So how come you spent your summers here when you lived in Venice?'

His eyes lowered, as if he was trying to figure out how to answer what should be a straightforward question. 'Things changed in our family. My mother...' he hesitated '...needed a little space. The summers were long and we had family here in Pisa. My sister and I were delighted to come and spend our summers with our uncle and our cousins.'

So much unsaid. Everybody had secrets—she knew that better than anyone. But what had happened in Gabriel's family? What about the tragedy referred to on the internet search engine? She hadn't read any of those articles.

It would be intrusive to just come right out and ask. But

curiosity was killing her. Time to try another tactic. 'So what about Venice? How is your father doing?'

He shrugged. '*Not what the doctors tell him* would be the most appropriate answer.'

'Isn't that the same as most folks?'

He sighed. 'My father is a law unto himself. I'm supposed to be taking over some of the day-to-day things for him—anything I can do electronically—to try and relieve the pressure. Trouble is, Dad just finds something else to do.'

She gave him a smile. 'Sometimes parents are worse than children.' Something curled inside her stomach, sending a lump to her throat.

Gabriel had moved a little closer, reaching up and catching a curl that had escaped from her clip. His fingers brushed her cheek as he tucked the curl behind her ear. His eyes had intensity she hadn't seen before. 'So what's your story, Francesca Cruz?' His body moved closer to hers as some people edged past them.

She could feel the heat pressing against her, but she didn't want to step away. It didn't feel intrusive. It felt natural. It felt comfortable. His other hand settled at the side of her waist.

'I don't know what you mean,' she whispered.

Then he moved even closer, his chest pressing against hers. 'You're one of the best nurses I've worked with, Francesca. Everyone in the team thinks really highly of you. But you seem to be the only person that doesn't think that. What's going on?'

She took a deep breath. If she told him the truth he would hate her. If she told him how she'd nearly sent Carly Glencross away he would be horrified.

She couldn't do that. She couldn't tell him about her

dad. She couldn't tell him she'd missed all the signs that could have indicated how low he'd been feeling.

Gabriel's breath was tickling her cheek. She was lost in those dark brown eyes. She didn't want to do anything to spoil this.

'What about our forfeit?' she whispered, a smile creeping across her face.

'Would you like to decide what your forfeit is, or should I?' His voice was husky, the implication clear.

She met his gaze and her stomach tightened. There was no way her heart was going to stop thudding now. At the top of the bell tower the light breeze cooled their heated skin. The beauty of Cathedral Square was just beneath them, but neither of them seemed to notice. He raised his fingers and captured another little chestnut curl that had stuck on her damp skin. He wound it round his finger slowly, never taking his eyes from hers. 'I think we might both have decided the same thing.'

She couldn't move. She couldn't breathe.

His lips bent to meet hers. His kiss was electrifying, the lightest, most delicate of touches. Nothing more, nothing less. With very little pressure his mouth teased the edges of hers. His hand brushed gently along her cheek, settling behind her ear and cradling her head in his hand. The kiss deepened slightly, the pressure increasing as he pushed forward then pulled away. Her first instinct was to grab him. To want more from this kiss. But he released his lips from hers and pressed his forehead against hers. It was perfect.

Their first proper kiss on top of one of the most famous monuments in the world. It could have been a moment from a movie. He might have kissed her outside her cabin. The air had been electric and atmosphere heavy, but it could never have matched this moment. A fleeting brush of his lips on her ear could never compare with this. She took a deep breath and stepped backwards.

He smiled at her, a thousand unspoken thoughts in his eyes. A promise of something else. Something for later.

Because she didn't need anything else right now. Her lips were tingling, the taste of him still there. The scent in her nostrils was that of his distinctive aftershave. The back of her head could still feel the warmth from his hand.

She'd thought everything about Gabriel would feel wrong. But it didn't. It felt very right.

A crowd of voices broke the silence seconds later as a horde of tourists reached the top of the stairs and joined them on the balcony, oblivious to what they had just interrupted.

Gabriel moved over to let some of them past. His hand rested on Francesca's waist. 'Do you want to take some photographs?' he asked, the lazy smile appearing on his face.

Francesca nodded. She wanted to capture this moment. She wanted to remember this. She pulled out her camera and was immediately accosted by a small grey-haired woman.

'Oh, let me, dear,' she said, grabbing the camera from Francesca's hand. 'You make a beautiful couple.'

Francesca looked over at him. Would he want to capture the moment, too? The enthusiastic woman gave them a prod to push them together again.

'Come on, then—give us a smile.'

They stepped together and both gave a smile. Gabriel's arm was still around her waist and he pulled her closer, nestling her beneath the crook of his arm. Her hand naturally lifted and rested on his firm chest. He smiled at her again, as if still reliving their secret moment.

Click.

'Perfect!'

The woman handed the camera back and wandered off.

Francesca felt her shoulders ease. She looked back over the balcony. 'Can we visit the *Duomo*?'

'Anything you want, Francesca.' His words sounded so simple, but she understood the hidden meaning. He was waiting for her lead.

'Great.' She turned and headed back down the winding staircase. It was becoming hotter now and getting busier. They walked across the crowded square towards the *Duomo*, the medieval cathedral at the heart of the square, his hand loosely grasping hers.

This felt different from this morning. Taking his hand, this morning had been a stepping stone. A starting point. What now?

An instant quiet fell on them as they stepped from the hot and bustling square through the massive bronze doors into the cooler air and hushed tones of the cathedral. Although it was filled with numerous tourists, there was a respectful silence and tranquil feeling inside. Francesca gave a little shudder as her body adjusted to the rapid change in temperature. The gorgeous gold-decorated ceiling gave a feeling of opulence and wealth, as did the decorated mosaics and the carved marble panels showing dramatic scenes from the New Testament.

Gabriel calmly kept her hand in his and walked with her in silence around the statues and elaborately carved pulpit. She was grateful for that silence. Even though she was wandering amongst some of the most beautiful artefacts in the world, Francesca felt as if she could hardly concentrate. She was conscious of him at her side. Of the dark curling hairs on his arm brushing against hers.

They had finished walking around the cathedral and had reached the bronze doors again. 'Are you ready for lunch yet?'

She gave a little nod. She was beginning to feel more relaxed and calm again. Lunch might be the perfect time to get to know the man she'd kissed a little better. They walked across the square and down a side street towards an Italian restaurant. Gabriel stopped just as they were about to enter the dark wood doors.

He shot her a smile. 'Prepare yourself,' he muttered as he pushed open the door.

Four hours later they stepped back out of the restaurant.

Gabriel had the noisiest and most welcoming family she'd ever met. The food and company had been delicious. The smells alone had been fantastic.

Her head was reeling. She'd barely caught a word of the rapid Italian. Her basic Italian was passable but so many regions of Italy had dialects and she struggled to follow the fast-paced words. Gabriel had flowed back into his native language with no hesitation whatsoever. His grasp of English was impeccable and she'd almost forgotten it wasn't his first language. But Gabriel, ever the gentleman, had obviously sensed her unease and had stopped time and time again to include her in the conversation.

Seeing the obvious affection he felt for his family had sent little pangs straight to her heart. It was at times like this she missed her mum and dad more than words could say. It made her realise what she'd lost.

'Francesca?'

The voice was a whisper in her ear, his warm hand touching her waist.

'I've something to ask you.'

A little shiver went down her spine. There was something about the way he was looking at her, the way he was touching her. All of a sudden her heart was beating furiously in her chest. Her breath seemed to have caught in her throat. They'd had a perfect day. Was it about to get better? Or was he going to spoil it? She held her breath.

'Want to do this again?'

CHAPTER TEN

'WHAT you doing, gorgeous?'

The words danced over her skin like the warm afternoon sun. She was standing on the adults-only sunbathing deck again. But instead of hiding inside a pod and reading, she was leaning over the rail towards the swimming pool underneath, watching the children play with the entertainers.

She took a sip from her long, cool drink as she turned to face him. 'I like watching the kids. I like watching people who don't seem to have a care in the world.'

She wondered what he'd say as a frown seemed to hover around his brow. The guy was a paediatrician, surely he didn't have an aversion to kids?

He leaned on the rail next to her. 'Families,' he muttered quietly as his eyes swept over the scene below.

There was a whole host of children dancing in the sun with the entertainers. A younger bunch was in the paddling pool, throwing balls back and forwards. Families of all shapes and descriptions were scattered around the loungers next to the pool.

Francesca laughed as one toddler dumped her ice-cream cone onto her brother's back. He screamed at the top of his voice and ran away.

'I should go down there and talk about sunscreen. Some of those kids look red already.'

She gave him a sharp nudge. 'Stop thinking like a doctor, Gabriel, and start thinking like a normal person and have some fun.'

She couldn't see his eyes as they were hidden behind designer sunglasses. Just like the part of him he kept hidden from her.

But, then, they were both a little guilty of that.

'I like your family. Your father's cousin and his family were great. Think we can go back and visit again? The food in their restaurant was amazing.'

He gave the slightest nod. 'If only the rest of the family was like that.'

'What do you mean?' She pushed her sunglasses up onto her head. 'Aren't you and your dad close? I thought you were back to help him?'

She hoped it sounded like a casual enquiry with no ulterior motive. He'd hardly said a word about his mother or his father. He leaned further over the rail, focusing on the people below.

A classic avoidance tactic. One she'd used herself.

'Gabriel?'

She wasn't going to let this go. She'd shared a kiss with this man. Surely she was entitled to know a little bit more?

'I do what I can at night online. My sister is helping with the day-to-day running of things.'

'Your sister?' She could feel her eyebrows rise. He had barely even mentioned her before.

There was the tiniest moment's hesitation. 'Sofia could run my father's printing company with her eyes shut. She eats, breathes and sleeps the business. Whereas I...' His voice drifted off. 'But she's a girl—that's the problem.'

Francesca felt herself pull back a little. 'Is your father really that old-fashioned? In this day and age?'

She couldn't read him. She couldn't see his eyes at all and it was driving her crazy.

He shrugged, his arm curving around her waist. 'It's complicated,' he said as he bent towards her for a kiss, pressing his body up next to hers. A smile was starting to flicker across his face as if he had other, more pressing things on his mind.

'All family business is complicated,' she said as her arms crept around his neck and she lost herself in his kiss.

Whatever it was, it could wait.

The next two weeks passed by in a blur of ports, beautiful cities, sexy sightseeing and crackling electricity.

And, of course, passengers.

Sunburn and blistering seemed to be the common complaint amongst the children on board, parents misjudging the strength of the Mediterranean sun. For the older patients the trend seemed to be fractured wrists, with falls from the tour buses, slips on the open-air decks and tumbles on the stairwells.

But for Francesca and Gabriel all this was just background noise.

It seemed only natural that when they were apart they would seek each other out. If they weren't working together they were eating together, visiting ancient monuments or watching the entertainment.

The electricity between them seemed to be gaining momentum with every second they spent together.

He'd kissed her again, of course. Each one more tempting than the last. The increasing intensity was driving her crazy. It seemed only natural that things would progress between them. The only question was when. The lack of privacy on the cruise ship was definitely restricting their activities.

But, tonight, for the first time in two weeks, they were finally on call together.

'What are you doing, Gabriel?'

He sighed and leaned back in his chair. The rest of the lights in the medical centre were off and his face was lit up by the computer screen in front of him. 'I'm just typing up some notes for a patient I've just visited.'

'Anyone I know?'

He looked tired and he ran his hand through his hair. He handed her some notes. 'I don't think you've met him. Jackson King, seventy. Chest infection.' He ran his fingers through his dark hair, as if contemplating his thoughts. 'I should probably put him off at the next port but he's waited a year for this cruise and, to be honest, I don't think he'll make another. I might bring him down and try him on some IV antibiotics next.'

Francesca could feel herself getting flustered. In the past she'd dealt with lots of patients who had died. It was part of the element of being a nurse.

But since she'd lost her dad she found herself getting emotional and irrational about these sorts of things. She'd made a conscious decision to try and take herself out of these scenarios and cruise-ship nursing had been a pretty safe bet.

Most passengers who became unwell were transferred off the ship. It was only in really rare and unfortunate conditions that someone died on board.

Nothing like that had ever happened since Francesca had joined the crew.

A wave of fear swept over her body. 'Is it serious? Do you think he's going to die on board?'

She saw him bite at his bottom lip, his dark eyes fixed on hers. 'Hopefully not. I'd hate to put him off the ship and dump him into a local hospital if all they're going to do is put on him IV antibiotics for a few days and give him oxygen—we can do that here.'

'But maybe that's not in his best interests.' She could feel herself starting to twitter. 'I mean, we may have an X-ray machine but sometimes people are better off in a hospital. We can't deliver the kind of care he might need in here. We could ventilate someone for a few hours at most. And if he reached that stage, it would be even more risky to transfer him. I think it's best if you put him off at the next port, Gabriel.'

Gabriel reached over and took her hand. 'Sit down, Francesca.' His voice was calm but firm. He pulled her over towards the chair next to him. He was looking at her as if she had just sprouted horns.

'Wanna tell me what's going on?'

Her skin felt jittery, the tiny hairs on her arms standing on end. Her brain was working ten to the dozen, she was agitated and she couldn't hide it.

'It's not that I'm saying I can't look after him because obviously I could.' She swept her arm around the state-of-the-art treatment room. 'But it's best for the crew if we don't really have patients overnight. It puts extra pressure on us that we don't need. And we don't have everything we need here.'

He was staring at her with those big brown eyes. She could practically read his thoughts and it wasn't helping.

The *Silver Whisper* had every bit of equipment they could possibly need for a man with a chest infection. An X-ray machine to determine the extent of the infection, IV antibiotics to treat the infection expertly and efficiently, oxygen supplies, monitoring equipment, and an emergency ventilator if needed.

At least once a week they had someone who needed to stay in the medical centre overnight and be monitored. It was part and parcel of the job.

'What's the worst that could happen?' His voice was deep and even, perfectly controlled.

Silence hung in the air. There was the slightest rise of Gabriel's eyebrows.

Francesca could feel her heart thump against her chest. She couldn't breathe. Her chest was tight. She was struggling to pull in air.

She couldn't focus. She kept seeing her father's body sitting in front of her. The terrible colour and tone of his skin. That horrible deathly tinge of grey. It made her want to be sick.

All her nursing life she'd dealt with dead bodies. From the very old to the heartbreaking very young. She'd always treated them with reverence and respect, almost as if they had been members of her own family.

But the cold, harsh jolt of reality had been a terrible experience for her. She couldn't face it. She didn't think she could deal with a dead body again.

Everything had changed now.

'I really don't want to be around someone who's about to die,' she blurted out.

Gabriel was more than a little surprised by her reaction. She was freaking out. His normally calm, capable nurse had turned into a jittery wreck. Her hands were flapping all over the place, she was pacing up and down, talking nineteen to the dozen. What was this about?

She was a nurse. She was used to dealing with death. What on earth was wrong?

She'd helped pull him from the water and resuscitated him. Essentially, until she'd put her hands on his chest, he'd been dead. Until she'd given him mouth to mouth he hadn't been going to breathe again.

But she obviously wasn't thinking like that. This was something different. Her actions in an emergency were automatic—without thought. This was something else entirely.

He stood up and put his hands on her shoulders.

'Francesca, calm down.' She wasn't listening, she was still ranting. 'Francesca.' The volume of his voice increased, bringing her to a halt. There were tears glistening in her eyes, threatening to spill down her cheeks at any second.

This wasn't a normal reaction. This wasn't a professional response.

This was personal.

He guided her into the chair once again and knelt in front of her. The time his voice was quiet, almost a whisper. 'What is it, Francesca? What happened?'

Her shoulders started to shake and the dam burst. Whatever had been threatening to erupt inside her had just taken over. He put his arm around her shoulder as she sobbed, rubbing her back and letting her rest her head on his shoulder.

'My dad,' she sobbed. 'It was my dad.'

He ran his hand through her tangled hair, smoothing it down with the palm of his hand. The shoulder of his shirt was sodden with her tears but he didn't care. At last he was getting to the bottom of what was wrong with her.

'What happened to your dad, Francesca?' She hardly mentioned her parents. It had always seemed like a sensitive area. He knew both her parents had died, but had no

idea of the circumstances. When he'd made tentative queries with the other staff, none of them seemed to know,
either.

'I missed the signs. I should have known. I should have
paid more attention.' He took a sharp intake of breath. Had
her father died of a chest infection?

But Francesca wasn't finished. 'If I'd just understood
how lonely he was then I would have known to pay more
attention.' No. This didn't sound like a chest infection.
This sounded like something else entirely.

Pieces of the jigsaw puzzle started to slot into place.
'How long ago did your mum die, Francesca?'

'Five years. I left London to come back home and help
my dad.' Her eyes lifted to meet his. 'It was hard for us
both and he was depressed after it.' She shook her head.
'But he was better, at least I *thought* he was getting better. He'd started to go out more, take care of his appearance. I thought the depression had lifted. I never would
have left him alone otherwise. He was all I had left.' She
doubled over, her body racked with sobs again and her
head in her hands.

Gabriel took a deep breath. Everything was fitting together. 'Did your father commit suicide, Francesca?'

Through her sobs she nodded.

Everything seemed crystal clear to him now. That's
why she struggled at work. That's why she didn't trust
her instincts.

She'd missed something in the person who had meant
the most to her in the world. She was crippled by guilt.
Anyone would be.

He understood it well. He'd only been a child when
Dante had died, but that didn't stop the feelings of guilt.
That he should have known something was wrong with

his brother. He should have tried to help his mother more. He should have chased after that obnoxious doctor when he'd left the house saying Dante would be fine in a few days.

He pushed a stray tendril of hair behind her ear and put his fingers under her chin, lifting her face to his.

'That wasn't your fault, Francesca.'

'Then whose fault was it?' Her voice was angry. She needed to vent.

He ran his hand along the length of her arm, stroking her skin. 'Francesca, often we can't see things in those we love most. You thought your dad was getting better. You were probably feeling relieved.' He shook his head, 'It's not till after the fact that you get to examine things. You must know by now that often people who are depressed seem to have a spell when they pick up, make improvements, and then something like this happens.' He clasped her hands in his.

'It's not your fault. This could never be your fault. I didn't know your father, or know his reasons. But he was an adult, Francesca. The decision to do that was his. It doesn't take away from how much he must have loved you.'

She was shaking her head slowly. 'But he was my responsibility, Gabriel. *Mine*. No one else's. I should have seen the signs.'

Gabriel nodded. 'I know that's what you believe. And I know that's what has been affecting your work. You think you've lost your instincts, you think you made a mistake.' Her eyes widened. 'But you haven't, Francesca. You're one of the most competent nurses I've ever worked with. And your instincts are spot on.'

A single tear dripped down her cheek and she lowered her gaze. 'I'm not, Gabriel. You have no idea,' she whispered.

'You're a nurse. I know you're scared. But you're going to have to learn to deal with death again. In this job, we have to be prepared. We have to be prepared for anything.'

He rubbed his hand over the top of hers. 'I'm going to tell you something that hardly anyone knows about me.'

Gabriel drew in a long, slow breath. He had to tell her. He had to share with her. She had to know she wasn't alone in feeling she'd let down her family. He had to be honest with her.

'I don't just have a sister.'

She tilted her head and looked confused.

'I used to have a brother, too. Dante died when he was a baby. I was six. Dante had meningitis—except we didn't know it at the time. My mother called for the doctor, but he was tired or drunk—or both. He was in and out of our house in less than five minutes, saying Dante would be fine in a few days. But my mother *knew*. My mother knew something was wrong. We all did. I've never heard a cry like that before. And by the time we took him to the hospital a few hours later it was too late.'

'Oh, Gabriel. I'm so sorry.' Her hand reached up and stroked the side of his face.

He caught her hand back in his. 'A mother's instinct is never wrong. It's the most valuable lesson I've ever learned. So I *know*, Francesca. I understand what it feels like to miss something in a family member. To question every day if there was something else—something different—you could have done.' He held her hand next to his chest. 'I understand in a way that other people can't. Because I feel guilty, too.'

Her reaction was instantaneous. She shook her head. 'But that's ridiculous. You were a child. You couldn't have done anything to save your brother. You know how it is with meningitis. It's so quick. It's so deadly. Even with all the technology in the world, we still can't save everyone.'

He pressed her hand closer to his chest. 'It doesn't matter what the logical explanation is, Francesca. It doesn't change what I feel in here. Just like it doesn't change what you feel in here.' He reached over and pressed his hand over her heart. He felt her pull her breath into her lungs, holding it in place, while she contemplated his words.

'Because our family was well known in Italy it was all over the press. Everywhere we went there were reporters following us, photographers snapping pictures. My mother was fragile enough as it was.' He shook his head. 'To add that into the equation...'

Now she would understand. He could see the realisation dawning on her of why he hadn't wanted any press intrusion about the incident in Venice harbour. Her hand pushed against him even more.

He was kneeling on the floor in front of her. In the dimly lit room she was beautiful, her eyes wide, her vulnerability shining through.

Did she know just how irresistible she was? Did she know how many times he'd wanted to kiss her? How much he wanted her?

'Sometimes we just need somebody.'

Her eyes met his. Dark brown, melting pools of chocolate.

'I need you, Gabriel.' Her voice had changed. This time there was no tremor—no vulnerability. This time it had a very determined edge.

Did she mean what he thought she did?

'Francesca?'

She moved from her chair. A decisive movement, kneeling on the floor to face him.

They were almost nose to nose, just inches apart.

She lifted her hand to touch the side of his face and ran her fingers through his hair.

He caught her hand in his. 'Are you sure?' The atmosphere in the room was so tense he could barely growl the words out.

'I'm sure.' There was no shred of doubt in her voice.

'Then not here.' It was all he could do not to push her onto the floor or up against the wall in the medical centre. But no matter how much he wanted her, he couldn't do that.

Anyone could walk in here at any time.

For Francesca he wanted uninterrupted time and pleasure.

He pulled her towards the door, striding down the quiet corridors of the ship towards his cabin—the two-minute journey had never seemed so long—fumbling in his pocket to find his card to open the door.

She could feel the electricity in the air between them; it felt as if any minute now a million fireworks could go off in a dazzling multicoloured display.

As the door sprung open she found herself slammed up against the wall, her hands above her head. His mouth was on hers in a second. Warm, scorching heat. His tongue probing, pressing her lips apart. This was no gentle kiss like the one on top of the Leaning Tower. This was pure passion.

She pressed herself against the blazing heat of his body, feeling his instant hardness across her taut stomach. Her fingers started tugging at the buttons on his shirt, struggling to unfasten them quickly. Her heart was thundering in her chest and her head was spinning. He pulled her over towards his bed and they crashed onto the mattress together. 'Tell me this is what you want,' he growled.

He bent forward and started leaving a trail of kisses behind her left ear, down the delicate, ticklish skin at the side of her neck and across her shoulder bone, carrying on downwards until he reached the skin between her breasts. Francesca squirmed in delight, feeling his breath on her electrified skin as he tantalised and teased her with his lighter-than-air kisses.

He reached up and wound his fingers around the strap of her bra, pulling it down roughly to release her swollen breast from the confines of her underwear. A wicked grin came over his face and he leaned over and flicked his tongue over the prize.

She groaned out aloud and her body reacted instinctively to his, arching her back towards him, thrusting her nipple further into his mouth. He devoured her endlessly before rising, brushing a kiss across her lips, and started his trail of butterfly kisses again under her other ear. She could barely stand the tension as she could feel the first involuntary tremors of arousal in her body. His hand lifted to move her second strap and release the other breast from its confines.

She pulled his shirt apart, pushing it down over his shoulders. She wanted to see him. She wanted to feel him. She didn't want anything between them.

His other hand wound its way downwards and inside her silk panties to find her moistness, stroking it with expert fingers. Francesca could stand the torment no longer. In his position astride her she could see and feel his erection brushing against her stomach.

'Don't play games with me, Gabriel,' she breathed. She wasn't waiting a second longer as she tugged at his trousers.

His reaction was instant as he fumbled from the bed

and threw his clothes across the floor. He stopped for a few seconds. There was a rustle of a wrapper before he was poised above her again.

Francesca used that time to push her silk panties over her legs to join his clothes in the puddle next to the bed.

Within seconds he was back on top of her on the bed. He gently pressed the length of his naked body next to hers. She responded immediately by opening her legs and winding them around his waist. 'Now, Gabriel,' she gasped. He was poised above her again and he hesitated, still waiting for her lead.

'Are you sure?'

'Come on, Gabriel.' She grabbed his shoulders. There was no doubt in her mind. If he stopped now, she would kill him.

She tilted her hips up towards him. Nothing else mattered. Nothing but right now and this moment. Nothing had ever felt this good.

He entered her in one powerful thrust sending shockwaves shooting through her body. The pressure increased with each stroke as his momentum increased, the tide of passion rising quickly. She wound her legs tighter around his body to pull him deeper into her as the first waves of ecstasy throbbed through her.

Making love had never felt like this before—everything about it was different. She'd never felt this kind of connection before.

Maybe it was because of what she'd shared with him? And what he'd shared with her?

She had never been able to do that before—to talk about her father and what he'd done.

She'd seen the hurt in his eyes, just as he must have

seen it in hers. It had given her this—the first time she'd felt truly connected to a man.

She was losing control. The sensations were sweeping over. Taking her to the place she wanted to go. Gabriel touched her face and whispered in her ear. Words of emotion. Words of tenderness. Words of passion.

And she let go.

She glanced at the clock on his bedside table; it was after midnight and Gabriel was already sleeping. She wondered what it would be like to wake up every morning next to this gorgeous man. A man who had spent the last few hours treating her as though she was the most important thing on earth.

She wondered what it would be like to share his bed every night.

The release of endorphins was obviously making her crazy because, in her head, she was picturing two dark-eyed children playing outside a beautiful house, with Gabriel and herself standing in the garden, watching.

Clearly, she was losing her mind.

She had never allowed herself to formulate dreams like this—she was so used to being alone. But Gabriel had evoked feelings in her that she could never have hoped for. His heat was enveloping her now like a warm blanket and ripples of fatigue were tugging at her. She dug her head into the feather pillow. This bed was much more comfortable than hers; she could get use to this.

It was almost as if a huge weight had been lifted off her shoulders. She'd hardly ever spoke to anyone about this.

She'd never known talking about it could have this effect.

But it wasn't just what she'd said. It was what *he'd* said that mattered.

He'd shared with her about his brother. How hard must it have been to dig up all those childhood emotions and memories? No wonder he never spoke about it. The pain had been etched on his heart, just like it was on hers.

Had she finally met someone who could understand? Really understand what this felt like?

Someone she could finally share with? Someone to take the aching feeling of loneliness away?

That could be too good to be true.

Her plans drifted through her mind, like feathers in the wind scattering aimlessly around.

Her letter from Australia? It might never be opened.

CHAPTER ELEVEN

TIME was beginning to drift for Francesca. Her letter had sat unopened in her bedside cabinet for weeks.

She'd been very busy. Busy spending every moment with Gabriel.

Today they were on duty. The boat had docked at Mykonos in Greece, with most of the passengers visiting the nearby town with its maze of tiny streets and whitewashed-steps lanes. Things had been quiet.

But that was about to change.

They heard a cry from the corridor. It was the most distinctive cry she'd ever heard.

Gabriel was on his feet in an instant, not waiting for the patient to reach the medical centre but striding down the corridor at lightning speed.

Seconds later he returned with a toddler in his arms. The scream was like nothing Francesca had ever experienced before. Something was really wrong.

Gabriel laid the little one down on the one of the examination trolleys, listening as the parents joined him, both talking at once.

Francesca picked up fragments of the conversation as she connected the little one to a monitor. 'Temperature… fretful…not drinking…screaming.'

Gabriel was sounding his chest. Francesca lifted the tympanic thermometer and put it in his ear. 'High temp, Gabriel. Thirty-nine point eight.'

She lifted a nearby chart and touched the arm of the child's mother. 'Excuse me, what's your son's name?' In the speed and confusion she hadn't heard it.

'It's Jake. His name is Jake. Jake Peterson.'

Francesca nodded. 'Date of birth?' She wrote down the details; he was only fourteen months old. She watched as Gabriel finished sounding his chest, checked his blood pressure and checked his ears, nose and throat.

'He had an ear infection last week,' said his mother anxiously. 'He had antibiotics but I'm not sure if they've worked. We gave him paracetamol but his temperature won't come down. He won't drink. He's been vomiting.'

Francesca was still watching Gabriel. Was that a tremor in his hands? Did he suspect what she thought he did?

On autopilot she reached over and touched Jake's hands and feet. While his body temperature was high, his hands and feet were distinctly cold. An indicator of meningitis in children.

She gave Gabriel a little nod. He understood instantly. He took a few more moments, placing his hand behind Jake's head and lifting it while keeping his other hand on Jake's chest. The movement caused an involuntary reaction in Jake, flexing his hips and knees. 'Positive Brudzinki's.' He glanced over at Francesca. And she could see it.

The pain written all over his face.

Was Jake the same age that Dante had been?

He pointed to the phone on the nearby wall. 'Phone the captain, tell him we have a medical emergency. Tell him not to leave port.'

Francesca glanced at her watch. The ship was due to

leave Mykonos in the next few minutes. The engines had already started up and the anchor probably lifted. It was vital they stop this. Every minute in a meningitis case counted. An emergency sea evacuation would take up precious time. She spoke swiftly and quietly then hung up the phone. 'It's done.'

'What's happening? What's wrong with Jake?'

Gabriel put his hand on Jake's mums shoulder. 'Jake is showing signs of meningitis.'

She looked aghast. 'No. He can't be. He's had those vaccinations. He can't have meningitis.'

Her hand stroked the head of her son lying on the bed. The screaming had stopped. He was floppy and lethargic. His heart beating too fast, his colour pale.

Gabriel appeared calm. But she could hear it. The tiny tremor in his voice. The absolute control he was exercising over himself.

'Unfortunately there are lots of different types of meningitis. The vaccines only protect against the most common. Jake has obviously picked up another type. We won't be sure which type until we can do some tests, but in the meantime I'm going to give him some intravenous antibiotics.'

The woman gripped Gabriel's arm fiercely. 'What if you're wrong? What if it's not meningitis? Don't you need to do that horrible test on Jake to find out? The needle in his back?'

Gabriel shook his head. 'There's no time. I'm going to give him antibiotics and arrange immediate transfer to a children's hospital. He'll need some steroids, too. We can't wait. We have to act now.'

He was moving across the treatment room, opening cupboards, obviously searching for what he needed.

'What IV antibiotics have we got?'

Francesca was at his side in an instant. She glanced at the small, pale child over her shoulder. 'What do you want?'

'Vancomycin.'

She shook her head. They only had the most basic antibiotics on board. 'Benzylpenicillin or cefotaxime, then.'

'We've got both of them.' She waited while he scribbled his prescriptions.

'I'll take some bloods and insert the IV cannula while you make up the loading drugs.'

She nodded and got to work quickly. This must be his worst nightmare. She couldn't imagine how he must be feeling. Outwardly he seemed cool, calm and collected. An experienced paediatrician dealing with something he must have seen before.

Jake's mother had started to cry. 'But he doesn't even have a rash…'

Francesca touched her arm as she hung the bag of fluids up and ran the infusion through the IV line. 'It's probably best that he doesn't. A rash is a really critical sign of meningitis. The sooner we get these started the better.'

It had only taken Gabriel a few seconds to collect the blood samples and insert the cannula.

Francesca joined up the IV and set the electronic pump. It was important that these antibiotics were delivered as quickly and as safely as possible. She handed Gabriel a scrap of paper.

'Here are the nearest hospital's contact details. I'm not sure who the paediatrician is there.'

He nodded and walked swiftly over to his office, leaving the door open so he could continue to observe Jake as he made the call.

It was all over in a few minutes. 'Ambulance should be here soon. They're sending a doctor to do the transfer.'

Francesca started a new set of observations on Jake. There was no change. No improvement, no deterioration. Gabriel never left his side, writing his notes at the bedside and talking calmly and quietly to Jake's parents.

Ten minutes later the phone in the medical centre rang to say the ambulance was at port side. There had been no time to make any alternative arrangements, and the family's luggage was still on board as the stewards hadn't had enough time to pack up their cabin.

One of the pursers brought the family their passports and money from the safe in their cabin and promised to arrange the transport for their luggage. It was as much as they could do.

For Jake, time was of the essence. Everything else would have to wait.

Ten minutes later Jake and his parents were in the back of the ambulance, speeding off to the local children's unit in Mykonos.

Francesca and Gabriel walked back up the stairs to the medical centre in silence. She was watching him carefully.

He was clenching his fists and his jaw was firmly set. It was clear his frustration and anger was building. He strode ahead swiftly and she jumped as something crashed off the wall in front of her.

'We need to get better antibiotics in here! That child could have died!'

She froze. She'd never seen him like this before. His anger was frightening, even though it wasn't directed at her.

She turned to face him. 'You did a good job, Gabriel,'

she said quietly. It was a calm, measured response, hopefully one that would permeate across to him.

'What if we'd been at sea?' He was pacing now. His anger clearly had not abated. His hands were shaking.

She walked over to the worktop in front of her and started clearing up the remnants from earlier. Discarded vials, packaging from the IV line, the plastic cover for the bag of saline.

She'd no idea how to handle this. She knew he was angry. She knew he was frustrated. But the anger spike made her recoil.

Was that wrong? Shouldn't she be trying to support him, the way he had her?

He was a wreck.

Francesca walked across the room towards him.

She placed a hand gently on his arm. 'But he didn't, Gabriel.' She could feel a tremor in his arms.

It was her turn. He was one of the finest doctors she'd ever worked with.

If she hadn't known about his brother she would never have understood his reaction.

But he'd shared with her.

He'd told her something he didn't share with anyone and she loved him for it.

There. The words had finally formed in her head.

The man she'd started out hating was the man she'd finally bared her soul to. The one who was stealing a place in her heart.

She lifted her hands up onto his shoulders. 'You did good, Gabriel.'

'If we'd been at sea you would have started the antibiotics and the steroids and arranged the quickest air ambulance you could.' She paused, watching the frown that puckered his handsome face.

'Haven't you had to deal with a child with meningitis before?' It almost felt disloyal to ask the question. But she had to know. He was paediatrician. Surely he dealt with this before?

His reply was abrupt, snappy. 'Of course I've dealt with kids with meningitis. Just not in the middle of the sea before. I've always had the equipment and people around me that I needed.'

His words stung. Did he think she wasn't good enough to deal with a severely sick child? And they weren't in the middle of the sea. They were in a port, next to a reliable and capable children's hospital that would have dealt with this condition on a hundred other occasions. Jake was in good hands.

She picked up the item he'd flung at the wall. His wallet. It must have been the closest thing he'd had to hand. It fell open in her hands.

There, under a clear bit of plastic, was an old photograph. Two young children and a baby.

It wasn't quite old enough to be a black and white photo, but the colours had faded with age. The little girl's dress had probably been a vibrant pink. Now it was a paler version, her hair in dark curls about her shoulders. The boy was barely an inch taller than her, his dark hair and eyes unmistakeable.

But what made her stomach clench was the pride in their faces as they held their baby brother between them. The innocence of childhood. The joy of family, as they held him on their knees.

Dante. This was Dante.

The tears welled up her eyes.

She sensed him next to her. His finger ran across the battered plastic.

'It's a lovely photograph,' she whispered.

He took the wallet from her hand. 'Yes, yes, it is.' He closed it tightly and slipped it into his back pocket.

There was hesitation, as if he was about to say something. What should she do? Should she wrap her arms around him?

He seemed so closed. So self-contained. She wanted to reach out but couldn't bear the thought of him brushing her aside. Maybe he needed time. Maybe he needed a little space.

Yes, that was it.

She should give him a little time to process what had just happened. It must be so hard for him. It must have dredged up a whole host of difficult memories.

The aspect of feeling out of control must have been the most terrifying of all.

And she could relate. Because it was exactly how she'd felt about her father.

He was still watching her. The tension crackled in the air.

If only she could take that step.

If only she could cross the treatment room and put her arms around him.

But something was stopping her. Something was gluing her feet to the floor and her arms at her sides.

He hesitated. 'We need to discuss this case at the next staff meeting and review the drugs we have available.' He nodded and turned and swept out the door.

Leaving Francesca rooted to the spot.

The feeling of regret swept over her like an icy chill.

It was the last time he was alone with her for three days.

CHAPTER TWELVE

GABRIEL looked furious.

And no wonder.

There, right in front of her, was the headline: *'Million-aire Doc Saves Drowning Teenager in Venice.'*

Her eyes swept over the newspaper thrust in front of her, a British tabloid that was prone to running scandal-ous stories of all descriptions.

And as she read the words her heart sank like a stone.

Gorgeous Doc Gabriel Russo, thirty-one, heir to the Russo Printing fortune, saved the life of a British teenager the other day after he fell into the harbour at Venice and was swept out to sea.

Eyewitnesses reported that Gabriel didn't hesitate and dived straight in, swimming to the teenager and making several attempts to bring him to the surface. Unfortunately he then had to be rescued himself as they were swept by the tide into the harbour wall and the Italian millionaire was knocked out.

He was resuscitated by British nurse Francesca Cruz, who serves on the same cruise ship as him.

Ryan Hargreaves, age thirteen, from Sussex, on holiday with his parents and younger sister, was suc-

cessfully treated on board and managed to enjoy the rest of their holiday despite his ordeal. He is now safely at home.

Dr Russo had been working as a paediatrician in the States but recently came home to help out the family business after his father's health failed.

His skills haven't been wasted on the Italian cruise liner Silver Whisper, *as he's reportedly saved the life of another child, diagnosing an unusual case that, if missed, could have resulted in the child's death.*

The accompanying photo made her heart turn to ice. It was the snapshot she'd sent to Jill, showing Gabriel dressed in his white uniform, directing the ship-to-ship transfer of a patient during a routine crew exercise.

Some of the words in the newspaper article were copied almost directly from her email. Why on earth had Jill done this?

Her brain was scrambled. She'd known that Gabriel had refused any publicity about the incident. She just hadn't exactly known why.

'How could you?' he hissed, before slamming the newspaper down on the table in front of her. 'After everything that's happened between us. You sold confidential patient details, Francesca. The first rule for any health-care professional—never break patient confidentiality. That's the first thing any medical student learns.' The volume of his voice was increasing on a par with his rage. His face was becoming redder and redder. She'd seen his rage before with the dining-room manager and over the antibiotics and that had been scary enough. But this?

Her head was spiralling. She tried to speak, 'Gabriel, wait—'

'Did you really need the money so badly? Did you? How much did they pay you? How much was it worth to sell me out? Do you know what this will do to the family business? My father is the patriarch of the family. He's the figurehead that everyone expects to see. This will ruin him. Share prices will plummet once people know he's been unwell. You've just ruined a business that's been in my family for generations—all because of your greed!'

'Stop it!' She thudded her hand down on the desk as she pushed herself up from her chair. She couldn't listen to this a second longer. He thought she'd sold this story? He thought she'd do something like this? Betray patient confidentiality?

How dared he? Surely he knew her well enough to know that she would never do anything like this?

'Stop it now!' She picked up the newspaper in disgust. 'I'm not responsible for this, Gabriel. I would never do something like this.'

'So who is their source, then, Francesca? Because they know things that shouldn't have left this cruise ship. And how the hell did they get their hands on that picture?'

She cringed. There was no hiding this. There was no getting away from any of this.

'I knew it,' he muttered furiously. 'I should have known you were just like your friend.'

What did that mean? She felt a cold chill wash over her skin. He thought she was a liar. The one thing in her life that she'd never been guilty of.

She couldn't stand this. She had to get things out in the open. 'Now…' She took a deep breath. 'Some of this I *am* responsible for.'

She pointed at the front of the newspaper. 'It was Jill. At least, I'm assuming it was Jill. She emailed a few weeks ago and I replied. I told her about the rescue and how I re-suscitated you. I also told her you'd saved another child's life. But I never, *never* revealed any patient details to her.' She shook her head fiercely. 'I would never do that. I don't know where they got Ryan's name from, but it certainly didn't come from me.'

Her fingers touched the paper. 'The picture, however, did come from me. She asked me what you looked like these days. And I sent it to her.' She lifted her eyes to meet his. 'And for that I'm truly sorry.'

She waited a few moments for them both to catch their breath.

'Now maybe you'll tell me what you meant about "being the same" as my friend Jill.' Her hands were shaking but she kept the tremor from her voice. Tiny jigsaw pieces were slotting together in her head—and she didn't like the picture they were forming.

He was trembling—still furious with her. It would be so easy to turn around and walk away. To storm off and open the Australian visa that was in the top drawer of her bedside cabinet. Book a flight and head off into the sunset.

But she didn't want to do any of that. She had to be grown up. She had to accept responsibility that some of this was her fault. Not the patient details but the Gabriel details.

For a few weeks life with Gabriel had almost crept into that dreamlike realm. The happy, blissful place where everything was tinged with pink. A few days of stolen kisses and secret moments.

But that had been before they'd looked after Jake. That had been before she'd seen his reaction to treating a child with meningitis.

Wearing rose-tinted glass was all very well but the reality check of life meant there would always be murky grey skirting around the edges.

And Francesca didn't want to walk away. Because for the first time in a long time she felt at home. At home with Gabriel.

It didn't matter that they were roaming the ocean on a cruise ship with no fixed abode. She felt relaxed and happy with Gabriel. And up until a few seconds ago she'd thought he felt the same with her.

For Francesca it was a revelation. It was the people that made the home, not the place.

She wanted to see this through. No matter where it would take her. She'd connected with him in a way she'd never experienced before and she wasn't about to let this slip through her fingers.

This was worth fighting for.

She took a deep breath. 'Tell me about Jill.'

His hands were fixed on the side of the desk, his knuckles white. His eyes met hers, his dark brown eyes almost black.

'Your friend is a thief. I threw her out when I discovered her hiding my watch in her bag. A few other things had gone missing and I'd had my suspicions. But this time I caught her—and her feet didn't touch the floor.'

She felt her throat close over. The hairs on her arms stood on end and an uneasy trickle crept down her spine.

There was no point in leaping to her defence. Jill had always been desperate for money. Francesca just hadn't known why. What's more, she hadn't *wanted* to know why.

'Do you know what, Gabriel? I'm sorry my friend did that. I have no idea why she did. It certainly wasn't anything that I knew about. But I have to be honest—to my knowledge, Jill never stole anything from me. Maybe I didn't have anything worth stealing. She was always diving from one get-rich-quick scheme to another but that didn't matter to me. What did matter was that when I really needed her, she was there for me. Just as I hope I will be for her. Particularly if she has problems.'

No one in life was perfect.

Not her. Not him. Not her father. And not Jill.

This was real life. Not some fairy-tale. Her father wasn't here to tell her those stories any more. He'd chosen a different path and it was time for Francesca to choose hers.

She reached her hand across the desk and touched Gabriel's cold skin.

Gabriel wasn't angry with her. He was angry at the set of circumstances he'd been dropped into. Things that were out of his control.

And she knew what that felt like.

Because she'd been there.

And so had he.

And what she wanted to do right now was help him. To prove to the man that she loved that she would stand by him through thick and thin.

She knew nothing about share prices. She didn't care about his money. Money had never been a factor in this relationship.

But what she did know was how it felt to have a family member to worry about. To want to ease the pressure and strain on them.

His hands were starting to loosen at the edge of the desk and she intertwined her warm fingers with his cool ones.

Hurt and confusion was written all over his face. And panic at the potential threat to his father's health and the family business.

This was it. This was the time to choose—between the dream job or the dream man. And she didn't hesitate.

'What can I do to help, Gabriel? Because I'm here for you. I'm not going anywhere.' She held his gaze and lifted his hand to her heart.

Gabriel was trying to control the anger he was feeling. Even as he'd shouted some of those words at Francesca he'd known couldn't be true.

Francesca could never be like Jill. The person he'd got to know over the last few weeks was warm and loving, not cold and desperate like her friend had been.

This was the woman who'd bared her soul to him and sobbed her heart out over her father's suicide.

She was one of the few people in his life he'd ever told about Dante. And he'd shared with her because he trusted her. Francesca Cruz was a good person. An honest person.

Even now, when he'd told her about Jill, she hadn't been reactive and angry. She'd immediately had some perspective and been rational about it.

He had to ask. He had to ask now. 'What are you running from, Francesca?'

He heard her sharp intake of breath.

'You've drifted from job to job, place to place. You hardly stay anywhere longer than six months. Hardly enough time to make friends—hardly enough time to get to know people. I heard that your next step will be Australia. When do you plan on going there? When do you plan on leaving?'

His head was swimming with how he felt about her. How he felt about everything. How he felt about his family.

'I'm not running, Gabriel,' she whispered as she tried to blink back tears. 'I'm just trying to find a place to call home.'

And it escaped. One single fat tear sliding down her perfect cheek.

But what would happen now? It would take the Italian press less than a few hours to pick up on the implication about his father's health.

Then it would be everywhere. He cringed. He had to get back home. He had to be with his family.

He'd come back to Venice to be near and to help his family, not to hinder it. There had to be a way to put this right.

'I need to go. I need to leave.'

He could see the expression on her face, the quiet determination masking the hurt in her eyes.

To him, she'd never looked so beautiful.

The next few days would be a nightmare.

And, as much as he wanted to, he couldn't possibly lead her into that.

It wouldn't be fair. They'd only really just met. They'd only spent one precious night together. He couldn't possibly ask her to...

'Just give me time to pack.'

He blinked. And in that moment he knew.

The person he'd always been looking for was standing right in front of him. She was prepared to come and walk into the lion's den with him—right by his side. Francesca had been searching for home.

And it was the one thing he could give her.

The words clogged in his throat. 'Are you sure?'

She looked as though she might cry again. Maybe she wasn't sure. Maybe she just wanted to walk away.

He looked across at the deep brown eyes as she tilted her chin up towards him. If he was lucky, it would be the

face he'd spend the next fifty years looking at. A force to
be reckoned with.

'I've never been surer.'

EPILOGUE

EVERYTHING passed in a blur. A quick trip back to Venice followed by four more trips around the Med to see out their notice.

A press officer to deal with media enquiries.

A quiet phone call to a tearful friend who admitted she needed some help.

Gabriel's sister announced as the new, entirely capable CEO of the company.

Francesca fingered the still unopened envelope in her hand.

Australia. Her dream job—at least, that's what she'd thought.

She still hadn't told him—and she probably never would. Because everything she'd been looking for she'd found here, with him.

'What's your favourite fairy-tale?'

She smiled as she felt the warm breath at the back of her neck and his arms steal around her waist. She leaned back against his warm body, looking over at the city of Venice.

It was twilight and the twinkling scattered lights bobbed up and down on the inky-dark waters. Gabriel's penthouse with its gothic façade sat on the Misericordia canal. It was surrounded by gorgeous buildings and a fourteenth-century palace. Every girl's modern-day fairy-tale, with the gondolas slipping silently by at night. A perfect setting.

She sighed. 'I like a little bit from each of them. Snow White being kissed by the prince. Prince Charming sliding the shoe onto Cinderella's foot. Rapunzel throwing down her hair, and Sleeping Beauty being woken by a tender kiss.'

He smiled, showing his perfect white teeth. She turned around, her arms reaching up and twining around his neck.

This was her Gabriel. The tiny lines, caused by the worry and stress of the last few weeks, were dissipating. The tension was gone from his back and shoulders.

'You called me Sleeping Beauty once before.'

She pulled back in surprise. 'You remember? I thought you wouldn't remember any of that. Why didn't you tell me?'

He raised an eyebrow at her. 'And spoil all our fun?' He whispered in her ear. 'Do you know which part of the fairy-tales I like best?'

She shook her head.

'The happy ever after. Everyone deserves one of those.'

She felt herself freeze. The cool evening air danced over her skin, sending the hairs on her arms standing on end. Her breath caught in her throat.

It was just a moment because Gabriel had dropped to one knee and was holding a black velvet box out towards her.

His eyes were staring earnestly at her. 'Francesca Cruz, will you do me the honour of becoming my wife? In sickness and in health, through good times and bad, from here until the end of time? Because I've found my own fairy-tale, here, with you. And I can't imagine spending the rest of my life with anyone other than you.'

She couldn't speak. The words just wouldn't form.

It was perfect. Her own personal fairy-tale with her own perfect hero. Her mum and dad would have loved him. Of that, she had no doubt. Just as Gabriel's family had welcomed her with open arms, making her feel instantly at home.

He opened the box and she blinked. Then smiled.

He stood up and slipped the ring from the box. 'You know that money was no object. You know I could have bought the biggest diamond in the world. But I wanted to buy something that was about us. Something about where we met.'

The ring was flawless. An exquisite aquamarine—the colour of the Mediterranean Sea—surrounded by a host of sparkling diamonds.

'It's perfect,' she breathed.

'Is that a yes?'

'Yes!' she screamed as she jumped up on him. 'Yes, yes, yes!' She smothered him in kisses as he laughed and held her tightly.

Her feet touched the floor again as he took a second to slide the ring onto her finger.

A wicked gleam crossed her eyes. 'It's not just fairy-tales I like,' she said.

'What do you mean?'

'Do you remember what I was reading on the boat?'

He remembered instantly, blood flushing through his heated skin. 'I remember,' he said slowly.

'Then I think it's time to act out my favourite part.'

And she held her hand out to him and led him to the bedroom.

* * * * *

Give a 12 month subscription to a friend today!

Call Customer Services
0844 844 1358*

or visit
millsandboon.co.uk/subscriptions

MILLS & BOON®

Why shop at millsandboon.co.uk?

Each year, thousands of romance readers find their perfect read at millsandboon.co.uk. That's because we're passionate about bringing you the very best romantic fiction. Here are some of the advantages of shopping at www.millsandboon.co.uk:

* **Get new books first**—you'll be able to buy your favourite books one month before they hit the shops

* **Get exclusive discounts**—you'll also be able to buy our specially created monthly collections, with up to 50% off the RRP

* **Find your favourite authors**—latest news, interviews and new releases for all your favourite authors and series on our website, plus ideas for what to try next

* **Join in**—once you've bought your favourite books, don't forget to register with us to rate, review and join in the discussions

Visit **www.millsandboon.co.uk**
for all this and more today!

MILLS_WEB

The World of
MILLS & BOON®

With eight paperback series to choose from, there's a Mills & Boon series perfect for you. So whether you're looking for glamorous seduction, Regency rakes or homespun heroes, we'll give you plenty of inspiration for your next read.

Cherish™

Experience the ultimate rush of falling in love.
12 new stories every month

Romantic Suspense INTRIGUE

A seductive combination of danger and desire
8 new stories every month

Desire™

Passionate and dramatic love stories
6 new stories every month

nocturne™

An exhilarating underworld of dark desires
2 new stories every month

The World of
MILLS & BOON®

HISTORICAL
*Awaken the romance
of the past*
6 new stories every month

MEDICAL ROMANCE
*The ultimate in romantic
medical drama*
6 new stories every month

MODERN™
*Power, passion and
irresistible temptation*
8 new stories every month

By Request
*Relive the romance with the
best of the best*
12 stories every month

Have you tried eBooks?

With eBook exclusive series and titles from just **£1.99**,
there's even more reason to try our eBooks today

Visit www.millsandboon.co.uk/eBooks
for more details
